Praise from readers

For all the readers who couldn't get their eyes off the "50 Shades of Grey" book, here is a story that will make the latter pale in comparison. Not because of its sexual content. "My Life Under Water" is all about raw life as it is, not as we imagine it. It's a page turner, that will make one laugh, because Alan Stamp writes with an uncanny humour, and it will also make one cry, for the lost opportunities of expression of love. In short, this story for me is not only about coming of age, but about love and friendship in all its forms and shapes, about pain and forgiveness, about the ugly and the beautiful aspects of life. This is a book must be read not only by older adults but by the young ones as well!

C. Katzen

This is a must-read novel for everyone. An engagingly frank, delightful novel of a young fellow coming to terms with himself by setting out on his own from a small burb in the Fraser Valley to the big city life in Vancouver. His trials and tribulations of coming out and being accepted are wonderfully engaging. His love of and prowess in the water are an ongoing theme in his novel. You will grow to love this young man and be sad when the story is over as you will want to keep discovering where his life will take him.

L. LeGood

I heard Stamp on a radio program in Vancouver and decided to pick up his book; and glad I did. I literally couldn't put it down. Stamp mixes beautiful prose, fast-paced and witty dialogue with recollections of his family, his competitions and his friends in late-70s Vancouver, BC. There are some incredible characters here - his best friend Lara, a frustrated singer whose talent is big, but her self-worth is low, Mrs. McBride, Pete and his mother...all very realistic and unforgettable.

Stamp is a therapist, and I figure that he's listened well, because the dialogue rings so true. He adds his own inner monologue through many parts and has a deprecating sense of humour that made me wince with recognition at times and laugh at others. Stamp and Lara also have a love story, but it's his coming of age story set against the water (water is everywhere here) and competitive swimming that really got my attention. This is a big book, but it moves as quickly as Stamp does in the pool.

It's undeniable that most gay youth struggle in a world that can reject them. Stamp gets this and yet the story is packed with humour and ultimately leads to a very climactic and satisfying ending. I loved this read!

J. Wilkins

Vivid, touching, honest, enlightening memories in technicolor. All of the above and much more. On the one hand, Mr. Stamp makes the process of growing up and coming out seem easy, even sort of beautiful in a hard-earned kind of way. It's in his description of his swim at Nationals where he gives the most real and accurate description of what it's actually like. He has a lot to say and says it so well.

T. Monroe

I absolutely adored this book. It is a beautiful coming of age story of a young man navigating through his youth with curiosity, confusion, and courage. I read this book in three nights and I caught myself giggling in some sections and gripped by youthful angst in others. The main character struggles with fear and acceptance of his sexuality and goes on a journey of discovery that encompasses family, friendship, athletics and a touch of romance. I hope there is a sequel!!!

M. Walsh

MY LIFE ABOVE WATER

ALAN D. STAMP

Dedications

The AIDS crisis began to ravage Vancouver's gay community in the winter of 1983. In the early years of the epidemic, we were witness to sorrowful deaths that continued unrelentingly until anti-retroviral treatments were available in 1995. I dedicate this story to the memory of sweet lives lost, and to those left behind who remember a profoundly sad and frightening time in our history.

I'm fortunate to have had wonderful friendships throughout my life, professionally and personally. Friends have seen me through unsettling times, and for that, I'm grateful. This story is about the importance and power of friendships, with thanks and deep appreciation.

For my mother, Margaret Rose. Never failing to be cheerful, supportive and stylish, I'm fortunate to have had a one-in-a-million Mum.

To Chico, for making me smile with your antics.

And, as always, for the amazing and extraordinary Laura Jean.

Foreword

My *Life Above Water* opens with a foreboding violent winter storm. It's February of 1983 and there's a plague striking Vancouver's gay community. The deadly infections are inexplicably and shockingly taking the lives of previously healthy men.

A struggling in-the-closet Vancouver swimmer and student, Shepard is one of the many "worried well" affected by the emerging crisis. He's trying to focus on his studies and training, however, he's having problems. Shep's being bullied by an unforgiving swim coach who is unimpressed by his inconsistent performances. At risk is Shep's spot on the national swim team and the loss of financial support. Complicating matters, his distant father suffers a near-fatal heart attack and requires surgery by an unfortunately named cardiologist: Dr. Deth. Shep's fashionable mother Rose needs help with her heartbroken husband, though her son's loyalties are divided between his surly father and an ex-lover who falls dangerously sick. Other problems surface when Lara — Shep's best friend and striving singer — frantically informs him that her agent is missing.

Flummoxed, Shepard's boyfriend can't help; Robby's working as a director in a third-rate dinner theatre in faraway Sudbury. And Shep's landlady and former distance swimmer Mrs. McBride has her own mortal problem and offers a potential, yet illegal, remedy to help revitalize one of their own in dire need.

My Life Above Water recounts how disconnected people reunite through a crisis at the beginning of the AIDS epidemic. To focus attention and to raise funds for the growing disease, friends and lovers make scarifies to carry out an adventurous and improbable plan: Shepard's attempt to swim 80 kilometres across the Strait of Georgia.

A Note About the Cover:
This is a picture of the author running on the Stanley Park Seawall during a very powerful winter's storm and serves as the starting point of the story. Surprisingly, it appeared on the front page of the Vancouver Sun. It was also a surprise that Stamp was soaked through with seawater the moment after this photograph was taken!

About the Author:
Alan D. Stamp is a Registered Psychotherapist who has practiced for more than thirty years. Stamp is a life-long swimmer, who competed until age 28. Stamp has resided in Vancouver's West End since 1986. This is Stamp's second book.

Table of Contents

"So long as we are loved by others we are indispens-able; and no man is useless while he has a friend."
Robert Louis Stevenson

1

The Wave Comes Ashore

February's bitter wind howled, causing hemlock branches to irritatingly scour my bedroom window as I lay awake. "Jezus," I moaned, unable to fall back asleep. I looked at my wrist-watch: 4:46 AM. I swung my legs from my bed, padded into the washroom and sat down to pee. *Might as well go for a run; there's no swim practice, is there? No, it's Sunday, right?* I gathered my thoughts as I staggered back to the bedroom. After pulling the duvet into a semblance of respectability, I went searching for my running tights in the darkness. Locating and pulling on my black leggings, I gazed out the apartment window. "At least it's not pouring," I muttered to myself above the screeching storm. I donned a long-sleeved top and a lime-green fleecy running vest. My grey Nikes were at the door. I laced up, went to the kitchen, opened the fridge and downed a huge glug of orange juice from the carton. I grabbed my keys, gloves and quietly headed out of the Queen Charlotte apartments. Just outside the building, I was surprised at the bracing air, my breath forming white steaming clouds, immediately whisked off by high winds. *Must be about minus 10.* The streets were deserted; the only thing moving was me — just barely — and the remains of autumn's leaves, whirling upwards in the cyclonic winds. I stretched for a couple of moments and began a slow, steady run, buffeted by the gale, bound for Stanley Park via Haro Street. I jogged past the tennis courts overlooking Lost Lagoon and along Chilco, connecting with the seawall as I quickened my pace. Beyond the Yacht Club, the lights of downtown towers shimmered against the cloudless sky and reflected in the black ocean. I noticed a precarious bobbing of the moored boats in Coal Harbour. *Even in protected areas, the swell is strong.* I started to perspire as I ran past the 9 o'clock Gun and towards Burrard Inlet. It was exhilarating to be alone in the squall. *That's a Canadian literary theme, isn't it? Man against winter ... very Northrup Frye.* The trees around me were crackling and snapping from the gusts, quickly ending my English 101 recollection. As I ran, I was surprised to see the amount of broken branches littering the trails and roadways. Every few seconds, I heard the sound of wood being snapped apart violently. *Is that a tree being split in two? Okay, that's a little too close. Better stay clear of the trails.*

The wind lessened considerably as I went past the *Girl in a Wetsuit*, just her trunk barely visible in the high tide. *I don't imagine the wetsuit's keeping her warm.* I headed north, eventually running underneath the soaring span of the Lions Gate Bridge, the water sloshing forcefully against the massive bridge pillars. After running for 30 minutes, I was nearing Siwash Rock when the full force of the wind began booming so loudly it hurt my ears. Starlight illuminated the whitecaps in English Bay, whipped into a foaming, churning, dizzying frenzy. The power of the gale pushed me backwards as I ran into it at full throttle. Every 5 or 6 seconds, the force of the ocean hitting the stone barrier produced a towering wave that crashed onto the narrow seawall. I stopped in my tracks. *Whoa, I've never seen waves like this.* With the cliffs towering above me and the raging surf beside me, I continued to run forward, vigilant of the danger, dodging the huge waves as they crashed onto the path. Suddenly, a giant wave moved rapidly towards the seawall, shot up over 20 feet and cascaded downwards, drenching me with frigid saltwater. *"Fuuuuuck!"* I screamed, my clothing and shoes soaked through. My wet hair made my head ache as the wind blew icily, immediately chilling every part of me to sub-zero. I plodded on, my running shoes squishing with water as I cut up from Third Beach, rocketing through the dark woods in an effort to become warm. Past the Teahouse I felt my groin chaffing, the saltwater adding stinging insult to injury. The winds were now so strong it was as though they blew me back home. A few minutes before arriving at the Queen Charlotte, I started to chuckle at my misfortune. *Would anyone believe that I was overcome by a wave?*

By 6:30, I entered my lobby, shivering, red-faced, dripping wet and utterly frozen. Collecting her Province newspaper, grey-haired Mrs. McBride stood in the entrance, staring at me with disbelief as I came through.

"My dear boy! What on earth were you doing outside?"

"Well, I —" Before I could explain, Mrs. McBride gave me a weather update.

"This storm is wreaking havoc all over the city. The ferries can't sail due to high seas. Power is out all through the suburbs. The hydro crews estimate there are hundreds of trees down in the park and elsewhere. It's the worst winter storm since 1974." Mrs. McBride clutched the front of her floral housedress and shuddered sympathetically at my appearance.

"You're right. It's like a hurricane, out there." I panted hoarsely as my landlady took in my drenched appearance. She scrutinized my wet runners rapidly dampening the red and blue Axminster carpeting.

"It looks like you've been hosed down by those adorable firemen from Station No.6. You know the ones I mean, don't you dear?"

Firemen? I know the ones or I'd like to. And why are they all so good-looking? Is that how they get hired? I gotta stop thinking with my penis. I'm a popsicle.

"Well, not really," I lied.

"So, do tell me. Why were you —"

"I couldn't sleep in this storm,' I shrugged. "So I figured that I'd go for a run on the seawall."

"Dear, it looks as though you *fell* off the seawall."

"At first, it was just cold and windy, but as I got near Siwash Rock ..." I rubbed my hands together in an effort to lessen the numbness. It wasn't working.

"What happened then, dear?"

"Well, roaring up from the bay, this massive rogue wave came ashore and hit me." Once the words were out of my mouth, I realized how bizarre it sounded.

"A *rogue* wave?" Judging by her wide-eyed look, she didn't look fully convinced. "How astounding!" she exclaimed. "You must be chilled to the —"

"Yeah, I'm a block of ice, so I gotta go, Mrs. McBride. S'cuse me." I fished keys from my water-logged vest.

"Of course, dear." She waved her newspaper at me. "I'm reading that this is one of our coldest winters on record."

My teeth chattered. "I believe it, Mrs. McBride. I don't think I've ever been more cold and wet. I better get warm," I said, starting up the 3 flights of stairs.

"Yes, yes. A hot shower is what you're wanting. And tea. Go along and do take care of yourself, dear," she called out. "We can't have you getting ill."

My fingers were cramped with cold as I unlocked my door and ditched my wet running clothes in the foyer. Naked, in the mirror I noticed my body was bright red. I ran the longest, hottest shower imaginable. For 30 minutes, the heat from the shower warmed me, though after towelling off and dressing in my faded Levi's and my favourite red wool sweater, I once again felt chilled. Well-informed Mrs. McBride was correct. It had been a bitterly cold winter by Vancouver standards. Still, no ice storm, no snow drifts, no block heaters, no frozen lakes and no mukluks — not here. *It's just February; there's more winter ahead.* I tumbled into bed and wrapped myself with covers in an attempt to raise my body temperature. *If Robby were here, he'd find a way to warm me.* My thoughts meandered. *Well, he's not here.* I mentally made a list as I lay motionless. *I gotta get my laundry done and clean this apartment ... so get outta bed. And I owe Lara a call. She should be coming back to town soon. Where'd she say she was singing? Oh, don't forget to phone Mum. Okay, before I make some calls maybe I'll just rest a few minutes under these warm covers ... just until I get toasty.*

Daylight seemed to be blown into my bedroom by the formidable and unrelenting winds. My frosty body warmed as I drowsily thought of Dorothy Gale. My eyelids dropped. In my mind, I saw an image of an old shoddy farmhouse, ripped from its foundations, spinning like a top as it hurtled skyward, sucked up by a wicked tornado as I quickly fell asleep.

2

Catching Up

The last few years had been hectic. I'd finished graduate school and was anxiously working my way through a family therapy program. My internship supervisors were supporting me as I was developing, albeit not without substantial constructive criticism. Frankly, it was not unlike the swim coaches I'd had, always pushing me to do better. My confidence as a beginning therapist was developing as I moved from theory and into clinical practice. Seeing clients at the school's clinic paid me only a small amount, so I was grateful for the stipend provided by the national swim team. It was sufficient to pay for my rent, though I also worked part-time teaching swim lessons. It was something I knew I was good at. Swimming remained the constant in my life — everything revolved around it. Early morning and evening practices at the Vancouver Aquatic Centre were gruelling — perhaps more so than any time. At just 26 years of age and after 20 years of swimming, I was finding it tougher to recover from year-round training. My times needed improvement to stay competitive, so I tirelessly worked at getting faster. But my results were mixed; medalling with some personal bests, but also losing badly at several key swim meets. Sensing my abilities were declining, I decided that this season would be my last. I planned to end my competitive swimming career in the summer at the 1983 Pan American Games in Caracas, Venezuela. I was concerned about qualifying for the competition, and for me, the pressure to do well had never been greater. My events continued to be the 400 IM, 200 butterfly and the 400 and 800 freestyle.

I wasn't alone in having challenging goals. Lara was performing in Canada and the United States since she debuted in spectacular style at the Festijazz in Montreal in 1979. Lara had carved out a name for herself in jazz circles. Her diligence paid off with reasonably consistent engagements, but her fan base remained small. She was trying to achieve a goal of having her first record, or I should say, CD, as they were now becoming popular. Pete continued to represent her, getting her appearances at clubs and small concert venues. Lara told me that Pete was "talking with the right people" about getting her a recording contract with a quality label like Verve. Still, nothing had come of Pete's efforts — yet. *Pete.* I saw him rarely, but when I did it was usually with Lara over dinner when she was in town. I confess those meetings were a little awkward for me. After all, Pete had been my occasional and secret lover years ago. Lara never knew that we'd been intimate, and I wanted to keep it that way. I remained indebted to Pete. He'd been instrumental in both Lara's professional growth and my sexual development. Though Pete was heading towards 50, he was a veritable *Dorian Gray* - maybe *Dorian Gay* would be more fitting. His stunningly glossy black hair was now tinged with a few strands of grey at the temples, but otherwise, he remained youthful, slim, swarthy and masculine. And, of course, utterly charming. Pete was every bit as irresistible regardless of his age.

Robby and I continued our relationship from a distance, as he was directing a dinner theatre version of Agatha Christies 'The

Mousetrap' in Sudbury. That's Sudbury, Ontario, home of the giant nickel. Work in regional theatre was sporadic at best, but Robby's work ethic was untroubled by such lesser assignments, though he didn't elaborate to many people that the show he directed also offered a 2 for 1 drink special. His absences placed a strain on us, but we'd made a commitment to figuring out things as they came along. Robby was someone with whom I had spent my life hoping to find, so a few months away wasn't going to dismantle our relationship. I guess you could say we had an unconventional romance on top of *being* unconventional. Robby and I maintained our separate apartments. I wasn't ready to live with him. The largest reason? I was afraid of telling my parents their son was sleeping with another man. I don't think that would have been well-received, to say the least. That time would come, but not for nearly a decade. The thing is, my parents could have handled that news. It was me who wasn't ready.

My mother, Rose, admitted being dissatisfied with her stay-at-home life. So, in 1981, she earned a diploma in interior decorating from a community college. Decorating was something that she was already skilled at; school polished her abilities further. When I moved into the Queen Charlotte, she transformed my apartment from drab to fab — and on a shoestring budget. Working from a home office, Mum had become self-assured, poised, vibrant and looking as stylish as her client's beautifully decorated homes. On her off-time, she cared for my sister's two children. My sister's husband was now an ex-husband, and Lynda needed Mum's help in order for her to return to full-time work. Lynda and I weren't particularly close, but I was interested in her struggles. Mum ensured that I had the 'skinny' on the various goings-on in her home.

As far as my father, he continued to work in his store 6 days a week and golfed on Sundays in town. He remained unchanged in my perception: distant, irritable, often surly, unceasingly puffing on his Buckingham cigarettes morning till night.

So, all things considered, for my friends, family and me, life was moving in a rather disconnected, yet stable and predictable fashion. But things can change in a heartbeat, can't they?

3

The Call

In the middle of my Family of Origin class, the office manager padded into the room, came over to me and whispered in my ear, "Come with me to the office; there's a call for you. Bring your books; your jacket, too." Anxious about why I was getting called in the middle of my class, I quickly went with Dora to her desk at the end of the hall.

"Here," she said, gently handing the telephone to me. One look at Dora's face and I knew that something bad had happened.

"Thanks," I uttered, noticing the pounding of my heart. "Hello?"

"Shepard, it's Lynda." Her voice was dry and tight.

"Lynda? Has something —"

"It's Dad. He's had a heart attack at the golf club. Dropped like a stone."

"What? It's not Sunday," I said, then heard how stupid I sounded.

"No, but at least he was closer to the hospital. Golfing in February? That old fool." Lynda's voice cracked with emotion.

"Jeez, is he —"

"No, he's not dead. He's at the Royal Columbian. They have to run more tests — an angiogram. Mum's spoken with the doctor. He said his oxygen level is very low and there's a blockage — Mum, what did they say about the blockage?"

"The doctor said his aorta is 85% blocked." My mother's voice was small and tinny.

"Gawd," I uttered, taking a huge breath. "Is he conscious?"

"Yes, in bed and he's been told there's to be no exertion," my sister added.

Well, surely that will be familiar.

"Do we know how he's feeling? "

"Oh, Dad's pissed. He keeps asking the nurses for a smoke. They've put him on oxygen. The doctor said if he lights a ciggie the ward'll explode like Hiroshima."

"Christ. How's Mum?"

"She's white as a sheet and can't believe what's happened, but I honestly don't know why. Dad's smoked like a furnace since he was 9, not to mention his all-meat diet."

I heard some rustling noises in the background.

"Listen, I'm not going to put Mum on because we're leaving shortly. Will you —"

"I'll meet you at the hospital. Be careful on the way in, okay? Bye."

I put down the phone and puffed out a deep breath and quickly told Dora what happened.

"I'm so sorry," Dora offered quietly.

"Thanks. Can you let everyone know I'll be away for a few days?"

Dora nodded affirmatively. "I'll give you a call soon," I cried out as I bounded downstairs and swiftly located my infamous (to me, at least) red VW Fastback in the student parking lot. The car lock was frozen again.

Shit.

I put my key in my mouth for a minute, then tried again. *Thank gawd.* I opened the door, slid in on vinyl seats. Placing the key in the ignition, I noticed my hand was shaking. *Take a breath.* After firing up the VW, I threw the gear into 1ˢᵗ and started a contemplative drive to New Westminster.

The traffic on the Grandview highway was heavy as I inched my way towards the freeway and started to recall what my sister had said. *Lynda's right, it was only a matter of time. His incessant smoking. Drinking Scotch like it was water. Not to mention a steady diet of red meat, white bread and potatoes drenched in a pound of butter. A meal he typically finished with an entire brick of Neapolitan ice cream and a pack of Buckingham's. Doesn't it all catch up with us in the end?* I wasn't watching the road as I merged onto a packed freeway at rush-hour. *Pay attention; this isn't the time to crash into a ditch.* I shifted into 3rd gear as I moved onto the crowded express-way. As I drove past the Villa Hotel, there was a huge bank of fog obscuring the opposite lane in the Burnaby Lake area. I clicked on my headlights as the winter light began to fade.

But people survive heart attacks, right? He's only — what? 50-something...57? Well, that's probably old enough. I dropped the Fastback into 4th and drove the better part of an hour, taking Brunette Avenue exit for New Westminster. In another 20 minutes I was walking through the doors of the Royal Columbian Hospital. I located the information desk, hardly noticing the mayhem of staff and patients around me. I recall how odd it was for me to rush to the hospital to see a father who had been a distant figure in my life. If he — as I told myself — was so unimportant to me, why did my hands tremble and my heart pound at the thought that he would leave us? *Perhaps he means more to me than I'd care to admit. Nah, you're wrong about that one, Sunshine.*

The nurse at the desk looked haggard; perhaps she was nearing the end of her shift. She glanced up at me, exhaled and asked, "Yes?"

"My father's been brought in today — William Stamp. What's the room, please?"

The nurse hauled out a giant black binder and leafed through it quickly.

"He's in Emergency," she stated plainly. "There's no room for him yet." She pointed to the left. "Head that way."

After checking at the Emergency desk, a nurse took me through the back end of the ward, past beeping equipment, bustling hospital staff, and moaning patients. I breathed in a troubling stench of disinfectant and decay.

"He's behind there," she stated, gesturing at the pale blue curtain.

"Thanks."

I pushed the curtain back to reveal the crumpled, ashen figure of my father. He lay slightly propped up, motionless on a chrome-railed hospital bed, wires attached to his chest, a plastic hose in his nostrils, his wrists cuffed for blood pressure and a monitor with a green circular display screen close by on a caster-wheeled cart. His snowy-white hair was askew and his hazel eyes were heavy-lidded and red. He stared back at what must have been my startled face.

"Number One," he deadpanned.

4

Rules of Attachment

Parents whose attachment with their own parent or parents is not achieved may have considerable challenges with their own child. There are many factors that influence attachment. Was I a child that proved difficult for my father to attach to? There's no doubt. I imagined my father sensed that I was "different" from a young age and both he and I began to distance. A gay boy may detach from his father unwittingly, perhaps because he fears disappointing him. Having a gay son is often considered shameful, so many gay boys or men keep themselves — as I did — locked away from their father. A boy's relationship with his father is where he learns whether he's loveable. If this primary relationship is characterized by distance — which it is for many gay boys — it has a great implication for how a boy develops his sense of worth in the eyes of other men.

It was confusing to sort out my thoughts when it came to my father being so unwell. His role in my life was peripheral at best. His collapse was disturbing — perhaps *because* of the lack of attachment that I experienced throughout my growing up. Additionally, I was troubled by my father's illness for what it meant to my mother.

But for me? *Do I have any right to be upset by a father who has never done so much as throw a ball with me? Go for a walk in the woods? A swim at the lake? Give me a hug when I was scared? Help me with schoolwork? No, it's hard to know how to feel.* That was something I just couldn't figure out.

5

Man & Superman

When I was a boy, I adored Superman. In fact, as a tot I learned to read by leafing through DC comics. It wasn't just the Man of Steel's red cape and blue tights, by the way. Superman's lantern jaw, blue-black hair, muscular physique and superpowers were thrilling, but there was something else that got my attention: his secret identity. Every gay boy or girl can identify with having an outside image which competes with their "real" persona. Superman was accepted both as an amazing hero and as Clark Kent. As a boy and as a young man, self-acceptance was a challenge. That's why swimming became such a critical activity for me. I had an unquestioned identity as a swimmer, nearly invisible beneath the water. Becoming visible was a riskier task than a race ever represented. Years before Stonewall and the politics of inclusion, being gay was reason enough for many of us to stay hidden. It created a tension that permeated nearly every aspect of my interactions — including those with my father. Kryptonite was Superman's nemesis, and clearly my father was face to face with his foe — the cigarette. Vulnerable in his bed, I struggled with what to do or say. I was stunningly reminded that we remained strangers for many years.

"What did the doctor tell you?" I inquired, trying to initiate a conversation.

"Where's your mother?" he asked, ignoring my question.

"She's on her way. I spoke with Lynda an hour or so ago. They both should be here shortly." *So answer my bloody question, already.*

"Bring that over here." He stabbed his finger in the direction of a red plastic chair. "I don't like you towering over me." I felt a quick flush of irritation before I retrieved the chair and dragged it close to his bed. I could smell his breath, a mixture of stale cigarettes and coffee. I took off my brown leather jacket and placed in on the back of the chair. There was a woman's scream from a few beds away, cordoned off by a curtain.

"Jezus," I muttered as I sat down, jolted by the agonized shriek.

"That's been going on for a while. I think she's on drugs. And she wants more of 'em," he said, rolling his eyes as the woman cried out.

"So," I ventured once more, "what happened, Dad?"

My father raised his hand, clenched it into a fist and pounded the hospital bed railings several times. "Like I was hit with a sledgehammer. I came in to play a round and was on the back nine — can't remember the hole — and thought I was having bad indigestion from the sausage rolls I had for lunch." He gritted his teeth from the recollection. "The pain got worse until I dropped to my knees. Then I passed out. Chip must have gotten help. I don't remember. Then I woke up here, wired to all this," he gestured at the variety of equipment that he was plugged into. "That's what happened," he said weakly.

"Do you have pain now?" I inquired.

"It's tolerable," he said, not elaborating further with my question. "It'd be better with a smoke."

"I'm sure," I said dryly.

A long period of silence followed, having spoken with my father more in the last few minutes than I had in years. I was thinking of the next question to ask when my mother and sister appeared, rushing into the ward, with worry etched on their faces. Mum kissed my father's mouth, then glanced anxiously at the hoses, wires and contraptions keeping him alive.

My mother and sister were a study in contrasts. Lynda was petite, her dark-hair cut in a pixie style, olive-skinned with eyes so dark they appeared black. She was dressed in a mint-green polyester uniform, having come directly from her job at a dental office. My mother's blonde hair was past collar length with bangs, her body shapely, pale skinned with blue-green eyes. She was dressed in black pleated pants, wore brown boots, a beige blouse and a long navy wool coat. I could see she'd broken out in a rash across her throat and upper chest.

"How was the traffic on the freeway?" he asked.

"Uh, it was — Dad, do you really want to talk about the traffic?" Lynda responded ruefully. "Where's the doctor? Who do we speak to?" Lynda bent over his head, fluffing the pillow.

"How the hell do I know?" he responded irritably. "Stop fooling with my pillow."

"I'll find out," she said, leaving his bedside to head to the nurse's station.

"Well," my mother watched as my sister went off in search of answers she doubted she'd receive. She turned her attention back to my father. In a voice that dripped with cheerfulness, she said, "At least we're all together, aren't we?" It sounded forced. She cast me a furtive peek as my father, pale and wan, lay sunken in his bed. "And whatever needs doing, we'll do and you'll live to see another day, won't you?"

"I don't want to hear any Goddamned schmaltz," my father uttered, then stared blankly across the unpleasant room he was in, past the machines that kept him alive.

"Will, I wasn't trying to —"

"I wish I could just fly away," he said closing he eyes. My mother looked at me and shook her head.

Hmmm. Just like Superman.

6

Introducing Dr. Deth

For another hour we sat with Dad in an attempt to comfort him when a tall man — perhaps in his late 30s — in the proverbial white coat came to his bedside, as per my sister's request.

"Mister Stamp?"

My Dad lifted his head and then slowly nodded. "And you are?"

"I'm your cardiologist, Dr. Deth," he said, waiting for our response. I jumped at the chance. "Excuse me, did you say your —"

"Yes, it's 'Deth'. I'm Belgian."

"*Jesus Christ*," my mother muttered under her breath. Dad's jaw dropped to the disinfected floor. Lynda looked horrified and I couldn't help but smile; it was grossly comical, in a macabre way. *This couldn't get any better.*

My father was shaken when Dr. Deth gave him the results of his angiogram, angioplasty and blood work. He informed him that he needed to have open-heart surgery to repair a nearly completely blocked artery and to replace his heart valve. And there was a sense of urgency: the operation was to go ahead within the next few days. For all my father's stalwartness, he was squeamish about medical issues. (The first time he gave blood was the last — he passed out when the nurse missed his vein a couple of times.) In his defence, the description of the surgery provided by the unfortunately named cardiologist would have made most people squirm. During the 7-hour operation, his chest would be cracked open at the breastbone to expose his heart. He'd be connected to a heart-lung bypass machine, then his heart valve would be replaced using a pig's heart for parts — a bit of irony for my Jewish father who operated an auto-part's store. After his chest was literally wired up, the healing process would begin — with a long period of recovery. Dr. Deth didn't pull punches — there were great risks during and after the surgery. The look of resignation spread across my father's face. He was clearly convinced that he was on the way out. When Dr. Deth left, we did our best to disabuse Dad of his prediction, but we weren't as assured as we made out to be. After spending a couple of hours with him, Dad was obviously exhausted. My sister held his hand for a moment and said goodbye, kissing him on the forehead. She and I left Mum and stepped into the hall so she could speak with her husband in privacy.

"I've gotta get back home to the girls. I asked the woman next door with the drinking problem to look after them, and God knows what's happening. If I'm lucky, she hasn't blacked out with a lit cigarette in her mouth." Lynda buttoned up her coat.

"Gawd, let's hope. I guess Mum is —"

"Going to have to stay with you," she said flatly, finishing my sentence. "That's okay, isn't it?" Lynda asked with raised brows. "She'll need to run back and forth to this place for the next couple of weeks. You do know that?"

Really? I couldn't have figured that out. "It's no problem," I lied. "Dad's really in a bad way, isn't he?" My father had spent nearly 50 years puffing on pack after pack of cigarettes. How much plague had formed in those arteries? His lungs must have been black with tar.

"I know about teeth and gums," she opined. "But like Deth said, open-heart surgery is a chancy procedure." Lynda tapped her wristwatch. "I'm sorry, but I *have* to get back to Abbotsford before my neighbour gets into my box of wine."

"She wouldn't, would she?"

"Please. She's likely four sheets to the wind and the girls are probably entertaining the boy's hockey team in the garage. You know how girls are."

Not really, but...

"Yeah, sounds like you better hustle, Lynda," I said earnestly.

"I'll try to see him tomorrow night. Tell Mum, 'k?" Lynda's tired voice croaked a bit, her eyes glimmered, perhaps holding back some tears. Then she left, walking swiftly from the ward. A few moments later, Mum emerged wearing a ghostly face.

"C'mon, Mum. We're going back to my place," I explained as brightly as I could. "It'll be a blast," I said, wondering if there was anything I should have put away from her view in my apartment. *No, I think everything's fine...*

"It's no bother? I don't want to cramp your style."

"Mum, we all know I have no style," I chuckled.

"I can always get a room at the Sylvia. Really, I —"

"Mum."

I put my arm around her shoulder as we began to leave the hospital. "Jeez," I began, the described surgical procedure burning images in my mind, "that's one scary operation."

"Yes," Mum agreed, then quickly changed the subject. "So, what would you like for dinner?"

7

The Visitation of Rose

W e walked across the barren parking lot and climbed into the Fastback. I wiped the mist from the inside of the windshield with a paper towel and fired up the VW.

"Well," my mother declared, "I suppose this brings new meaning to the term, 'Golf Widow'," she said dryly.

Or Merry Widow.

"Mum, isn't that a little premature? He hasn't even gone under Dr. Deth's knife yet," I said, hearing the preposterousness in the statement as I tossed the Fastback into gear. Mum grew quiet for some time as we sped home to my apartment, having missed my evening swim practice, dinner and now, much-needed sleep. Thankfully, after 9 PM the roads were nearly empty as we zipped past Burnaby and approached the Vancouver boundary.

"You know, your father's been feeling unwell for a while," she reflected.

"I didn't know that. How so?"

"Well, for example, after cutting the grass this past summer he'd be utterly exhausted. Drenched in sweat as though he'd run a marathon. So he hired that boy next door to do the lawn. The tall boy."

"Yes, I recall."

The tall, very good-looking young man with the long brown hair who prefers to cut the grass shirtless. I certainly do recall.

"Your father said he was tired of the chore, but that's rubbish. Even going upstairs has become a struggle for him — just gasping for air. Will says it's his allergies, but I suspected something was seriously wrong with his breathing. He's also sleeping 11 or 12 hours a night and he's become hard to waken — so unlike him. When I implored him to go to his doctor, he nearly took my head off. And he's even more irritable," she added.

"Is that possible?" I asked rhetorically.

"I hoped this was a just a part of getting older, but … I knew better." Mum shook her head. "And though he never said so, he's been worried, too."

"He's going to have to quit smoking. Really, somehow he's gotta stop."

"Perhaps this'll be the scare he needs," she stated.

I chose not to respond to my mother's last statement and tried to focus my fading attention on staying alert as my eyes grew heavy. My father had never been able to quit smoking, though many attempts had been made. From the moment he woke to the time just before his head was on the pillow, his perennial companion hung from his mouth. It was impossible for me to think that he could willingly give it up. Mum explained the "boys" would look after the store for my father so that he needn't worry. Of course, he worried about his business most of the time. The remaining half-hour of the drive was spent in silence. Exiting the freeway, we travelled west on 1st Avenue, past old wooden homes with the contrasting modern towers of the downtown core and the high-rises of the West End coming into view. I adjusted the heat; it was too warm in the car and it was making me even groggier. The VW heat control was mercurial. We drove along the Georgia viaduct, the air-cooled motor clattering comfortingly. As we turned off Dunsmuir and right on Georgia we approached her former place of employment: The Hudson's Bay.

"Oh, I wasn't thinking," she blurted as we went past the large building.

"Sorry?"

"I have nothing — no change of clothes, no toiletries. I'll have to go to the Bay tomorrow."

"Of course," I clucked as we cruised along vacant streets on the way to the Queen Charlotte apartments. After finding parking, we stepped from the Fastback and felt the stinging bite of cold air.

"It's like Winterpeg out here," I said, locking the car as a gush of icy air pushed my hair off my forehead. We walked, empty-handed, up Nicola Street towards the apartment, our breaths forming clouds of white. *Usually, when Mum comes to stay with me for a weekend she's got enough luggage for a 6-month stay — but not this time.*

My mother and I tiredly went through the lobby. Instead of taking the stairs we moved to the ornate bird-cage elevator with the brass door. Pushing it open, I pressed the floor number. Immediately, the gears groaned as the lift slowly shuddered its way to the 3rd floor. I unlocked the apartment, and as we went through I noticed the blinking light on my answering machine. After removing our shoes and coats, Mum went to the small galley kitchen.

"Hungry?"

"I'd love a glass of wine," she said. Though I rarely drank, I stocked wine for my mother and most certainly for Lara when she was in town.

"There should be Chardonnay in the fridge. Be warned; to get at the vino you'll have to bypass some very furry leftovers."

"Bypass, eh?" Mum frowned at me, then started her search.

"Yeah, not the best turn of —"

"It's okay. Look, I found some," she exclaimed happily, holding it up. She found a glass, uncorked the bottle and poured herself a large drink.

"I'd better fix you something to eat with that. How 'bout an omelette?"

"With buttered toast? And marmalade? I mean, if you have any."

"Of course. Go sit down on the sofa. I'll just be a few minutes."

She smiled, gave me a squeeze of my hand, then slowly moved to my velvet peacock brown and teal sofa. I busied myself with cracking eggs and whisking them in a glass bowl, slicing some sharp white cheddar cheese and making some toast with bread from the Paris Bakery on Denman Street — my favourite. I cut up some tomatoes, spread the toast with margarine (I wasn't fond of butter) and Seville marmalade. I heated up the cast iron pan, poured in some olive oil and made a large cheese omelette for my mother and me. By the time I came back to the living room, she had fallen into a heavy sleep. Her wine was barely touched. I stared at my sleeping mother. At age 51, she remained youthful. Her face had few lines; hair well-coifed and coloured; an hourglass figure fashionably attired. I stood for a moment longer, cheese omelette and toast on a bamboo tray, and marvelled at how untroubled she appeared. Her deep and regular breathing promptly turned into light snoring.

"Mum," I said softly. "Here's your dinner." No response. I took the food and left it on the small round kitchen table, retrieved a blanket from my bed and came back to the living room. I lifted her legs all the way up onto the sofa. She sighed slightly. I placed the blanket snugly around her and left the room without a sound. I used the toilet, neglecting to flush because of the noise, and went to my bedroom. I pulled off my socks, stepped out of my faded Levi's and dropped them to the floor. *I gotta get up in a few hours for swim practice.* I fantasized about skipping practice more than I'd care to admit. After all, I wasn't going to class for a few days. *No, you have to go to practice.* I crawled under the duvet, ruminated for a few moments and slipped into unconsciousness.

8

Beat the Clock

I woke at 5:00 in the morning. I used the washroom, brushed my teeth, tugged on my sweatpants, a white tee-shirt and a bright green sweater, then soundlessly walked to the kitchen table where I stood and chowed down on my mother's uneaten omelette. I noticed Mum didn't seem to have moved from the night before. *She's dead to the world. Or maybe she's dead? Oh, there's a snore.* I collected my swim gear, wrote her a note telling her how to get to the hospital on the most direct bus route, slipped on my Nikes and left for practice.

After hurrying to the Aquatic Centre in my foggy Fastback, I changed into a black Speedo, grabbed my goggles and cap and walked onto the pool deck. I looked at the posted workout schedule for my group written on a huge green chalkboard. The contingent of swimmers in my training group hovered with me to review the schedule, but I'd never describe them as friends. There were a few swimmers that I exchanged pleasantries, but otherwise, I maintained my distance — even after all this time. It was a great risk to be an "out" athlete, male or female.

For the past 3 years, my coach was Tom Thompson — not the famous Canadian painter — but a former freestyler from the 1960s who became an elite coach for high-performance athletes. I was challenged to meet his expectations. In fact, Thompson openly questioned my abilities. He had good reason; at most, I'd been inconsistent at key meets this and most of the previous year. There were several other swimmers looking at the board and a dozen others in the water when Thompson came up beside me.

"And where were *you* last night, Stamp?" he barked. Several swimmers smiled at my apparent embarrassment.

Shit.

"Sorry. It's my dad. He's sick in hospital. It was all unexpected," I offered. "Sorry."

"You already said that. You're expected to call and let me know. There's no excuse. Get in your lane and start your set. *Now,*" he said crossly.

I pushed my long hair under my swim cap, adjusted my goggles and jumped in to start my practice. *And thanks for your kind words of consolation, asshole.*

Like the other swimmers, I began with a warm-up of freestyle, back and breaststroke — my least successful stroke, but a necessary one when swimming the Individual Medley. I'd been grinding out demanding physical practice sessions for much of my life. It was really taking a toll. As in my youth, swimming distance day in and day out yielded a well-developed and flexible physique with powerful arms and large shoulders. My 170-pound body remained strikingly free of injuries, although the aches associated with elite training were constant. I'd become accustomed to them, but I found it fatiguing to be in a recovery phase for most of the year. My workout was 6 kilometres. It consisted of a kick set, 400 IM sets, a pyramid set of 100-metre sprints, another kick set and repetitions of free, back, breast and free with a cool-down of 500 metres. For portions of the swim, I had the displeasure of Thompson yelling at me either at the gutter or the length of the pool. During the IM, I lost my concentration —thinking of how my father was managing in hospital. Thompson soon noticed.

"Hey, you! Pick it up! Pull, pull!" Thompson hollered at me, loud enough for the rest of the swimmers to briefly cock their ears from the water to see if the coach was screaming at them. I picked up the pace as ordered. With a tough 400 IM to complete, I willed myself to compensate for my lack of rest. I pushed off from the wall, dolphin kicking deeply. My extra-long arms and wide feet gave me bonus power as I felt the familiar movement of my body, nearly kicking from my sternum as I undulated underwater for 15 metres, my 6-foot body fully extended, then surfaced and took my first pull, the water pushed behind me. My body arched as I coordinated the movement of kick, kick, pull, pull over and over again, creating a boiling wake in the process. After completing one length, my lungs burned. I repeated the stroke, gaining speed as I reached my maximum speed, breathing explosively timed, closing on the wall. *Just a few more metres.* Arms completely extended, I kicked one final time, grabbed the gutter, then flipped to my back, pushing off the wall with exhausted legs. I started the backstroke with a slight foot cramp, then it was gone as I kept my eyes on the ceiling, moving quickly to the end of the lane, then a flip-turn as I went into the last 50 metres, swimming well, churning the water, shoulders pulling me through the water easily, breathing rhythmically as the water rolled over my face. I kicked harder, reaching the end and onto my breaststroke. I did one underwater heart-shaped pull and whip-kick before surfacing. For me, the 'fly was strenuous, but it was the breaststroke that continued to challenge me throughout my competitive swim career. I only swam it during IM's and could never compete in it alone. Though I'd made necessary improvements, the breast remained a struggle for me. When I took an inhalation at the end of the stroke it was more of a nausea-inducing gasp. After the turn, the second 50 was significantly more difficult than the first. I felt my knees ache from a whip that didn't propel me effectively; my shoulders stung, too, and my bursting lungs signalled I was running out of fuel. My last few metres saw me falling off the pace — Coach Thompson (unfairly) called my stroke 'leisurely' at this point of the IM. The relief was enormous for me as I got to the end of the lane and began the freestyle — a stroke I *could* do, and fast. In Montreal, I did the impossible — winning the 400 IM with a blistering final kick that sent me scorching past the other competitors. Lara called it 'turning on the jets'. In practice, I lit the fuse and rocketed the final 70 metres, touching the wall in 4:39 — very respectable for a swim practice, if not fully competitive. Still, my chest was heaving from the exertion at the end of the lane as I pushed off my goggles and found Thompson glaring above me on the pool deck.

"That's more like it, Stamp. Now do it again and knock off 5 seconds. Go!"

I regained my oxygen and pushed off the wall. 22 swimmers and me playing beat the clock.

After a punishing swim, there was a workout in the weight room with our trainer followed by an ice-bath before trekking home at 10:00 AM. The sun was hidden by ominous grey clouds as I walked to my apartment. *Weather's changing. Certainly it's warmer.* I unlocked my door and immediately saw the flashing light of the answering machine. *Shit, I forgot about this last night.*

I heard the shower running.

Mum's still here. I thought she'd be at the hospital by now.

After I plunked down my swim-bag on the table, I touched the play button.

Two messages. Gotta be Robby. I should have called to let him know what's —

"Sunshine, it's me. I tried calling last night after practice, but you weren't home. I have to talk to you. It's about —" she left her sentence tantalizingly unfinished as the machine cut out.

"Damnit," I said, shaking my head in disappointment, waiting for the next message.

"Hey, it's me. It's 10 PM your time, but guess you're out, unless you're asleep. Call me and if I don't hear from you tonight, I'll try you in the morning. I miss you."

Robby. I smiled at the sound of his bright voice, even if it was on a cassette tape. I replayed his message.

"Oh, you're back," Mum cried as she peered down the hall wearing a large bath towel. "I didn't hear you come in. Did you get your message from that nice boy?"

"Mum," I said, feeling my face flush, "why do you think he's a nice boy?"

Jeez, did you listen to my messages?

"Well, he sounded very pleasant when I spoke with him this morning."

"Huh? You were speaking to him?" I tried not to sound as surprised as I was.

"Of course. He woke me up when he called. Who is he?"

"He's my friend Robby," I gulped. "You've heard me talk about him — he's the guy directing a show in Sudbury." I'd cautiously mentioned Robby in passing several times — never any details.

Gawd, don't look embarrassed. Perhaps I should spill the beans. Yeah, Mum, let me tell you all about Robby. He's a hot blond guy with a killer body who picked me up at Lost Lagoon a few years ago. Whaddya think of that?

"Sudbury? Well, he seemed anxious to speak with you." Mum retreated to the washroom. "You'll have to reach him."

"I'll ring him after tonight's practice," I called out. "It's long distance."

Mum stepped from the washroom in her bra and yesterday's pants. Her white flesh was still mottled with splotches of red across her chest. She dabbed at her bare arms with the towel. Her brow was furrowed. "Aren't you going to the hospital this evening?"

"Mum, Thompson almost tossed me off the team for going AWOL last night. I can't miss practice again," I explained. "Dad'll understand."

"Your father's going to need your support. *He's your father*," she needlessly emphasized as she stepped back into the small bathroom.

Yes, he's my father. But, were the situation reversed, would he stop his work — and that's what swimming was for me — to be "supportive"?

"Besides, nothing's happening for a few days, right?" I asked.

"I expect we'll get more information today," she sighed. "First, I've got to get a few things downtown," she said. "I look like a ragamuffin," she said, viewing herself in the mirror. "Don't worry, I can take the bus ..." Mum pulled on her blouse. "Yech, this smells like the hospital," she said disdainfully. She drew bright red lipstick across her mouth, pursing her lips and wiping the edges of her gob.

"No, I'll run you downtown, Mum. Lynda said she would try to see Dad tonight."

"He'll want to see you, as well." Mum smeared her eyes with blue eyeshadow that she'd located in her purse. Her unwashed hair was uncharacteristically jutting out at various angles leaving an unpolished impression. "I think I need a scarf, don't you?" she asked, pushing and pulling at her unruly dark-blonde hair. "I look like Mrs. Lovett in 'Sweeny Todd'," she moaned.

"Mum, " I sighed, grabbing the car keys, "you're beautiful — let's go."

9

The Smoking Friend

After a 3 hour buying frenzy at the Hudson's Bay and Eaton's across the street, my mother was pleased to have amassed a wardrobe suitable for a week's worth of hospital visits: 2 pairs of slacks in taupe and navy, 5 blouses in a variety of shades of blue, peach, ivory and green, a handful of silk scarves in coordinating colours and subtle patterns, a new pair of beige boots and a couple pieces of costume jewelry. For lugging her bags around and patiently providing my style opinion, Mum rewarded me with an aqua polo shirt and a pair of khaki pants from Eaton's. "For the summer," she said. Such spring or summer weather was outside the realm of consciousness — at least, for me. Winter in Vancouver is not for those who require sunlight. The coast is a wet, cold and for some, depressing season. As the Fastback's motor securely whirled to life in the Bay parking lot, I put on the lights. Though it was just 2 PM, the overcast skies were quickly darkening, and as I pulled onto Dunsmuir, the rain started to fall. I cracked open the window, tried in vain to get warm air moving across the seemingly permanently fogged windshield and drove towards New Westminster.

"Mum," I cautiously ventured, "if something happened to Dad, would you be okay?"

"What do you mean, 'okay'?"

"I mean, would you be able to take care of the house, the bills, all that stuff?"

"Well, yes, I suppose that I would. I'd have to learn a few things, but … I'd have to. After all, I'm not an idiot. What choice would I have?"

"Right. I was just cur —"

"You don't think your father will make it through surgery, do you?" she asked pointedly.

"I didn't say that, Mum. And I'm certain that he will," I answered half-truthfully. As we drove, I kept thinking about the procedure Dr. Deth described and felt slightly nauseous. *Cracking open the sternum? An operation lasting 7 or 8 hours? Jeez. And if he didn't come through, what would it mean to me? I'd have lost a father I never really had. Would that be worse than not having one at all?* I couldn't wrap my head around it as I continued to move along the highway.

"I've been so caught up with your father that I've neglected to ask what you think."

"About?"

"About your father having a heart attack."

"Well, Mum." I gave myself a moment to breathe deeply. I didn't want to upset my mother.

"Yes?"

"I think Dad's lucky to have gotten this far."

"I thought you might say that."

"It's just —"

"That he's spent his life puffing on Buckingham's and downing Scotch?"

"Yeah. And working 15 hours a day. I think it caught up with him — especially the smoking. And it's not as though he didn't have the chance to quit, is it?"

"When Will was shipped to Canada from overseas he was just 13 and on his own. No adults to care for him and certainly no schoolmates. Maybe cigarettes eased his loneliness and were — I don't know, like having a friend."

"Did he tell you that, Mum?"

"Your father? No, I doubt he'd think about it that way."

"Maybe if he had found different friends … he wouldn't be visiting Dr. Deth," I stated ironically.

"You simply love to use that doctor's name, don't you?" Mum admonished me.

I smiled slightly as we continued on our way to the Royal Columbian Hospital.

10

Getting the Goods

As anxious as a family emergency can be, it tends to inspire members to be on their best behaviour. That was the case for my family. I told myself to be more patient, more conciliatory towards my father. My other family — Lara and Robby — were being neglected. They were unaware of what was going on and I had to find some time to apprise them of the situation. *I'll call them both when I get back from here.*

"He's been moved to the cardiac ward. Private room," the starchy nurse said crisply when Dad wasn't found in the Emergency area. "Elevator to your left, 6th floor. East wing."

The stench of this place. What is that? Dettol plus bleach? A bit of overkill. Oops, wrong term again. We made our way to my father's ward. We stepped into a room with four sickly-looking adult males. In the corner, looking agitated, was Dad. He was wearing paper-thin powder-blue cotton pyjamas. My father *never* wore pyjamas. The prongs of a clear plastic oxygen cord continued to be attached to his nostrils.

"Rose. I've been waiting all day for you to get here. What took you?" He looked as before; ashen.

"I had to get a few things," she blanched at his criticism.

"I can see that," he said accusingly, noticing my mother's new outfit.

"How are you? Need anything?" she asked, moving towards him for a kiss. He turned his cheek so that she could peck it.

"I need a smoke."

"Yes, well that's not going to happen," a nurse boomed as she moved to his bedside. "You the Mrs.?"

"Yes," my mother warily answered.

Like me, my mother was instantly cognizant that we were dealing with Nurse Authority.

"He keeps asking me to wheel him out for a cigarette. He doesn't take 'no' easily, does he? Used to getting your way, are you?" The nurse, a small-framed woman with frizzy red hair, looked to be in her 40s. Small and wiry, she was nonetheless intimidating in every respect and seemed weary of my father's ridiculous requests.

"Did you bring me something to eat?" he asked my mother. Before she could answer, he swore, "They're starving me with poached fish and limp lettuce."

"No green Jello?" I inquired. My father was not amused.

"Number One, go to that deli on 6th — the one near Woodward's — and get me something I can sink my teeth into. A corned beef sandwich with lots of hot mustard. And some real coffee, not this decaf crap. My wallet's —"

"Oh, Mr. Stamp, there'll be no such thing," Nurse Authority interrupted immediately. "Your father's been put on a low-fat diet."

"It's hell on earth," he declared, scowling at the nurse.

"He's such a charmer," the nurse commented. Her name-tag was askew, but it looked like it read, 'Nurse Parrot' although I preferred the moniker I provided. "I'll be back," she warned my father, waving her 1st finger in mid-air.

"I'll be holding my breath," he muttered. Nurse Authority heard his sarcastic comment, grimaced and said, "That wouldn't be advisable," as she left.

"Well, Dad. It looks like you've made a new friend," I joked.

"She's got it in for me, I tell you," he reported in complete seriousness.

"Will, let's change the subject. Has the doc —"

"No, I haven't seen him this afternoon, if that's what you wanna know." He slid lower in his bed and pulled the flannelette covers to his neck. I'd never seen my father look resigned before. He didn't wear it well.

"Where's Lynda? Isn't she coming? She told me she'd be here."

Wow, you are stressed. What's going on with you? Is this what a scare does? Oh, of course; it's like that woman screaming for drugs the other night. It's not merely about being frightened — it's also about what's been lost.

"You're *really* missing your smokes, aren't you Dad?"

My father glowered at me in his most intimidating manner. "Sorry. I just ... well, I think I should head out soon. Practice is at 5:30."

"How is your mother getting back? Rose?" My father looked very concerned.

"I'll take the bus. I know the one to catch; Shepard told me," she calmly responded.

"You're not taking the bus at night. Do you want to get your throat slit? Lynda can drive you back. Or your son can."

"He's not coming back for me tonight, Will," she sighed. "He's already done enough driving for me. I won't have it."

Ignoring her, my father asked, "What about those brakes?"

"Huh? What about them?"

Don't snap at your father ...

"The cylinder broke," my father reminded me.

"Yeah, Dad, but that was 2 years ago," I said curtly. "Dad, don't worry about my brakes. Worry about —" *Ooops.* I paused in mid-sentence.

"About myself? About being sliced open like a sturgeon?" He glared icily.

"I just meant, that, well, yes, you s*hould* be thinking of getting better." I looked at my Timex blatantly. "Jeez, I don't want to be late, I really need to go before the traffic is too —"

"Yes, yes. Go. Swimming's *very* important," he sneered sarcastically. I looked at my father in disbelief, as though he'd changed into a completely different man in 48 hours.

"Will," my mother intervened, "he's just trying to —"

"Rose, give me a moment with my son," he said firmly. "Get a coffee. *Do it.*" My father thumbed at the door. My mother looked startled and offended. As she left the room, my heart thudded. "Come here," he commanded, though in a rather feeble voice.

I came closer to my father; too close for comfort.

"Dad?"

"I spoke with that doctor. Dr. Deth. *Jesus H. Christ.* What a name. He gave me the goods."

"And?" I nervously asked.

"And I want you to promise that if something happens, and I don't wake up after this surgery ... you'll make sure your mother's taken care of. And the store ... God, *my* store."

"*Dad.*"

"Promise me. Your *oath.*" His eyes were misted with the moisture of tears I'd never before seen.

"There's no question. Of course I will. Okay?" My throat was tight and my voice was scratchy. Suddenly my crusty, cantankerous father looked relieved.

"Good." He let out a sigh of relief. "That's all I'm asking. That store is your mother's security."

"I understand," I said. "Dad, I hafta get going, okay?"

"Alright. Now, before you go, give your old dad a kiss goodbye."

I couldn't believe my ears. After a few telling moments of hesitation, I leaned over the railing of the bed, looked down on a man that I always thought of as robust and vigorous, albeit disconnected from me. That same man I viewed was vulnerable, frail and grey. I placed my hand on his chest, kissed my father on his lips and felt the plastic of his oxygen hose against my face. He seemed to completely relax under my touch. He dropped his head to his chest and closed his heavy eyes, his lids speckled with minute spider veins. I stood, touched his white, Brillo-pad hair, smiled at my father and quietly left his side.

11

The Anxiety Starts

As I'd anticipated, swim practice that evening was a shambles. Thompson was apoplectic with my lack of focus. I came home, exhausted and made up the bedroom for my mother. There were a few, ah, periodicals that I nestled away in the linen closet. *Hmmm, you're not the only things heading into the closet during Mum's visit.*

After putting on some fresh sheets, I plumped pillows, shook the peach duvet cover, dusted, vacuumed, scrubbed the bathroom with Comet and dumped some bleach into the toilet. *She'll like that. Mum has an affinity for Javex.* I was out of fresh towels, so I took a heap of them with jeans and some tee-shirts bound for the dark and definitely creepy basement where the laundry was located. During my 3-year tenancy at the Queen Charlotte, the building had seen some upgrades, though for the most part, its days of glory were decades earlier. I took my wash into the cramped elevator and descended to the murky basement, where my imagination conjured up ghostly visions that simply did not exist. *Jeez, did that shadow just move?* I took a quick breath.

How did I become so fearful? The dark gloom of the cellar was lightened considerably when I stepped into the florescent-lit laundry room. As per usual, there wasn't a soul in sight. After dumping in my clothes, I ran back upstairs to see what I could make for supper. *It's nearly 9 o'clock. What's happening at the hospital? Jeez, I gotta call Lara and Robby.* I stepped into my apartment and grabbed the phone, dialled and sat down in my brown leather chair. Robby answered on the 3rd ring.

"Hello, handsome," he said.

"How do you know who this is?" I asked, smiling at the sound of his voice.

"It's after midnight. Who else would be calling me?"

"Well, it could be any number of those actors that you're working with. I'm sure they all have crushes on you."

"Oh, yes," Robby stated sarcastically, "I'm shooing them away by the thousands."

"Big cast."

"Everything about Sudbury is big, including the actors," he laughed. "Seems as though fast food is a way of life in Sudbury. The only fresh fruit here is me."

"I'm sure that's not the case. They're actors, after all."

"You'd be surprised."

"I've sorta got a surprise, too, Robby, and not a good one."

"What's that?"

"My father. He's had a heart attack and —"

Before I could finish my statement Robby interrupted. "Oh, is your dad, umm, is he —"

"He's in hospital waiting for open-heart surgery."

"Christ. Sorry to —"

"Really," I broke in, "it's okay, I think. Although Dad's convinced that he's on the way out — typical. My father's a bit of a catastrophiziser."

"How's your mother managing?"

"Mum's okay. She's staying with me for a few days while she visits Dad at the Royal Columbian — that's easy, relatively. The hard part'll be when he goes home. He'll be a beast — and one without any cigarettes. I can't imagine how's he's going to do it."

"Maybe he won't."

"Well, he'll have to. Anyway, I wanted you to know."

"Thanks. Listen, with this play, I can't really come —"

"No, of course not; I'm not asking —"

"Have you talked to Lara yet?"

"She's next on my list," I said. "But I don't know how to reach her. She's back east somewhere. Toledo, Ohio?" I postulated.

"Leave her a message at home. She's bound to pick them up."

"Good idea," I said. Robby was right. Lara was sure to call in to retrieve messages on her machine. "She had something important to tell me, but her voice cut out before she could explain what it was. I'm kinda anxious about it."

"C'mon, you know Lara," Robby stated. True, Lara could get worked up about seemingly minor things. Her confidence had grown substantially, though she could be plagued by self-criticism. She'd learned to deal with good and bad reviews in the past couple of years in her professional singing career, though how positive she thought about her own abilities could waver with the tides.

"So … I miss you," I said sincerely.

"Me, too. I won't be here much longer; just until April."

"Seems like forever since we ran the seawall," I said, thinking of Robby's and my first unofficial date — running through and around Stanley Park before having some of the most satisfying sex I'd experienced.

"We certainly wouldn't be running here," he laughed. "There's snowdrifts the size of Mt. McKinley," Robby chortled. "Lake effect snow, they tell me. I'm amazed anyone can live through the winter. It's inhuman."

Just talking to Robby settled me. Even if it was talking about the weather.

"Have you been following what's happening in San Francisco and New York?"

You mean with —"

"There's been more deaths, and not just there, but in Vancouver now, too. It's bad, Shepard. *Really bad.*" Robby said soberly. He was referring to the phenomenon of gay men who were being diagnosed with unusual illnesses such as Kaposi's sarcoma and pneumocystis. Reports coming in from the East and West coast were detailing the growing numbers of people with the illness called GRID, or Gay-related Immune Deficiency. "Nobody knows what's coming next. They're calling it the gay plague. And there's no treatment other than chemotherapy for lesions, but even that's not working on most."

"Jezus," was all I could muster.

"I'm just so ... scared. It's overwhelming to think about the impact this could have. Researchers think it's gonna be huge — all over the world, perhaps."

"Gawd." I had a fleeting moment of paranoia. Save for one time at the beginning of dating Robby, I never had sex outside of my relationship; had he? Was he telling me something? *No, he's just fearful like everyone else, right?*

"I'm sorry. Your dad is sick and I'm going on."

"No apology needed. I'll call you in a few days, okay?"

"Deal. I'm sending you a hug. Can you feel it?"

"I can, but I'd rather be feeling something else," I said in my best husky tone. "I'll try Lara now. Get some rest, it's late. Sweet dreams."

"G'night."

I hung up the phone and plopped down on the velvet sofa for a moment, worried by the rapidly changing and highly dangerous situation.

Well, if you needed another reason to stay in the closet ...

I closed my eyes for a minute, felt my throat for enlarged lymph glands and gathered my thoughts before calling Lara's Vancouver phone number. "Lara, it's me. Call me when you can, ok? I'll be home all evenings after 9 or so. Where are you? When are you home? Bye." *Gawd, I hate these things. At least I didn't stutter this time.* I did a set of pushups, some stretches, then distracted myself with thoughts about dinner once more but did nothing about it. I stuffed a few pieces of bread in my mouth when I heard the door open.

"I'm back," my mother said tiredly. "I've got to wash my hands. That bus ride was like a trip through Bangladesh."

"Mum, it can't be that bad," I said, glancing quickly at my Timex. "It's nearly 10; you stayed late. How's Dad?"

"Miserable." Mum scrubbed her hands at the sink with Sunlight liquid soap until her hands were red.

"So no different than usual?" I jeered. Mum didn't seem to think much of my attempt at humour. "Hungry?" I offered her a dishtowel to dry off.

"Peckish," she said offhandedly. My mother was never peckish.

"How 'bout," I hesitated, as I opened the fridge and saw few things that could constitute a dinner. "Grilled cheese and salad?" I looked closely at the suspicious hunk of cheese and rusty romaine lettuce. "Cheddar cheese shouldn't be dark blue, should it?" I held it up to the light like a high school chemistry experiment.

"Blue?" she looked apprehensively at the blue cheddar I was examining.

"Maybe we should go out," I admitted. "I'm thinking Greek. There's a great Souvlaki place on Davie, if you're not too tired."

"Souvlaki?" My mother was suspicious. "Do they have wine?" she asked pointedly.

"I guess so, Mum." I tossed the chunk of cheese in the trash.

Though exhausted, my mother quickly stepped to the foyer and donned her coat, opened the door and said, "Hurry and get your shoes on. We're going out," she said firmly.

12

Not There...Yet

My mother and I were out, but being in the closet — at least with my family and others — was my reality. In retrospect, I probably sold my mother short. Perhaps I could have told her. After all, she was patient, understanding, adaptable, supportive, kind and giving. It was possible that she would have come to accept me for who I was. On the other hand, my father's "softer" traits were meagre and I'd anticipated that coming out to him would be unsettling. It's not that I found fault in them; both parents were products of a time when traditional gender roles were adhered to without question. Or so it seemed.

As far back as I can recall, my mother played the 1950s conventional wife and mother role to great aplomb. Most certainly, there were many women of that era whose main focus was their husband and children. I'd bet — though I'd never asked — that my mother would have been pleased to be called a 'housewife'. While being married to a house sounds anything but liberating, Mum found meaning and satisfaction in her position. And while she enjoyed her brood, her husband was utterly disinterested with his children. Dad directed his energies towards earning money and doing so limited his time in my mother's fashionably decorated home. Along with his striving for greater income came plenty of moves; deeply trouble-some for an awkward secret-keeper like me who experienced great difficulty in making friends with every change of school and city. My sister — to me always assured — wasn't inhibited with every new town or school. I think if a person is a confident extrovert, then life's an adventure. If a person is timid and guarded, then life is about finding ways to be invisible, fearing the consequences of being known. Isn't that what being in the closet is all about?

Even at age 26, I was careful and cautious about how I presented myself to my family, my school and swim team. I'm sure that though some people may have suspected, only a handful of people knew I was gay — Robby and some of his friends and of course Lara — she was the first that was told several years earlier as we strolled on a rainy afternoon atop the seawall. Because I was competing, only a select few knew that I was gay. If I was "outed", the repercussions would have ended my swim career in disgrace. I can't describe how stressful it was to be hyper-vigilant. I fantasized — maybe many gay young men and women do — about the time when I could give up the oppressive role I'd created for myself and live as I was meant to — but I wasn't there; not yet. Clearly, my lack of courage and my conviction not to fully come out was a source of irritation to Robby. He believed that it was unethical of me to stay hidden. Of course, he was right, but being out for me as a competitor was a risk I was unable to rationalize. And as a son, it was a risk I wasn't prepared to make … just in case it left me ostracized from my mother. So, for the duration of the time my mother spent with me, I was on my best behaviour. Meaning? I only allowed a portion of how I lived to be communicated. Besides, it wasn't as though she or anyone else was asking about my personal life. At least, in the West End, I could be comfortable in my skin, if wittingly creating my own illusion.

13

What Would It Take?

The garish store lights glistened in the drizzle on Davie Street. The unpleasant weather didn't prevent scores of sex workers from plying their trade along the street. Usually bound up in same-sex groups of two or more (though there were several individuals hunkering in doorways), young men and women in their colourful uniforms — tight-fitting jeans or leggings, low-cut tops, tall heels and overdone make-up — stood in the damp cold, some smoking, others clearly under the influence as they tried to entice both male pedestrians and drivers by asking if they were "looking for a date".

"What a dangerous life. Anything could happen. Look at this one," Mum commented in a subdued tone as we dodged a wild-eyed tall woman in a curly blonde wig, an open faux-fur coat, purple halter top and white Adidas gym shorts, walking unbalanced on purple stilettos.

Um, I don't think this is a woman.

"I dunno, Mum. We all have something to sell, don't we?" I asked in a subdued tone as we made our way to Sue's Souvlaki Palace.

"You're being rather naive, dear. These girls put themselves at risk … probably all for drugs. It's a very dangerous path."

I wondered if she noticed the young male prostitutes or if she chose not to discuss their presence.

"Good God, it's a sea of Spandex out here," she observed with a critical voice.

"*Mum.*"

"We used to call them 'Ladies of the Night'. But I think there's a new name for them now."

"Sex-trade worker, Mum." I sighed audibly.

"Delightful," she groaned.

"*Mum.*"

"They look like they're in need of a hot shower, a good meal and a dose of penicillin."

"You really are a mother, aren't you?" I asked, smiling. "Here we are."

She's right. Perhaps even more than a shower and a meal, these young men and women needed a family that cared for them the way my mother did. Really, how lucky have I been?

Though late, Sue's was packed with patrons. The smell of garlic and grilled fish wafted on the air as we strode in and seated ourselves at a small white table near the window. A harried server with dark hair and eyes wearing an extremely short black corduroy skirt and a crisp white cotton blouse quickly came to deliver a menu and water. As per usual, Mum ordered a half-carafe of dry white wine.

"What's the news about Dad?"

"He's stable. They're going to operate — what day is it?"

"It's Tuesday."

"Thursday," she said, exhaling deeply.

"Did you want to talk about —"

"No," Mum responded lightning-fast. "Tell me about Lara. Have you spoken with her?"

"Not yet. I left a message on her machine."

"Where is she?"

"I think she was in Toledo. She's in one city for a few nights, then off to the next."

"And she's happy?" Without letting me answer, my mother added, "She's doing what she wanted, isn't she?"

"Well, yes. Singing is everything to her. But it means that she's never settled; always moving on to different towns. It's such an irregular life. I'd hate it, but Lara's never complained — not to me."

"Perhaps her family was right, then." Mum was referring to Lara's parents who distanced from her when she'd decided to pursue performing rather than finishing university and teaching French. To them, her choice was more than shameful folly. Her family was convinced she was tossing her life away for a "dubious" profession. In response, Lara had nearly lost touch with her parents. Her brothers were disconnected from her, too. She figured that her parents instructed her brothers to limit their contact with her, perhaps as a form of punishment for an offence she never committed. Lara compensated for her family's disdain by creating her own group of cherished friends, though she wasn't seeing any of them — including me — with any consistency. I thought she must be lonely at times, and I yearned for the days when she and I were close. I missed all the fun — the conversations, the laughter and the unique connection. It was bizarre that Lara in effect "came out" to her family as a performer and was penalized with non-acceptance and disapproval. My thoughts were interrupted when Mum's wine came. The server poured her wine in a sparkling glass, she took a long sip and sighed contentedly.

"No, Mum. She's doing what she *has* to. Lara's got a plan, performing everywhere they'll take her. That way she can … uh, jeez, what's that term?" I searched for words.

"Pay her dues?"

"Yes. That's why she's on the road so much. Lara's determined to make it, whatever it takes. Pete's always said there's something special about her. She's willing to play all kinds of clubs — some mediocre places included — to be successful."

I'd stated it many times: Lara's talent was as big as her appetite. In possession of a glorious soprano voice, she sang the American Songbook with the same ease as the music of Hayden or Puccini. She'd been polishing her craft, improving each year. She was recognized as a thrilling performer whose voice was rich, powerful, plaintive and rangy. Jazz lovers compared her to a young Sarah Vaughn, while classical aficionados likened her silvery soprano to Lucia Pop. Some critics didn't quite know what to make of Lara. Was she a singer of art, jazz or popular song? For Lara, that criticism was unimportant; she sang what she loved. That made for a very exciting evening of music as she blended a smattering of opera with traditional folk songs, Canadiana and Tin Pan Alley. Lara had the ability to galvanize audiences with a voice of many colours and tones, whispered high notes and booming low tones without the need for amplification. A slight person, Lara's voice was impressively large. Travelling with her trio across North America, she was very much a working singer. *To get what you want, you have to give something up.* That was a motto that I understood well. Lara had sacrificed home-life, friendships and perhaps her family to be able to become what she'd dreamt of since a child — a performer who expressed herself through lyrics and music.

The server arrived with our meal — a large platter of roasted lamb, rice, potatoes, Greek salad and pita for my mother and chicken souvlaki, rice, roasted peppers and tomatoes for me.

"I'll never eat all this," my mother moaned, viewing the huge dinner heaped on her white and blue plate.

"Take some leftovers to the hospital tomorrow," I suggested.

My mother looked at me and shook her head. "Not allowed to."

"Well, this would constitute a Mediterranean diet. I guess he didn't eat a meal like this tonight." I removed the grilled chicken from the skewer and speared it with my fork. One of the great pleasures for me was food. I ate mountains of it each day to keep fuelled for the pool.

"Your father had poached skinless turkey and lumpy mashed potatoes. I could barely tell them apart," she said with disdain as she munched her salad.

"Ugh."

"Both were off-white and dry as dust. Have you ever seen poached poultry? Not appetizing. The turkey was plated with mushy canned peas — they were grey, not green in the slightest — and a piece of Wonder bread. Your father pushed it away and asked that nurse for liver and fried onions."

"Nurse Authority? Yeah, I doubt she ran into the kitchen to whip that up."

Mum nodded affirmatively between bites. "Oh, that's delicious lamb," she murmured, forking some additional onions and peppers from my plate. "The nurse wants your father to get with the program. Isn't that what you young people say?"

I nodded and commented, "At the very least, he's not smoking. Too bad it took this long to get him to stop, isn't it?"

"Let's be realistic, sweetheart." She tasted a few of her roast potatoes before continuing. "It'll take more than open-heart surgery to stop your father from sucking on his Buckingham's," Mum said ruefully as she picked out the black olives from her Greek salad.

"Hmm," I wondered aloud as I bit into a warm slice of grilled pita. "What would it take?"

14

Is Getting Close Enough?

When my mother and I were out for dinner, I had hoped that Lara might have called. Gazing down at the answering machine I could tell that she hadn't. I busied myself in preparation for the morning practice by tossing some gear into my swim bag.

"I've been so worried about your father that I've neglected to ask you about school and swimming." My mother kicked shoes off her tired feet and hung her's and my coat in the closet.

"That's okay, Mum," I called out from the bedroom. I came back, finding Mum stretched out on the velvet sofa. "School's great. Swimming isn't going as well as I'd hoped."

"How do you mean? Is it that nasty coach?" My mother knew about my ongoing struggles with Thompson. I flopped onto my sumptuous leather chair — the one my mother had bought for me at Woodward's when I'd moved into the Queen Charlotte.

"It's not just him, Mum. I'm having a hard time keeping up with the expectations. I'm afraid I'm not as competitive as I need to be. I'm getting into finals, but I'm not medalling — I get close sometimes, but…"

"But it's not just about winning, is it?"

"Mum, of course it's *all* about winning. It's how I'm getting through school. No wins and I'm SOL."

"Excuse me?"

"Shit out of luck."

"That's rather vulgar, dear. But you *do* love the water."

I'd ruminated on that without end. I'd spent most of my life competing in the pool and of course being under water had become my shield. However, my shield was leaking. *Did I love the water? Yes. Was I loving competing?* That was a bigger question. *I loved swimming … no, I loved winning races in the pool, too.*

I didn't know if I would finish my career with a big splash or a little dribble. I pushed myself harder than ever before, and yet my results were lacking. It was a massive worry.

"Yes, I love the water, Mum," I said, preferring not to explain that my medal winning times may have been over. It was impossible for me to admit it to myself, let alone to anyone else. *But I'm more than a competitor, aren't I?*

"You remember when we spent summertime at Boulevard Lake?"

"Of course, Mum. That's where I learned to swim."

"Well, one day — you must have been 6 or 7 and you'd already been swimming for a couple years in summer swim clubs — you swam out a bit too far. I'd been watching you and when I got up to call you back, you'd disappeared. I panicked and ran screaming into the lake. I made *quite* a scene. My friend was at the lake and shouted that you were fine and pointed where you were. You'd taken off fast as a rocket towards the other end of the shore and left a wake behind you — wasn't that incredible? A little boy with a motor in his tiny legs. People were startled when they noticed how fast you swam. I told them that *rocket* was my son." Mum laughed and took

a breath as she recalled her memory. "You and the water … insepa-
rable, ever since you were a child. You'd have slept in the water if
it were possible. The competitions, all those medals I've kept in the
shoeboxes, the newspaper clippings, the happiness in the wins and
the disappointment in your losses — they were so horrid for you."
She shook her head sadly. "You were a very sensitive boy — you
cried inconsolably when you lost."

"*Mum.*"

"I don't know if you'll win more races, but what you've achieved
is enough, isn't it?"

"But I wanna go out with another win … something spectacular."
Spectacular was how Lara described my win in Montreal. She was
proud of what I'd done and I was *as* proud of her accomplishments.

"And if you don't get it?" Mum asked pointedly. She asked a
good question — and one that I didn't have a ready answer. Could
I accept a loss after a lifetime of competition? I didn't answer.

"I'd better get some zzz's before practice." I rose and collected
a yellow comforter and started fluffing up the pillows on the sofa.
"Going to the hospital in the morning?" I asked, knowing the answer.

"Oh, yes. I'll be there, bright and early-ish."

"You mean lunchtime, don't you, Mum?" I asked sarcastically.

"Don't be clever with your mother," she said curtly, then gave
me a hug and readied herself for bed.

15

Heartbroken

Following my Wednesday morning swim practice, I went to the Paris Bakery and bought several huge cinnamon rolls with caramelized sugar and spiked with currants for our breakfast. I managed to eat one of them on the return trip. When I arrived back home with my fragrant treasures I was surprised to see my mother busying herself in the kitchen.

"You're up?" I asked, not hiding the surprise in my voice.

"I thought you'd like a proper breakfast," she said, motioning towards the table where she'd put a large bowl of segmented grapefruit. She'd kept plates of scrambled eggs warm in the oven and Mum was stirring a large cast-iron pan of hash-brown potatoes with onions. On the table was a French press of jet-black coffee, which I rarely drank. "What've you got there?"

"Um, breakfast. Gooey cinnamon buns," I said, putting them down on the counter. My mother immediately opened the bag and took a whiff.

"Oh, don't these smell deadly?" She pulled a small section of a roll and popped it in her mouth. "Couldn't resist," she added. "Here," she piled the deeply browned potatoes into a bowl. "Sit down and have something to eat."

At breakfast, which would be the second one I'd had, my mother asked, "Are you taking me to the hospital?" Mum and I put the plates of eggs on the table. I collected the sinful cinnamon buns and we sat down.

"I can't, Mum. I'm going to class. I shouldn't miss more than I have to."

"Tomorrow's the surgery. You'll —"

"Mum, I'll be there, just not today. I've got practice and Thompson's looking for any rea—" I was interrupted by the sound of the telephone. I grabbed it by the second ring. "Good morning. Yes, this is he," I answered cautiously. It was the duty nurse, informing me that my father had a difficult night with "complications". The nurse explained that he was being prepped for surgery a day early. "Of course. I'll let her know." As I said that, my mother's ears perked up. She put her fork down and listened to what I was saying. "Thanks. Bye." I put down the receiver slowly.

"What's happened?"

"Um, well, it seems that Dad had a rough night with his breathing and they're getting him ready to go earlier than expected." I swallowed. "Actually, he's being taken in for surgery in the next hour."

"Oh, no." My mother looked instantly alarmed.

"Mum, it's okay. I'll take you in." I gathered up my leather coat as Mum collected her things. Grabbing the cinnamon buns, I doubled back and turned off the oven and put the food in the fridge.

"What about —"

"I'll cancel school and practice for tonight when we get to the hospital. Thompson's just gonna have to understand."

By the time that I'd made calls to the school, notified Thompson's office and my sister, it was nearly 11 in the morning. As we were fighting the traffic, my father had been wheeled into surgery. We arrived at the hospital it was just after lunch. As the procedure would take up to 8 hours or longer, we took our orange plastic seats in the cardiac ward section with several other worried-looking people and silently waited for the appearance of Dr. Deth.

As I waited, my mother sipped burnt coffee and absently leafed through National Geographic magazines that were at least a decade old. My sister arrived just after 5 PM, finding me drowsily sitting with my legs propped up on an opposing table. My mother remained seated as Lynda swept into the waiting area.

"What's happening?" Lynda inquired in a loud, assertive voice.

"Well, hi, Lynda. Nice to see you," I said, dripping in sweetness. *A bit of social grace could go a long way right about now.*

"Hi. You, too," my sister begrudgingly acknowledged. "Sorry. I've been juggling a thousand things. Finding someone to watch the girls was a nightmare. Their father bailed on me at the last second. Decided to go skiing at Whistler, instead."

"Who'd you get to look after the girls?" Mum inquired. Normally, my mother cared for her grandchildren whenever possible or needed.

"I had to beg that neurotic woman —"

"The neighbour with the drinking problem?" I asked.

"No, Natalya. She's from a babysitting service and has worked for me before."

"So that's good, right?" Mum asked.

"Well, last time she was here, the girls told me that Natalya, who's from Kazakhstan, thinks she's the reincarnation of Billie Holliday."

"Gawd," was all I could say.

"Apparently, Natalya sang '*Strange Fruit*' as their bedtime story. They both had nightmares for a week."

"Christ," my mother commented. "Where do they get these people?"

"It was my last option. Either the neighbour who replaces rum in her Coke can or her. At least Natalya's insured." My sister's strain was showing. I stood and gave her a hug. She looked at me with expectation.

"Okay, Nurse Authority's told us the operation's in progress." I looked at my Timex. "That was a few hours ago."

"A few hours ago? We really need an update." Lynda began to frenetically walk in circles in the small room.

"For God's sake, sit down, Lynda," my mother urged in a whisper. "Your pacing's making me sick." My mother patted a chair, encouraging her to take a seat.

"Aren't I allowed to be a bit anxious?" Lynda glared at my mother.

My sister looked more than anxious. She looked scrappy. Several individuals were tuned into our conversation. An older woman wearing a bright blue wollen hat and thick black glasses piped up, "The waiting is a real trial, isn't it, honey?"

"Yes," my mother offered. "It's a worrisome time for us," she added, looking at my sister. "That's why we have to be composed and calm, don't we?" Lynda removed her red parka, sat down and put her head in her hands. "I hate waiting," she emphatically stated to no one in particular.

By 8 PM, my mother and sister were worried *and* hungry. I decided to go hunt for some turkey sandwiches and coffee. I found the cafeteria and a couple of innocuous-looking tunafish on sourdough with suspect past-their-prime lettuce, three pieces of red cherry pie

and collected coffees in cardboard cups. *Not exactly Umberto's, but it'll fill the void and distract them for a bit.* I came back upstairs to the cardiac surgical floor precariously balancing all the food in flimsy paper containers. When I arrived back in the waiting room, only the older woman was there. *That's odd.*

"Excuse me, but did you happen to know where my mother and sister went?" I asked the older woman wearing the woollen hat.

"Oh, a man came in to speak with them and they all went off with him," she said softly.

"Did they say where —"

"No, they seemed in a rush, honey."

Jezus, what could it be now?

"Thanks." I left the bundle of food on the table and quickly walked over to the nurse's station. "My family was waiting here a minute ago and now they're gone. Do you know where they are? Are they with the doctor?"

"Let me see," the nurse said. "Looks as though your father's out of surgery and in the recovery area in ICU. Down the hall to the left; room 611, just past the chapel."

I fairly raced down to room 611 where I found my mother and sister both standing at my father's bedside with the doctor. Nurse Authority was closely hovering at a bank of machines. I slowly moved into the space and saw my dad, looking more vulnerable than I thought possible. It was a shock. His chest was covered with layers of paper sheets, but they did not obscure the taped lines going from his chest, arms and mouth leading to ventilators, an ECG machine, pumps, tubes, pressure monitors and IV lines. Restraints kept his arms in place. A catheter was used to drain off urine. His eyes were half-open and his skin-tone was slightly yellow. Dr. Deth seemed to be discussing how the surgery had gone, but I couldn't hear much of what they were saying. I was too stunned by my father's appearance. I tried listening to his physician as he was in mid-sentence.

"… with the breathing tube in place he won't be able to speak for a short time. And the valve obstruction was much greater than we thought. Your husband is very fortunate. He's got a new valve — from a pig. We'll watch for infection or any problems. He'll be instructed to do breathing exercises to reduce complications every hour. Nurse Parrot will get him out of bed and walking — probably tonight. She'll be turning him in his bed frequently, too. When your husband has stable blood pressure and oxygen levels and when he's tolerating food and water, he can go home. Perhaps in 5 days."

"Really? Home in 5 days? He looks like he's been run over by a truck," I gasped.

"I know it's very distressing. However, patients can heal quickly when they're getting quality hospital care."

"Yes, but how can I look after him at home?" My mother asked anxiously, looking down at her husband. "He looks like death warmed over. No pun intended, Dr."

Deth looked over at me and smiled knowingly. *He's heard it all before.*

"None taken," he said plainly.

I don't know why I didn't notice it before, but Dr. Deth is a bit of a fox, isn't he? I can't believe I'm thinking about that right now…in front of my corpse-like father. Well, why not? He's a great-looking guy. What is he — 38 or so? Quite handsome. Curly brown hair. Green eyes. Sort of sparkly. Nice Belgian accent. Is that the same as French? Lara would love him. And fills out those low-rise slacks very well. He must work out when he's not saving lives. Stop it. You're missing what's being said.

"So let's see how Will does with the post-op routines. Nurse Parrot will be working with him."

Gawd, my father's going to absolutely love that.

"He'll receive a lot of medical attention in the short term as he recovers. The nurse will instruct you in how to care for him when you return home in the next week. Of course, home care is available to assist with the transition."

I could hear my mother swallow hard.

Maybe she didn't think he could get this far. Maybe she didn't want him to. No, that's not a reasonable thought.

"I'll be monitoring him over the next few days," Deth said as he departed, speedily exiting the room.

I looked over at my sister. She'd been silent the entire time. She came up beside me, out of earshot of our father.

"He's got a long way to go, doesn't he, Lynda?"

"I'm speechless," she managed to whisper as she watched our mother smoothing her husband's white sheets with only the noise of heart-rate monitors piercing the quiet. Lynda looked stunned at the appearance of my father.

"Maybe you're hungry?" I oddly offered.

"Hungry? Uh, well, not rea —" my sister started to say.

"I bought sandwiches. I'll run and get 'em. Back in a minute."

I bolted down the hallway, and nearly crashed into Dr. Dethly handsome.

"Oh, sorry. Not watching where I'm going," I apologized.

"You're a swimmer, aren't you?"

"Uh, yes, how did you —"

"Your father. He told me all about you. You're on the national team?"

"Yup." I started to turn red. *Jeez, why do I have to turn into a beet?*

"Very accomplished. And going to school, too? Your father's very proud."

"He is? Huh." That didn't sound like *my* father. "Are you sure you're not referring to another swimmer's dad with a heart condition?" I laughed as I flirted a bit.

"You're in quite a hurry. Were you wanting to see me?" Deth caught and held my eyes as he beamed an off-kilter smile that said volumes.

Okay ... the reliable gaydar was kicking in.

"Oh, no, not really. You see, I'm just looking for my tunafish."

Gawd, how brainless must I sound?

"Your tunafish? I see. Here," Deth said, reaching into his white coat and extracting a business card from an inner pocket. "You're in the West End, right?"

"Uh, how did —"

"Your father listed you as an emergency contact," Deth smiled, showing a few crooked teeth.

Kinda nice to see that you're not perfect.

"Oh," I softly responded.

"The reason why I ask is that I'm at St. Paul's Hospital several times a week." Deth stopped to see my response, which was one of curiosity.

He's trying to pick me up in my father's cardiac ward? Isn't that in bad taste?

The doctor went further. "This is my number. Call me if you have any questions, or call me even if you don't. It would be great to go for coffee sometime if you'd like." I looked at his card. He smiled again and extended his hand. "It's 'Serge'. My name." He shook my hand firmly, lingering slightly before releasing it.

Okay, I got it. You're definitely one of the tribe.

"Thanks, I'm really ... I mean *we're* really grateful for what you did; putting a pig in my father's heart, that's just, umm, unreal," I stumbled.

"Well, technically, it's a valve from the pig's heart," he said without mocking my ignorance.

"Yes, the valve, that's what I meant." Uncomfortable in the silence I added, "I'll give you a call for a coffee. Um, I guess I better find those sandwiches."

"Salut," he said, grinning crookedly and then continued down the hallway amidst the cries of distressed patients and past the harried nursing staff. The cardiologist was surely moving on to an urgent case. Comparatively, my next urgent matter was locating my mother and sister's tunafish and then preparing for a long night of sitting with my heartbroken father.

16

Missing

To my surprise, my father's recovery progressed with no complications the first week after his surgery. He was expertly cared for by Nurse Authority and the rest of the medical staff with clear directions from Dr. Deth. Unless he was being incredibly friendly, I presumed my Dad's life was in the talented hands of a gay cardiologist. Throughout his hospital stay, my mother dutifully visited Dad morning and night, arriving by bus or hitching a ride with me whenever possible. She attended cooking classes at the hospital so she could confidently prepare him a low-fat diet when they returned home. Though my father's palate was not sophisticated, he vocalized his diet was missing several things: bread slathered with butter, red meat, fried eggs, sharp English cheddar, Buckingham's and his favourite Scotch. Like cigarettes, his unquenchable thirst for liquor represented a challenge and one which he would not overcome. Mum would be curtailing my father's wonts as much as possible, and if anyone could make fatless food taste fabulous, it would be my mother. I wouldn't have called his diet one of deprivation. There was fish, poultry, lean meats, grains, a bounty of vegetables and salads — my father previously deplored salads — with fresh fruit replacing large blocks of ice cream and giant wedges of raisin pie for dessert. Alcohol was to be restricted and smoking was off the menu. Ironically, the dietician that was putting together my father's meal plan was — how to say this kindly — plump. Dad would say she was "as broad as a battleship," and question how a portly nutritionist could counsel on proper eating habits. Every time she came round to advise him, he rolled his eyes to the back of his skull with shameless disrespect at her Rubinesque figure. However, my surly father was compliant with the well-padded dietician's guidelines and promised to adhere to them. After all, he'd been given another chance at living. Why squander it?

My father was slowly but clearly regaining his strength. Though he had great difficulty getting out of bed, he was walking well, coughing less, looking generally brighter and had good colour. He was eager to leave the hospital and go back to Abbotsford, though he had not received notification of his discharge. His worries about his business may have provided further impetus for his continued improvement. He wanted to get back to his store, but actual work was only allowed after 2 further months of recovery. Earlier in the week, Dr. Deth consulted with him on his new regime of pills - Beta-blockers, anti-platelet meds, ACE inhibitors and medications to reduce blood lipids. My mother was to ensure he adhered to his drug regime. In fact, my mother would be his primary care provider; attending to his needs from this point on. Mum confessed that she was anxious about her upcoming changed role. Instead of merely running the house, she would be overseeing my father's day-to-day health.

I'd taken Mum into the hospital on Sunday — my non-swim day. Bored out of my mind, I played cribbage with my father on his bed. While his physical health continued to improve, his mind was consistently sharp as he beat me at the game. My mother sat and flipped through the pages of a 'People' magazine she'd purchased at the hospital tuck shop. As my father looked annoyed at my inability to count during the crib game, my mother blew out a long breath. I was happy to take a break from cribbage (so was my exasperated father).

"Anything interesting?" I asked, turning my attention to my mother.

Because this sure the hell isn't.

"It's such a shame about Karen Carpenter. She wouldn't eat, poor thing. Someone should have strapped her down and stuffed a ham and cheese sandwich down her throat."

"Mum, it's not that simple. Anorexia is really hard to treat."

"And that tennis player you liked with the long hair retired. And he's so young!"

"Björn Borg?" I asked. *You mean the incredibly handsome Swede with the blonde hair, the shy smile and an ass that launched a thous —*

"That's him," she affirmed, interrupting my fantasy. "Just 26 years old, too … the same age as you. Isn't that something? That Mary Hart's been talking about it on Entertainment Tonight, as well."

"Another good reason not to have a TV," I muttered. Hart's piercing voice and perpetual sunniness made my brain hurt and my stomach ache.

"Hart said his game was faltering because he was too old to win against the likes of McEnroe and the top —"

"He's not old, Mum," I cracked, slightly annoyed at her possible reference to my failings in the pool. "Maybe there's another reason he's tossing his racket." Both parents knew this was my last year of competing and were cautious when discussing my swim times and lack of hardware. "Perhaps he just didn't feel excited about tennis any longer. Does it say that?" I asked.

"No, doesn't seem too," she said, scanning the article and inspecting the pictures. "He's such a good-looking man. One of my clients says that Swedish men aren't ones that you'd chuck from your bed. I see what she means, can't you?"

I swallowed as my father turned his head towards me, observing my rapidly reddening non-verbal response. Before I could construct a feeble answer, my father's cardiologist stepped into the room and came towards him quickly.

"Mr. Stamp, how are you feel —"

"I'm *feeling* like I'm ready to go home," my father snapped before his question could be asked. I could see his irritation start to rise the moment Dr. Deth arrived. The doctor smiled and placed his stethoscope on Dad's chest to hear his heart.

"Oh, I imagine that it's going to be happening soon enough. That sounds good, very steady," Deth said, as though to himself. "You spoke with Nurse Parrot tonight?"

"Yes." My father looked at my mother.

"And she went over your medications?"

"Yes."

"And do you have —"

"When can I get outta here?" he snarled.

Ungrateful, irascible, cantankerous, obstreperous ...

"Well, we want to make sure that your home-care is all set up, and that we have you scheduled for —"

"Home-care? My wife is doing all the home-care."

"I see." Deth looked at my mother quizzically. "That's not what we discussed."

"Will, the doctor is trying to help," my mother said, embarrassed by her husband's behaviour. She gazed at the doctor and mouthed 'I'm sorry'. I put my hands on my neck and squeezed until it hurt.

"I have my family. If I need anything," my father stated firmly, "they'll look after it."

Right, because we're all here to look after your needs. Makes sense, doesn't it?

"I've got some paperwork for you to go over, then we can arrange a discharge first thing in the morning, Mr. Stamp." Dr. Deth looked eager to complete his business, especially considering my father's truculent behaviour.

"Well, it's about time," he stated, smiling with yellowed, tobacco-stained teeth.

"I've arranged for an ambulance to take you back to Abbotsford late tomorrow morning."

"Is that right?" My father huffed, "Let's hope it's not a female driver."

My mother and I said our good nights to my badly behaving father and travelled back to the Queen Charlotte. It was late. I was bone-tired and I couldn't wait to have my apartment back to myself again. Though I loved my velvet sofa, sleeping on it for the past week was causing lower back pain. As well, I'd missed many classes, and though I'd been attending swim practice, it was critical that I catch up with my schoolwork. I wasn't the only perturbed person. My mother's considerable worry about caring for my father was weighing on her. Mum was visibly anxious when she started talking about what was soon to come.

"In the hospital," she started, "everything is looked after."

"Yep. Being home with Dad's going to be a monster of a challenge, Mum."

"Well, he may not like it, but I'm going to arrange some home-care, regardless of what he thinks. I spoke to the nurse about it already. I've got my own work, too. I don't want to give that up," she said pensively, running her hand through her blonde hair and mussing it completely. Mum's clients were small and represented no more than 15 hours per week. Still, those 15 hours were important to my mother.

"Of course, Mum. You won't have to." I didn't know what I was talking about. I'd never had to look after a sick person before, nor did I understand the complexity of caring for a previously autonomous and now completely dependent man. *There's no control over what happens to others, is there? So knowing that ... now what?*

We had a snack in the living room, munching on scraps I found lurking in the fridge: crusty mustard seed bread from Paris Bakery, some large Manzanilla olives, sliced apples, cheese and for my mother, a large glass of white wine. After a quick bite and a chat, I went to brush my teeth when I heard the phone chime. Because of all the concerns about my father, a ringing phone late at night startled me. As I crossed to the living room to answer it, I felt my heart beat in my chest. My mother came into the room.

"Hello?" I warily asked.

"Sunshine! I'm so glad you're at home." Lara sounded relieved.

"Lara, I've been trying to reach you," I exclaimed, happy to hear her voice. "But it's so late ... where the heck *are* you?"

"I'm here, Sunshine."

"Here in —"

"Yes, I'm in Vancouver. Just a couple of hours ago."

"But aren't you meant to be away for —"

"Yes, another week. I had to cancel. But we've got a problem," she said in a hushed tone.

"A problem?" Listening in to a one-sided conversation, my mother raised her eyebrows with interest. *No more problems, please.*

"I can't believe what's happened..." Her voice was unsteady and dark.

"Lara, for gawd's sake, tell me."

"What's wrong?" Mum whispered.

I could hear Lara begin to cry.

"It's Pete," she sobbed. "He's disappeared."

17

Lara's Return

I told my mother Lara was having some 'agent-related' problems as the reason why she needed to come over to speak with me. Mum understood and decided to head to bed while I waited for Lara to arrive. By the time she got to the apartment, it was nearing 11 o'clock. I opened the door to a very fretful Lara. Her slender frame was dressed in khaki pants, a black tee-shirt and brown boots. She had a bulky Cowichan wool sweater in cream with a brown moose knitted into the design. Her red hair was pulled back into a ponytail. As always, Lara was very thin. It made her make-up-free face look more drawn and strained.

"I know, I look like shit," Lara said as she entered my apartment. I gave her a huge hug and she held on tightly. Her body was small in my arms. I let go.

"Just so you know, my mother's here, she's in the bedroom."

"Oh, she's —"

"Here because my father had open heart surgery."

"Sunshine, I didn't know. How's he doing?"

"He's doing fine. Sit down. I'll get you something to —"

"I don't want anything to drink." Lara collapsed on the sofa.

"What's happened to Pete?" I sat beside Lara.

"That's the question, Sunshine. The last time I saw him was 2 weeks ago, in Rochester. He'd been so good in coming down from Toronto to see the show and wanted to take me for dinner." Lara took a tissue from her slacks and wiped her velvet-brown eyes.

"Was he okay?"

"Well, yes, except for looking tired and thin. He said he'd been dealing with a bad cold; had a bothersome cough. I told him he needed to slow down and get some rest. He laughed at me and said that I should be thankful that he was working so hard for me. For *me*." Lara looked scattered and frenetic. She got up from the sofa and paced. "I don't know if there was anything wrong. We didn't talk about his problems, just mine," Lara sobbed. "Typical. Then he flew back to Vancouver."

"Lara, when did you think something was wrong?"

"We had a meeting planned for Monday — Valentine's Day — with a studio to see if we could get a deal with a recording label in Detroit. I mean, it wasn't Verve, but it was something."

"That's great," I said.

"Yes, except when I got to Detroit on Monday, Pete never showed up for the meeting. So we called his office and they said they hadn't heard from him for since last Thursday. His office said that other clients were looking for him on the weekend. I called and left messages for him at home, but no response. Pete's never out of touch for more than a couple of days and never for nearly a week. That's when I really started to freak out."

"Maybe he forgot about the meeting in Detroit?" I asked, though I now understood Lara's worry. Pete stuck to his commitments.

"No, he'd never miss that meeting. He was very excited about it."

"Could he be - I don't know — with a boyfriend on a getaway? Does he even have a boyfriend?"

"No, no, no," Lara said, shaking her head. "That's not what Pete is all about. He likes being unattached, you know that."

"Have the police been contacted?"

"No. I was afraid that I was being too neurotic. Am I?" Lara looked exhausted.

"Lara, if you've called around and no one knows where Pete is, then the police should be notified. Could he have gone away … maybe to see his family in Montreal?"

"From what he's told me, he's not close with his family. I can't imagine that he would have gone there. Besides, Pete always lets me know if he's planning a trip. And he would have let his office know. This doesn't make any sense, Sunshine."

"Was he depressed? Was the agency in bad shape?"

"Pete depressed? No way. The agency is in good shape, far as I know. Pete has no shortage of clients. Pete's the best."

"I think we gotta give the RCMP a call, sweetie. It's too out of character for Pete."

"Now?" Lara looked apprehensive, as if calling the police would mean Pete was truly in trouble.

"Yes, now." I got up and walked to the small table where the phone was. Lara joined me, her face flushed with anxiety. I handed her the phone and dialled for the operator.

"I think I'm gonna pray to the porcelain God," she said, bowing her head and putting her hand to her mouth to quell her nausea.

"Lara, you have to be calm," I advised as she tried to settle herself by breathing deeply before holding the receiver in her hand.

"Hi," she started speaking in a shaky voice. "My name is Lara Jean," she croaked. "Can you please connect me with the police?" Lara pleaded. "The reason? My agent," Lara's voice broke. "You see, he's gone missing."

18

Looking for Mr. Gauthier

After Lara made her missing person report to the police, I did my level best to reassure her that Pete would be located, but I had no legitimacy about such matters. Lara and I were both fatigued, so we only spoke for a short time before I called for a taxi to take her back to her apartment in Kitsilano. We'd planned on talking the following day. I was beyond tired, but completely unable to sleep, tossing myself around on the sofa. *What's happened to Pete? Who could I contact? No one. All these years and I can't find anyone to call? Pete's been a phenomenal help to Lara and to me, too. I gotta help him, don't I?* At around 2 AM I finally drifted off. At 4 AM, I heard a noise and saw my mother in the kitchen pouring herself a drink.

"Mum? You okay?" I asked groggily. Her image was made ghostly by the light from the open refrigerator.

"Sorry I woke you." She came into the living room with her glass of orange juice. "I'm having a hard time staying asleep."

"Me, too," I said, rising from the couch and rubbing my eyes. My hair was messy and a scruffy beard had sprouted as I didn't usually shave during the weekend. My tee-shirt was crumpled and my boxer shorts were stuck in my butt. "Pete's missing."

"Pete? Lara's agent? How do you mean, missing?"

I filled in my mother with what Lara had told me. She listened patiently as we sat at the kitchen table.

"Lara's come home early. She's cancelled a bunch of work dates. I said that I'd try to help, but I really don't know what I can do." I hated feeling powerless.

"Well, it's good the police are involved. You'll know more when they've been able to investigate. Let's hope that it's all been just a big mix-up." Mum couldn't offer more than that. I locked my hands in vice-grip and wished I could believe her assessment. She yawned and finished her juice and left her glass on the counter.

"Why don't you go back to bed, Mum?"

"You're right. I should try to sleep. Tomorrow's going to be a trying day going back home in an ambulance with your father." My mother groaned slightly. "Thank you for taking me back and forth and waiting and ... everything."

"Of course, Mum." She sleepily made her way back to the bedroom. I pulled the yellow comforter up to my neck and I was left to wonder where Pete was.

Swim practice did not go well. Thompson had something critical to say about each set I completed. *Not pulling hard enough, bad flip-turns, no explosion, poor kick set, no energy.* I was wondering if I was being targeted, but then I decided that Thompson was right. It seemed as though my instinct for swimming had deserted me. My timing was off in the butterfly and I was not coordinating the kick in the breast. *How long have you been swimming?* I completed 5 kilometres and after a quick shower, spent another hour in the weight room. As I went through my routines of squats, levers, ropes, shoulder and chest presses, I was in my own head, hardly noticing any of the other swimmers groaning and sweating all around me. After the weight room, I had my second shower. I stood under the water, shaking my head, trying to clear out the fog, but it wasn't working. I dressed and headed out to the Institute for my studies. My classes proved a good distraction. We were studying Bowen's theory of differentiation, an interesting concept that left me wondering how individuated I was. After class, I gave Lara a call — she wasn't answering — dashed home, ate a couple sandwiches and rested for an hour and went back to the Aquatic Centre for my workout # 2 with my dear friend, Coach Thompson. My last practice was worse than the first. Thompson decided to suspend his critique of me — thankfully. Instead, he glared at me and continually shook his head in disappointment. *Maybe he's resigned himself?* I had lost seconds off my best times in every stroke and in every distance. I told myself that I was just going through a blip. A very long blip. *We all have them, right? I just have to wait this out. I'll find a way to get faster.* Try as I might, my thoughts were preoccupied with Pete. It was impossible for me to get him off my mind. I knew I should also be worried about my father. My mother, too. But Pete's disappearing act was getting most of my mental attention.

Just after 8 PM, I called Lara's home. She answered on the first ring, saying *'Hello'* nervously.

"It's me. What did the police tell you?" I stood and paced as long as the phone line would permit.

"They went to his place —"

"And?"

"Let me finish, Shepard, please."

"I'm sorry."

"Well, they said they didn't see anything unusual — I think they meant there wasn't any sign of violence — though they found his wallet there."

"His *wallet?* Well, jeez, that's unusual in itself. No man goes anywhere without his wallet."

"That's what I thought. So they've put out an APB for him, they're talking to people in his office, talking to anyone who knew him."

"Are they saying it's suspicious?"

"No, they haven't said that, but of course it is."

"Do they have any hunches?"

"If they do, they're not telling me."

I shook my head. "It's been a week, Lara. People don't vanish off the earth like this."

"Pete has. Pete's left no trace; not that anyone or I can find."

"Maybe we're not looking in the right places."

"Like...?"

"I dunno, but we have to trace where Pete's been, the last people who had contact with him, something that will give us a clue as to what's happened."

"Isn't that what the police are doing?"

"Lara, Pete's gay. The police aren't going to give a flying fuck about him."

"That can't be true, Sunshine. I refuse to believe that." Lara upset was palpable.

"I'm sorry, it's just that the police can be thoughtless when it comes to gay men and women," I explained. "So, Thursday night, that's the key. We have to find out what he was doing that night."

"Agreed, but how?"

"Let's start with a picture. Do you have a headshot? What did the police use?"

"They pulled a driver's license. It doesn't even look like him. I must have something at home," Lara thought aloud. "Yes, I'm sure I do."

"Let's get it. I'll make some photocopies and start showing Pete's picture around town; places he'd go to. Pete's handsome as any movie star. Someone's going to remember seeing him somewhere."

That night, I drove Lara back to her apartment where we searched for Pete's picture. Lara was relieved when she found it in a tall pile of papers, contracts and sheet music. I left Lara's place and took the shot to school that night — I had keys for the clinic and therefore had access to the office after hours. While at the office, I used the typewriter to draft my own missing person poster and I attached a blurb:

Missing since February 10th, 1983:

> **Pete Gauthier, male, 6' 2", 175 pounds, 47 years old; looks younger, medium-length dark hair, brown eyes, olive skin, mole on cheek. Well-dressed, good-looking, outgoing, friendly personality. Works in the entertainment field.**

I listed my name and number with the posting and did a makeshift combination of picture and the missing person report, stuck it together with Scotch tape and made 100 photocopies. I stuffed them into a manilla envelope and left the office.

As I was driving back home I strategized: *Okay, now I've gotta go to some clubs, gay clubs. Maybe to the baths, too. Pete goes there, doesn't he? I should go at night. Tonight. It's late and I'm tired, but I can't wait on this.*

That night I saw more of gay nightlife in one evening that I had in many years. I didn't drink or smoke, so I rarely attended clubs. I found out early as a young adult that though nightclubs were an important part of gay life, they were only one part. For me, I was completely at sea in a gay disco. Consistently, I was ill-equipped socially to know how to look, act or otherwise behave in a manner that the wild throngs of the most attractive men would rush to speak with me. *Yeah, that never happened.* So, I contented myself with other pursuits such as athletics and my vitally important friendship with Lara. Those were the things that centered my experience with being gay.

I clambered back into the Fastback in pissing rain and headed out. By 11:30, Faces nightclub on Seymour Street was packed — even on a Tuesday evening. I handed out Pete's picture and explained my predicament to a mostly interested crowd. The noisy disco music made discussion difficult, but I persevered. I played out the same scene in several bars that night, including The Playpen Central, The Shaggy Horse and Streets, then got back to the car to drive to Hamilton and spoke to several people at the Gandydancer. So far, no patron knew much about Pete, though there were a few men who said that they had seen him in the previous month or so. *Not very helpful.* I headed over to Hornby Street where The Garden Baths were located. I had to leave my posters at the front office, but the young man working as the cashier promised to distribute the information. On recommendation from the attendant at the bathhouse, I motored over to the Richards Street Service Club, which I had previously thought was a garage. Inside the door, there was a steep flight of wooden stairs that led up to the entrance office. The place stank of rot. It was dark, dank and oppressive. Through a glass partition, I spoke with the attendant, a bald, short, heavy man wearing a leather harness and not much else. The harness pushed his pendulous breasts from his body in a very unappealing manner.

"Hi, I'm hoping you might help me."

"What with, son?" He looked disinterested with my plea for assistance.

"It's my friend," I pulled out Pete's picture. "He's missing. Could you let some of your customers —"

Leather Harness interrupted me. "I don't have to."

Great, thanks a lot.

"No, you don't have to, but if —"

"No, I mean, I think I know who this is. Pretty sure he's the guy that collapsed here a few nights ago."

"What? Collapsed?"

"Yup, he'd only just gone through the door. Called the ambulance, what was it? Thursday night; well late into Friday. Poor guy, wasn't in good shape. Maybe he was high; dunno. They took him to hospital."

"St. Paul's?"

"Do I look like I have a crystal ball?" Leather Harness's voice was sharp.

"Hey, I'm waitin' back here, ya know."

Behind me was a middle-aged man itching to get into the bathhouse.

"I've told you what I know. Now, unless you wanna come inside, move off, son," he said impatiently.

"Thanks, you made my night," I shouted as I darted down the steps. I fired-up the VW and trekked over to St. Paul's. I parked on Burrard and raced into the aging brick-facaded hospital, quickly finding the Emergency Department. A tired-looking nurse was at the information station. Drenched like a rat, I approached her.

"Excuse me." I pulled Pete's picture from the envelope. "This man, he's my friend, and I think he's here, but you might not have his name because his wallet isn't with him and I"m really worried that he's —"

"Hold on, hold on, young man." The nurse took the picture from my hand. "We have a lot of patients here. I'll send it along —"

"No, please, listen, don't do that. There's gotta be someone that I could talk to. Someone who treated Pete. Pete Gauthier. He could be here, a John Doe. I think he collapsed early Friday morning and was brought in here. Please, someone's gotta help me." I thought I was going to burst into tears. "He's my friend and my friend's friend."

"Give me a few minutes," she said calmly. "I'll check right now, okay? Try to calm yourself. Here," the nurse passed me some tissues. "Sit down, have some water and wait for me right here. It could be a little while."

The nurse smiled warmly, then took the picture and left her station. I sat down and tried to control myself. I had a lot of fear that was bottled up inside me. I took a glance at my Timex and was surprised that it was after 1 AM. It had been a long day and now it was turning into a very long night. I took the nurse's advice and got a drink of water from the ancient water cooler, downed a couple of cups, then sat back down. My clothes were soaked, I was cold and exhausted from the worry I felt. I removed my jacket and put it over me like a blanket and closed my exquisitely tired eyes. *Maybe if I catch an hour's worth of sleep I'll be okay for practice.* Nearly an hour later, I woke when I heard my name being called.

"Shepard?"

I opened my heavy eyes to the sharp glare of fluorescent lighting and thought I must have been dreaming.

"Dr. Deth?" I gave my head a small shake.

"I think we've found your friend."

19

The Double Duty of Dr. Deth

"I'm seeing you a lot on the wards, aren't I?" Deth said as he led me down a long corridor to see Pete who was now in a cardiac ward.

"Did my friend have a heart attack? What's happened?"

"He was brought here several nights ago by ambulance. He has a type of pneumonia and sepsis, which caused his heart to become enlarged."

"He's had a heart attack?"

"No, we don't think so. However, everything is complicated by the pneumonia. His right lung collapsed and we had to intubate him. He's unable to speak —"

"Because of the tube?"

"Well, yes, but he's been so unwell that he's been in and out of consciousness. He's also been given sedation because when he comes to he tries to pull out his tubes and catheter."

That sounds like Pete.

"He can't pee on his own?"

"Not yet. We have him on antibiotics for infection, but he's not doing well right now. I'm handling his coronary-pulmonary concerns, but others are working on his overall health situation. We're still running tests, but I can say that we're struggling to figure out what's happening. He was very febrile and refused giving us his name. Your friend had no identification on him, just a roll of cash."

Yes, and that's probably because he was at a squalid bathhouse and didn't want to have any valuables with him, including his wallet. Now I understand.

"No? Well, I can tell you who he is. We've been scouring the neighbourhood for him. The police, too, apparently, though I'm surprised they didn't bother to look here."

Maybe they weren't looking that hard.

Deth pressed the elevator button. This entire scene seemed like a continuation of what I'd been doing for the past week at the Royal Columbian.

"I have to call my friend, Lara. Pete's her agent. She's worried beyond belief."

"There's a pay phone off the hall in the cardiac ward. You can call her after you see your friend, okay? He may be contagious. We've got gloves and a mask for your protection, but make sure you scrub your hands very well after your visit, as well." Deth passed me the gloves and mask. "And, just warning you, he's going to seem very ill and out of sorts."

"It can't be any worse than my father, can it?" I asked, leaving Deth. I put on my protection and stepped into a room shared with 4 or 5 others. In the middle lay Pete, half-awake, semi-prone in bed. His eyes became round as saucers when he spotted me. Underneath his beautiful brown eyes were dark purple bags. His gorgeous hair was matted and greasy, his face covered with stubble.

"Jezus Christ, Pete, am I happy to see you!" I cried out, rushing to his bedside. I pushed down my mask to my chin and quickly removed the gloves. Deth was right. Pete looked gravely ill. There was a plastic tube in his throat, a respirator helping out with his collapsed lung, IV's of antibiotics going into his veins and yet he smiled at me as though he hadn't a care in the world.

"So tell me," I whispered, pulling up a chair and grabbing his large hands with my own, careful of the needles in his wrist, "what the fuck have you done this time?"

I had a long visit with Pete. I told him that we'd all been frantically searching for him. Mostly, Pete smiled at me. It was more than the sedation; he was pleased I was with him. I got up so that I could call Lara, and Pete's eyes flashed fear.

"Hey, I'll be back. I gotta let your favourite singer know you've been found, that's all. See you in a few minutes. And don't go anywhere." Pete relaxed into his bed, almost disappearing into it. His body was terribly thin ... too thin, even for Pete.

Even though it was very late, I called Lara who answered the phone on the first ring.

"Lara, it's me," I said quietly.

"Do you have news?" Lara's voice was extremely hoarse.

"Yes. Pete's at St. Paul's. He's got pneumonia and he's in rough shape. He's full of tubes; he can't talk. I've spoken with the doctor. Jeez, Lara, he's the same guy that did my dad's heart operation. Dr. Deth's doing double-duty, for fuck's sake. What're the chances?" I asked, amazed at the coincidence.

"I'm getting a cab right —"

"Lara, don't be insane. Do you know what time it is? Come tomorrow. Pete's going to need your help and you've gotta be rested."

"Sunshine, I've been so worried. I can't tell you ..." Lara began softly crying.

"I know, Lara. But he's safe here. Try to sleep, sweetie."

"Are you going home?" Lara asked.

I thought for a bit before answering. "No, I'm gonna spend the night with Pete. He's afraid, I'm sure of it. I think he'll be more comfortable if I'm here with him. It's what family does."

"Sunshine," Lara uttered admiringly.

"It's what my Mum says. And Pete's part of *our* family, isn't he?"

Lara and I agreed to meet the next night after my swim practice. I finished my call with her and went back to Pete. I thought he looked anxious for my return.

"I spoke to Lara. She thinks you're staging all this as a ploy for attention."

Pete rolled his eyes for a moment, smiled then extended his hands. I held his large, cool paws and thought back to a short time ago when Pete seemed to have the world tightly in his firm grip. With my foot, I pulled up one of the chairs to sit on, close to Pete. His liquid eyes with the incredibly long, dark lashes, grew weary. He closed his eyes and his grip on my hand lessened, then it fell away completely as he dropped off to sleep. I stroked his hair as I'd done when he'd been in my bed years earlier, smoothing his mop against his forehead. It made me think of doing the same to my father a short while earlier. As I sat with him, I didn't allow myself to think what Pete's dangerous illness might have meant for him ... or me.

20

The Suggestion

I woke disoriented, dry-mouthed, my body as stiff as the plastic chair I'd been sleeping on. My Timex read 5:20. I rubbed my scalp and looked over at Pete. He was asleep, breathing normally, considering the equipment he was plugged in to. He looked unwell. I didn't want to disturb him, but I had to leave to go to practice. As it was, I'd be late.

Terrific. And I've still gotta go home to get my swim gear. Shit. I rose, grabbed at the base of my neck for a quick massage and yelped softly from a tender spot and unintentionally woke Pete. He looked at me and smiled groggily. I gave him a brief and gentle hug — as well as I could hug someone lying in a hospital bed.

"Morning. Did you sleep okay?" Pete nodded. "Do you have pain?" Pete shook his head. "Listen, I have to run to practice, alright?" He nodded once more. "I called Lara last night. She was going to jump into a taxi and bust your ass, but I told her to wait till this morning. I'll come back to visit. Stay out of trouble; don't pick up any male nurses, got it?" Pete winked once and closed his eyes. I made my way out of a dead-quiet hospital, feeling my gritty teeth with my tongue as I ran out to find the Fastback, dashed to my apartment and headed to the pool for what was going to be another grim swim practice.

Thompson noted my lateness for practice but chose not to say anything. I moved through the other swimmers to get to the pool deck. After studying my itinerary, I jumped in the bracing water with Pete on my mind. I'm no fool. Pete's haunted appearance was worrisome to say the least. I'd seen him perhaps 4 or 5 months earlier at dinner with Lara, and while very trim, he looked healthy. *Healthy can be an illusion.* As I reeled off the metres, I recalled the first time I met Pete. It was at Oil Can Harry's, a jazz club where Lara had persuaded me to listen to an American singer. Pete seduced me that night in the club's toilet — with no protest from me. It was perhaps the most intoxicating sexual experience I'd ever had — exhilarating, electric, sensual — with a man for whom I'd had an instant crush on. I doubt I ever lost that feeling with him. Everything about Pete radiated what I lacked — confidence, sexuality, charisma. Subsequent meetings with Pete were had been infrequent, but each tryst had been memorable. Through the years, he'd been strategically involved in Lara's successes and never failed to take an interest in my athletics. Pete was himself a success; a self-made man. He was someone that I looked up to and marvelled over.

By the time I reached the kick-set portion of my swim, I was fatigued. I'd had perhaps 3 hours of sleep and was not swimming well. Thompson wasn't screaming at me, though, which I was grateful for. *Guess I'm not gonna be your whipping boy this morning. That's unfair. I'm swimming like a hack. Admit it. Take responsibility.* I completed the swim and did not go to weight training. Instead, I showered-up, avoiding the coach, and headed to class. At the office,

I called Lara, but she didn't answer. *Perhaps she's at the hospital already?*

Late for class, I scrunched in at the back of the room, hopefully unnoticed. In my therapy studies, there was an emphasis on discussing personal challenges. After all, therapists have to be able to explore their past, master their present and construct a future that is congruent with their principles and values. However, during the experiential and discussion forum, I wasn't about to talk about spending the night flitting from one gay bar to the next and pleading with a bathhouse worker in a frenzied effort to locate my once-secret male lover. As I moved past my middle 20s, I was disappointed that I still lacked the mettle to be myself. It angered me and kept me hidden.

I was able to get some rest after class and before the last swim practice of the day. At home, I changed out of my sweats and into my uniform — Levi's and a white tee-shirt. I tidied my apartment and made a peanut butter and raisin sandwich and drank a litre of milk from the carton. Just after 8 PM, the door buzzer sounded. Knowing who it was, I buzzed Lara through. In a few moments, she appeared, looking haggard. Her face was lined with worry and she was moving slowly. Her thin frame was wrapped up in a long black coat. We had a lengthy embrace and she updated me with news from the hospital.

"When I was visiting Pete I spoke with the doctor." Lara took off her coat and sat down at the kitchen table. I went to the kitchen, grabbed a half-empty bottle of wine and poured her a drink. She thanked me and had a sip, leaving lipstick on the rim of the glass.

"Dr. Deth?"

"No, it was someone else. Can't recall her name." Lara wiped lipstick off her glass with her forefinger.

"What did she tell you?" I sat down across from her with an OJ.

"Pete's doing a bit better, but she said he's got a huge recovery ahead. Might take a couple of months or longer for him to get back to form." Lara sighed. "They're taking out that nasty breathing tube tomorrow to see how he manages."

"Great. You know how much Pete likes to talk. Right now he's writing things down on paper. Did they tell you anything else?" *What I really want to ask but I'm afraid to, does Pete have AIDS?*

"Just that it's an unusual type of pneumonia. Sunshine, he looks so sick." Lara took another sip of wine.

"He *is* sick, Lara."

"I never asked you. Where was Pete found?"

"Well," I hesitated. *Some things are private; like where Pete had been.*

"Where?" she persisted.

"He collapsed at a ... gay club."

"A bar?"

"Um, yeah; can't recall which one. I was in a hundred of 'em it seemed. It was on Richards," I said, altering the truth for Pete's sake. I really didn't want to explain that Pete had been at a seedy bathhouse. Changing the topic, I asked, "So, did the doctor say when he'd be outta there?"

"That depends," she answered. "If there's someone to care for him, probably in a week."

"I'm not sure what you —"

Lara interrupted me, "I mean, he can go home if he has —"

It was my turn to jump in. "Hold on. Are you saying that someone has to be at home with him?" Unlike my father, I couldn't see Pete being cared for at home; he was too independent.

"Not all the time, just until he's recovered. We can do —"

"*We?* Just a second, Lara." Being best friends often meant that I had a good idea what she was thinking about. "Are you suggesting that *we* look after Pete? You and I?"

"Well, yes, that's what I'm suggesting. I'm very caring," she offered carefully.

"Please. You can't even keep houseplants alive," I stated unfairly.

"So sometimes I forget to water them. That's no crime," Lara said defensively.

"You're missing my point, Lara."

"Yes, I'm suggesting we look after Pete," Lara stated firmly. "Like you said, Pete's family. I owe him that much. He's given me a career. I'm not going to turn my back on him when this time *he's* the one in need."

I also had an obligation to Pete, who had been instrumental in my own development.

"Lara, Pete won't have it. He's too proud and inde —"

"You're right, Sunshine. He's proud, but right now he's terribly sick … and vulnerable. We could nurse him back to health. Maybe he'll be fine in a few weeks," Lara added optimistically.

"Have you spoken to him about this?"

"No, but the doctor thought it was a good idea. And besides, Pete's going to have to accept being a patient."

"How do you propose that we do this?" I asked, thinking on her scheme.

"Well, he could stay here with you — my place is too small, and he'd need his own bed. You could sleep on your sofa." Lara had a studio apartment in Kits compared to my roomy one bedroom. "And I'd help out when you were at school or at swim practice. It can work, Sunshine, and it's not forever. Please, let's not fail him. I couldn't live with myself if I failed him." Lara's eyes glimmered with emotion. No one says 'no' to Lara easily, and though there were logistics to be thought out, she was making perfect sense. "I could even do some cooking," she offered, screwing her face up in the process.

"Lara, let's be pragmatic. Everyone knows you don't cook."

"I could learn, Sunshine," she said imploringly. "I'm no Julia Child, but there are cookbooks, aren't there?"

I had to smile at the thought of Lara stirring a pot of bubbling bouillabaisse. Then reality struck: *What am I going to tell Robby? My mother? Jeez. What am I getting into? I'll have Lara's help, but still ... hold on. Make this simple — Pete's family like I said.*

"I don't know how we're gonna do this, but you're right, Lara. When the time comes, let's bring Pete home."

21

Starting Over

Robby was very understanding of when I explained that Lara and I were going to be nursing Pete. My mother was worried that I'd become ill with pneumonia, no matter how I reassured her. (Probably ditching my mask and gloves on my visits at the hospital wasn't the brightest thing I could have done.) I never spoke with my father about it, but I was certain he would be impassive about the matter. Lara and I committed ourselves to provide our friend with excellent care, as he'd had in St. Paul's. Pete had a very attentive medical team. Doctors, nurses and a respiratory therapist all came together to help him sufficiently recover so that he could leave their care and go home. Of course, not his home at 'Vaseline Towers', as he called it, but my apartment at the Queen Charlotte. Pete had been in hospital for 12 days, sharing his space with several other patients. The tubes were out and he was able to speak, if his baritone voice was a bit on the rough side. The larger concern was his low weight. Pete had continued to lose muscle mass during his stay at St. Paul's. His appetite was insignificant and it showed. His tall frame was now weighing in at a paltry 153 pounds. I arranged for him to be released on a Sunday afternoon because I had no practice. I asked the nurse if I could speak privately with the on-duty physician, a small Jewish woman named Dr. Gelmon. Gelmon seemed efficient, but wasn't the warmest person I'd come across.

"What would you like to know?" she asked brusquely as we stood in the ward corridor.

"Well, I'm taking Pete home to recover," I started, then paused for a moment, unclear how to ask the next question.

"Yes?"

"I just want to understand. Is he, um, sick, you know, with something else?"

"Your friend has had a type of pneumonia that's found in AIDS patients. Is that what you're asking about?"

My heart sank.

"Uh huh. And does that mean that —"

"I don't know. *We* don't know what that means. We're at the beginning of something that's already proving deadly. We're getting reports of AIDS across the US and Europe and now here in Canada. Are you following the news?"

"Yeah, what I'm hearing is … really shocking."

"It's as alarming as you're hearing." Gelmon briefly glanced at her clipboard.

"I can't believe … how this is all …" My breathing was shallow and I suddenly wanted to run away. *Sort of how your father felt, isn't it?*

"Have you been intimate with your friend?" She scribbled on her board.

"Huh? Intimate? No. Why do you —" Gelmon interrupted my falsehood as I blushed crimson.

"There are researchers in France who believe a virus that causes swelling in the lymphatic system may be the cause of AIDS and is transmitted —"

"Through sexual contact?" I anxiously finished her sentence with a question.

"Their work isn't complete, but yes, that's correct. There's a Dr. Gallo who's suggesting this is a type of infectious retrovirus," Gelmon stated. "If you were asking me for advice, I'd say to curtail sexual contact — until more is understood."

It's a little late for that.

Gelmon continued. "At this point we just have theories. I don't know if your friend has AIDS, but he's got a pneumonia associated with GRID and he's certainly in a high-risk group. Beyond that ..." Gelmon didn't finish her sentence, but shook her head. "Take Mr. Gauthier home. Make him comfortable. Force him to eat, if you have to. He should improve with the good nutrition and rest, but we're not clear about how much or if his immune system will recover."

I felt faint as a nurse came by. "Mr. Gauthier is ready for discharge, Dr. Gelmon."

"All right. Now, we'll see him again in one week for follow-up, so he'll need to make an appointment. You understand how important it is for him to come back?"

The lump in my throat made it difficult to swallow let alone talk.

"Yes. I'll make sure he's here next week. Thank you, doctor," I croaked.

Gelmon nodded, turned with the nurse and headed back to the ward. I was left to nervously digest what I'd been told as I moved into Pete's room. He sat expectantly, thin, fatigued but very eager to leave. He was wearing clothes from when he came to hospital; jeans, a black polo shirt and a light brown leather bomber. All were now far too large for him, though his coat covered his bony shoulders. I came up beside him and put my arm under his forearm, helping him to stand up from the chair he had been in, chatting with several ill-looking men. I gathered up his medications and stuffed them in my coat pocket.

"C'mon, Pete. We're blowing this hospital." Pete responded with a devious smile and was about to make a crack at my bad and unoriginal faux pas. Before he could say a word, I shook my finger at him and said, "Don't even think about it."

22

Pete Speaks

"It's not a Porsche, but it'll get us home," I said, as we exited St. Paul's and slowly walked along Burrard to find the Fastback. Of course, stylish Pete drove a series of gorgeous Porsches ever since I'd known him. Pete stepped slowly and cautiously. His pants were nearly falling off, catching on the sole of his shoes. With his apartment key, I'd gone to collect some of his clothes to bring back to my place, but I doubt any would have fit him. He was initially ambivalent about staying with me, but Lara had convinced him. "I should have brought you a hat," I said, worrying about the cold rain pelting down on him, bouncing off the sidewalk as people scurried home in the fading afternoon light.

"No," he said. "It's good to feel the rain on me." Quickly, Pete's and my hair were soaked. As we climbed into the VW, I looked over at him and donned my biggest smile.

"Lara's got a surprise for you." No response from Pete. "Okay, you beat it outta me. She's made supper for us." I fired up the VW and started the short trip home.

"Lara?"

"Yup, she's a new woman. I haven't actually seen her cook, but she's been talking about making dinner for the past 3 days."

"Our Lara, the singer?" Pete asked skeptically and briefly crowed. Pete put his long arm over my shoulder as we continued to drive down Davie. Pete was quiet the rest of the way. I couldn't help but think of all the men walking on the street. *Were they facing a potentially frightening future, too? Was I?* I stopped outside the Queen Charlotte to let Pete out so that he didn't have to walk.

"I'll be up in a couple of minutes after I find some parking. Here's the key," I said, passing the extra one to him. "And use the elevator, okay?"

I looked at Pete through my foggy windows and watched his ghostly image move to the apartment entrance as I motored off. After luckily finding a spot close-by, I rushed back home, climbed the stairs and entered my apartment. In the past few hours that I'd been with Pete at the hospital, Lara had busied herself in the kitchen. As I entered, she was standing nervously in the dining room, tomato sauce smeared across her pretty blue silk blouse, grease marks on her beige wool slacks, remnants of whipped cream unfathomably on her collar, in bare feet, hair completely askew and looking unlike the fashionable woman we knew. Pete was beside her gazing at the feast that Lara had created. Shockingly, on the dining table was chicken cacciatore with angel hair pasta, Caesar Salad with fried croutons and red wine for Lara, OJ for Pete and me. A tall multi-layered cake sat nearby, heaped with pastry cream and layers of cake and glazed fruits. French bread, olives and cheese were sitting on the end of the table, just in case the orgy of food wasn't sufficient.

"My Gawd, Lara. What have you done?" I was stunned.

"What does it look like?" Lara answered off-handedly. "I cooked … sort of."

The spectacular meal looked suspicious. I wandered into the kitchen and surreptitiously looked in the garbage and found paper bags and containers from Mannheim's. "Looks terrific, Lara. What do you think, Pete?" I turned to see him sliding down onto the sofa. "You okay, buster?"

"I have to sit for a bit," Pete said, then raised his legs onto the couch. "Give me a minute, okay?"

"I don't think he likes my cooking," Lara said wryly, viewing the immense amount of food piled across the table.

"Pete, let me fix you a plate and you can eat it right there, okay?" I urged.

Pete shook his head, obviously disinterested in eating. He put his hand over his eyes and deeply exhaled, coughing as he did so.

"Sunshine, I think we need to get Pete into bed. He's tired."

"No. He has to have something to eat," I insisted. "Right, Pete?" He lay still and ignored my question. "Dr. Gelmon told me eating should be his top priority."

"Yes," Lara added, "but perhaps later is best, when he's had a chance to rest —"

"How much rest can he need? The doctor said he needs to start gaining some weight so that —"

"I spoke to the discharge nurse; she said he'll eat when he's had a chance —"

"No, no. Lara, the doctor ordered —"

"*Fuck the doctor!*" Pete screamed.

"Huh?" Pete's forceful and gruff voice took Lara and me by surprise.

"Listen to me. I'm not hungry. I appreciate all this," he pointed at the dinner sprawled across the table, "but I just don't want anything. Not now, please. The very sight ..." He turned his head from the table and blew out a breath and coughed slightly.

"Of course," Lara swept towards Pete. "I'm sorry. I overdid it. Well, you know what's best for you, naturally." Lara sat beside him. "Just tell us what you need, Pete, and we'll do it, get it, screw it, sing it — whatever. All right?" She kissed him on the forehead, looked at me with worry, then got up and began removing food from the table. "Christ, Sunshine, help me clear this food. You know I'm not Betty-fucking-Crocker."

"Hah!" Pete howled. "That's the kind of line I've been waiting to hear!"

Lara scowled at him and stepped closer towards our sick friend.

"Now you listen to me, bub," Lara raged. "All this work for you and all I get is a ruined Port's blouse," she uttered angrily, as she grabbed her chemise. "Look! Demolished with tomato sauce. So this is the thanks I get for being a happy hooker?"

"I think you meant 'happy homemaker', Lara." I corrected her faux pas.

"Putain ça," she cursed, then started to chuckle. By the time I joined in, Pete and Lara were laughing so hard they were gasping for air. "For God's sake," Lara managed to say between breaths, "don't *ever* ask me to make another meal," she cackled. "Look at me," she cried, pulling at her damaged clothes and running her fingers through her seriously mussed hair. "Don't you know who I am?"

Lara's statement was like a lit match to fuel. In a few moments, all of us were howling, together again on my velvet sofa, chortling, sighing, hugging and loving each other.

An hour later we had gently persuaded Pete to eat a tiny amount of angel hair pasta and drink some juice. He took his antibiotic medication and thanked both Lara and me for our support before going off to my bedroom, exhausted.

"You won't mind the couch?" Lara asked as we finished cleaning up the dinner dishes and were chatting in the small galley.

"Actually, I'm kinda getting used to it." I explained that I slept there when my mother was staying with me during my father's hospital stay. "I owe them a call, too. Tomorrow," I yawned. "Or the next day." I had a lot to balance with Pete's care being a prime concern.

"Sunshine," Lara began. "With everything that's happening in the world right now. I mean, you know, health-wise … I don't want Pete to have … you know … Christ, I can't even say the word."

"Then don't. Don't say it. Not now." I put my arms around my best friend. Lara held on tightly, nearly squeezing the air from my lungs.

"Nothing is the same," she said quietly. "Is it?"

After calling a cab, she put on her coat and shoes, kissed me gently on the cheek and silently left the Queen Charlotte.

Pete wasn't the only tired man. I was feeling the pinch of managing swimming, school and having to adjust to having a new housemate. As I brought the yellow comforter back to the sofa, I heard muffled sounds coming from my bedroom. I listened carefully as I padded down the hallway barefoot, pausing outside the closed door. It was Pete, softly sobbing. My heart throbbed. I wondered what to do for a moment and then I went through the door. Pete was lying on his side, hunched nearly into a ball, with tears coursing down his cheeks. When he saw me, he covered his face. I moved to the bed. Pete was so frail, looked so vulnerable and appeared in so much emotional pain. His suffering was palpable. Wordlessly, I went around to the other side of the bed, climbed in and lay beside my friend, gathering him up in my arms and rocking him gently until his tears subsided and he fell into a deep sleep.

23

The Problem with Pete

Over the course of several days, Lara and I did our best to inspire Pete to eat, but we failed miserably. His appetite had deserted him. Food became the enemy, something to avoid. He was taking fluids such as orange juice and tea with milk, but that was all Pete explained he could stomach. No matter what I made, or what Lara bought, most foods remained untouched by my ill houseguest. I spoke with my mother about it, the nutritionist at St. Paul's and Pete's physician, too, but no change in his eating behaviour occurred. I made soft food, textured food, bland food, spicy food, blended fruit and avocado smoothies and offered gallons of chocolate milk but his appetite was the same — zilch. My mother thought Pete might have been depressed, and even though I didn't tell her the whole story, that seemed to be a reasonable assessment. Even Mrs. McBride knew of his difficulties. I talked to her about in the laundry room. She didn't have the full picture, but listened to my worries regarding Pete and his rapidly decreasing weight. She was wiping the inside of the washers as I was folding my clean clothes on the large table.

"… and it doesn't matter what type of food, he passes on all of it."

"Dear, does he have pain?"

"No, Mrs. McBride. Not that he's said."

"And what about his cough? That can make a person nauseous and less inclined to eat."

"He's not coughing much, hardly at all now."

"Fever?" she inquired.

"No, he's not feverish either. But he's become so terribly thin … and weak."

"Well, yes, he's wasting away, dear. I saw him in the hall when you were coming back from the hospital yesterday afternoon." The building manager completed wiping the drum of the machine and went to the large concrete sink to rinse her cloth.

"Did you?" I finished folding the towels and was working on putting my dress shirts on hangers. I was so focused on Pete I never saw her.

"Yes, dear. He's not the man that ran up the stairs with my groceries a few years ago, is he?" Mrs. McBride asked sadly, hanging her cloth on the side of the sink to dry.

"I'm afraid not. Yesterday the doctor said if he doesn't start eating they'll have to admit him to hospital and put a feed tube in his stomach. Can you imagine that?" I was horrified at the thought. "Pete said he'd never let them do it."

"Well, dear, there might be another way to get your friend's appetite back."

I stopped hanging out my shirts, turned to her and inquired, "Please, what is it?"

"It worked for Mr. McBride when all had failed to provide relief from his cancer. He was in terrible unrelenting pain and couldn't eat. Nothing helped him."

"Oh, I never knew." Mrs. McBride rarely spoke of her husband.

"Yes, dear, so much pain that Harold couldn't face food, either." Mrs. McBride sighed as she sat in a battered rattan chair, her diminutive frame dissolving in the seat. Though she was small, Mrs. McBride had been a champion swimmer in the 1930s, famously crossing English Bay in a startling race between herself and legendary swimmer Percy Norman. Back then, she was called 'Clockwork Carrie' for her steady, assured front crawl stroke. She continued on with her story. "Mr. McBride became skeletal." She rotated her ring on her finger absently.

"Poor man. So what did you do?"

"Well, we had a friend. What was his name?" she pondered momentarily before continuing. "Of course — Cecil, that's right. And such a lovely man," she smiled at her memory, then went on. "He gave me something for my husband's pain, and my word, it was a miracle — it took away his pain and his appetite returned within a few days."

"Was Cecil a doctor?" I asked as I plunked the shirts on top of my laundry basket.

"A doctor? No, dear. Cecil was ... how should I put this? Cecil was a supplier."

"Mrs. McBride, are you telling me that your friend was a drug dealer?" I asked, eyes wide with disbelief.

"Not drugs, dear. Herbs. That's what Cecil preferred to call them. After all, he was a florist by trade."

"A florist? But —"

"I know what you're thinking, dear. But when someone you love is suffering, you'll do anything to alleviate their pain."

"Even if it's illegal?"

"You're being rather puritanical. One does what works," she advised. "It's how I've managed to cope with my bad back," Mrs. McBride expressed, shifting her weight in the creaking chair. I thought about Pete's alarming weight loss for a moment.

"I wouldn't even know how or where to get —"

"You won't have to. I have my own plentiful stash, right here."

"You do? From Cecil?"

"No, dear," she laughed. "I'm afraid that Cecil is long gone. But he did teach me how to grow my own. I have a private spot on the roof that I've turned into a small greenhouse. Most people think it's for my geraniums."

"But it's —"

"For my herbs. I've gotten quite good at production. You should see how much I've got in my flour canisters," the landlady said proudly. "There's enough for all of Kits."

"But, Mrs. McBride, you're growing —"

"Mary Jane," she smiled and finished my sentence. "Don't look so shocked, dear." Mrs. McBride rose from her chair and took a deep breath. "Would you like to give some to your friend?"

The image of Pete's fading weight flashed in my mind.

"The thing is, Pete doesn't smoke," I answered. I finished folding my remaining clothes and put them into my basket.

"Then, dear," Mrs. McBride said with a sly voice, "you'll have to make him an herbal convert."

My landlady and I climbed into the birdcage elevator and it groaned and heaved its way to the 3rd floor. I left my laundry outside my apartment door and accompanied her to her home.

"I'll wait here?" I asked.

"No, you'll come through. Excuse my mess."

After removing my shoes and leaving them at the door, I stepped into her decidedly *unmessy* living room for the first time. It was painted a sunny yellow and had a coffered white ceiling. Mrs. McBride had a cream-coloured sofa and two cherry-red chairs with a dark green blanket draped over one of them. Along one wall were tall wooden bookcases completely filled with a variety of tomes. I glanced volumes of leather-bound works of Shakespeare, Mario Puzo, Arthur Miller, several cookbooks as well as editions of Robert Burns' poetry jostling with 'Harlequin Romances'. There were a few 'Women's Daily' magazines littering her oak coffee table.

"Sit, dear. I'll be back in a moment with Pete's herbs."

I did as instructed, and plopped into one of the chairs. Underfoot was a plush red and blue oriental carpet. There was an abundance of light coming in through her windows covered with filmy off-white sheers. The overall appearance of Mrs. McBride's apartment was one of conservative elegance. Of course, conservative wouldn't accurately have described the pot-smoking 68-year-old former swimming champ. As I waited, I noted a scent of sweetness that permeated the air. In 5 or 6 minutes, she reentered the living room with a large zip-lock bag of cannabis. I stood up.

"Now, you'll have to crumble this up a bit, then put a few good pinches into a rolling paper," she said, reaching into her pocket. "These are them," she said, handing a packet to me. "Roll and light — perhaps in the morning and early evening by an open window, if you don't mind. Can't have our neighbours complain, can we?"

"Thank you, Mrs. McBride." I walked to the door and put on my shoes and started down the hallway.

"Dear, do tell me how he makes out with my herbs," she called out hopefully.

24

A Puff for a Pouf

I have a motto that I've lived by most of my life: "To get what you want you have to give something up." It's meant many things to me; to strive to be a good swimmer, I had to give up a social life. Or to be a therapist, I had to be willing to give up holding on to presumptions about myself or family that may have been myth. The biggest one: to be openly gay, I had to give up the notion that I couldn't manage the potential backlash from my family, my school or the swim community. It's a motto that many people, including Lara, identified with. After all, to become a professional singer, she gave up hoping that her family would accept her decision. For Pete, if he wanted to restore his health, he had to give up a certain attitude that he'd held, well, for years.

"I don't smoke, you know that." Pete looked unimpressed as I presented him with Mrs. McBride's appetite-building idea. We were seated at the kitchen table after my morning swim practice.

"I know, Pete, but it's not tobacco, and it's not supposed to be bad for your lungs, I checked. Jeez, this isn't as easy as I thought,"

I said, struggling with the fine motor skills needed to place pot on a tiny piece of paper and roll a joint.

"Where'd you get this stuff, anyway?" Pete watched as I fumbled with the task.

"A friend recommended —"

"Lara doesn't smoke pot."

"It wasn't Lara." I licked the rolling paper and started to slowly form the joint.

"You don't have any other friends," Pete said flatly.

"That's not true. I have —"

"Well, I don't care who it was, I'm not smoking pot … I'm not a stoner. That's it. Period." Pete declared, sipping his juice slowly and with effort.

"Why are you being so obstinate? It's just herbs. And what if it makes you feel like eating? What if it got you back to where you were? What else has been working? How 'bout, 'nothing'?" I asked forcefully. My first attempt at a doobie was complete. "There," I said with satisfaction, viewing my work — a bent, damp, craggy joint. Pete looked at me with eyes dark as the most threatening of storm clouds. "I'm assuming that you want to get better so that you can return to work? Turn Lara into a megastar?"

Pete batted his long lashes at me. "Of course I do. By the way, Lara already thinks she's a megastar. She has a healthy ego. It goes with her appetite."

I passed the joint over to him. He took it cautiously. "It's not a nuclear weapon. It's just some grass. Try it. For me? Just one puff."

"Is this some kind of warped Jewish guilt you're trying?"

"Is it working?" I pushed a Bic lighter towards him. "My friend said twice a day and you'll be back to form in no time."

Pete put down his juice, flicked the Bic, placed the joint in his mouth and lit up, taking a deep breath and promptly started coughing.

"I hope this stuff isn't gonna make me go run naked up Davie Street like a lunatic," he deadpanned, blowing out a cloud of smoke and inhaling once again, this time, less deep and without a cough.

"Ah," I said, "you mean like the old Pete?"

In the winter of 1983, not much was known about the devastating virus that would wreak destruction and pain around the world. I suspected that Pete had it. He — like many gay men —- had unshackled themselves from the tyranny of sexual oppression during the turbulent 1970s and claimed their place with pride. Horrifically, gay men were falling prey to an outbreak that seemed to be targeting them. Of course, the so-called 'Gay Plague' was not confined to homosexual men, but at the start of the epidemic, most thought it was. To say I was worried for not only him, but for myself and Robby, was an understatement. Caring for Pete meant there was a constant reminder of what may lie ahead for me and for a community that I was just learning how to be a part of.

After initially rejecting the cannabis, Pete eased into a twice-daily routine, thanks to Mrs. McBride, who kept me stocked up with the stuff. He passed on smoking joints and switched to a glass pipe I bought in a sketchy shop in Gastown. It was far easier for him to use. Pete smoked beside the open French doors, so the telltale scent could drift out of the Queen Charlotte. Contrary to his initial concern of reefer madness, Pete wasn't running stark naked through the streets, but rather Mrs. McBride's magic marijuana made Lara's agent relaxed and calm. At first, there wasn't any change in Pete. Within a few days, however, he was able to nibble at some cheese, then a bit of bread, a small bowl of clear broth, a few boiled potatoes and eventually fish and chicken were not only tolerated, but he was hungry for more. On the afternoons that I was at school, Lara made a trip with food from the deli, and no longer had to worry about how to stuff broiled chicken down Pete's throat. In fact, he wasn't fighting Lara or me any longer. By the middle of March, Pete had been with me for over 2 weeks; longer than anticipated. He began looking appreciatively better and had stopped losing weight. His energy was much lower, certainly, but his strength was reappearing, albeit slowly.

March is a time when Vancouver's cold, wet, dark weeks of winter disappear and are fascinatingly replaced with brighter days where many plants and trees wake up, bud out and turn a vibrant green. *Pete's also a part of this springtime renewal. He's growing stronger, sunnier, livelier.*

As before, to get what both Lara and I wanted — for Pete to improve — also meant that we gave up some things. Lara put all music dates on hold, resulting in lost income for her and her trio. I missed many classes, however, I attended every swim practice and plowed my way through with as much gumption as I could muster. Unfortunately for me, gumption alone does not a champion swimmer make. On Sunday, I rose, stiff from the sofa or perhaps sore from the previous practice session. It was difficult to tell as I was experiencing frequent muscle tenderness from my workouts. I cracked it up to being older and needing more time to recover than was possible. I was just barely awake and looking in the fridge when the phone rang. I dashed to get it before it woke Pete. It was my mother.

"Jeez, Mum, you're up early. Is everything okay with Dad?" I looked at my Timex: 7:45 AM. I had uncharacteristically overslept.

"It's not that early. I haven't heard from you in a while, so I thought I'd call."

"Oh, I thought I spoke to you just … you're right. It's been a few days. Sorry, I've had a lot going on."

"I expect you'd like to know how your father's been?"

"Uh, of course. How's he been?" *I noticed that you didn't ask how Pete was.*

"He's back at work a couple days a week. Can you believe it?"

"Yes, I can, Mum. Did you think he would stay away from the store?"

"It's just over a month after his surgery. I think he wanted to go back so that he could light up."

"Jeez, Mum, don't tell me that he's smoking,"

"I can't do that," she sighed.

"Have you seen him smoking?"

"No, but I don't have to. He's been going out for drives every evening and coming back stinking of cigarettes. Lynda told me just last week that she went by the store and he was outside near the rear door puffing away." My mother sounded exasperated.

"Well, if the surgery didn't kill him, the Buckingham's surely will."

"Maybe you could come out and have a talk with him?"

"Me? Oh, I dunno, Mum. I've got my hands full with Pete." The thought of having a conversation with my father about his smoking turned my blood cold.

"It seems that your friend is more important than your father," she said with more than a touch of accusation.

"What? No, I wouldn't say that, exactly." *I should have said, "Of course you're correct."*

"How does next Sunday sound?"

"Huh? Next Sunday? Ah, I think I have…." *C'mon, come up with something fast.*

"You can't lie to your mother. Bring Pete … and Lara, too, if she can come."

"Well, Pete may not be well enough."

"Perhaps the country air will do him some good."

"Mum, you live in a ditch that smells like rotten broccoli."

"How can you be so unkind?"

"All of us, eh?"

"Yes, we'll have a lovely evening, and —"

"Mum, I dunno, I've got an early practice Monday morning."

"Then brunch. Yes, we'll have a nice, big, friendly brunch next Sunday," she said confidently. "I'll make that shrimp quiche you love."

"I, ah …"

"Good, then it's all settled," my mother said triumphantly. "We'll see you at 1 PM."

"Thanks, Mum, but how 'bout a rain-check? Maybe in a few weeks?"

My mother didn't wait to say goodbye, instead she sighed, signed off and hung up before I could explain why we weren't able to come to "the country".

Pete wandered into the living room wearing only a pair of underwear that was too large for him. His bones jutted out sharply from his shoulders and hips.

"Sorry if the phone woke you," I said, having disturbed Pete.

"No, I should have been up. I've spent too much time in your bed." Pete rubbed his mop of black hair and asked, "Mother?"

"How'd you know?" Pete staggered into the kitchen. I didn't tell him about Mum's invite.

"Tone of voice. You know, I feel incredibly well this morning," he said, yawning and scratching his belly. "After I get cleaned up, I'm going to make us some breakfast for a change."

"You sure you're up to it?" Pete had been doing a lot of nothing for 2 weeks.

"Shep, it's breakfast. It's not like I'm running a marathon. How 'bout some eggs, French Canadian style?" He took a carton of eggs from the fridge.

"Sure, what's that?"

"An omelette." Pete grinned, his teeth wide as a Cheshire cat.

"Oh. What makes it French Canadian?"

"Me." Pete laughed and pulled the cast-iron skillet from the cupboard, left it on the gas stove and went off to take a steamy shower. I could hear him humming and singing. I was surprised at his change of energy and while he was showering, called Lara excitedly.

"Hell, I mean hello?" Lara groggily responded on the 5th ring.

"Lara, it's me."

"What's wrong?" she asked sharply.

"Nothing," I started.

"Hold on, Sunshine. You're calling me at — what does that clock say? *Good God.* Do you know what time it is?"

"Lara, stop kvetching. It's Pete. He's better this morning."

"Better? How?"

"He's fired up, talkative. Says he feels great. He's going to make breakfast for us."

"That's wonderful news."

"By the way, Mum invited us to come out to the Ditch for brunch next Sunday. She's making shrimp quiche."

"Us?"

"Us. You, Pete and myself."

"You told her …" Lara waited for me to finish her sentence.

"I told her 'no', and now she's pissed at me."

"*Brunch* … all of us with your father? That's a little out there, isn't it?" she asked in a now-strong voice.

"Isn't it?"

"I don't think sharing a quiche with your father … well, no disrespect, but …"

"I know; my stomach's heaving just thinking about it."

Pete emerged with wet hair, cleanly shaven, wearing a bright blue polo shirt and khakis that were cinched tightly on his small waist with a wide brown belt. He stage-whispered, "If that's Lara, tell her to come over for breakfast."

"Pete's asking you to come over for something to eat."

"Sunshine, je vais me rendormir. Avoir un oeuf sur moi, s'il te plait."

"I'll take that as a no," I laughed, said goodbye and hung the phone up.

The omelette Pete created, and we wolfed down, was filled with fresh asparagus, mushrooms and some briny Feta cheese found in the back of the fridge. He also made some instant coffee and sweetened it with several spoons of sugar and added a large pour of cream.

"I want to thank you for what you've done the last while." He stirred his coffee in a big ceramic blue mug.

"Oh, no, you don't have —"

"It's been rough for you, too. Looking after me. I appreciate it. You know that I don't like people hovering around me, but I'm glad that you persisted. I'm glad I'm still here." Pete smiled widely and took a big sip of coffee before continuing. "And now it's time for me to get back to my apartment."

"Pete, you sure that's a good idea?" I had doubts that he was well enough. *Maybe this burst of energy isn't going to last.*

"Yes, and I think in the next week I can go back to work. And Lara, she needs to get on the road and make some money for me," he laughed. "We never talked about ...well, about what me being sick means." Pete's eyes locked on mine. "I might have this plague that's happening —"

"You don't know that, Pete." And I certainly didn't want to believe it.

"No, but ..." He left his statement unfinished. "Still, it was brave of you and Lara to look after me; you could have gotten pneumonia at the very least."

"I don't think that's even —"

"There's been a lot of ... hysteria around this. Like at the hospital everyone was gloved and gowned as though I was a leper. But you and Lara have been positively angelic and very patient." Pete put his coffee down and fixed me with his dark eyes. "Thank you. Being sick sure isn't for the weak," he reflected.

"You know, that Dr. Gelmon said that she thinks that people like us should stop having sex until they know more about what's going on medically. Maybe that's good advice for people who've never had sex, but for me it all seems too late," I blurted.

"I'm divided, frankly," Pete offered. "I mean, I surely don't wanna die, but how did fucking become synonymous with death?"

I understood exactly what he meant. From the first time I had sexual relations with Pete, I knew how life-affirming the act could be. I once described Pete as a sexual athlete. He was masterful at it, as I could attest. His skills were ones I envied and admired. Though I revered him for those abilities, Lara's perception of Pete was that he was a "player", which may have been true. In fairness to Pete, Lara had a significant amount of partners herself. But to me, Pete remained the quintessential (and paradoxical) man's man: tall, great-looking, successful, oozing confidence, hyper-masculine, with beautiful large brown eyes that could melt a glacier, a Roman nose, shampoo-commercial hair and a sex-drive as big as his cock. Honestly, to *be* Pete meant that sexual encounters were a natural extension of his identity and ironically might be the reason for his ruin. Of course, Pete was more than merely physical or sexual; he'd been a mentor to Lara and me. He was largely responsible for Lara's musical success. His intellect was razor-sharp and was noted for being an excellent dealmaker in the entertainment biz, not to mention being in high demand as an agent. *And, he's hot as fuck. It's simply impossible to ignore that part of Pete.*

That Sunday after we munched on Pete's French Canadian omelette, we gathered up his too-big clothes, personal effects, medications and, of course, his alternative medication — Mrs. McBride's home-grown herbs.

"You figure it's okay for me to drive with all this weed in the car?" I asked worriedly, thinking of being stopped by the police and thrown in jail like the unlucky Billy Hayes in '*Midnight Express*'. "I mean, there's a sizeable amount you've got there," I said, pointing at the large bag on the bedside table.

"We can put it in the trunk to be safe," Pete said, picking it up.

"It worked, didn't it? You have your appetite back, right?"

"Seem to. I think I'll keep using it … at least for now. Some of the guys in the hospital I spoke to use it, too. A couple of guys even turn it into brownies. They seem to think it's good for the immune system."

"If that's possible, then keep puffing 'em. A little safeguard can't hurt, can it?" I asked as I bundled up the remaining clothes and toiletries in Pete's overnight case.

"Who'd have thought?" Pete laughed, showing his even, white teeth and flashing a killer smile.

"Huh?"

"That Aquaman, who's half my age, has turned me into a hard-core, twice-a-day stoner." Pete stuffed his herbs into his bag and shook his head in disbelief. "I don't know if you should be taking me home or taking me to Rehab," Pete mocked.

"What can I say? I had a divine intervention from a little Scottish woman," I said, laughing as I told Pete about Mrs. McBride's remedy. We were ready to leave the Queen Charlotte and return Pete to 'Vaseline Towers'. I hefted his bag over my shoulder and we started out the door. Pete took a fleeting glance at the apartment that he'd called home for a few weeks, his health markedly improved, even though his condition was clearly not fully restored. "Okay, Bob Marley," I said. "Let's rock on."

25

The Most Important Season

Vancouver residents are rewarded for enduring the long, water-logged winter with spring — my favourite time of year. Spring meant renewal, and this spring was no exception. Surely, there had never been a more important season for Pete. He seemed to take in every moment, from the startling blaze of golden sunlight, the piquant breezes from English Bay and the displays of sunny-yellow daffodils in city parks. As spring hurtled along, Pete's mood moved from despair to optimism. Conversely, my mother reported that a change of seasons did little to alter my father's irritability. After a period of recovery at home, and with much support, he returned to his work (part-time) and routines, surreptitiously sneaking cigarettes on his breaks (and fooling no one). He had insufficient smokes to reduce his prickly behaviour but enough guile to deny any allegations of lighting up. After all, he wouldn't want his wife — who managed his health like a clinical case manager — to think that he was doing something dishonourable by ignoring all medical advice. Spring had an all-encompassing psychological benefit for Pete, but for my father,

spring primarily meant a return to the golf club and his cronies —
perhaps what he valued most.

By late Sunday morning, the sun shot through the clouds and
turned the wet streets into dreamy layers of steamy clouds. With a
mug of sweet tea in hand, I peered out the window and pondered the
situation. Though not back at work, Pete was undeniably better and
improving every few days. He had regained several pounds, though
his strength continued to be poor due to inactivity. To help, Lara
walked with him almost every afternoon — rain or shine. By the last
week of March, Pete was looking more like himself. Perhaps Mrs.
McBride's herbal remedy was also a great boon for Pete. Since he'd
been taking it, there'd been a discernible improvement in his appetite. Lara and I continued to help him, but Pete was slowly requiring
less assistance. My father had Mum, Lynda — even me to a lesser
extent — to care for him. If my father was grateful, his was silent
appreciation. With Pete, he told Lara and me how thankful he was
for our (sometimes annoying) help. That was the clear difference.
*Am I obliged to be caring towards my churlish father when his life
was spent being indifferent to me?* I wish that I could respond that
my father's nonchalance about me didn't matter, but frankly, I'd be
lying. When Dad was in hospital, I was moved by his vulnerability,
however, it seemed to be a brief moment not to be repeated. Pete
regarded Lara and me as active and welcome players in his recovery. We were unwaveringly positive without — I hoped — being
cloying. But, even with Pete's resurgence, there were unanswered
questions for him and all of us about what the future had in store.

26

Crisco Isn't Just for Pie Crusts

"How excited are you to see Robby?" Lara puffed heavily as we ran past Lumberman's Arch in Stanley Park. "It's been what — 4 months?" She led up the trail onto the steep incline that would eventually lead up to Prospect Point and I followed, working out a cramp in my calf.

"Yeah," I panted. "Since December."

As we started to climb the hill, I felt my quads ache. I wasn't nearly the runner that Lara was. My lungs were burning as we took the first 400 meters of the bluff at a pace that was proving challenging to me.

"Hey, can we slow down?" I gasped.

"I think you're out of shape," Lara laughed, zipping up with decidedly less effort than me. My blue running shorts were wringing wet with sweat running down from my chest and back. Lara still looked fresh after 40 minutes of running on the seawall and ascending the trail leading under the massive Lion's Gate Bridge span. "Running hills is great for my diaphragm," she said, pumping her arms for extra power as she moved up the near-vertical climb. The deep-green of the cedars encompassed us with their heavy scent as we continued to run, then staggered, to the highest point in Stanley Park — towering a hundred meters above the sea. The view from the point was worth the effort. To the northwest, the ocean glittered as though lit with thousands of tiny lights. Freighters carefully eased their way under the bridge's span, silently gliding towards the harbours in Burrard Inlet. The shore of West Vancouver was aglow in late afternoon light. Further west, the lighthouse beacon flashed at regular intervals. I breathed heavily, grabbed my sweaty knees and bent over. *Why am I so winded? Maybe I should be running more. Is that why?*

"Sunshine, you okay?" Lara came and put her hand on my heaving back.

"Yeah," I exhaled forcefully. "The last bit got me," I wheezed as I finished massaging my calf. "Let's go." I wiped the last bit of sweat from my eyes and started off with my best friend beside me.

"What are you doing for Robby when he gets back home?" Lara asked, her voice unstrained as we started to run the gradual descending slope.

"Doing? Whaddya mean?" My calf was better as I picked up the pace, thankful for the downward portion.

"Sunshine, he's been away forever. You gotta have a welcome home party or do something special for him. What's wrong with you?"

"A party? I hate parties. Maybe I'll just make him a nice dinner."

"Make him dinner?" Lara sounded slightly aghast.

"Sure. My Mum gave me her recipe for meatloaf and —"

"Great, why don't you follow up the meatloaf with a glass of warm milk? Maybe you can finish off the night watching Barbara Frump in matching flannel pyjamas?"

"Huh? You know I don't have a TV. And it's Barbara Frum."

"You haven't seen Robby in months and you're thinking about your mother's meatloaf?" Lara's head shook, making her red hair bob and sway even more.

"Well ..." I pondered what Lara was saying and felt sweat running off my forehead as I pounded the trail leading to the Hollow Tree.

"You should bring Robby home and not leave your bedroom for a week ... or at the very least the weekend."

"Lara, it's just that ..."

"What? Tell me." Lara hurtled past the Hollow Tree, increasing the pace, running quickly downhill. "What is it?" she persisted.

"I haven't been feeling very sexy," I admitted. My breathing was easing as we continued down a steeper part of the trail. "So, I thought when he came back I'd greet him with a nice meal. Is there something wrong with that?"

"In so many ways. You should greet Robby with a tub of Crisco and a set of black rubber sheets," Lara stated emphatically, darting under a massive awning of trees.

"Lara," I panted. "Crisco? Are you serious?"

"It's not just for making pies. Well, not that I'd know," she admitted.

"You don't understand. It's not like that anymore. Not now." Pete's thin face flashed in my mind for a moment.

"You're wrong, Sunshine," Lara asserted. She picked the pace up further. "More than ever, it's *exactly* like that." She zipped down the hill, heading for the Tea House Restaurant, kicking up dirt in the process and literally leaving me in the dust.

"Jeez, Lara, can you run any faster?" I shouted from 10 metres back.

"C'mon, keep up!" Lara whipped past the Tea House and started running on the sidewalk high above the seawall. I, the well-trained swimmer, fell back further, gasping, then began sprinting towards my friend in a vain effort to catch up.

27

Before & After

There are at least two distinct times in the lives of gay men of a specific era: before AIDS decimated the lives of millions, and after, with the eventual medical and psychosocial management of the virus. The time in-between was one of collective dread. The greatest irony? After hundreds of years of oppression and living secret, cautious lives, by the late 1970s, a grudging acceptance of homosexuality took root in Western society. By the early 1980s, that favourable change was quickly reversed and replaced with fear and hatred — of gays, of gay sex and a belief held steadfastly by many that gay men got what they deserved. Once again, gay men had become the vilified outlaw. For some gay men, nothing — including the mounting panic that was seeping in and sweeping through the community at this time — was going to prevent them from changing the manner by which they believed they had the right to live.

By the early 1970s, Vancouver had a large and growing gay and lesbian population. There were no shortages of places to connect. Most certainly, there were plenty of bars and bathhouses, but also there were gay baseball and bowling leagues, choirs, running clubs, reading groups, political think-tanks, pot-lucks and socials. The community had been well-established by 1983, though even the most organized community would have been ill-equipped to grapple with the staggering loss of lives about to take place over the next decade in Vancouver and around the world. Pete was one who availed himself with what gay life had to offer — and why not? Pete had killer looks. The same looks that years earlier left me stuttering and stammering in a failed attempt to make intelligent conversation when we'd first met at Oil Can Harry's. Pete had the semblance and carriage of a film star and an easy elegance in everything he did. If I could choose a gay or any male archetype, it would be Pete. So, I wasn't surprised that he'd collapsed at a seamy men's spa because Pete liked — no, loved — sex regardless of where that activity took place. Pete received much attention, so to be him and move through the world with such allure and sexual power must have been addictive. Of course, it was concerning that he must have done something that compromised his health. *Don't forget, you also had a few romps with Pete, not to mention others, as well. How do you know if you're not sick? You don't. The thing is, presently no one knows if they're okay, do they?* As spring turned grey Vancouver into a white-blossomed paradise, there was a pervasive unease of a monster in our midst — a germ, a bug — that was responsible for GRID, but as of April '83, nothing was clearly understood. *There's such dread in the unknown.*

28

Homo Homecoming

I took Lara's advice on creating something special for Robby. However, black rubber sheets and Crisco just weren't my style. I settled for a Meyer's lemon cake from the Paris Bakery. All things considered, a measured and conservative choice. Robby was due to arrive in Vancouver at 7 PM on Saturday night. Like we'd done in the past, I was going to collect him. I was freshly showered, cologne on, wearing my best white dress shirt, my weathered leather jacket and my favourite pair of faded Levi's. Dripping with rain, the VW moved quickly through light traffic as I travelled south down Granville, over the Arthur Laing bridge and was at the airport arrival area in less than a half-hour; 20 minutes early. The airport was swarming with at least a hundred people at the gate as I waited, expectant and slightly nervous. I watched where passengers would move through to exit. I pondered the long time that we'd been apart. *Over 4 months.* I thought back to when he'd left then suddenly saw a golden-haired young man gliding effortlessly down the passenger plank, a leather bag slung over his shoulder. Robby's trim body was outfitted in a pair of tan chinos, a purple window-pane check shirt and a brown wool sweater. His winter coat was slung over his arm. He hadn't seen me yet, and in an instant of recognition, I felt a familiar tug in my groin.

"Robby!" I cried out, raising my hand in a wave. Seeing me, his smile became radiant. He rushed past other passengers, nearly leaping his way over to me. I couldn't take my eyes from him. He looked strong, healthy, vibrant, alive, albeit a bit tired. In a moment, Robby had wrapped his arms around me. He felt good. He smelled good, too. He moved his hands to the back of my head and gave me a long kiss. His stubble from his beard scraped my face as he kissed me. Immediately reddening, my internalized homophobia kicked in. Those nearby shot looks of contempt — or that's how I perceived it. It didn't matter to Robby what other people may have thought of our passionate greeting, but I continued to be affected by the heterosexual norm and was very aware that men relating to each other in a loving way could represent great danger.

"Miss me?" Robby asked innocently as his hand moved deftly to my butt for a quick squeeze. I raised my eyebrows and nodded.

"What, away for a few months and now you're a top?" I joked. "What has Sudbury done to you?"

"Man, you have no idea," he smirked. "You look great," Robby stepped back and gave an appraising once-over. "Really great," he emphasized and I smiled at the compliment. "Let's motor. I've got something that I want to show you, and I can't take it out here."

"Really?" I played along as we speedily moved through the crowd and to the car park. "I can't *imagine* what that might be," I laughed as I placed my arm around his shoulder, squeezing, nearly delirious with anticipation.

Though I'm loathe to admit it, the world is primarily heterosexual and all institutions or systems reflect that. I've always found it striking that gays and lesbians have adjusted to a world where they are, by default, excluded rather than included in the "ordinary" aspects of life. Think of simple things like songs on the radio, films, commercials on television, romance novels, storybooks for children — even comics. All and more are geared towards heterosexuals, and I understand why — they *are* the majority. However, I wonder how many of those same people would be able or willing to understand the experience of being an outlaw in all facets of life. I'd like to help non-gay individuals understand that a simple kiss at an airport between two men in love can be the basis for rationalizing hatred and violence. Do straight couples experience the fear of retribution for being themselves? Many gay men come to understand the role that shame plays in their lives, often from very young and sometimes until the time they "join the choir", so to speak. Worry and fear in being different in a world that's threatened by differences? Well, that's a reality — mine and others — too important to forget. While I had made strides in living as a gay man, I would describe it as a relative degree of "outness". I certainly was not out with my family or with my swim team or coach. Outside of the West End, life became riskier, so while my sense of comfort with who I was developed, I nevertheless maintained my vigilance. It's an unfortunate and an anxious way to live, a kind of balancing act where the wrong action — such as a smooch at a public place, or merely being oneself — could result in being beaten, or worse. With the flourishing "gay plague" progressing at a horrifying pace, the public's attitude towards gay men was regressing as the press publicized every unsavoury death from AIDS. The religious right found new ways to justify their hate of their old and convenient demon: gay men.

The drive back found us catching up — the kind of talk much more satisfying in person compared to the chatting we did on the phone every week. Robby's hand was on my thigh for the trip home. I was aroused by his touch and found it hard to concentrate on the traffic. After driving for 25 minutes, the downtown peninsula came into view from the Granville rise. Through the rains, the towers shot up into a darkened sky. The lights of the Lion's Gate Bridge glimmered in the distance, winking through the relentless drizzle. The mountains of the North Shore were blue-black, spectral images in the background. Robby wiped my foggy windshield with the back of his hand to get a clearer view of the familiar metropolis that opened up before him.

"Wow," he uttered admiringly at the expanse of the city. "I missed this place." Robby noticed the increase in building projects. Vancouver was booming, and massive towers, their tops obscured by mist and clouds, juggled for space. Vancouver had won a bid for a worldwide exposition — Expo '86 — and though the fair was 3 years away, many building projects, including a train line, were vigorously underway. We drove past the Stanley Theatre where *The Right Stuff* was playing. Robby noticed the marquee.

"Hey, there's a movie I should take you to," he laughed. Robby knew that my father had named me after Alan Shepard, one of the Mercury 7 astronauts who indeed had the right stuff, being the first American in space. "I heard it was pretty good," he commented. "In that over the top, American way," Robby added. I had seen it with Lara and Pete a few weeks earlier and had enjoyed it immensely.

"I'd love to see it with you," I said as I stopped at the light. I looked over at Robby.

"That's a date, then." He smiled, but looked fatigued, with dark circles under his hazel eyes. *Funny that I didn't notice that at the airport.* He had spent many hours with connecting flights from Sudbury to get back to the west coast.

"Did they feed you on your flight?" I asked, knowing that they had. "Some rubber chicken?" Robby nodded. "Because if you're still hungry, we can get something at Fresgo's or wherever you'd like." Fresgo's was a diner on Davie with a decidedly gay clientele.

"When we get to the Queen Charlotte, I think you'll know what I'm hungry for." Robby grinned widely, showing his impossibly white, if uneven, teeth. We hadn't had sex for over 4 months, and truth be known, I was unsure about it, especially with everything that was happening with Pete and in the community at large. *How quickly things can change.* After motoring up and onto the Granville Bridge, Robby looked east and noticed a massive structure. "It's garish, isn't it? Looks like a puffy concrete quilt," he criticized.

"BC Place? Yes, it's hideous," I agreed. "It seems as though it doesn't belong here," I said as we turned left onto Davie and headed into the West End. The village was quiet and the streets and side-walks were saturated with rain. A few people were out, probably about to have their supper. I looked at every man as we went up the street, trying to decipher who was unwell. *That man, he looks sick. Is he? Stop it, you can't tell by looking, can you? Focus yourself. You haven't seen Robby in forever. Don't ruin this for him. Take a breath. Pay attention.* Robby moved his hand to my hair, tousling it the way that Pete did. *Pete. Fuck. Is he all right? I wonder if he's feeling better? Did he eat today? Did Lara see him? Will he need —*

"You okay? You look as though you're miles away," Robby added.

"Jeez, sorry. My head went away for a sec. I didn't ask you if you wanted to go back to your place first." Robby shared an apart-ment — not too far from me — with a male UBC student. It was an effective financial arrangement for him, and it also meant that Robby and I could maintain a healthy physical distance from each other. I liked that we weren't in "each other's pockets".

"Nope, I wanna go home with you. Oh, you're in luck," Robby exclaimed as he pointed excitedly at a parking spot on Nicola a half-block from the apartment. I squeezed in between a panel truck and an old Chevy. I retrieved Robby's leather bag from the rear seat and we made our way to the apartment.

"It's so warm here," Robby said as we walked. "And green. In Sudbury there's a foot of snow on the ground and Lake Wanapitei is a mass of ice."

"Lake Whatawape?" I laughed.

With winter lasting in northern Ontario for up to 6 months, it wasn't surprising that the residents enjoyed theatre. Sure, Robby wasn't directing a stellar cast of classical actors performing Ibsen, but like Lara, he had to pay his dues, too. Robby was only too willing to do what it took — including dinner theatre in a nickel mining town — to get to more rewarding assignments. After all, he had worked hard to earn his MFA in directing over 3 years ago. As we made our way up the terracotta steps to the Queen Charlotte, Robby took a deep breath. "The air is so soft," he exhaled. "Vancouver's a world away from where I've been." We went through the unlocked lobby and climbed the stairs. I searched my pockets for the key and we entered 302. Before I could place Robby's satchel on the floor, he wrapped me up in his wiry arms, pulling me close to his chest to hold me in a vice-like grip. So much had happened from the last time we'd been together until now. My throat was constricted. I wanted this evening to be about us, not about my fears and anxieties of a future that hadn't happened yet.

"Can I grab a shower? I smell like the inside of a stale airplane," Robby sniffed. I hung his coat on a clever coat hook over the door frame that my mother had purchased when she had decorated my apartment.

"Let me," I said, tugging off his wool sweater and unbuttoning his shirt. I eased his chinos past his hips and he stepped from his pants. His body was lean — even leaner than a few months ago. His pale skin was smooth, his ectomorphic frame defined with muscle and ropey sinew. Robby slid his briefs down past knobby knees, which allowed his large, beautiful cock to jut from his body. I stood in silent awe at the spectacle of Robby, marble-like, nude before me like a Renaissance statue.

"You sure you wanna shower?" I asked. "I've got a lemon cake from Paris Bakery," I added, which was rather odd, considering the situation. Instead of cake, Robby moved towards me, then pressed his mouth on mine, deeply kissing me with a probing intensity that felt like an electrical current to my groin. We moved down the hallway and into the bedroom. I, fully clothed, and he naked, kissed for an hour before I removed my attire. I admit that I had been at sea, worried about having any type of sex, a kind of plague paranoia. But being with Robby in my bed ... well, it vanished my fears —– at least for the moment — and I was charged with excitement. I covered every inch of his body with kisses. Robby's body was peerless; lean, lightly muscled and sumptuously designed for sex. His cock throbbed when I sucked on it aggressively. His bottom was hungry for me to be inside. It was then that I was ambivalent.

"Are you sure that you —"

"Of course I'm sure. What are you —"

"It's just that, well, is it okay to do this?" I asked, panting slightly.

"I'm not sick, you're not sick ..."

"But we don't know that. No one knows if they're sick or not. How do we know if our number's up?"

"Listen to me," Robby pleaded, more serious than I'd ever seen him. "If your number's up — if my number's up, we'll both draw another."

"So we should just go ahead and —"

"Fuck," Robby asserted. "*Fuck me*," he repeated.

I pulled the bedside drawer open to collect the lubricant as Robby lay turned onto his stomach. In a few moments, I lay on him, feeling his supple skin, slippery as glass. I massaged his tired body, starting with his tense neck, then kneading his upper back, then his buttocks. He groaned softly as I slowly pushed my cock into him and established a powerful rhythm. Robby drew to his knees I felt his heat on my cock as it stroked deeply, aware of the risks, unsure of the consequences, but willing away any fear to be with the person that I loved as much as life itself.

29

Failure or Player

Lara suggested Robby and I not leave the bedroom for a week, but that wasn't realistic. After an amazing night of sex, conversation, a few unforgiving slices of a decidedly decadent lemon cake and more sex, I fell profoundly asleep. I woke on time — 5 AM, and gazed over at Robby who was sleeping on his side. His mouth was slightly open, snoring every so often. I watched for a few minutes. I wondered if he was dreaming, or if he'd slept well. He was a handsome man — awake or asleep. I pulled the cover over him gently, kissed his hair and left the bedroom, soundlessly closing the door behind me. I staggered into the kitchen to down some water and I stuffed some bread with peanut butter in my stomach. After brushing my teeth, I pulled on my swimsuit, then donned my shorts and a tee-shirt. At the door, I found my Nikes, picked up my swim-bag, then paused to write Robby a note.

Morning Robby,
Hope I didn't disturb you when I got up, tho you seemed catatonic. If you're hungry, there's eggs & juice in the

fridge, plus all that lemon cake! For gawd's sake, eat the cake. I'm happy you're back. You were gone far too long, and in Sudbury?

XOXO

I stuck the note on the fridge with a piece of electrical tape. Robby planned on going back to his own apartment Monday morning. He had some business to attend do. He had to begin a search for his next directing job. *Hopefully, closer to home, not another dinner theatre gig in Kenora or Medicine Hat.*

Perhaps because of the previous late night, swim practice was even more challenging for me. It was yet another one of many trainings where my speed was elusive and reserved for finishing lengths. However much I put into the swim, my results demonstrated that I was consistently off my best times, and by a considerable amount. Still in my 20s, I couldn't be considered old, though with such difficulties, I began to seriously wonder if my prime days of competing were behind me. Adding more fuel to my worrisome fire was that Coach Thompson seemed to be ignoring me since I dumped practice when my father became ill. *Well, Sunshine, that can't be a good sign, can it? Has Thompson given up on me as well?* I started to wonder if I was going to be ditched from the national swim team. *Does that even happen? Of course it does — swimmers that aren't performing get suspended all the time. What a slap in the face that would be. Do you want to end your swim career in shame? You've gotta find your way back to form, and fast.* I was doing everything I knew to be competitive, and yet I was failing. I was directed by an experienced coach (even if he appeared to loathe me), received extra strength training, had nutritional help and coaching for weight training. I had all the pieces and all the supports. *So, you're an intern therapist; you should be able to figure out what's wrong.*

Could it be my preoccupation with Pete? My ailing father? Is it my own health? Perhaps my age? Christ, I'm just 26, that's not old, is it? Why are you so distracted from the thing that's been the only constant? Because there's a lot of shit going on, that's why. There was a swim meet in Calgary at the first week of May to kick off the summer season. I had to show Thompson — and myself — that I was still able to take my place on the medal stand. *Somehow I have to regain my status; be a player — just one more time. What irony. You once told Lara that Pete was a player. Looks as though all the "players" are struggling to keep their heads above water; pun intended.*

30

The Surprise in 207

At 7:30 PM I arrived home from practice — dog tired. I went to hang up my swimsuit and towel to dry in the washroom when I heard a knock on my door.

"Mrs. McBride?" My landlady stood before me, appearing upset. "Is there something wrong?"

"I'm so sorry to bother you at this hour, but have you seen Tommy of late?"

Tommy was a burly window dresser who helped me move several heavy items from the basement and into my then-new apartment years earlier. He was not exactly a friend, but he was always friendly and talkative whenever we met by chance in the lobby or laundry room. I found him to be a very likeable guy.

"Tommy from downstairs? No, why?"

"Well, he missed paying his rent at the first of the month. He'd had a horrible cold with a bad cough last week, so I thought that he'd pay when he was feeling better. Tommy never misses, dear. Not in 9 years. I knocked on his door, but there's no response. I called him, too, but the phone just rang off the hook. I've become worried." Mrs.

McBride was fingering a large set of keys in her troubled hands. "I wonder if you could come with me to his apartment?"

"You mean —"

"Perhaps he's hurt himself or he's become more ill and, I don't know, can't get to the phone." Mrs. McBride's face was flushed with emotion.

"Do you have —"

The landlady held up a dangling set of keys.

"Of course I'll come with you, Mrs. McBride." I took off my leather jacket, tossed it on the velvet sofa and went with her to the staircase.

"Thank you, dear. I'm afraid of going in on my own." She walked purposefully downstairs to apartment 207, adjusting her cornflower-blue housedress as she walked. She gave the door several knocks and we waited for a few moments before she used the key. She opened the door to a silent apartment. "Come through," she urged as I warily went in. The unit was dim. I could see that the blinds had been shut in the living room. She flicked on the light switch, revealing a tidy-looking residence. "Tommy? It's Hannah. I'm here with Shepard." There was no response. Looking around, I started to feel a growing sense of unease. I could hear music faintly playing.

"Do you hear …"

"Let's check the bedroom, dear." Mrs. McBride's voice was shaking. I swallowed as I moved past the living room, and into the darkened hallway that led to Tommy's bedroom.

"Maybe he's just working out-of-town and forgot to give you a cheque," I offered, not liking how I was feeling. Slowly, we stepped along the hallway, the weight of our feet making the wooden floors groan. Orchestral music was playing softly from the bedroom. "Perhaps he neglected to turn off the radio when he left," I said, not believing myself as we entered Tommy's bedroom. "It's pitch black in here," I said, reaching for the light on the wall. The burst of light cruelly illuminated a body lying crumpled in a mass of blankets. Mrs. McBride covered her mouth with her hand and uttered, "Dear God." I breathed in the decay that filled the room and instantly wanted to vomit. His face was discoloured and blotchy with accumulated fluids, but we could tell it was her tenant. His body was twisted, contorted among the sheets. Tommy's naked torso was marked by numerous purplish-reddish, crusty-looking spots. On his night-stand were two blue glass tumblers; one was likely filled with water and the other empty, as were bottles of drugstore cough medicines. Beside his bedside lamp were open photograph albums, letters and a small St. Christopher's medallion on a silver chain that he'd worn around his neck. A CD had been playing and he'd programmed it to replay the same disc. I knew right away what he'd been listening to because Lara had played it many times for me and I'd loved it — Dvořák's *"From the New World, Symphony No. 9." Did Tommy want to die with music? Maybe he didn't want to go in silence. I'm assuming that he knew he was dying.* I turned the player off and looked at Mrs. McBride.

"Tommy, Tommy," she repeated softly as she gazed upon his motionless body and began to weep.

"Maybe he's not dead," I said hopefully. "Should we take a pulse?" I moved towards the body, the stench overpowering. Mrs. McBride grabbed my forearm to prevent me from going further.

"No, dear. He's gone," she sniffed. I stepped back from the bed, not wanting to view the body. She reached out to take my hand to steady herself, but in truth, she was providing me with support so I could stay on my feet. Silently, we walked from his death chamber in a daze, bound for her apartment to call the authorities. In the next half-hour, police were at the Queen Charlotte, and a half-hour later, several people dressed in peculiar coverall-type suits with masks were collecting Tommy's corpse and inspecting his home. Apartment residents streamed into the hallways in worried curiosity.

Mrs. McBride did her best to assuage any fears. After speaking with the police, I asked Mrs. McBride to my apartment for tea, hoping to calm the shock of it all. She sat in the leather chair and I wordlessly brewed some Earl Grey. I watched her from the kitchen. She seemed as stunned as me, and I worried about her being in shock.

"Here," I said, offering her a strong cup. "It's hot, careful." She took the steaming mug, holding it in her veiny hands, perhaps grateful for the warmth it provided. I sat down on the floor beside her.

"Much appreciated, dear." She smiled wanly, mindlessly pushing grey hair from her furrowed brow before taking a quiet sip. "People don't die from having a cold."

"No, they don't. No people I've ever known."

"It was something else. Wasn't it? There were marks on him, like the pox."

So, she had seen the marks on Tommy's body. His torso looked like the paintings of sufferers of the plagues from the Dark Ages, riddled with boils.

"I saw them, but perhaps —"

"Tommy was a lovely man." She sipped her tea. "I can't believe he's gone. And for him to die alone ..." Mrs. McBride's voice trailed off as she struggled to complete her sentence.

"I know, it's so hard to —"

"He was 37, dear. Just 37. It's impossible ..." Mrs. McBride's frail body started to shake. I ran to get a warm blanket which I wrapped around her sagging shoulders. "Thank you," she said, holding tightly onto her mug. "This is a terrible blow. Am I meant to call Tommy's family?"

"No, that lady police officer said they'd do that. I'm not sure exactly what we do. Does he even have a family?" I stupidly asked.

"Tommy has a mother; she's been here. Such a pleasant woman, too. I'd imagine that she was very proud of her son. To be predeceased by a child," she pondered with wide eyes. "I can't imagine how she's going to take this news." My landlady looked reflective and added, "He was very kind to her as he was to me. I don't know about his father; never saw him here and Tommy never spoke of him. I never inquired." She took a long sip of tea, soothing herself as much as possible. "Perhaps we can do something for him … something here? He loved his apartment at the Queen Charlotte."

"Some kind of get-together?"

"Yes. Good people need to be remembered." Mrs. McBride finished her drink, stood and gave me the blanket. "I'm exhausted, dear. I must go home. Thank you for the cuppa. We'll figure out what's next later, when I'm … more myself," she said, her lilting voice breaking as she passed me her mug. I walked her to the door and said good night, then immediately called Robby. He picked up on the 2nd ring.

"Robby, can you come over? Something horrible has happened here tonight."

"What are you talking —"

"A man died —Tommy — in 207." I started to blurt out the details.

"The window dresser? Jesus, do you think he had —"

"Yes, I saw lesions all over his body. I swear it."

"Christ …"

"He's died from this fucking gay plague."

"You don't know that, "Robby countered. "I'll be right over."

31

The Story Breaks

Though I was very grateful that Robby came by, he nor anyone had a remedy that by all reckoning, was beginning a lethal sweep in the large urban areas of North America — and Vancouver appeared to be a place the "plague" was hitting hard. Robby stayed the night that Tommy's body was discovered, but still I'd been unable to sleep. This made for a disastrous swim practice the next morning. At school, I was tight-lipped when I should have talked it out, but the events seemed so raw and so linked to my being gay that I was unable to share what had occurred. I knew that I had to talk to Pete about what had happened, but I just couldn't wrap my head around it. When I voiced my concerns with Lara the next day, she agreed that it was better if we waited a bit. That might have been more due to our dread about how to have *that* type of conversation with someone to whom we both were indebted. We thought that Pete was slowly improving, so she and I worried that this kind of news would only serve to devastate him — it was literally too close to home. After class, I scooted to Super Valu to pick up something for dinner.

At the checkout, only 2 days after Tommy's death, the Vancouver Sun newspaper headline was emblazoned on the front page:

DEADLY INFECTION SPREADS TO VANCOUVER

A 37-year-old man named Thomas (Tommy) Minouge was found dead in his apartment in Vancouver's West End. Minouge was a freelance window dresser for department stores such as The Hudson's Bay, Woodward's and Eaton's. The coroner's office has ruled that there was no foul play, violence or any suspicious cause of death. The medical examiner confirmed the presence in Minouge's lungs of "an overwhelming Pneumocystis carinii pneumonia." As well, the deceased was thought to have Kaposi's sarcoma, a rare cancer associated with recent AIDS diagnoses and deaths. Minogue was known to have travelled to San Francisco recently, which is considered a hot spot and high-risk area for the AIDS epidemic. The Centre for Disease Control is currently investigating Minogue's death, along with a growing number of gay males who are being seen at St. Paul's Hospital, where there are currently few treatment options available. It remains unclear how the lethal infection is being spread.

"Jezus-fucking-hell," I said under my breath, feeling the blood pounding at my temples. I left my cart of items at the checkout and dashed out of the store. *I've gotta talk to Pete.*

I don't mean to "straight-bash", but when gay men starting becoming gravely ill, I suspected that many heterosexual men were — at the very least — unsympathetic. Perhaps that's unkind to say, but history has a well-known antipathy regarding gay men that goes back hundreds, if not thousands of years. So, when this plague raised its hideous head, many stuck their own heads in the sand. I'm not sure if some were pleased or if they simply didn't give the suffering of gay men much thought. One thing was going to become remarkably clear in the next short while, and that was that gay men would be supported like never before by their gay brothers and straight *and* gay sisters. Those coalitions would serve to galvanize the members of the gay community through their exceptional hard work and be a shining example of how to care for those most vulnerable. But, those infected had to manage with the present, and that was going to test every societal, health, legal and family system.

I drove to Pete's apartment on Beach Avenue. He called it "Vaseline Towers", which is a moniker that formerly had been amusing to me. It was across the street from where I worked out at the Aquatic Centre. Pete's place was on the 32nd floor and had a commanding view of English Bay. After finding a place to park, I strode to his building, got to the elaborate entrance and went to press his buzzer — then stopped, my hand freezing in mid-air. *How do I approach this? What should I say? How are you? Oh, by the way, a friend passed away from AIDS in my building a couple nights ago. I found his tortured-looking body with my landlady. Covered in lesions, too. Really, it was right out of Edgar Allen Poe. You might have heard about it? It's been in the papers and probably on the TV, as well. Seems as though you and he had the same pneumonia. Just thought I'd let you know.* No. I can't do this. I gotta talk to Lara first. I turned away and started to walk back down to Beach, then went past the Fastback and jogged down the hill to the seawall. The breeze coming off the water was fresh, with the scent of spring permeating the air. There were many people out walking — as per usual on a late afternoon without rain — though I wasn't paying much attention to who was around. I removed my socks and running shoes and strode along the sands of Sunset Beach, finding a weathered and worn giant piece of driftwood to sit on. The sand felt cold underfoot as I pondered recent events. *Nothing is going right, is it? In my youth, I hid under the water so that I could remain invisible, or so I thought. But as I've gotten older, life above water — in school, in relationships with my family and friends — is proving much more of a challenge. My mother's pissed at me because I'm dedicated to Pete's recovery and in the process not supporting my father — but he's got her, right? Pete only has Lara and me. My father's disappointed in me for a hundred possible reasons. My boyfriend can't understand why I'm being a "coward for not taking the leap" and coming "all the way out". What happened to the young guy that was to live his life "without fear and without apology"? Well, because now everything is different. We've got men dying from something that nobody understands ... my gawd, we found Tommy's corpse in my building. No one knows what's ahead, and this infection just keeps growing. If Pete's sick with this, could he have infected me?* I grabbed at the side of my throat to feel for swollen lymph. *If I'm sick, does that mean that I infected Robby? Jezus. And to cap it all off, the thing that I do or did better than anything — swimming — I hack my way through, and mostly with times I did 4 years ago. It's not good enough, not by a long shot. My coach looks as though I'm a liability not worthy of investing any more time in.* I looked out to the faraway freighters in English Bay as the filtered sunlight faded, streaking the sky with shots of deepest orange and turned the waters blood-red. Taking stock, I was feeling as important as one of the grains of sand my feet were under. Missing swim practice, time vanished as I watched the orb descend to the horizon until it dipped below Vancouver Island and was gone.

32

The Novice

Apoplectic best describes how my coach reacted the next morning as I sheepishly came onto the pool deck.

"Stamp, get over here," he commanded, his eyes bright with anger. In my Speedo's, I walked with Thompson up a flight of stairs to his small and phenomenally stuffy brick-walled office at the Aquatic Centre. At least a dozen pictures of prominent swimmers hung on the wall, including Thompson. Even though I'd set a couple records myself in Montreal, I noticed my picture was not included. Perhaps they were the "well-behaved" and obedient swimmers, I suspected.

"Sit down," he barked, pointing at an old vinyl chair. As Thompson closed the door, I did as directed, and immediately my bare back stuck to the plastic. I shifted in my seat, thinking it was ridiculous to be having a serious meeting wearing a skimpy bathing suit. Thompson's eyes glared at me with contempt — I'm sure that's what it was.

"I'm not even going to ask you why you ditched practice last night," he started, seating himself down behind an old grey metal desk. "At this point, it's irrelevant."

"I'm sorry, but …" I stopped, realizing that so much of what had been happening I couldn't inform him about. I thought about saying that my father had taken ill again. *No, don't get caught up in another lie. Really, what can I say?*

"I'm not interested in another apology," Thompson's anger flared. "Not only are you swimming like a novice most of the time, you're failing to attend practice and with no explanation given. Swim Canada is paying for you to put in the hours and get results. We expected better from you — much better."

"But, I told you, my father's been —"

"Not interested in your excuses, Stamp."

"But …" I didn't know what to say.

"I've spoken with Swim Canada this morning."

"Swim Canada?" *Fuck.* I swallowed hard and expected the worst.

"You're a hair's breadth from suspension. They're prepared to issue you a formal warning of as soon as I give 'em the word. You'll lose your scholarship and any other income, to boot. You won't swim at Caracas — off the table. I'm assuming this is what you wanted?" Thompson's sarcasm dripped effortlessly from his thin lips.

"Of course not," I said, shaking my head.

"You *were* a high-performing swimmer. You're fit, you get the best athletic support that money can buy, the best trainers and I've seen you get excellent times. But your results are a faded memory at best this year. What the hell's goin' on?"

I thought about responding honestly to his question, then, knew that it was impossible.

"And there's something else," Thompson added, this time with him looking decidedly uncomfortable. "Rumour is that you don't like girls. That true?"

I squirmed and must have looked guilty as charged.

"Untrue. I, um, like girls," I stammered. *I love Lara … she's a girl.*

"Well, it would be an even bigger embarrassment for you to be off the national team because …" Thompson didn't finish his statement, but I got the meaning easily enough. "So here's the deal. You're gonna take 2 weeks off from training."

"What?"

"I'm ordering a 2-week suspension. We'll see if you're fit enough to compete in Calgary. Pull yourself together, Stamp. Aren't you in school to be a shrink?"

"Um, well …"

"Figure out if you are willing to put in the effort to warrant the expense we're givin' you. I'll let you come back at the beginning of May, but if you so much as miss a practice — *one practice* — I'll suspend you immediately. And that'll be how you finish up on Canada's team. A big fuckin' failure. Got it?"

"Yes." My face burned with anger.

"It starts now. Get your gear and leave." Thompson unnecessarily thumbed towards the door. My sweaty back had adhered to the chair to such an extent it came with me as I rose to leave. Deeply humiliated, I did as I was told, went to my locker to collect my things and left the Aquatic Centre, more worried about my future than I ever had been.

33

The Used-To-Be

"That's outrageous!" Lara cried as I told her about my recent unplanned swimming sabbatical. I'd asked her to come by for dinner. I stirred the pasta sauce with turkey meatballs on the ancient gas stove. "Can he really do that?" Lara tore some romaine lettuce and angrily dumped it into a large wooden bowl. From the fridge, she took out a bottle of Caesar dressing.

"Apparently he can," I said, resigned to my coach's decision. I checked the spaghetti, which was furiously boiling on the stove. "He also wanted to know if I liked girls. I'll bet he's heard from my so-called teammates," I said with as much scorn as I could muster.

"I bet Thompson's a homophobe or a closet case. After swim practice he's probably down at the adult bookstore glory-holes wearing out his knees."

"Lara, you know about —"

"*Please*. Doesn't he appreciate what you've accomplished?"

"Lara," I deadpanned, "I'm a nobody. I'm a used-to-be. At least in the water. And frankly, Thompson's right about a few things. I've bombed at meets all year, I've missed practice numerous times, I've been a lousy swimmer and I'm definitely preoccupied with stuff I can't even talk about — with him, at least. Part of me thinks that I can medal again, but a bigger part of me says that I'm just not good enough," I said pensively.

"Vous avez besoin d'un retour," Lara stated firmly.

"I need a humpback?" I was dumbfounded. My Francais was as good as my 1983 medal count.

"Sunshine, I said you need a comeback. That's exactly what you need," Lara said brightly. She dressed the salad, put a handful of parmesan cheese on top, tossed it and put the bowl of greens on the table. "Oh, where are the —"

"The croutons are in the cupboard — there," I pointed to the location. "Judy Garland makes comebacks, not me." I lowered the heat and went back to the table. Lara retrieved the box of croutons, scattered them on the Caesar salad and sat down with a large glass of red wine.

"Garland's dead, Sunshine," Lara added.

"I rest my case," I said, sitting down and toying with the cotton table napkins. "What did Judy used to say? *People are always talking about me making a comeback, but I never went away. I've been working the whole time'*. I've never been away from the water, so maybe … somehow … this'll all work out in the end," I said, not fully believing my statement. "You know, Lara, even if I get dropped from the national team, I'll always love the water. Thompson can't take that from me."

"C'est la bonne attitude!"

"Okay, that I understood," I said, grinning. "Lara, what on earth would I do without you?"

Lara smiled back radiantly. For nearly 10 years, we'd been trooping along together. Becoming an adult was fraught with hardships, but having a best friend made every challenge possible.

"When are you going away next?" I asked, getting up to bring plates to the table and check the pasta.

Lara adjusted the belt of her jeans slightly and straightened the collar of her emerald green blouse. "Well, it depends on Pete." She took a sip of her wine before continuing. "He's definitely better. He's working a few days a week, but his energy seems low. I'm not going anywhere until I'm confident that he's at the very least, stable. I'm rehearsing some songs while we … just wait. Sunshine, I'm worried about him."

"I'm worried about all of us. None of us have lived like nuns the past few years, have we?" I drained the pasta in a red metal strainer at the sink, creating a cloud of steam so large it made me cough.

"From what I hear, some nuns have a vastly better sex life than me," Lara responded mischievously, tipping back the rest of the wine. "But you're right." Lara reached for the Chianti and poured herself another glass. "We all have reason to be very concerned. In the Province this morning they're reporting 7 more AIDS cases at St. Paul's, with more expected. And in New York, Toronto, LA and San Francisco the numbers are shocking. Vancouver's right up there, and that's a dubious distinction." Lara twisted her long red hair in her hand. "The worst part is that no one understands what this is, other than a cluster of illnesses. There's no test to run, no vaccine to get, no medication to take. So far, I've only heard of gay men and hemophiliacs getting it; no women that I know of. Is that right?"

"I don't think so, Lara." I put the spaghetti in a large blue and white bowl and poured the meatballs and sauce over top, then brought it to the table. "If this is spread through sexual contact, like that doctor at St. Paul's thinks, why wouldn't women get infected? I think anyone could be at risk." I collected the pepper and sat down. "Robby told me there's an information meeting planned this Friday night at 7 o'clock at the West End Community Centre," I said. "We're going, and I was wondering if you were interested —"

"I'll be there," she answered my question before it was asked. I piled a huge amount of pasta on her plate, the meatballs spilling onto the table. "Sunshine," Lara refrained from eating for a few moments; an indication of her high anxiety. (After all, she had an appetite that was legendary.) "I don't want to freak you out, but as this story develops, aren't you getting more and more afraid?"

"Afraid?" I took a moment to gather my French. "Lara, j'ai peur sans merde."

Nailed it.

34

The Talk

I wasn't officially training for a couple of weeks, and classes were on hiatus for the next 10 days. Before the information meeting at the Community Centre on Friday night, I thought I'd try to squeeze in a surprise visit with my family in what I not so fondly called the "Ditch", or Abbotsford on Wednesday morning. I knew that my father wasn't working that day, so I could chat or try to chat with him as my mother had asked in the previous month. My mother had told me that he was "back to being himself again", and that wasn't necessarily a good thing. Perhaps I should have stayed in town and spent the day with Robby, but he had several interviews booked that required preparation. With a song in my heart — really a dirge — I motored off on a beautiful spring day. When I got stuck in a traffic jam about 6 miles east of the Port Mann Bridge, I wondered if I'd made an error in my decision. I never liked stop-and-go traffic, especially with the Fastback. With nearly 200,000 miles on the odometer, there was always the risk that it would stop and never go again. With my radio tuned in to the CBC and my feet alternating on the clutch and gas, I inched my way past a terrible road accident near the Cape Horn interchange, where I saw that a BMW had flipped over with medics and police scuttling the scene. *There's danger everywhere.* The traffic improved immeasurably once I got onto the bridge deck and it was more or less smooth driving into the valley, arriving nearly 2 hours after my departure from the West End.

The valley isn't an awful place ... not exactly. It held several very bad memories for me, including where I'd been gay-bashed when I came home from high school the night before Halloween. A pickup truck had driven up beside me at the top of Hazel Road with several men — rocks in hand — in the back of the truck. They cornered me, then pelted me with rocks as I tried to escape. I managed to bolt away, bleeding and broken, eluding them by hiding in the underbrush. It was perhaps the pivotal moment that confirmed it was essential to keep myself hidden. But, it's also the town where Robby spent several years, and though at the time I only knew of him, it nevertheless gave me the opportunity to recognize him many years later when our paths crossed accidentally at Lost Lagoon. Lara liked saying that it was destiny that he and I met that day, but I was of the belief that most gay boys will find a way out of a ditch — any ditch — and into the city.

After arriving at my parent's home, I checked the time — 10 AM — and cut the motor. Like before, the beautiful and enormous maple tree stood watch, its leaves not quite fully leafed out. My father's new grey Camray was in the carport, shining in the reflected light of the morning sun. I took a deep and long breath, blowing it out forcefully in an effort to relax, and stepped from the Fastback. The large 4-bedroom Cape Cod home was painted cobalt blue. I preferred the previous sunny yellow, but my mother was the colour expert. Showing a bit of age — the house, not my mother — it was overall well-maintained with flower boxes everywhere in raging bloom. I rang the bell and waited, but no one answered. In my pocket, I fumbled for the key, which my mother gave me years earlier. Before I could find it, the door swung open.

"Morning, Dad," I said, astonished that it was he who answered the door.

"Number One," he responded flatly.

"Surprised to see me?"

"I thought you'd come out eventually."

I winced — hopefully unnoticed — at his comment. He stood impassively at the door. The maple tree had been considerably more welcoming. Inconceivably, my father looked more glum than usual, his eyes heavy, his skin a dull olive colour. His frame was thin; he'd lost more weight as compared to the last time I'd seen him. Dressed in dark-blue polyester pants and a floral lavender golf shirt, he stood implacably at the doorway.

"Come in."

"Something up?" I asked as I went through.

"Your mother," Dad responded. "She's not talking to me."

"Oh," I said, regretting the schlep out to the Ditch. I removed my loafers. "Had a tiff, eh?"

Pushing past my father, Mum moved towards me. "What a lovely surprise," she cried, giving me a warm hug. "Come through; don't let your father get in the way," she said archly. "Maybe while we're visiting, Will can have a smoke," she enthused sardonically.

So, that's what this is about.

My mother was the closest thing to a being selfless that I'd come across. For my father, she'd been devoted, adaptable, moving seemingly a hundred times for his benefit and tirelessly creating a wonderful home regardless of where we lived. My father was the beneficiary of my mother's efforts. All he had to do was work. She took care of all the rest, which included raising my sister and me. Perhaps not the most balanced family or relationship, but it seemed to work for them. My father's refusal to participate with his own health by following the rules — primarily not smoking — incensed my mother. To her, it seemed as though he was having an affair with his smokes — a kind of bizarre, twisted tobacco betrayal.

"You're not in class? Oh," my mother was about to answer her own question, "of course, there's a break. In my time, we had a couple of days off for Christmas and Easter. Now the kids are hardly in school. No wonder most of them can't spell their names."

Perhaps it was the strain of caring for my father, but my mother looked uncharacteristically tired, with a definite change in her usual sunny disposition. Still, she was — as always — fashionably dressed wearing a pink linen blouse and dark brown pleated slacks and a jewelled tan belt circled her waist. She ushered me into the living room, leaving my father in the hallway. "Have a seat," she said graciously. "Do you want a coffee or tea? What about something to eat?"

"No, I'm okay for now, thanks, Mum." I quickly noticed that the room had been redecorated, with fresh royal-blue and beige French wallpaper, a stunning deep camel-coloured sofa and modern arm-chairs in a red and gold stripe. The plush area carpet in tones of red was also a recent addition. "Looks like you've been busy, Mum." My father came into the room meekly, not saying a word. He sat down on one of the new chairs and looked completely ill-at-ease.

"Well, I have to have a home that looks smart. This time it's French Provençal. What do you think?"

"It's beautiful," I commented, taking in the colour, texture and impression that she'd created.

"I have clients coming here, after all. It can't look as though I live in a trailer."

"Of course. And how's that going, Mum?"

"The business is coming along. Always need new clients."

I turned my attention to my father. "And Dad, how're doing with your recovery?"

"Not bad for a man of one hundred," he answered. The same answer he always gave when I asked how he was. *So why do I keep on asking the question?*

"Right," I said, thinking of planning my escape. I looked at my watch. 10:15. "Been to the doctor of late? Everything healing up?" *For fuck's sake, you had open heart surgery. Don't you want to tell me how you're managing with all the changes?*

"I'm fine," he said. "Adjusting to medications. Working a few days a week."

"That's great, Dad." *Okay, now you've completely run out of things to ask.* "Um, so Pete's doing better," I said to my mother.

"Who's Pete?" My father asked.

"Don't you listen to me, William? Pete is Lara's agent. He gets her bookings. You know that." My mother's annoyance was palpable.

"Rose, don't tell me what I know. If I knew that I wouldn't ask," he snapped.

Well, it seems that you're both talking again.

"Like I said, Pete's better," I mentioned quickly, noting my mother's increasing crossness.

"Well, that's very nice to hear," she said warmly.

"Funny coincidence … he was treated by the same doctor as Dad."

"Imagine that. You mean Dr. Deth?" she asked.

"Uh huh. Guess you could say that Deth strikes twice," I said brightly.

"You could, but it wouldn't be a very humorous pun, would it?" My father was clearly unimpressed at my attempt at a bon mot.

Well, this is going well. Perhaps I should come out here more often.

"I'm surprised that you didn't bring Lara with you. She's in town still, isn't she?" she asked, ignoring my father's earlier comment.

"Yes, she's here for a while. She's been helping with Pete, of course. I think she's rehearsing some new material." I thought for a moment. "Yes, that's what she's up to."

"How's swimming?" Dad asked abruptly. I wasn't really sure of how to respond.

"Well, not great, actually. My times have been poor this year. Not really sure —"

"Not working hard enough, eh?" My father's criticism came fast.

"*Will.*" My mother's eyes narrowed and she shook her head. "I'm sure that's not the case."

"Well, what *is* the case then?" he pointedly asked me.

"Ah, it's sorta complicated." *That should put you off any more questions. Unless you really want to know, and then I can tell you that life's been tricky because my boyfriend is struggling to find work, my friend may have AIDS and one of my young neighbours passed away from an illness that no one seems to know anything about, putting the entire gay community in potential crisis mode. How's that for starters?*

"Are you injured?" he persisted, making my discomfort grow.

"Injured?" I thought quickly. "Um, yes, I'm having some shoulder … I mean some rotator cuff problems," I lied. I never had any shoulder problems other than fatigue and muscle soreness.

"I'll get you in to see Tom," he stated firmly. "He'll fix you up." Tom Manley was my father's GP in New Westminster.

"Oh, thanks, but I've got a physical therapist that takes care of those things."

"You have to stay healthy," he said.

My mother picked up on that immediately.

"Well, isn't that the pot calling the kettle black," she blurted out smugly and appeared far too satisfied with her remark. My father had enough, gave a look of great displeasure, rose and left the room.

"Mum, what's going on? It's unbelievably tense in here."

"I caught him smoking like a chimney on the balcony this morning at 6:30." My mother was a late-riser; he'd have known that was a good time to suck on a Buckingham's without her catching him.

"You were up at 6:30 in the morning? That's more shocking than him puffing away on a ciggie."

"Don't be clever. This is serious."

"What did you do?"

"I told him that he could dig his own grave and toss himself in it. He hasn't been very happy with me since."

"No, I guess not," I agreed.

"I've worried myself to a size 10, endlessly run around for him, talked to his doctors, taken low-fat cooking classes. I've supported him in every way I know," she complained. "With no thanks, no gratitude. And with all I've done, he lights up like a misbehaving teenager."

"Maybe you have to do less, Mum. Get him to be responsible for his own health."

"Perhaps," she sighed. "Clearly he's not giving up smoking."

"If the scare — literally the scare of a lifetime — doesn't get him to quit, I don't know if you or anyone can convince him."

"Beyond my frustration, it defies logic, doesn't it? Will you talk to him?"

"Ah … you mean about what happened this morning?"

"Yes. He'll lis—"

"Dad's not going to listen to me, Mum," I interrupted her, shaking my head. What about Lynda? She seems to have more luck talking with Dad than I do." Clearly, my sister had a much better relationship with my father than me.

"Lynda asked your father about his smoking just a couple of days ago." My mother drummed her hands on her desk.

"What happened?"

"He told her to leave *his* house. And, she did, furiously."

"Oh …" *Poor Lynda. That must have been a horrible scene.*

"Can you try?" she implored, the tension showing on her face. "Please," she implored.

The thought of having a discussion with my father about his nearly life-long addiction set my teeth on edge.

"I suppose I can give it a whirl," I said, swallowing hard. *You've had all kinds of tough conversations with Pete and Lara in the last couple of months; how hard can this be?*

"Thank you." Mum smiled, relief lighting a spark in her beautiful green-blue eyes. "I've got phone calls to make, so I'll check with you later, okay? Good luck." She got up and went to my former bedroom, which she had converted into a home office, and I went in search of my father.

My father wasn't a chatterer like my mother. He didn't banter humouroulsy or regale people with long-winded tales or otherwise look to make conversation. For the most part, Dad gave measured, brief and succinct responses to questions and when he had something to say, he was clear, to the point and always dead-serious. If he was interested in others — including family — it was never outwardly shown, leaving the impression that he was distant and aloof. As a gay boy growing up, I assumed that who *I* was increased the distance between himself and me. Bridging that gap proved to be a complicated endeavour because I was never sure — *was it him or me?*

I found my father at the kitchen table, drinking instant coffee from his faded black and white checkerboard cup. Routine was important to my father. All that was missing was the constant companion of a cigarette hanging from his mouth and the omnipresent billowing cloud of foul smoke.

"How's the coffee?"

My father rose from his seat and walked to the counter.

"Your mother didn't put enough sugar in it, like usual." He dumped a large rounded teaspoon of sugar into his mug, gave it a stir and sat back down.

So make your own bloody coffee the way you like.

"Oh ... well." I sat down across from him, looking at his weary face. "I remember that you always had a smoke with your coffee," I said, hoping to engage him. No response, just a sour stare. I tried once more. "So, has it been hard, you know, trying not to smoke?"

"Did your mother tell you to ask me that?" He glared at me and I felt my stomach churn.

"No, not at all," I croaked, caught in a lie. "I know that ... um, that it's tough to quit."

"How would you know? You never smoked," he said plainly.

"No," I agreed, clearing my throat. "But I do know that there's help — like medications, or," I actually gulped before continuing, "support groups in the community." The thought of my father sitting in a support group was improbable at best. *He'd never do that, so why suggest it?*

"I've tried gums and patches before; they didn't work. And if you think I'll sit with a bunch of crack addicts talking about a higher power in a church basement you've got a few screws loose."

"It's just a sugges —"

"I expected more from you. You'll never understand how hard it is for a smoker to quit cold turkey."

You're right, I don't understand. I also can't imagine why you would want to intentionally turn your lungs into bags full of poisoned tar.

Describing my father as a smoker is like calling Pierre Trudeau an elected official. There was so much more to the description. For a half a century, from morning till night, my father lit-up, puffed, coughed and punished his lungs with 4 packs of Buckingham's per day. If there were more hours in the day, he would have filled them with smoking. Ironically, he needed to smoke in order to live, and yet smoking would be the eventual cause of his death.

"No, but it doesn't mean that I can't —"

"This conversation is over," he said sharply, clearly offended, rose slowly from the table without his coffee and walked from the kitchen.

"Dad, I didn't mean to —"

"If your mother wants to talk to me, there's nothing stopping her. I'm not about to get health advice from any child, including my own." He collected his keys from his golf pants. "You can tell your mother I'm taking out the garbage." My father's footsteps trailed off as he moved down the hallway and out the front door — without the trash. A few moments later, I heard his Camray startup. Of course, he was off for a smoke.

Well, wasn't that a successful little chat? At least he didn't tell me to leave. He left instead, so it's really the same thing.

I went to find my mother. In her home office, she was on the phone at her small writing desk, pouring through a large wallpaper book and adding clippings to a colour-board, presumably for the client she was speaking to on the phone. As I entered the room, she looked at me with hopeful anticipation, then noticed my facial expression. She drew a deep breath, covered the mouthpiece and shook her head in exasperation.

"Why do I think your father's taking out the garbage?"

35

Something Strange
This Way Cums

My visit with my parents was pretty much what I'd expected. My father's prickly attitude and reticence to make a change in his life nevertheless helped me understand human nature a bit more. *People will change if and when they want, and not because someone else thinks it's a good idea.* My father's behaviour demonstrated how attached he was to his smokes. Without them, he resorted to being dishonest — his way to keep his nicotine level satisfied. I'd like to be able to say that I was sympathetic to his dilemma, but it wasn't the case. At 58 years of age — and he appeared much older — my father continued to demonstrate that his need for cigarettes and alcohol superseded his health. My mother was unable — like most people living with a person with a reliance on substances — to crack the nut and sway him in a different direction. We were all left to watch him deteriorate at an ever-quickening pace.

After spending a few more hours with my mother (my father must have had a truckload of rubbish to unload as he arrived home

90 minutes after he departed), including a tension-filled lunch of egg-salad sandwiches and canned cream of tomato soup, my father sulked his way to the family room to watch golf on TV. I thanked my mother for the meal, gave her a hug and headed back to the West End. On the way home, I thought of how similar and how very different my father and Pete were. Initially, Pete resisted Lara's and my help — like my father resisted my mother's — but within a short time, he allowed us to provide as much assistance as we could, and was certainly better for it. The largest similarity? It was the struggle to give up something that represented such pleasure; my father's incessant smoking, and for Pete, it was relinquishing his very high sex drive — if indeed he had.

The gay community was on notice: sex was potentially dangerous and perhaps fatal. Panic was what many gay men felt, but paradoxically that fear did not necessarily mean a change in sexual behaviour — not yet. That included Robby and me. Absurdly, we made no changes in what we did in the bedroom. Perhaps due to massive anxiety about the "gay cancer", misinformation was rampant and speculation was abundant. Theories for the epidemic included: receiving the Hepatitis B, oral polio or the smallpox vaccines, having a promiscuous sexual history or using amyl nitrates or party drugs like cocaine that depleted the immune system. Some conspiracy theorists thought the CIA had chemically engineered the infection in a diabolical scheme to eradicate all homosexuals. Cooler heads were at a loss as to the reasons why this sickness was moving through the gay community with such alarming speed, and for many, with devastating results. For Robby, Pete, Lara and me, the hope was that the information meeting would address the range of worries that we and others were experiencing.

A day before the meeting, I was bored out of my mind at home reading the DSM and wondered in which category I fit. Sprawled out on the sofa, I was stuffing Cheezies into my face with abandon. *I gotta stop this or else I'm gonna look like Mama Cass.* I rose, went to the Juliet balcony and squeezed my 6-foot frame outside. It was about 20 degrees, with a little breeze wafting offshore. I inhaled deeply then came back into the living room. After viewing my fluorescent orange tongue and lips in the mirror, I hurried to the washroom, brushed my teeth and dropped my Levi's to the floor, searched for a clean pair of running shorts and a light top. After getting geared-up, I headed out the door for a run in the remaining hours of filtered light. Being outside felt terrific as I began jogging. It was after 5 PM. *Hmm, in another hour, Thompson will be barking at his swimmers. The fast swimmers, Sunshine.* I felt a surge of anger as I picked up the pace. Clipping along Pendrell, I headed for the park. *Thompson's an asshole. Or maybe he's been right all along. "You swim like a novice." Isn't that what he claimed? Is it my pride that's hurting? Well, of course it is, right? Face it, you can't get a handle on this.* I continued running through the heavily treed area, heading past the very busy, car-packed Denman Street, which was the main entry for the Lion's Gate Bridge and the North Shore. My hamstrings felt tight as I waited for a green light so that I could cross. It smelled good on Denman with odours drifting from the Greek Donair and pizza places — roasted meat, onions and garlic. *Always the stomach, eh?* Zipping past throngs of pedestrians, I soon passed the Sylvia Hotel, where Lara had triumphed years earlier as my mother and I cheered her on. The stately hotel was now a heritage building. *That's good; no one can rip it down, unlike so many other buildings that have fallen to the wrecking ball.* I scampered along, noticing the lime-green of the freshly leafed-out trees that lined Beach Avenue before I dropped down to the seawall. Teaming with walkers and runners, the winding path offered the best view of the sea. The wind was low and the tide was out — way out — as I gathered my thoughts and sped past Second Beach, dodging people as I started to establish a rhythm. The winds coming up from the sea smelled of fish and slightly of decay. I wiped the perspiration from my brow and continued, heading onto the trail on North Lagoon Drive. The sunny late-afternoon turned dim as I entered the forest. It was dark and cool as I moved under the awning of cedars, pines and firs, deeply inhaling their heady scents. I went further up to Rawling's Trail, the light scattering speckled patches on the soft forest floor. I turned left onto Cathedral Trail for several minutes before heading to Lees Trail, a rather infamous area where — and how shall I say this — gay men were known to — ahem, socialize. I slowed down to a light jog. I wasn't looking, but I did like to be around that kind of male energy, even if merely passing by. Being warmer, there appeared to be a fair number of men frequenting the park, which I expected. However, what I didn't expect was to see someone that I knew skulking about in the dappled light of the trail. I stopped jogging and moved beside a giant cedar tree, my head darting out to confirm my sighting. *Could it be? Maybe I'm wrong.* I surreptitiously continued to steal glances at the man about 15 metres away, clearly cruising on the trail. Though he was dressed in bulky, dark clothes and was wearing a red baseball cap to partially cover his face, he was nonetheless recognizable. *Coach Thompson.* I was spellbound, voyeuristically watching as my purported swimming mentor tried to pick up men who appeared half his age. *So Lara was right. Should I announce my arrival with a, "Hey Coach! Lookin' for some cock?" No, probably not the best tactic.* But though I was unprepared to coerce my coach as a way back to the national swim team, I admit I fantasized about it for more than a few moments. *Should I just step out and make him cringe with embarrassment that way he's shamed me? Tempting, but then I'd have more problems, wouldn't I?* Somehow, I could see Thompson managing to turn everything around and I'd be penalized. I maintained my secretive presence, waiting. Thompson looked like a thug, kicking the ground, hands in his pockets, trying to draw attention to himself. *Well, you're no prize.* He used to be fit, like the pictures of himself in his tiny office … maybe 25 years and 40 pounds ago. Thompson circled round a young man with reddish/blond hair, wearing grey fleecy jogging pants and a white singlet. *That dude must have low self-esteem to want to go with Thompson,* I rationalized, perhaps erroneously. I continued to take furtive glances from behind the tree, moving discreetly as I kept watch. *Wait till I tell Robby — wait, can I tell Robby?* Thompson started talking with Fleecy. I thought I could hear someone laugh. *Can't be Thompson. I've never heard him so much as … gawd, they're walking into the woods together.* I looked at my Timex; 5:48 PM. *He'd better get it out and finish the job, 'cause he's due on the pool deck in only a few …* I stepped forward in the growing dusk until I once more caught sight of my swim coach and Fleecy. Thompson had dropped his pants, and Fleecy was on his knees, blowing him. *Jezus. There's no accounting for taste.* I had to go, and yet the freakishness of the scene kept me nearly frozen beside the tree. A few men sauntered by me, indicating their interest with a smile. I shook my head and kept my eyes on Thompson and Fleecy. Several men didn't seem as though they approved of my behaviour, considering their disdainful glances. *Well, I look pretty sketchy spying on a couple of guys in the bushes.* I heard a few grunts followed by rustling noises. Thompson emerged, load apparently dropped, shuffling nearer to me as he tucked in his shirt. Quickly turning away, I bounded off like a sprinter from the Rainforest of Fairies.

36

Meeting of the Minds

On Thursday night, Robby brought over take-out vegetarian from the Afghan Horseman restaurant. We chowed down on sambosa's, lentil humus, baked eggplant and pawkara. Because it was meatless, the calories didn't count, so after we stuffed ourselves with relatively healthy food, I hauled out the triple-chocolate ice cream — still in the carton — topped it with roasted peanuts, drizzled it with Hershey's syrup and with 2 large spoons, we dug in. Watching Robby enjoy his desert, I decided that I couldn't tell him or Lara about seeing Thompson in the woods. After all, how could I explain my presence in *that* area of Stanley Park? I couldn't. Instead, I put my mental energy back where it belonged — staying fit, swimming sans teammates, seeing Robby, going to class, working in the clinic and thinking about the community meeting set for Friday night.

The real calories eaten, we stretched out on the sofa, his arm cradling my head as our bodies coiled around each other. Robby asked, "Pete confirmed for tomorrow night?"

"Yup. Lara, too. I spoke to them yesterday."

"Who's gonna be on this panel?"

"Well, the flyer states, 'health officials', but no names were given."

"I might be a bit late. I'm meeting with that horrible old queen at UBC at 6 PM."

"Oh, Dr. Hockington? Better watch out, I hear he likes the young, athletic type." I smiled. I knew who Hockington was. Very old, very overweight, and yielded immense control of the UBC Theatre Department.

"I dunno if he likes anyone. He was disrespectful to every student in the department, but we all turned a blind eye."

"Really?"

"Yeah. Lemme tell you, when I was a there, he never bothered to learn my name. Only referred to me as "the blonde boy". One time, he was observing one of my voice classes —"

"Wait, you had to take voice?"

"Directors have to know how to act and speak. So, in voice class, he came over to me and instructed me to "breathe from my sex.""

"Breathe from your —"

"Yeah, from my ass, apparently. He proceeded to push his hand down the front of my pants to show me where my diaphragm was. This was in front of the whole class, mind you. What a first-rate jerk. He also missed my diaphragm by a foot."

"And you're meeting with him because?"

"I told you, Shep. Because I wanna be one of the hopefuls that gets to direct a play at the Freddy Wood this year. If I get selected, I'll have a better chance of doing some work, including teaching at UBC. I can forgive his bad form years ago to find my way into the circle," Robby stated, meaning the relatively small, but growing, Vancouver theatre and film community.

"And selling yourself to Satan is what you need to do?"

"Now *you're* being dramatic. Hockington's not Satan. He's just one of those old-school directors who drips with narcissism. The last time he had any acclaim was in the 60s when he directed *As You Like It* with an all-male cast. Very avant-garde at the time."

Hmmm. That Forest of Arden would have been much like Stanley Park at night.

"Well, you don't have to be Werner Fassbinder to figure out why he created a Forest of Fairies," I added sarcastically.

"True enough," Robby laughed. "But Hockington knows people that I'd like to work with at UBC and in the theatre community downtown. He can help with the connections, if I play my cards right."

"It's a bit — I dunno, smarmy — isn't it?"

"Of course it is," he retorted. "It's the politics of theatre, Shep. Lara'll tell you."

"Lara *does* tell me, but I don't much like it."

"No one likes it, but it's how to be a part of the system. The people who are connected are the ones that get work. It's what we have to do, at least at first."

"And after?"

"After I'll get to make my own rules," Robby stated firmly.

"Speaking of rules," I took a gulp of oxygen, sat up slightly. "You don't want to screw around with other guys, do you?"

"Whoa. That's an odd question," Robby answered, clearly taken aback. "Where is *that* coming from?"

"That's not the response I was hoping for," I said, furrowing my brow. *Winters were very cold in Nickeltown, after all.*

"You might have lots of stuff to worry about, but you don't have to worry about me being faithful. A guy doesn't screw with his lover *and* his best friend. Especially now. Why would I? I've got the cutest boyfriend in the country, and he's a smokin' fast swim—"

"A once smoking fast swimmer," I added quickly. "And I'm not cute."

"Let's see," Robby said, giving me the once-over, moving his fingers through my locks. "Long wavy hair, blue eyes, muscled body."

"Please," I said. "Say more," I chuckled.

"A cute, hard-working and very fast swimmer," Robby completed the words I worked hard at negating. "I think I've covered all bases. Come here," he said. "I'm betting you're worried about the meeting?" Robby took one look at me and gave me the world's best bear-hug. Then he pummelled me with a hundred kisses. I could taste the mint of the wintergreen candy he'd eaten after our dessert.

"Yes, but it's more than that. On the CBC this morning, they announced that members of a holy roller church believe that gays are receiving *'just punishment for their evil ways.'* Pat Buchanan said gays should be *'put to death.'* Can you believe it?"

"I have a harder time believing the CBC called 'em holy rollers."

"Can't I have a bit of dramatic licence? It was some evangelical sect. The thing is, there's already a backlash against us historically, and not just from the religious right. I think that people have found yet another reason to hate us."

"There's always gonna be people who despise us regardless of AIDS," Robby interjected. "AIDS will make 'em hate us even more. That's how it is and why we gotta keep our cool, be smart, stand together, not lie down." Robby spoke in a firm, reasoned voice. "Those times of being passive died before Stonewall. This thing — whatever it is — it's gonna be another test of our collective character."

"I hate tests," I said, shaking my head and thinking of calculus tests in high school, which routinely prompted me to vomit in the boy's washroom shortly before writing them. I could almost taste the acid in my throat as I remembered.

"Well, think of it this way," Robby started, with a grand hand gesture to the ceiling. "The great Liza Minnelli once —"

"Wait, you're not really about to belt out a Liza number, are you?" I asked, slightly aghast. Before he could respond, I added, "No disrespect, but I've heard you sing. You're as rotten as my sister."

"I'm not singing anything, so let me finish," Robby said sternly, hand gesture still intact. "Liza once said, and I quote, '*Reality is something you rise above.*' Isn't that great? I can almost see those shiny red sequins." He dropped his hand and ruffled my hair.

"How did I ever wind up with such a theatre-queen?" I asked, tickling him under his armpit with my one free hand.

"Yeah," he said, "I bet your parents ask that question every single day," he said, squirming and gasping with uncontrolled laughter under my continual prodding.

On Friday evening, Pete and Lara were to meet us at the Community Centre on Denman. A modest building, it housed a decent library, a skating rink, meeting rooms, some music studios, specialty arts rooms and a good gym. It was popular with old and young alike. As Robby and I ambled down Denman, he started describing that his meeting with Hockington didn't prove to be as optimistic as he'd hoped. I listened carefully as we made our way to the centre. Though the skies threatened to rain, the streets were dry and full of mostly men seemingly bound for the forum.

"Hey!" Lara cried out. She was dressed in a long oatmeal-coloured sweater-coat. Underneath was a plain cotton shirt in soft grey. Her jeans were well-faded and she wore a pair of mid-calf brown boots. Just behind her slightly, jockeying for position in the large swarm of people, was Pete. Even in a crowd, he stood out. Of course, he was thin — too thin — but that wasn't what made him so noticeable. His brilliant white teeth flashed a dazzling display when he spotted me. And though he needed to increase his weight, he seemed to have regained the appearance of health. Wearing a pair of well-fitting new charcoal-grey pants, his black shoes shone, his glossy dark hair was immaculately gelled in place, his sharp features were softened considerably by a short and scruffy beard that few men could pull off. A crisp, fresh white shirt was beneath his expensive tan leather jacket. For all he'd gone through, Pete looked very much like the man of a year ago. He gave me a wink, his long, dark lashes lining his soulful deep-brown eyes. They were reddened, I presumed, by Mrs. McBride's twice-daily herbal treatment. However, Pete didn't seem to be stoned, but was in excellent spirits.

"I'm glad you're here," I said to them both, hugging Lara first, then embracing Pete carefully.

"I won't break," Pete said, grinning. "I'm not made of glass."

"No, you sure aren't," I agreed, giving him a firmer hug.

After Lara and Pete said a quick hello to Robby, we entered the centre and made our way to the lecture room. I felt my blood pounding in my head as we scurried and found 4 seats together near the front of the stage area. There were television cameras from both the CBC and CTV set up along the sides of the room. Reporters were already taking shots of the group and asking some questions, presumably for the 11 o'clock news. *Probably for tomorrow morning, too. Fabulous.*

"See anyone you know?" Robby asked me as we watched the panel coming to sit down. I scoured the group of men.

"I don't think … jeez," I said, startled at who I saw.

"What is it?" Robby asked.

"The man with the curly dark hair," I pointed discretely. "It's Dr. Deth," I whispered. Just 15 feet away, Deth noticed me or perhaps Pete and quickly began leafing through his papers.

"I recognize him from the hospital," Lara said. "But I never thanked him for taking care of Pete." Lara rose from her seat and went up to the panel to speak with him. Deth immediately stood as Lara extended her hand. I couldn't hear what she was saying, but I could see that Deth seemed pleased to speak with her, presumably about how he had helped her agent. After a brief exchange, Lara came back to her seat, the room settled down and the discussion started. Along with several physicians, in attendance was the Executive Director from the recently opened AIDS Vancouver and a social worker. First up was a soft-spoken Dr. Willow, who explained what was currently known, which wasn't a great deal, and gave updates of various large urban centres in the US and Canada as the number of cases continued to increase alarmingly. Willow discussed the lymphadenopathy study that was being conducted in Vancouver. There was a collective gasp when he mentioned the number of patients enrolled in the investigation was 700. Other panelists, including Deth, shared how the various ailments affected the body's ability to deal with respiratory infections of the lungs and the effect on the cardiovascular system. We — and not just our group — listened carefully to their assessment and then a microphone was set up for taking audience questions. There was no hesitation for members of the audience to line up and wait their turn as the questions started.

"We've heard a lot of opinions, so what's the cause?" a young man asked. Of course, almost everyone in the room probably had the same worried query.

"Well," one of the physicians answered, "we think it's a rare virus that, once introduced to the body, attacks the T-cells and kills them. Needless to say," the doctor raised his voice against growing grumbles of concern, "we all need our T-cells to function. Without them, we can't fight off a plethora of ailments. And that's what we're seeing in unprecedented numbers."

Another man wanted to know, "Who's at greatest risk?"

"Let me try to answer," Willow responded. "We think that it's presently gay or bisexual men who have or have had many sexual partners."

Or just about everyone in this room, you mean.

"Also considered a high-risk is shared needle use for the injection of drugs," he added. "And Haitians that have recently immigrated to Canada. Those people with hemophilia who receive large quantities of blood products through transfusions are also considered a high-risk group."

"So anyone who's had transfusions?" someone shouted out.

"It's possible," replied Willow. "And additional risk factors may include communicable diseases ... like hepatitis, herpes, gonorrhea, syphilis and amebiasis."

To my surprise, Pete had moved to the microphone. I'd been too engrossed in the discussion to notice that he'd left his seat until he spoke.

"Are you telling us that anyone who's had the clap is at risk for AIDS?" The room bristled. "Why would that be a risk?" he asked.

"It may be," Deth pointed out, "that repeated exposure to or ingestion of semen or other bodily fluids will carry this virus into the body," Deth postulated, "and sexual infections provide additional openings — opportunities, really — for the virus to invade and begin to break down the immune system."

"Then you're saying every gay man and straight woman in this room, and all over the city, is at risk, aren't you?" The murmuring ceased as Deth turned to an epidemiologist, and the physician gave his careful response.

"At this point, with still much that is unknown, we are saying that *gay* men, in particular, appear to be a very high-risk group."

"How long," Pete asked, "do people live once they have AIDS?"

I swallowed hard at Pete's question, a question that many wanted to have answered. Lara shot me a look, her brown eyes glimmering on the brink of tears. She, like I and perhaps many others, knew exactly what our friend was asking. Pete moved back to his seat. I noticed the camera had been on him during his questions.

"We can report that it may depend on the health of the person. For some, it can be slower to progress, and for others, well, it can move quickly to cancerous lesions like Kaposi's sarcoma or PCP or other infections that the person can no longer fight off. It could be as short as a few months or perhaps over a year. You must understand, even at 3 years in, we are really just at the beginning of this, and from what we've been charting, seeing, reading and hearing, the mortality rate is extremely high."

"What are the things that we should be looking out for?" a woman from the back of the room inquired, as more people disregarded the microphone line and began shouting their questions from the audience.

"Bear in mind that some symptoms may not be associated with AIDS, but generally, if a person is fatigued, has night sweats, fevers, swollen lymph glands, diarrhea, a persistent cough, thrush or any nodules on or beneath the skin," the epidemiologist continued, "in combination with being in a high-risk group, then …. well, then there's cause for great concern," he concluded. Robby and I looked at each other. As far as I knew, and though I felt fatigued at times, I seemed to lack the symptoms as described — at least at this point in time.

"What about tests for this?" an older man asked near the front row.

"I'm afraid we have no tests to determine if someone has AIDS — many researchers are working on it worldwide, though, and I'm hopeful in the next few years there will be more options for detection, diagnosis and treatment."

From the rear of the crowd, a man called out, "But we don't have years, do we?"

"And," another man cried, "there's no treatment for those who are suffering, is there?"

"No, that's not precisely true. There are experimental treatments like interferon and proven antibiotics that can be effective against pneumonia, but you're correct that nothing presently exists that cures this condition. What we hope for is the ability to, well, slow it down so we can understand how we can treat those affected. Right now, we are still looking for solutions. The medical community is working on this with great effort, let me assure you." The epidemiologist was doing his best to respond to the growing anxiety that was flooding the meeting like a Vancouver rainstorm.

"Then, what do we do for now?"

"If you want to lower your risk, abstaining from the exchange of bodily fluids is the CDC's recommendation, along with limiting your sexual partners, never sharing needles, maintaining a healthy diet, exercise, being monogamous in relationships, and knowing your partner's sexual history before being intimate. Some physicians are recommending using condoms for anal sex as we think the receptive partner is more at risk. We don't believe that casual contact such as shaking hands, hugging or air-borne particles spread AIDS. That's what we know at present, but our information is frankly very limited; there's far more that we don't know."

The panel members took a few moments to allow the medical information to sink in before proceeding with the social problems correlated with the virus. The Director of AIDS Vancouver spoke to a very shaky audience. The short man with receding hair seemed to gather himself before making his opening comments.

"The CDC's latest report is sobering — cases of AIDS are doubling every 6 months since they've been recording data after 1980. That's a staggering statistic. To provide some context, there have been 3,000 cases reported this year in the US. Of those, 1,000 people have died. There are easily 10,000 people infected in North America — and that's an extremely conservative estimate. We think that twice as many people are unaware that they're infected and won't know for 1 or 2 or perhaps more years. Of course, unwittingly, they could be infecting others, and those people infected will continue to do the same." There were loud gasps from the audience. "It may take a couple years, or even longer, for symptoms to show up. By that time, infected people could be in the hundreds of thousands. When we start to calculate the rates of affliction, the future is, well, incredibly worrisome." People shuffled uncomfortably in their chairs. Some appeared immobilized, others shook their heads in disbelief. "This is a call to arms. AIDS Vancouver will need your assistance to help those affected."

I looked around at an audience that had been stunned into silence, including Lara, Robby and even Pete. I wasn't sure why, but I stood up from my seat. Me, the secretly gay swimmer, the secretly gay son with a secret boyfriend and living an all too secretive life. For a few moments, I was unable to speak. I felt the eyes of the group and the panelists on me, in anticipation of words I'd yet to formulate. I cleared my tight throat with a dry cough, took a breath and steadied myself.

"There was a man in my building. Not just a man, but someone who was always friendly and helpful to me, and to others." I faltered, feeling my head pound. "And just a few weeks ago, my friend and I, we …" My social anxiety kicked in quickly as my throat constricted, recalling the shock of finding Tommy's contorted, lifeless body. "We …" I couldn't continue and sat down. Lara grabbed my hand and Robby placed his arm across my shoulder. Pete's eyes met mine in a steady stare.

"We found him," a woman's voice crackled from the middle of the room. She stood up. "His name was Tommy. Dead at the age of 37. His mother told me he'd drowned in his own fluids from a pneumonia that resisted any treatment. Our lovely Tommy died alone, with music playing … music that he must have loved. A beautiful, kind young man …" She took a moment to retrieve a tissue from her coat before continuing. "Several funeral homes declined to take Tommy's body; they flatly refused. Outrageous disrespect. Is this how a civil society cares for those who have fallen?" Mrs. McBride's voice shook with contempt as she covered her mouth for a moment in the still room. "This … pestilence ravages lives and leaves nothing behind but shame." Mrs. McBride wiped her nose with a tissue. "We can't allow another Tommy to perish with no one's hand to hold, can we?" She slowly walked from the room in complete silence, head down, exhausted.

"So," Robby directed a question to the panel and breaking the hush, his strong baritone inflamed with emotion. "How do we help?"

37

White Tower

By the time the meeting had finished and we stepped out onto Denman Street, rain was mercilessly pelting down.

"That meeting didn't go like I thought it might," Lara said as she pulled up the collar of her sweater-coat. "But no one has answers to the big questions right now, do they?" Our group didn't respond as Lara tied the belt of her coat. "How about White Tower?" she asked. "I'd love something to eat."

"You can eat now after that?" Robby was surprised that she or anyone could contemplate a greasy pizza. We continued to stand under the green awning of the Community Centre.

"Well," Pete said, "I could certainly nosh on something. I'm really getting the munchies." Mrs. McBride's product certainly was helping Pete maintain his food intake.

I gotta call or see her tomorrow to make sure she's okay.

"C'mon," I said, snatching Robby's hand. "Let's go."

The four of us broke into a half-run in the downpour to White Tower, one of Lara's and my favourite hangouts from years earlier.

Going for something to eat was a good idea. We needed to decompress from an overwhelmingly trying meeting.

"It's just pissing!" I shouted over the roar of the relentless rain. Not one of us had an umbrella.

"Pete, you're soaked," Lara said, catching my eye. She and I worried that being wet and cold would affect him adversely.

"Don't start," Pete warned. We got the message easily enough. Lara took his arm as we jogged up Robson Street. The rains let up just as we were about to enter White Tower about 10 minutes later. We waited for a table, rubbing hands, arms, legs and various other body parts in an effort to warm up. I took a gander at the three others. *Wet as sewer rats*. Lara's red hair was plastered against her face. Pete's jacket seemed to do little to prevent his white shirt from becoming saturated, showing his dark chest hair underneath. Robby somehow looked refreshed and handsome. I appeared as though I'd been through the rinse cycle of a washing machine.

"You'll make sure that Pete's getting a cab back, okay?" I whispered to Lara. Lara didn't drive, so she'd be taking a taxi home, too.

After we got seated, 2 large vegetarian pizzas were ordered, along with hot coffee and tea. There seemed to be so much to say, but we all were avoiding *that* conversation. I eased into it cautiously.

"I thought I'd give AV a call tomorrow. There's gotta be something that I can do," I added. Just a family therapy intern, I didn't have any real legitimacy as a professional, but I wasn't about to give swimming lessons. "They're gonna offer a volunteer counselling program. I'd really be interested in helping with that."

"And you'd be perfect, Sunshine. Everyone needs someone to talk to, especially when there's, you know, uncertainty with what lies ahead." Lara refrained from looking at Pete. "AIDS Vancouver will need money. Maybe we could think about doing some kind of benefit to raise funds? Perhaps something that Robby could direct?" She turned to him with raised eyebrows. "I can't wash cars or bake muffins or run a telethon or sell chocolate-covered cherries," Lara explained apologetically. "But I can sing my ass off right into Tuesday."

Robby looked at my dearest of friends. "I'll find out what we can do, okay?"

"I'm not sure what, but I wanna help, too," Pete affirmed.

"You can continue to get stronger," I offered. "That's what I'd like. That's what everyone would like." Pete smiled, then winked at me. His impossibly long eyelashes were still damp from the rain. He warmed me just by his presence. Robby watched me as I gazed at Pete, his efforts at getting his health were inspirational. I was protective of him as he'd been with me over the years. Surely, his fight left him more vulnerable, and yet he retained the power of attraction that belied his physical appearance. *Mesmerizing.*

"I wonder," Pete thought aloud, "where we'll all be a year from now."

"What do you mean, Pete?" Lara asked somewhat apprehensively.

"Well, you see, before I got sick, I took life as it came. I didn't plan too far ahead; just let things unwind as they did. And now … well, I'm inclined to be more aware of time and what I do with it." He turned to Lara and gave her a peck on the cheek. "Like having dinner with my friends. It's special and it … it makes me so happy." Pete's gorgeous eyes shone across the table as we sat for a brief moment reflecting on what he'd said.

"Pete," Lara's voice broke with emotion, "I refuse to let you get maudlin on me and ruin my appetite."

"Lara, let's be honest, when have your emotions *ever* prevented you from having a meal?" Pete laughed, with others following suit, thereby breaking any tension and ending the sadness, but certainly not the worry, that had permeated the evening.

As if on cue, our server brought a couple of immense pizza's to the table, blazing hot and smelling of onions, garlic, roasted tomatoes, peppers, pesto sauce and riddled with a near-blanket of stringy mozzarella cheese.

"Oooh!" Lara exclaimed. "Let's tuck in!" In a few moments we dug into our shared meal, stuffing ourselves with slice after slice, sipping coffee and tea, laughing, telling stories about bad dates, evil siblings, stage disasters and otherwise cherishing our time together. Underneath the laughter, we were scared for Pete and worried for each other. We were mournful of the early and tragic losses of life — like Tommy — where love and sex had become dangerous and linked to a dodgy future. A future no one could have predicted.

38

Tommy & Friend

I've been told since I was young by both family and friends that my imagination "got the better of me". As a child, I had lions and tigers under my bed at night for years. The terrifying, beady-eyed Wolf with red eyes and a salivating mouth from Red Riding Hood was an unwelcome visitor at my window for more nights than I would like to recall. As an adult, I was mostly free of the scare-fest that plagued me as a youngster. As a boy, I may have created such images because I — like many children of a certain age — could find nighttime terrifying. Childhood was far behind me, however, I once again was finding bedtime perturbing, given all the recent and unsettling events.

The night of the meeting, Robby decided to go back to his apartment. I walked back to the Queen Charlotte in the drenching rains, and though the night had ended very happily at White Tower, it had nevertheless been a taxing evening. It was late — nearly midnight — when I climbed the stairs to the 2nd floor, pausing to gaze at Tommy's apartment, which was still not rented out. I had a sudden burst of the 'what if''s' as I stood on the landing. *Perhaps, if I or someone else had been aware, Tommy could have been taken into St. Paul's, like Pete had been. What if his mother would have stayed with him? If she'd been with him, wouldn't she'd have gotten him the medical help he needed? If that had been my Mum, she would have called the ambulance. If, if, if ...* I heard a low moaning sound and snapped my head around. *Nothing there. Foolishness. It's just the hot-water heating starting up, isn't it?* I exhaled, shook my head and went up the next flight of stairs to my apartment. Unlocking my door, I stepped through, not turning on any lights. I was soggy from the rain, so after removing my coat, I stepped out of my jeans and tee-shirt. I went to the kitchen to take a swig of orange juice. Standing in front of an open fridge in the darkened kitchen, I had the uneasy sense that someone was behind me. I wasn't courageous enough to turn around and look; instead, I was frozen in place. I put the juice back and took another deep breath before turning around. *See? No one there.* I went to the bathroom to brush my teeth. It was quiet — dead-quiet in the apartment. *Why am I so unsettled? There's no reason to* — I heard a cough, or I thought I heard a cough, and felt my ears perk up like a dog. *Jezus, what's wrong with me? Maybe it was someone above or beside my apartment. There's no one in here. Calm down.* I sat down to pee, didn't flush the toilet because I was intent on listening for any peculiar sounds. Satisfied, I pulled up my boxers and padded my way down the hallway to the bedroom. I'd left the window wide-open and it was very cool in the room. I half-closed the opening, noticing the rain was again forceful and was being pushed sideways by a stiff breeze. I shuddered, rubbing my arms with icy-cold hands. I heard a wheezing sound, startling me. I turned on my heels, but of course there was no one there. My skin felt clammy. *What the fuck is the matter with me? I really need to get some sleep. At least I don't have to worry about getting up at 5 for practice. No, that's because I've fucked that up, too.* After I had sufficiently beat myself, I punched the pillows a few times, crawled under the duvet and closed my eyes. I tossed from one side to the next, struggling to sleep. From what seemed like a distance, I heard music. *Shit, who's got this on at — what time is it?* In the blackness of my room, I peered at my digital alarm clock. 12:48 AM. The music was soft, but it was sufficiently loud to annoy me. The music was familiar. *What is that?* Then I knew … *the New World Symphony No. 9 — Dvořák. The music that Tommy died listening to. And this is not my imagination. This is real.* Panicked, I sat up and was stunned to see, at the foot of the bed, a gauzy figure glowing, seemingly lit by a light from within. I blinked, rubbed my eyes. But there he was. *Tommy.* I took a sharp breath as I watched him peering at me. I couldn't accept what I was seeing, so I looked away, then slowly moved my sight to the end of the bed once more. *Good gawd; he's still there.* As I looked at him, the beautiful, soaring music grew louder, insistently playing. I heard a small, plaintive moan — not of pain, I didn't think — more of a sigh. His eyes were dark as night, set in a face of palest white, and steadfastly he continued to gaze at me. His image didn't frighten me, strangely enough, though I was astonished at what I was seeing. And as I looked at Tommy, there was something else. In Tommy's hand he held a light-green bird — the edges of him and the bird were slowly becoming indistinct and blurry. He brought the bird close to his upper chest, and as he did so, I could see the faintest smile cross Tommy's lips. The small bird was beautiful, and it pressed itself against his neck, making a chirping call, barely audible and hollow.

"Oh, you're not alone," I said, elated for him, yet scarcely believing what I was seeing. His image began flickering, dwindling, dissolving as he moved away from the bed.

"Tommy," I whispered as my throat ached. "I'm so sorry for what happened to you." I gently caught my breath, and felt my eyes sting. The music began to fade, becoming softer and softer. As their images disappeared, the music echoed in my room, the horns lingered like a lonesome cry. Then all was eerily quiet in my dark bedroom.

39

The Day After That

I didn't have any more unexpected visitors that night, which I was relieved about. As I was making up my bed, I thought about telling Lara or Robby about my visitors, but decided against it. *Maybe it was the fabrication of a tired mind? Perhaps I was asleep when it occurred? Impossible. I was awake, wasn't I? Or could I have constructed something in those moments?* I smoothed the duvet and topped it with green pillows. *Green, like Tommy's bird. Oh, stop.* The incoming morning light glinted off the frame of the brass bed. *Perhaps it's better to just get it out of your mind; call it some kind of delusion due to stress.* Mrs. McBride's apartment was a few doors away from mine, but on the same floor. I wondered if she heard anything. *Can't hurt to ask, could it?* It was difficult for me to get the image of Tommy out of my mind. I ate a small breakfast, skipped a swim and dug out my unfinished assignment. *I've heard that some people think that ghosts are just leftover energy. That's too new-agey for me. But I heard the music, I felt my tears forming, I saw a bird, for Christ's sake. But did you?* I made a large mug of tea, sweetened it considerably with buckwheat honey, pulled out my schoolwork and dumped it on my kitchen table. I was finding it hard to concentrate on the task and was relieved when the phone rang. I bolted up to the small table near the front door before the answering machine picked it up.

"Good morning," I said, thinking it might have been Lara or Pete.

"How's the TV star?" my mother asked.

"Excuse me?"

"Your father and I saw you and Lara on the news last night."

Of course. There was coverage of the community meeting. *Gawd, and I thought seeing a ghost was bad.*

"Um, yeah, I attended an information meeting."

"About the AIDS," she stated.

"About *AIDS*, yes, Mum."

"I saw Lara talking to someone on stage, but only for a moment."

I guess you couldn't see that it was Dad's cardiologist. This is getting far too incestuous.

"Uh, huh. Some of my other friends were there, too."

"Really? Who were they?"

"Huh?"

"Which friends were you with?"

And why do you want to know?

"Well, Pete was there, and my friend Robby, too."

"I thought that was Pete, but he looked very different. Very thin."

"Oh, yes, but he's —"

"Sick?"

Great. What are you really asking me?

"No, he's getting better every week. Pete's very strong," I said a little defensively.

"He looks unwell."

"*Mum.* He's improving. Lara and I are really looking after him."

"Well, just be careful, dear."

Okay, I don't know exactly what you're trying to tell me, but I'm ready to change this conversation. "Mum, I always look after myself," I stated. "You know that."

"Are you eating?"

"*Mum.* No, I'm starving myself. Of course I'm eating."

We spoke for a few more minutes. I inquired about my father, who was apparently doing better.

"Perhaps I can come in for a visit this spring?" she asked, hopeful for a positive response. "Now that your father is stable. Work is slow for me and I'd love a break."

"Of course, Mum," I said. "It's great having you here."

She soon ended the call and I stretched out on the sofa. I'd slept poorly last night — ghostly visitors are like a shot of adrenaline, I'd discovered — and dozed for a few minutes. When I woke, I looked at my Timex and was surprised to find that I'd slept for nearly 90 minutes. *You've gotta get yourself into the pool today.* I had 4 swimming lessons scheduled at the Aquatic Centre — that was $100.00 worth of fees. I pushed myself up and fixed something to eat, brushed my teeth, had a hot, steamy shower, shaved the scruff from my face, collected my gear and biked to the pool.

The suspension from swimming was lousy. As I cycled to the pool in the rain, I thought that perhaps one of the friendlier swimmers on the team might have called me to see how I was, but there had been no contact. I wondered what my coach — when he wasn't picking up tricks in the park — had told them. Still, it wasn't forever, and the break in the routine was probably therapeutic for me. I was able to cram in more private lessons, too. That helped my bank account considerably. For a young man whose life revolved around swimming, this leave was a significant change. I locked my bike up outside the pool. After I donned my suit in the change room, I stepped out onto the deck and waited for my first client — Jenny or Ginny — I couldn't recall her name. She showed up a bit late, paid her fee which I stashed in my swimbag, then we got to work. Teaching swimming was enjoyable when a person had some basic fitness. But, she hadn't. In fact, she wasn't fit; she was fat, with rolls of flesh spilling out of her suit. She didn't take direction well, and giggled when I put a pull-buoy between her legs so that she could focus on her arms (which were flaccid and flabby, with no muscle tone). After 45 minutes, she was done, and I had a few minutes before my next client. So, I positioned my goggles and started with a few laps of butterfly. I was surprising myself — I felt smooth and powerful in the water, easily churning up a huge wave behind me. The next 100 metres I watched the large-handed timer on the wall. I was knocking off each 100 in 56, then 54 seconds. Decent times, considering that I only was pushing off from the wall. I stretched out at the end of the lane. I moved my goggles up to my hairline.

"Pretty impressive. Can you teach me how to do that?"

I looked up and onto the pool deck. A man with curly, dark hair wearing a pair of orange bathing trunks had been watching my butterfly.

"Dr. Deth." I was surprised to see him at the pool, of all places.

"Serge, please."

"I thought that you'd be working. Don't physicians work around the clock?"

"I'm a cardiologist," he said with a crooked-tooth smile. "I have specialist hours." Deth jumped into the pool. His curly hair appeared to be elsewhere, including his slight chest. His legs were slender and he was generally trim. I decided that he was more attractive when he was wearing his doctor garb at the hospital. Still, there was something appealing about Serge Deth, even in his long, flowered-print orange swim shorts.

"I saw you and your friends at the meeting the other night, but of course I couldn't speak with you due to privacy."

"No. I appreciate your confidentiality. Thanks."

"So, Mr. Gauthier, the one we treated, was he your boyfriend?"

"Pete? Oh, no. He wasn't."

"Oh, interesting," Deth said. "You were also with a redheaded woman wearing a long sweater; very pretty — she could have been a model. I think I've seen her before, but I can't recall where. She and I spoke for a bit before the meeting. You're fond of her?"

"Yes, we're very close," I responded, a little unsettled with his questions. "What did you talk about, if you don't mind me —"

"She thanked me for attending to Pete. Her concern was touching."

"She's super-tight with Pete; he's mentored her along to success." I gave him the minimal amount of information and chose not to tell Deth that Lara was a singer. It was interesting to me that he didn't inquire about Robby, who clearly I was in close contact through the meeting. Changing the topic, I added, "I haven't seen you here before — not that I recall. Swim often?"

"Not really. I live close by on Thurlow and thought swimming would be a good way to relax. I do enjoy the water. In fact, I have a small boat that's moored in False Creek just beside Granville Island. It's just 26 feet, but well-equipped."

"That's great. The ocean's like a playground, isn't it?"

"Oh, yeah. It's great to spend a hot summer's day out in English Bay with treats from Granville Island."

"I bet." *So, where's this going?*

"You like boating?"

"Boating? Uh, well, I haven't rea —"

"If you're ever interested, let me know. I'd be happy to take you out. Maybe some of your friends would like to come, too?"

"That's very kind of you," I said, with no intention of taking him up on his offer. A heavyset boy jumped in a metre from me, splashing stinging, chlorinated water directly into my eyes. As I wiped it away, Deth continued with another question.

"You were going to call to go out for coffee, remember?"

I did remember. "Yes, I just have a lot going on right now, what with my father *(lie #1)* and Pete. I'm also going to school, swimming on the team *(lie #2)* and working. I'm actually doing swim lessons all day today. I'm on a break for another few minutes."

"Yes, I was watching you teaching that woman."

"Oh, were you?" *That's peculiar ...*

"I picked up some tips. You're a good instructor. I could use a few lessons," Deth said, raising his brows in anticipation of a favourable response. "Especially my backstroke. It's sort of wobbly. I bet you could straighten it out for me."

"I'm pretty booked up for the next while," I expressed untruthfully.

"Well, when you can, some help would be appreciated." Deth waited a beat. "Great arms," Deth commented, appraising my upper body.

"Huh?"

"Very well defined. I can tell that you've worked hard in the water."

"Um, thanks. I've swum for a long time."

"It shows," Deth said, firmly grabbing my shoulders. "Very developed muscles. Many men would be quite envious." He released his Deth grip *(sorry, couldn't resist)* and added. "Really, I'm serious about the lessons. I can pay you — generously."

"Um, no need. I'm indebted for, you know, putting a pig's heart in my father's chest," I said, feeling uncomfortable with Deth's "generous" offer.

"A pig's valve, remember?" He smiled at my second-time error.

"Of course, sorry. Boy, I really should go — there's my next swimmer, and he's a little afraid of being in the water; he's what I call a sinker. Give me a call and I'll be happy to give you a few lessons *(lie #3)* in the next month or so. Cheers."

"Salut." Deth gave his biggest and most crooked smile. I swam under the lane rope to my next client who was shaking with either anxiety or cold in the shallow, open area of the pool.

I called my mother the evening after I had completed all my lessons.

"Twice in one day, how lovely," she said, referring to my additional phone call.

"Mum, were you speaking with Dad's cardiologist recently?"

"How odd that you asked. As a matter of fact, he called here just a couple of days ago. Wanted to give your father some test results and book a time to review a few things."

"Oh … and did you chat with him, too?"

"Yes, only I spoke with him. He didn't wish to have a word with Will, just with the case manager."

"Funny, Mum. What did you talk about, if you don't mind me asking?"

"Well, let's see," Mum paused before going on. "He wanted to know if your father was taking his blood thinners, if he was being physically active. I told him Will's already playing a bit of golf — of course. Dr. Deth wanted to know if Will was a swimmer — like you — as that's considered a very good way to increase the lung capacity following surgery."

"Oh," I said, feeling uneasy with Deth's questions once more.

"I told him that you were the only swimmer in the family. Deth seemed quite interested in your efforts, though. He commented that you must be very dedicated to attend school and swim at the same time. I told him you even teach swimming at the weekend."

"My, that was quite a friendly conversation."

"Should I not have —"

"Mum, did you mention *where* I gave swim lessons?"

"Hmm, I don't know. Perhaps I did. Why?"

"Small world, I guess, 'cause I ran into him today at the Aquatic Centre."

"Really? Isn't it strange how things like that happen by chance?"

"Yes, isn't it?" I doubted there was chance involved with Deth showing up on the pool deck. "Well, I'll let you go. Say 'hi' to Dad for me."

"Oh, he's around here somewhere. Why don't I find him so that you can —"

"That's okay. Bye, Mum."

40

The Killer Amidst Us

I didn't like that Deth was making inquiries about me and "coincidentally" appearing at the Aquatic Centre, though perhaps I was overreacting. He could have had a real interest in swimming, or wanted to merely be friendly. I'm assuming that he was as in the closet as I was with only select people in the know. It would have very risky for a physician to be out, especially as the tide was turning against gays. And being from Belgium, he might not have many friends in Vancouver. After all, Lara had been my only companion for many years. Vancouver can be a difficult place to establish new friendships. But, I couldn't deny there was something curious about the situation, though I chose not to share with Robby that he'd appeared at the pool.

I had over a week to go before my swim suspension was over. I was determined to show myself — not just Thompson or anyone else — that I had the ability to compete. But first, I had to find a way to push distractions from my mind — including worrying that I and others were potentially ill — and focus on getting fast enough to qualify for the Pan Am Games. Lara, Pete, Robby all dedicated time, effort and energy to move their careers along successfully, making concessions along the way. I wondered aloud what else I needed to sacrifice to get to where I wanted to be.

"Sacrifice? Whadya mean?" Robby asked, surprised to hear me ask a question out of the blue. I was so used to talking to myself that I forgot how strange it might sound to another person. He and I were spending Sunday morning together. Sprawled out on the velvet sofa, he'd been reading Saturday's Vancouver Sun and Lloyd Dykk's bad-tempered review of The Vancouver Playhouse production of Shakespeare's *The Tempest*. Robby was having his 3rd cup of strong, black coffee and munching on a large Cadbury's chocolate bar. I was sitting in my comfy leather chair, sipping tea and going through Michael Kerr's textbook on family assessment, failing to concentrate on the task.

"Oh, sorry. Thinking aloud."

"About?" Robby folded the newspaper and left in on the coffee table and looked over at me.

"I want to go to Caracas this August," I said firmly.

"I know that. So?"

"I'm worried that I won't qualify, and part of me is *as* worried that I will."

"I know that, too." Robby took a big bite of chocolate and chewed for a bit before continuing. "Competing's still a messy business for you, isn't it?"

"I don't think I was ever built for it compared to other swimmers. I mean, I love to swim, but I have an ambivalent relationship with competing. If I'm well and fit, it's mostly okay, but when I'm out of sorts it's a whole new game."

"I don't have to ask if you're out of sorts, do I?" Robby asked anyway. "Even the other night, when we are all out for pizza, I could tell that you're stressed. Maybe 'cause of Pete? Even though he's better, you've still gotta be worried about him."

"Well," I started. *Of course I was worried about Pete.*

"At dinner, I saw how you looked at him. You love Pete, don't you?"

Robby's comment took me by surprise. "Love him? Yes, but not like I love you," I managed to say. I certainly had my times of infatuation with Pete. And, there was a time that I was smitten with him beyond words, but I didn't feel a romantic love for him since Robby and I started seeing each other.

"Hey, it's okay. Loving Pete doesn't bruise my ego," Robby said calmly.

"Robby, it's just I've thought that Pete was a kind of gay super-hero," I confessed. "I thought he was indestructible. But, I was wrong. Like my father, with illness, he's much less than what he used to be."

"Or more than what he was," Robby added, getting up from the sofa and stretching as he paced in the room.

"Meaning?"

"Well, think about it. We've got this killer plague, taking us out in the prime of our lives. Gay men are dealing with their mortality in their 20s or 30s — 50 years earlier than they should be — when they're meant to be living life to the fullest. We've never been challenged with anything like this. It's unparalleled, and from what we're hearing, it's the beginning of an epidemic with no remedy. What Pete's doing shows incredible character, doesn't it? To face AIDS with courage instead of resignation? That doesn't diminish him; it only makes him and the others braver and stronger. It's the ultimate of tests. People like Pete are showing us what gays are made of. He gets my respect, whether or not he's Superman." Robby stopped pacing and crouched down beside me, putting into words the things that eluded me.

"And what's going on puts my father's heart surgery into perspective. I know it's been risky and dangerous, but he's recovering. Maybe it's a long process, but he'll get all the treatment, the medications and the support he needs." *Pete wasn't offered home care or a nutritionist or a litany of specialists to get him back to health.*

"Yes, he'll steadily improve until he's back to a degree of normalcy, won't he?"

"Yeah, and I don't think my mother understands the difference. She's pissed that I'm not as involved with my father as she'd like. It's partly because we hafta look after Pete." I took a sip of my cooled tea and went on. "I mean, the reason why I get so stirred up about Pete and the others has to do with their vulnerability." Robby's quiet attention inspired me to continue. "There's no operation, no drug, no support or magic potion to make them better. Just the cold reality of what's next — like lung infections that don't resolve, cancers that attack the immune system, that horrible wasting. I don't want to negate my father's situation, but he's had a pretty long life already. For people like Pete, and for younger people, their future's been cut … no, their future's been stolen. It's massively unfair."

"Exactly. Isn't youth all about having a future?" Robby asked rhetorically.

"And what can we do? I'm not used to being helpless. I feel as impotent as Rock Hudson on his wedding night to Phyllis Gates."

Robby laughed at my reference before continuing.

"That's why we have to find a way to affirm life," Robby stated emphatically.

"What do you mean?" I asked, curious to understand Robby's statement. "Affirm to who?"

"To everyone who thinks that this epidemic doesn't really matter to them — the gay *and* non-gay community." Robby's voice rose with excitement. "We gotta get a message to the mainstream; a political message. Maybe it's through media, or protests or marches. Maybe it's doing some volunteer stuff with AIDS Vancouver. And maybe it's none of those things. But somehow, we gotta bring attention in a way that draws people in. Shows 'em we're not disposable and that we count as much as anyone, healthy or sick. Even with this plague, we aren't going away without a fight. We've organized before, we know we can do it again. That guy from AV was right — it *is* a call to arms." Robby took the last bite of his chocolate bar.

"You're a bit of a provocateur, aren't you?" I asked, marvelling at my boyfriend's activist leanings. "How do you suggest that we carry out this —"

"I dunno yet," Robby interrupted, "but first, let's consider your earlier comment about impotence." He stood from his crouched position, and moved his hands across my chest, stroking downwards to my groin, where something was rapidly stirring.

"Uh huh?" I asked innocently.

"Well,' he said, bending so that he could smother my mouth with seductive kisses that tasted deliciously of sweet mocha, "I'm hoping that was merely a metaphor."

41

On The Cool Side

The last days of April were dissolving in the endless rains across the city. Though wet, it brought forth cherry blossoms, looking like clouds of frothy pink candy floss. Other trees turned a vibrant emerald green and provided a comforting haven for hundreds of thousands of birds. The air was fresh with the fragrance of new growth and the scent was carried by the oncoming ocean winds. When the sun sporadically graced us with an appearance, its light stretched out longer, the decreasing evenings reduced by a few more minutes every week. I was also stretched out — by my flexibility coach, now that I was back in official training at the pool. A no-nonsense woman, Charlotte was Polish, having come to Vancouver a decade earlier to work as a physical therapist, which she was not licensed to do in Canada. Instead, she'd made a name for herself helping out with dry land exercises and stretches that I could only call torturous. She had my arms behind my back, both wrists held together and was pulling them up. Way up. I was grunting in pain and sweating through my tee-shirt.

"You're tight like husband's money belt," she stated.

"What?" I asked, not getting the reference. Charlotte's English was a little broken, which made for some occasionally mistaken, but usually humorous exchanges.

She pulled my arms and shoulders higher until they released the tension. "You okay now." Charlotte let go, and I dropped my hands to my side, then shook the pain away.

"We have work on hips." Charlotte pointed at the blue mat in the gym. "Drop to one knee. I pull you apart like roasted chicken." Then she chortled a bit. "I go easy. I go easy on men," she added. "Let's go."

Many people don't know that swimming is more than sheer muscle power. At a high level, it also entails being very flexible. I was fortunate, because in some key areas — mostly my shoulders and torso — I had been "bendy" for as long as I'd been swimming. I also maintained good flexion in my ankles, though my whip kick (for the breaststroke) demonstrated poor flexibility and limited external rotation of the hip joint. This was essential for a good whip kick and my inflexibility helped to explain why this stroke was my nemesis. Problem was, I swam the Individual Medley, and needed to knock off 100 meters in the breast portion of the event, where I consistently fell behind. I compensated with faster times in all other parts, which helped me stay competitive. (Ann Ottenbrite was an example of a breaststroker with amazing power in her kick which had a short dolphin kick at the end. I attempted to emulate, but could never approximate her incredible propulsion nor style.) Because of my shortcomings, I devoted extra time and effort just to stay in any competition. I included a powerful finish in the freestyle, where I "turned on the jets," as Lara described the races in which she watched me compete.

Charlotte had me on my back with my feet together and was pushing my knees down to the mat. I grimaced, gasped, perspired and mugged, but it didn't impress her at all. Nor did my various machinations get her to let up the pressure.

"It hurt bad?" she inquired.

"Yes, very bad," I strained to respond.

"That good," she happily replied, seemingly delighted in my pain. After one last pump to my groin, she clapped her hands together in triumph and said, "We're done," and left me in a wet puddle of sweat. I let out a huge sigh of relief, but nevertheless I was limbered-up for my 6-kilometre swim.

It was odd walking out onto the pool deck and getting ready to swim. In my personal life, there were friends like Pete and Lara — and of course Robby — who related to me (and I to them) in a warm, compassionate and interested manner. And while I was all-business in the water as a way to distance myself from my teammates, part of me wanted them to offer — I don't know — a handshake, a hug, a "welcome back" or even just a smile. But, that didn't happen. There was a good chance that my own aloof attitude to other swimmers was the reason. I'd set myself up years ago to remain unapproachable so that no one could discover my sexuality, but it was tiresome and cost me potential friendships. I liked several of the men and women I swam with — and I saw them twice a day, up to 6 days per week for the past 3 years, but never attempted to get to know them beyond the cursory. *Face it, there's a lot of your father in you. How sad is that?* I must have appeared to be a one-dimensional character. And, if I was out to the swimming community, what could the repercussions be?

I started my swim with 500 meters of warm-up, 2.5-kilometres freestyle, 1-kilometre kick, then the main part, blistering repeats of the 400 metre IM for the next 2 kilometres. With the exception of the breaststroke, my swim went reasonably well, and my times were mostly competitive.

With things more stable in my personal life, swimming seemed less of a challenge. My relation with Thompson was still on the cool side. His coaching was minimal at best. My hunch was that he was waiting for me to fail at the upcoming swim meet so that he could boot me off the team. Swimming, perhaps like all organizations, is in part political. Now that Thompson thought that I "didn't like girls", I was imagining all kinds of lurid scenes. Both morning and evening swims were decent, with my times beginning to come back to where I was a year ago. If Thompson was pleased, there was no mention of it to me. *That's unimportant. What counts is that I'm pleased, right?* Right.

By the time I got back home at 8 PM, I was too tired to make a proper meal. After hanging up my swim gear in the washroom, I lurched to the kitchen, hauled out the peanut butter, spread it thickly on some crunchy Dutch Oven bread and topped it with sliced bananas. Standing at the counter, I ate my dinner. I poured a large glass of milk, drank half, poured more, then sat down on the sofa and turned on the radio. The CBC was playing jazz, which I loved. I stretched out on the sofa, listening to Count Basie. I was still hungry, but before I could think about making another sandwich, I fell fast asleep.

42

The Fairies Go For a Walk

School was going well. I was learning a tremendous amount by working in the clinic, where student therapists turned family therapy theory into practice. I saw a variety of clients with an equally impressive array of presenting concerns. Paradoxically, I found working with families, rather than individuals, to be not only more interesting, but was much easier, as all perspectives of the story were in the room. Perhaps because of my father's aloof demeanour, I was mindful of how I approached my questions with men who seemed similar — less communicative, distant, irritable. Of course, family therapy is all about having excellent questions wedded to the elegant theory that Dr. Murray Bowen provided. Questions helped to do reframe a client's experience, promote awareness and move towards their expressed objectives. Always in the background, there was theory. *Theory, theory, theory!* It was clear that this would be a life-long work for me. Therapists work at their craft with a deep dedication, consistently upgrading and acquiring greater skills, with clinical supervision and mentoring required to ensure that the "product" being provided was not only helpful, but grounded in practice, theory and ethics. When competitive swimming ended, I looked forward to working full-time and continuing my therapy training on a part-time basis until all of the pieces were complete — but in fact being a therapist was really a career-long endeavour. It was important to me that I had a plan for myself that would carry me through life — one that would hold my interest and reflect my belief that the provision of therapy could make a positive difference. Most certainly, that was the intent. However, in a city where the spectre of death hovered like a Vancouver raincloud, planning ahead was tempered with questions. Would I and others be provided with a long life? Or would life be severed prematurely, like the unnerving deaths of young men across North America and Europe? In 1983, it was impossible to know which way the dice would roll.

"Surprised?" Robby asked from the kitchen as I came through the door after class. I had about 90 minutes before I had to leave for my second swim practice. As Robby and I didn't have each other's keys, it was a surprise for me to see him in my apartment. I dropped my books on the coffee table and gave him a hug.

"Um, very. What's all this?" I asked after spying pieces of cut vegetables, scraped fresh ginger and the remains of several zested limes scattered along the chopping block. On the counter, white cubes of moist tofu were heaped beside a jar of opened Skippy peanut butter. With the exception of the onion that Robby had been dicing, all looked ready to be heaped into a large frying pan. He went back to his onion as he answered my question.

"Tofu stir-fry with peanut and lime sauce." Robby answered, looking slightly smug. "I haven't been around very much," he explained, "and so I broke into your place to make dinner."

"Mrs. McBride let you in again, eh?"

Robby answered, "Of course. Besides, she couldn't possibly say no to a famous director, could she?"

"Oh, has she heard about your Agatha Christie triumph?"

"You mean the impressive *'Mousetrap, with All You Can Eat Schnitzel?'"* he quipped.

"That's the one," I agreed. "I can't recall the last time you made us supper."

"It's all very *'Play Misty for Me'*, isn't it?" He was referring to the movie where Jessica Walter stalked the hapless Clint Eastwood and tried to knife him in the final scene.

"Should I be worried with how you're holding that French knife?"

Robby gave me his most diabolical look and raised his eyebrows menacingly.

"Well," he waved the blade of the knife contemplatively.

"You'll never get away with it," I said firmly.

"Hmm, you're right." He smiled and went back to chopping the large yellow onion, his eyes watering and turning red. "The sacrifices I make for you," he said as he dabbed his eyes which made them water further.

"You know, the more we see each other, the more Jewish you're becoming."

"Don't be such a putz and help me with this," he joked as he turned the gas stove to a high flame. After sequentially dumping in each veggie into the smoking-hot pan, the ginger, tofu, soya sauce and peanut butter were added as the food sizzled. Lime juice was squeezed on the cooked concoction. It smelled delicious and he placed the mixture in a large white bowl, topped with chopped cilantro and toasted sesame seeds.

A few minutes after we tucked into the tofu stir-fry — with chopsticks, no less — I said, "You know, speaking of stalkers …" pausing to swallow a large mouthful.

"Yes?" Robby looked at me quizzically and with anticipation.

"I saw Dr. Deth at the pool a couple Saturday's ago when I was teaching." I struggled to coordinate the chopsticks and dropped an unattainable piece of broccoli.

"Well, that's hardly stalking. Maybe he lives around there." Robby ground fresh pepper generously onto his dinner.

"Yes, he does."

"How did you —-"

"Because between lessons, he came over and started gabbing."

"Uh huh …" Robby chewed vigorously on some crunchy peppers.

"That's when he told me that he lived nearby, on Thurlow. But that's rather uncanny for him to be at the pool at the same time as me, isn't it?"

"Well, not really. The West End's not a big place. Didn't he ask about your father?"

"No, he was asking if Pete had been my boyfriend and wanted to know more about the woman with the red hair. He said that she looked familiar," I ventured.

"Perhaps he's seen Lara singing before."

"Maybe. Lara's pretty well-known in Vancouver. Then Deth asked me if I wanted to go on his boat," I blurted.

"Pass the soya sauce, please. He's got a boat?"

"Apparently. He asked me to go for coffee and if I could give him some swim lessons." I passed Robby a bottle of soya, and he shook some sauce on the last remaining bites of his stir-fry.

"Oh, of course," Robby said confidently. "He wants to fuck you." Robby finished his tofu and took his plate to the kitchen. "More?"

"No, thanks. So you don't think that Deth was just being friendly?"

"How many straight men come up to other men to ask for a coffee date because they want to be platonic friends?" Robby asked rhetorically. He chuckled for a moment. I rose from the table with my unfinished plate and scraped it into the trash bin.

"He also said that he liked my shoulders." I suddenly felt embarrassed.

"He said that?" Robby looked surprised as he stood at the counter near the sink.

"He touched 'em and said that it must have taken a lot of work, or something like that," I recalled.

"Hmm, that's ballsy. That also seals the deal. My hunch is that he wants to put you in a leather sling for the weekend." Robby ran the hot water in the sink and squeezed in some Sunlight soap.

"I prefer my leather chair. To be fair, he also asked if my friends would like to go boating. But, I don't want to have coffee with him. And I'd prefer not to give my father's cardiologist tips on his backstroke. It's just ... wacky."

"Completely understandable; it crosses a boundary. Send over the glasses." I collected glasses from the table and dumped them in the sink with the plates and some cutlery. I turned off the hot water and grabbed a sponge to do the washing up.

"Besides, should I really be thanking him for *saving* my father's life?"

"*Shep,*" Robby chided me. "What did you tell him?"

"I told him I'd give him a few free lessons. I dunno, maybe that was stupid. I didn't really commit to anything, including his boat idea. I found the whole situation a little creepy, to be honest. But maybe I was overreacting. I tend to do that." I washed, rinsed, then stacked the glasses and plates onto a wooden dish drain rack then placed the frying pan into the sink to soak for a few minutes.

"So," Robby paused for a few moments before continuing. "Didn't you tell him that you had a boyfriend?" He leaned up against the counter, watching my response.

"He's my father's doctor, Robby. I can't. Who knows what he might say to my dad." I fetched the Brillo pad and started to scrub the burned pieces of vegetables and tofu from the skillet. "And he's never said that he's gay. Maybe his forwardness is a European thing?"

"How 'bout picking up men in a pool? I'd say it's a universally *gay* thing."

I glanced at my Timex: 4:40. "I gotta run soon." I dried my hands on a tea towel.

"Got another surprise for you."

"What's that?"

Robby collected his weathered backpack. "I'm going swimming, too."

The Aquatic Centre had to keep lanes open other than for the swim team. Robby could take a dip in one of the alternate lanes. He wasn't a particularly good swimmer but was an excellent runner. The two activities required a different skill set.

"You're joking, right?"

"Nope, got everything here. Thought we could go down together; burn off this tofu. It's sitting in my gut like lead. And it's a great night for a walk. How does that sound?"

"Great! Let me grab my stuff and we're off quicker than Elton John's towel in a men's sauna."

The walk along Beach Avenue with my boyfriend was made even more special by the dazzling sky, shot with streaks of vermillion and orange above a calm dark-blue ocean.

"This sure isn't Sudbury," Robby enthused as we could barely take our eyes off the phenomenal sight of a scarlet sun blazing its final hour of light. Affectionately, he took my hand as we continued to quickly stroll along the street, running down the hill to the seawall, and observing the staggering sky. I was apprehensive for him to be clutching my hand as we walked, but many male-female couples were doing the same. *So why not us?* I put my internalized homophobia on hold and in the next few minutes we approached the Aquatic Centre. *After all, we've passed lots of other couples without any weird reaction, so there's no reason to wor —*

"I knew it!" A voice boomed from the Sunset Beach parking lot. Robby and I followed the voice. Standing beside his van, with bags of equipment and several other swimmers in tow, stood Coach Thompson.

"Stamp's a fag!" one of the male swimmers shouted. Several of the younger women swimmers giggled as they saw us. I uncoupled from my boyfriend's hand and stopped dead in my tracks.

"He's a fairy!" one of the girls cried, pointing her finger. Other girls started shouting out "faggot" and "gay-boy" and laughed with scorn. Robby looked at me briefly and mouthed, "Christ". Then he took several deliberate strides towards them, which appeared to take the group aback. Raising his hand that he clenched into a fist, he said, "Listen, you backwoods breeders," he snarled with a look that would liquefy glass. "I'll give you one warning to keep your ignorant mouths shut." Robby's tone was intimidating and his menacing attitude silenced the swimmers immediately. Thompson glared at me, his beady eyes searing right into mine.

"Keep your distance," he commanded to Robby. "Stamp, get your ass in the pool," he directed his terse words at me. "We'll talk about this after practice. Move it."

I didn't know what to do, say or think. I did know that in a few minutes, several young people would be telling every swimmer on the national team that their teammate was gay. Robby turned to me with a defiant stare as he shook his head in disbelief. "I'm gonna wait for you." I nodded at him and made my way to the pool. After nearly 20 years of hiding under water, my jig was up.

43

Put The Bite On

Subsequent to a shaky and poor swim practice, Thompson ordered me into his tiny office. I kept him waiting, having showered and dressed leisurely. I told Robby in the upstairs lobby to go back home.

"No, I think I should be there when —"

"Nope, I'm going to speak with Thompson alone."

"But what are you gonna —"

"I haven't figured it out yet. I'll call you later tonight. Oh, by the way ... *backwoods breeders?*"

"I used it in Sudbury more than a few times." Robby knew how to stand up to bullies.

"Seemed quite effective." I smiled. After giving him a hug, I walked over to my coach's office. His door was partly open and he did not look happy. When he saw me, he rose, closed the door, locked it and told me to sit. I declined and stood instead.

"This is how it's gonna go," he began. "My swimmers will tell every parent in this city that their teammate is a faggot. And those parents are going to be calling me and complaining that the man, naked in the showers with their son, is a deviant cocksucker."

"Oh, and which man is that?" I asked boldly.

Thompson looked up at me, completely startled. "What did you say?"

"I asked you a plain-enough question. I'm not — as you so poetically put it — the only deviant cocksucker around here, am I?" I smiled knowingly.

Thompson's colour changed, the blood quickly draining from his face.

"If you know what's good for you, you'd better watch your fuckin' mouth." Thompson pointed his finger at me threateningly.

"Because, you see," I continued, ignoring his caution, "I have some fascinating accounts of a swim coach who likes to frequent Stanley Park at dusk." As I said those words, Thompson froze. "Lees Trail, actually. I'm sure parents would be interested to hear all about it, not to mention ... you're married, aren't you?" I managed a devious smile.

"You little shit," he said under his breath. Thompson had the look of murder in his small eyes.

"Now it's *my* turn to tell you how it's gonna go," I said, my voice brimming with confidence. "I've given my life to swimming, and I refuse to be railroaded by you. I'm gonna finish my stint on this team — a place that I earned. I'll leave on my terms, not yours." Thompson's glare made my skin crawl. "Got it?" I demanded boldly.

"Get outta here," Thompson said, turning his head away from me.

"It's been such a pleasure, Coach," I said sarcastically, exiting his office and stepping out of the Aquatic Centre in utter elation.

"Shep!" Robby's voice cried out. He had been waiting for me just outside the glass doors of the building. "What happened in there?"

"I just put the bite on my swim coach," I said, surprising myself. In a few short minutes, I explained my meeting with Thompson to Robby.

"Jesus. You just extorted Tom Thompson." Robby was astounded. "So you actually saw him cruising Lees Trail?"

I was worried that I was guilty by association, but I continued to tell Robby my tale.

"Oh, yeah. Unmistakable. I hid behind a tree and watched for probably 10 minutes — just to make sure, of course."

"That makes you a bit of a voyeur, you know." Robby smiled as we slung our backpacks over our shoulders and started walking on Beach Avenue.

"Does it?" I asked, concerned about what he thought.

"Hmm," he murmured, grabbing my hand tightly as we strolled home, unconcerned about who might see. "That's kinda hot."

44

The Letter

The next few days of swim practice included more many taunts and sneers than I could recall. I was also asked if "I had AIDS yet?" by several male and female swimmers who, I suspect, hoped that their open bullying might make me want to leave the team. I did my best to ignore what I could, perhaps more focused than I had been in more than a year. I was able to tune out the contempt that select swimmers had for me. At school, the overwhelming response to me being gay was supportive. The difference between the pool and class was immeasurable. I was advised to "stick it out", with the belief that things would settle. When I got home Wednesday morning after practice, there was a letter in my mailbox that I was apprehensive about opening. It was from Swim Canada. I carried it up to my apartment. I had a sick sense about the contents. Dropping my swim gear on the floor, I opened the envelope.

```
April 25, 1983
Dear Mr. Stamp,
We regret to inform you that effective imme-
diately, your contract has been terminated
with Swim Canada. The reason for this is due
to consistently decreased performances, poor
meet results and absenteeism over the past
12 months as reported to us by Mr. Tom Thomp-
son. We appreciate your past contributions
and wish to acknowledge the importance of the
Canadian records you set in the 400 IM and the
400 Freestyle in 1979 and the Canadian record
broken in the 200 Butterfly in 1982. The NSC
of Canada will honour your contract with a
payout (cheque enclosed) for the remainder
of your term.
Best of luck in your future endeavours.
Sincerely,
Jordon West
Cc, Tom Thompson
```

I read it 3 times. "Thompson, you're one dirty bastard," I said aloud. I looked at the cheque. Nearly $6K worth of a settlement, but not nearly enough to compensate for the humiliation. I folded the letter and placed it and the cheque in a folder on the dining cabinet, deeply troubled that I wouldn't be going to Caracas to end my swim career in distinction. The letter had been written one day after my incident with my coach, so he must have got to work quickly to dismiss me. *Nice.* I plunked myself down on the sofa. The early morning sun was streaming through windows that needed cleaning. *Guess I'll have some extra time to do that, now.* I felt a mixture of disbelief, embarrassment and relief. *Suspension was one thing; being terminated is an entirely different outcome.* I thought Thompson wouldn't have risked moving ahead with his plan, but I was wrong. *Thompson used his power and influence, didn't he? What do I tell my parents? Jezus, I can only imagine how disappointed they're going to be.* I blew a long breath from my lungs. I felt restless. Still dressed in shorts and a tee-shirt, I grabbed my keys and headed out for a walk. *It's okay, you'll figure this out.* I bounded down the 3 flights of stairs and left my apartment, heading for the spot I adored at Second Beach — the tiny cove just past the empty saltwater pool. The seawall was already busy with runners and walkers getting their morning exercise. I trotted along, taking in the slightly sweet scent of air as I ruminated on my firing — what else could I call it? Of course, I'd been underperforming, but my times had been improving. I believed that the real reason for being terminated was my knowledge of Thompson's foray into the Fairy Forest. I'd failed to understand his position in the greater scheme of things. *I'm just a swimmer; Thompson was on top.* I could appeal, but that would bring more attention to the matter. *What's wrong with that? Well, many things. Can't I be satisfied with the good things that have happened? But the ending was not what I had planned; it's so demeaning.* I slowed my pace as I came up to the cove, luckily devoid of any other people. The worn logs, scattered along the beach, beckoned me to sit on their smooth surface. After finding a spot, I stretched my fatigued body and gazed out at beautiful English Bay. To the southwest were the shores of Kits, and further out, green Point Grey. Boats shared the bay with massive freighters, plying in and out of the harbour. The visuals helped to centre me. The waters were calm. The sun on my face was warm. I closed my eyes. I heard the sound of screaming gulls flying overhead. The ocean lapped against the shore soothingly. Any noise from the seawall seemed to fade away to a low mumble. I kicked off my shoes and removed my socks, feeling the cool, white sands in the crevices of my feet.

Though only late April, the sun nevertheless heated the air sufficiently for me to feel a trickle of sweat at my temple. I pulled off my tee-shirt, instantly feeling cool air on my chest. For a few moments, I let the sun warm my bare upper body. I looked around; I remained alone in the small cove. I stood, then removed my shorts. I had no underwear on, having come from my practice. *My last practice.* I took another brief glance around me, and noting I was still alone, carefully moved to the water. I felt the coldness of the ocean on my feet, icing them instantly. As I continued to move deeper into the salty ocean, the familiar shock took place. Even though I knew it was going to be frigid, it surprised me. Naked in the sea, I pushed off, first with a few breaststrokes, clearing any potential underwater rocks. The water was cold, but certainly toasty in comparison to the many ice-baths I'd had. *Dropped from the national team. Fuck.* I was getting used to the temperature, and started the front crawl. *The tide must be on the way out. The water's really working with me, carrying me along; not having to swim with much effort. There, I can feel the rip of the tide.* After swimming for a few minutes, I looked with un-goggled eyes to determine my location. I was surprised to see how far I'd swum in a short period of time. Pushing my long hair from my eyes, I treaded water comfortably, looking out towards Vancouver Island. I thought of the many times I'd come to the beach and found myself inexplicably moving into the ocean. The water truly was my medicine. Embraced by the sea, it rejuvenated me, perhaps healed my hurts. Flipping over, I viewed the lush green forest of Stanley Park, then turned to view the Gulf Islands far across the bay. That's when the idea struck me like a bolt. After a few minutes, I swam back to the shore, convincing myself that my audacious plan was captivatingly clever. *Or you're an utter dreamer. Which is it going to be?*

45

The Audacious Plan

Like the Agatha Christie murder mystery that my boyfriend had directed, the players gathered, curious to know why I'd asked them to my apartment on Thursday evening. At 7 PM, Pete, Lara, Mrs. McBride and Robby were seated in the living room, enjoying some cheese, olives, wedges of melon, wine and an incredible loaf of bread from Paris Bakery, studded with seeds and herbs. I'd told them — Robby of course knew — about my termination from the national team. The notification was met with disparaging comments about Thompson, but I took responsibility for my lacklustre performances in the past year. Though it was a cordial collection of my friends, there was another topic that I was about to bring to their attention.

"Okay," I began slowly. "There's something else that I wanted to tell you. Something that sounds a little, umm … out there." I shuffled in my seat and took a sip of orange juice. "With all that's going on right now, health-wise … I wanted to find a way to bring attention to something — in the way I can." I looked around at my friends. They'd stopped noshing and were heeding my words. "After that community meeting, we talked a bit about what we can do — in practical terms, like volunteering at AV. But I'm suggesting something that has little to do with being practical." I hesitated, knowing that my next few words would sound, well, nuts.

"What are you proposing, Sunshine?" Lara asked as she put down her wine.

"I want to do a distance swim."

"Dear, do you mean a swim-a-thon? Swimming laps for dollars?" Mrs. McBride queried curiously.

I took a breath. "No, I mean a distance swim across the strait." The room grew still for a few moments as the words settled in.

"Pardon me," Lara said, "but hasn't a swim across the strait been done before?"

"Yes," I answered. "From Nanaimo, a much shorter distance, but never one from Ladysmith."

"Hold on." Lara looked at me in disbelief. "Are you suggesting a swim from Ladysmith across the Strait of Georgia to the Mainland?"

"Yes, exactly. I figured it's an 80-kilometre swim." I noticed the odd look on my friend's faces before continuing. "Like Lara said, there's been a few crossings from Nanaimo, but Ladysmith is considerably further. No one's attempted that."

"My dear," Mrs. McBride piped in, a famous former distance swimmer in her own right, "I can assure you that there's a reason why. Forgive me, but it's daft. There's so much that would work against you," she said, then counted them out on her fingers. "Wicked tides, huge swells, cold water temperature, ships, seals, even killer whales. And the sheer exhaustion of such a venture that would take … how long?"

"Two days and one night," I said. "I've done rough calculations."

"And how about swimming in the night? I don't wish to be a Doubting Thomas, but …" She was lost for words as she tried to comprehend my proposal.

"I know, it sounds wacky, but in training I swim up to 80 kilometres a week. I'll just be doing that distance at one time. It can work." Casting a look around the room, I noticed dubious faces. "I mean, I haven't figured this out precisely, but we could ask donors to contribute money for every kilometre completed. And it'll bring attention to AIDS and those people suffering, not to mention generating funds for AIDS Vancouver. Like that Director said at the meeting, there's going to be hundreds, if not thousands, of people right here that'll need support. We can help, with swim donations going directly to services. We could raise huge money, if we do it right."

"I get *why* you want to bring attention to this, and it's incredibly dramatic, but I agree with Mrs. McBride — it's folly to think you — or anyone — could pull this off," Robby declared. By the look of the group, I presumed that others thought the same way.

"I know it sounds improbable, but ..." I gathered my thoughts. "With all the right people on board — literally *onboard* — this is possible."

"Who are the right people?" Lara asked.

"Well, Pete can be the media and press contact to get coverage. He could do some promotional stuff and generate a buzz. I'm still on the books as a Canadian record holder; that's gotta count for something — notoriety, at least. And doing something that hasn't been done before? Swimming to raise awareness and money for AIDS?"

The group remained unimpressed with my argument, with the exception of Pete, whose interest seemed to swell like the waters of the strait.

"Go on," Pete said, showing his pique by fixing his deep-brown eyes on mine.

"And I'm sure that when we pull this together we can create a catchy name."

"I've got one. Swim for Life," Pete announced. "I mean, just off the cuff."

"See?" I smiled at Pete. "This is why we need him."

Pete's eyes lit up with excitement. *Perhaps he needs this project as much as me.*

"And we need Mrs. McBride," I commented, "who completed her own open water swim and almost beat Percy Norman in —"

"Dear," she interrupted, "that was only 10 kilometres, not 80 kilometres or more." She shook her head. "Deep water is cold, dear … very cold. We had to prepare for the temperature; it takes many weeks to do that correctly. You *have* heard of hypothermia?" Mrs. McBride was being tongue in cheek, but it was a serious concern.

"Yes, but I read that the swimmers that cross the English Channel smear fat all over their bodies to keep warm. And I've got the time to prepare properly for the conditions. If the summer's been hot, the top layer of the sea really warms up. I've been doing some research on climate patterns. Currents and tides can also help move me forward, too."

"It's possible, she mused. "However, tides also reverse, dear, and twice per day. This distance is also twice as far as the Channel."

"Yes, that's what makes it so captivating … and why I'll need your help to prepare for the swim, maybe help me understand how to manage with the cold water like you did. And, of course, to keep us organized."

"Well, dear, I am *very* organized," she puffed proudly.

I figured I was swaying her, so I spoke to Robby with growing enthusiasm. "And Robby can *direct* the swim crossing. Really, the water's the setting for a real drama."

"What about me?" Lara asked plaintively.

"You're going to be my moral support in the water," I said lovingly.

"In the water?" Lara looked horrified, thinking that I was asking her to jump into the drink with me — in fact, she was a very good swimmer.

"The boat, Lara. I need you in the boat."

"I tend to get a little nauseous in boats."

"There's medication for that. I hoped that you could talk and maybe even sing to me from the pilot boat to keep me alert."

"What type of boat?"

"We'll need a powerboat and a pilot who knows about tides and currents." I directed my question at Pete and Lara. "You two must know some sailors, right?"

"I resent your assumption," she said defensively. "Well, there was this Vice Admiral — he *said* he was a Vice Admiral — from Halifax, but after a weekend with me he went back to his wife," Lara said, with others raising their brows with their curiosity aroused. With our eyes on Lara, she said, "I didn't know about Mavis. Who can blame me? I liked the white uniform."

"Ah, okay," I said, then turned to Pete with expectation.

"I don't think you'll wanna know about my last Querelle," Pete winked. "Though I now can do a few rope tricks." Lara groaned as Pete continued. "Hey, they can come in handy. But, you're right, you need an experienced mariner to navigate you through the strait. You don't wanna make a wrong heading and find yourself in Taipei. That's not a good place to land."

Mrs. McBride chirped up, "The vessel must also be outfitted with powerful lighting at times of darkness. That's when it's most dangerous for the swimmer and the boat."

"Yes," Pete agreed enthusiastically. "We'd need a well-equipped craft and a savvy sailor, and preferably one with a uniform. I mean, if Lara would like." Pete's devilish smile reminded me of a different time.

Lara shook her head. "Forget the uniform. We'd need a skilled sailor," she surmised.

"Huh, there's actually someone that just came to mind," I said. "Perhaps he's not the savviest, but I'll inquire."

"How long would you need to train for?" Robby asked.

"Well, we have 3 months, which should be more than enough time. In order for me to make landing at Second Beach on BC Day, I'd have to begin the swim roughly 40 hours before, which is Friday, July 30th."

"Doing this on a holiday's a good idea, Sunshine," Lara said. "There'd be more interest on a long weekend, and there's bound to be hundreds at Ceperly park."

"I thought so. And now that school's nearly finished, I'll have oodles of time to dedicate to training. English Bay is a couple of blocks away. I can swim along the shoreline to the Lion's Gate Bridge."

"But, don't get close to the narrows, dear, or you'll get caught up in a dangerous riptide," Mrs. McBride added with concern in her voice.

"I understand that I'll need my wits about me. Even swimming in the bay should help me adjust to the strait water temperature, right, Mrs. McBride?"

"Well, yes, it shouldn't be too much colder in open water. As long as you are swimming well, your body will generate some heat to offset the water's temperature."

"I shouldn't need a boat until the day of the crossing —"

"No dear," Mrs. McBride interrupted. "You'll need several days of practice with the boat and the full crew. All efforts must be seamless in the boat and may require much rehearsal. We must practice for every possibility — what to do with any unanticipated changes — so that we are completely prepared for the crossing."

"I know about preparation. I'm not a novice," I said in an attempt to defend myself. "I'm a well-trained swimmer." I was doing my best to make for a convincing argument.

"Yes, dear, in a 50-metre pool. It's not the same as being in open water for 2 days and a long night. A challenge of this type cannot be underestimated." Mrs. McBride's tone was serious.

"I know it's a challenge, but with your help, I think that we can do it."

The room was solemn. Each person was looking at the other, in contemplation of a perilous crossing.

"I couldn't do this alone," I said quietly. More silence. "Whadya say?"

Robby was the first to speak. "There's a lot to consider, Shep. You'll have to see a doctor to be looked over."

"I expected that; no problem," I nodded vigorously. "Dr. Taylor's terrific, he'll check me out."

"Logistically, there's likely permits, consents and releases to satisfy." Robby turned to Pete. "Can you contact Shep's cousin, Ryan Stamp, before we do anything? He's a lawyer."

"Of course," Pete agreed. "I'd be delighted." He looked at my landlady. "There's probably a whole bunch of legalities with open water swimming, right Mrs. McBride?"

"Oh yes. During the swim, he can't touch the boat or anyone else. He'll need to pass a drug test, too. I expect Swim Canada will request an official on-board to verify the crossing."

"Swim Canada?" Robby asked. "That's ironic."

"How does he eat and drink?" Lara put forward. Of course, she was thinking with her stomach, the organ of which was a critical part of any endurance attempt.

"Food would have to be passed to him on a device, like a kick-board or pole. Fluids can be thrown to him in a bottle. It's very strict," Mrs. McBride said sharply. "Like I mentioned, if anyone touches him, he'll be disqualified straight away."

Robby added, "You'd be swimming in shipping lanes. Massive swells come from those freighters and BC Ferries. There's real risk. I'm not about to watch my boyfriend get swamped to his death in the middle of the night."

"That's never going —"

"If I'm directing this so-called drama, you have to agree if there's any trouble that we see or anticipate, the swim is stopped immediately."

"Tout suite," Lara added for extra emphasis.

"Absolutely no questions asked," Robby said firmly. "Understand?"

"Yes, of course," I agreed.

"We'll have to plan each hour of the swim — when you take breaks, when you'll eat and drink, how to rest treading in the water. How to ensure that you're not swallowing too much saltwater; it can cause terrible cramping, you know," Mrs. McBride noted.

"This is all so treacherous," Lara blurted.

"That's why the crew will be well-prepared and ready to assist in a heartbeat," I said, thinking of my father. "That'll minimize any risk."

"Sunshine, still …" Lara looked concerned.

"I don't have a death-wish; I wouldn't be suggesting this if I didn't think there was a good chance of completing it." I felt a surge of anxiety at the thought of what I was proposing. "If anything bad happens, a crew member can simply toss me a line and pull me back into the boat. I'll be swimming with help just a few arm lengths away," I added. "Don't forget, I'm a lifeguard; I know how to manage my safety."

"A very stubborn lifeguard," Robby added.

"I might be stubborn, but I'm not a fool — contrary to what my statistics teacher told me."

Robby smiled at my comment. "It's true. He's horrible at math." After I provided more reassurances, the tide turned, at least in my living room.

"Even if we fail to complete the distance, we'll still bring attention to a crisis that's happening in our backyard. And with the best outcome, we'll raise funds for AV to distribute to those who need help." I waited to hear someone say that I was being ridiculously idealistic or naive, but after several moments of quiet contemplation, I could see the group was — albeit tentatively — accepting my audacious proposition. There was one part that I didn't share with the group, and that was that I also needed an opportunity to redeem myself after being ousted from the team, though it was just a small part of the plan. I wasn't a fatalist, but in my mind I thought that if I was one of those who was infected, this might be my last chance to do something important in the water. I listened carefully as Lara, Pete, Mrs. McBride and Robby started sounding out ideas about how to make an intrepid plan come to life. Looking around the living room, I saw a singer that got seasick, an elderly, frail woman whose own distance swimming event was 52 years earlier, a talent agent in potentially dangerous, if not fatal health and my director boyfriend, whose greatest achievement was a dinner theatre production of Agatha Christie in small-town northwestern Ontario. Perhaps one might consider us a rather odd group, however, there couldn't have been a more caring potential crew.

"All right," Robby posed. "We're going to need to do some thinking about this scheme; talk to some experts to see if this can be done."

"Sure. But I'll start training in the interim, okay?"

I noted the faces of the group. There was a mixture of excitement and disbelief in what I had proposed. Pete raised his glass of OJ.

"Swim for Life?"

The members of my alternate family raised their glasses of wine, and without missing a beat, announced together, "Swim for Life."

46

Begin Again

If I had not been unceremoniously terminated from the swim team, the first week of May would have found me competing at a huge swim meet in Calgary to qualify for Caracas. Instead, I was changing from my warm rain gear, stuffing my clothing into my rucksack, locking them up at the English Bay bathhouse — another type of bathhouse, mind you — and walking to the water's edge in a Speedo. I held onto a pair of goggles and looked out over the ocean. On my head I wore 2 rubber swim-caps over my earplugs. One of the areas where significant heat loss could occur was from my head, so I was hoping a double-wrap would help me stay warmer. Around my mid-section I strapped a running belt that held a large plastic bottle containing a blended drink of high-calorie anti-cramping concoction including banana, dates, orange juice, blueberries, peanut butter and skim milk powder. I tapped the starter on my hopefully water-proof Timex. My plan was to swim for 4 hours in the chilly waters of English Bay on a drizzly and grey morning. The beach didn't open until the Victoria Day long weekend which was 3 weeks away, so I had the water to myself, sans lifeguards. It would be quite a change from swimming laps in the pool, as Mrs. McBride had stated. Once I had braved the water past my groin, I pushed off and headed to open water. The shock of the water's temperature surprised me, and it initially made my head pound with pain. I seemed to adjust to it after 10 or 15 minutes of swimming front crawl, and I found that including a hundred metres of butterfly every so often was very useful, the exertion easily warming my body. The conditions of the water were gratefully calm, and I was able to avoid any swells of saltwater going down my throat. After going out a few hundred metres, I tried to swim parallel to the shore. It was not as easy as I hoped. I had a hard time with my bearings. I had to stop to see where I was in relation to where I needed to be. I used the towers of the West End as a point of reference, but to do so meant that I was looking back to where I'd swum, rather than being sure of where I was heading. Though the water had appeared to be very calm on shore, in the bay there was a swell that intensified the further out I went. In an hour I was moving up then down the rolling water with almost every stroke. I watched my hand position underwater during the front crawl, but my vision of the landscape was consistently obscured by fogging goggles and by the rising and falling of the ocean's swell. I thought I'd been swimming for at least 2 hours, but checking my Timex, only 70 minutes had elapsed. I stopped and treaded water using a water polo eggbeater kick. I tried to reach for my bottle, positioned on my back, but my hands were too cold to remove it from the Velcro strap. *Shit.* My feet were cramping and my face felt as though someone was rubbing ice all over it. My ears were ringing. I managed to rip open the Velcro and downed my drink as I moved my legs in the frigid ocean. Putting the empty bottle back, I took notice of where I was — about 200 metres from Third Beach. *Wow, this is close to where that huge wave hit me on the seawall. Focus ... what's the pace? That's about 2 kilometres an hour. That's about what I'd calculated. Not bad. It'll be easier to go further if the water's warmer. Then I'm on track, aren't I? Good. Now, go back and do it again.*

I didn't last for the full 4 hours during my first long ocean swim, but stopped and came ashore after 3 hours and an estimated 6 kilometres. I was shaking with cold, and despairingly a little motion sick from merely gentle swells. I staggered back onto dry land and ignored some of the startled looks from those people who had stopped to watch a crimson swimmer emerge from the bay. Walking on the sand, I realized that I couldn't feel my feet. I grabbed my bag from the locker and wrapped myself with a fluffy white towel. Shaking with cold, I pushed my numb feet into my Nikes, pulled on my fleecy shorts, sweatshirt, raincoat and teetered back to my apartment, my arms wrapped around my chilled body. I spent nearly an hour in a scalding-hot shower, and as the hot water billowed clouds of welcome steam, I thought of Robert Service's poem, *The Cremation of Sam McGee*. Needless to say, I wasn't feeling confident.

47

Baiting The Hook

For the first 3 weeks of May, I trod down to English Bay to swim, rain or shine — but mostly rain. I would be in the water 2 hours before daybreak, 4 times per week, steeling myself for a long and always challenging swim. The darkness was by far the most disjointing part of the swim, so I was glad that with each passing day there was an earlier sunrise. I had to become familiar with the disorientation of swimming without any light. In the time that I'd been training in the ocean, the weather was consistently the marker by which I had a good or bad swim. In the previous 12 or 13 swims, I'd been in torrential rains which warmed the top layer of the water, fought through choppy whitecaps that battered me and prevented much progress, swam atop rolling swells of 1-3 metres, which made me queasy and battled strong tides far before the First Narrows that nevertheless threatened to pull me into Burrard Inlet. Open water swimming put a great deal of tension on my shoulders, so I eased into the kilometres in a graduated manner. Interestingly, I didn't have much in the way of long-lasting muscular pain in my shoulders. I presumed that being in cold water may have prevented strain or inflammation of muscle tissue.

By the beginning of the last week of May, there was a definite shift in the temperature of the water by as much as 2 degrees. I could safely stay in the sea for up to 8 hours. It was also possible that my physiology was adjusting; I was no longer feeling seasick, however at the conclusions of my swims, I was routinely a shaking, near-incoherent icy mess. I continued to be extremely cautious about staying no more than 300 metres from the shore. That protected me from any underwater rocks, but not from another danger — pleasure craft and their large wakes. I quickly learned how to swim along a wake rather than hitting it head-on. To do that meant I was rewarded with a mouthful of brine, which I tried my best to avoid. I truly had it easy in the pool. Open water swimming was an entirely differ-ent game, and I needed a clear awareness at all times of potential hazards. *Hard to do with a face underwater and looking through foggy goggles.*

Lifeguards were going to be patrolling the beaches beginning on Victoria Day, and I wasn't too sure about the reception that I was going to get from them. I anticipated that they would not be pleased with my efforts. I made sure that the Park's Board and the lifeguards were aware of what I was doing, and I'd asked that they keep it confidential.

Though I tried my best to be mindful of many things during a swim such as my location in relation to landmarks, the tides, wind, waves, temperature and risks, there was a tedium to endlessly stroking the water that was at best boring and at worst, hypnotizing. I caught myself, in cold water, letting my mind dangerously wander. Other times, I felt groggy, as hard as it is to believe. As much as I could, I played tricks with myself during the swims. In my head I played whole albums of music, sometimes mouthing or even singing the words underwater. I thought of clients that I was seeing and tried to think of questions to ask them. I tried to see the written text in my schoolbooks. I thought of my assignments and what I'd like to further study. I ruminated on Robby and Lara and how they were helping me to do the improbable. I also wondered how I would tell my parents that I'd been dropped from the national team. Would they be ashamed of me? What would my family think of me swimming to raise money for people suffering with AIDS? And, I thought of Pete and all the people I hadn't met who were facing dread in their lives. *This is important. So, don't screw it up.*

While I'd been swimming distance in the bay, Robby had been working at securing my registration with the Open Water Swimming Association, which was a part of Swim Canada. The rules were, as Mrs. McBride reported, clear and stringent: an official had to be with the pilot boat, no touching or any type of interference from any other person or thing was allowed during the swim, food and drink had to be tested for any substance, a urine test was to be performed on me before and after, the pilot boat operator had to prove their proficiency navigating through the Strait on the pre-approved course with no deviation, and a test run had to be done — with the swimmer, of course — at least 1 week before the attempt that approximated the distance and included swimming in darkness.

In addition to rehearsing new songs for a potential album — some of which were her own compositions — Lara had taken on the task of figuring out my nutritional needs and was spending a great deal of time researching the best ways to keep my food intake at an appropriate level during the swim. I estimated that I was expending up to 500 calories per hour or more in open water, so Lara was charged with finding easily digestible foods made of complex carbohydrates, proteins, fats and fluids that I could consume in the water with little effort. So far in practice sessions, I was taking in a liquid diet, but I knew that in the longer distance, what I was eating was insufficient. Not having adequate nutrition in the water was very dangerous, as being out of glycogen stores would end the attempt. Additionally, I had to eat and/or drink about every 45 minutes to an hour, which meant a large quantity of foods had to be kept on board the boat, then legally delivered to me in the water. Warm fluids were also important to balance out my decreased body temperature.

Mrs. McBride busied herself with finding ways to keep me as warm as possible in the water. She was experimenting with several forms of grease to see which might keep my core body temperature from falling dangerously low. Additionally, she was looking at insulating my bathing cap to mitigate heat loss and a type of garment that could potentially help inhibit loss of heat from my groin.

Pete was putting a donation strategy together for larger corporations like Speedo. Already, the swim company was interested in the attempt, and though we had yet to formally announce the Ladysmith to Vancouver crossing, they were willing to donate some funds if I would wear a Speedo suit and goggles (I always did, anyway). As well, they requested their company name would be painted on the pilot boat — the boat that we'd yet to secure. Pete was also devising a campaign for donations, all under wraps. Pete thought that timing was a vital part of this swim, and announcing it at the best time was something that I left to him. He did mention that AIDS Vancouver was excited and willing to be a sponsor.

Robby was in his element as the director of our planned watery spectacle, as he began overseeing and coordinating all the moving parts. Any small detail or query from our crew went to him for discussion and he made all operational decisions as we continued to move along. I wasn't fully aware of all the machinations, but I was cognizant of the difficulty required to cobble together all the various pieces. Another vital part of the swim was the pilot, whom we'd yet to hire and didn't know how we'd pay — perhaps from the donations we also couldn't predict we would have. According to Mrs. McBride, the pilot would follow a specific and approved course. The pilot would need to study the tide chart carefully for the planned 40 plus hours I'd be in the water and be vigilant of potential dangers during the crossing — especially in the dark. En route to Vancouver, I'd be swimming through the Gulf Islands, where the seas could run high and fast due to the topography in the narrows and the climatology of the region. Weather conditions could turn flat seas into churning and dangerous waters throughout Georgia Strait. A crossing attempt was contingent upon conditions that made such a venture possible. We needed good weather for an estimated 40 hours — minimum.

For the past 20 years, Sunday was my day off from swim practice. I continued to take that day off so that I could catch up on studying, cleaning, laundry and even do some cooking in large amounts for later in the week. In the laundry room, I emptied out the pockets of my Levi's before dumping them and other clothing items into a hot wash. Along with some loose change and a few scraps of paper, I found the phone number of someone I'd been avoiding calling. I stared at the number, sighed, then stashed the paper in my shorts and ran up to the third floor so that I could use the phone. Sitting on my sofa, I grabbed the telephone and placed it in my lap. *Now what? Make the call, already.* I dialled the number and thought how much I hated asking for help.

Huh, no one there? I'll have to leave a —

"Hello?"

"Hi. It's Shepard. Will Stamp's son? From the pool?"

"Of course. What a nice surprise. So are you finally asking me to coffee?"

Again with the coffee?

"Um, well, not really."

"Oh, what a shame for me," Deth said with a slight laugh.

"Well, sorry, but the reason I called was … you see, I was going to tell you about what my friends and I are planning. It's an event of sorts."

"An event?"

"Yeah, and I wanted to see if you'd be interested in helping us." Over the next 5 or 6 minutes, I told Deth of the planned crossing. He was silent until I finished the description.

"And you want to try this to bring attention to AIDS? There's no shortage of attention worldwide on this epidemic."

"That's true, but we also want to drum up some funds for people who are suffering or who'll be in need." I reminded him of AIDS Vancouver's efforts to fundraise.

"What you're talking about …" Deth paused for several seconds. "It's idealistic certainly, but I'm not sure that such a swim is even possible. Have you ever swum in open water before? Like you described for that length of time? Do you understand what can and will happen to your body?"

"I had my doctor check me out. Dr. Taylor said I'm fit. He's told me about the risks, mostly hypothermia and what it can do to the internal organs. But, I've been training in open water for the past month, and I'm already accustomed to the temperature," I exaggerated. I still found it hugely challenging, especially the last 2 hours. Somehow, I had to quintuple the time in cold water to get through the swim crossing. "Now we just need a pilot. And you're much more than a pilot — you're a *cardiologist* with a boat."

"Yes, I have a boat, but I'm not a mariner, for heaven's sake. You need someone more skilled than me out there. It's deceiving how dangerous the strait can be."

"Yes, but we have a crew, a dedicated crew that's going to lessen any danger. They won't allow me to get into trouble." I said confidently.

"Getting into the ocean for a 2-day swim is sufficiently troubling," Deth said sternly. "Who's the crew?" Deth sounded suspicious, with good reason.

"Well, uh, well," I stumbled for a moment. "There's my land-lady —"

"Your landlady?" I could hear the disbelief in Deth's voice.

"She was a famous distance swimmer. Clockwork Carrie."

"I see. Never heard of her. And who else is —"

"There's my boyfriend," I said cautiously.

"Oh, and he's been involved with distance-swimming events?"

"Not exactly. He works in the theatre," I said with enthusiasm. "He just finished directing an Agatha Christie play. In Sudbury, Ontario." I gulped a bit.

"Right. A director's helpful when you're swimming with sharks."

Wait — there's sharks?

"Well, I know how it sounds, but he's very skilled at managing people. Well, actors, but that's the same thing as people. Sort of."

"Uh, huh."

I could hear that Deth's interest was flagging.

"And of course there's Lara. She'll be with me — the others, I mean — on the boat."

"Lara with the red hair?" Deth asked with apparent interest.

"One and the same. She's my best friend. I wouldn't attempt this without her onboard." There was a pause on the line. "You still there?" I faintly asked.

"And I'm betting that Lara isn't a physical therapist, or a nurse, or a medic, correct?"

"Lara's a singer," I managed to say without hesitation.

"A *singer*?" Deth asked without masking his incredulity.

"A soprano, actually. She's a very good singer." I said, heavily emphasizing 'good'. Promptly moving on, I said, "You'd have to familiarize yourself with all the tide charts and learn the swim-course so that we don't stray. It'll be a long swim, and I have to be economical by travelling the least distance possible. We'd have to try a few practice runs out in English Bay, maybe near Bowen Island to get a feel of what it'll be like."

"You're serious about this, aren't you?" he asked flatly.

"Deadly."

"Not the best choice of words."

"Perhaps not," I conceded. "We really need your help. So, are you in?"

"I'd have to barter for a lot of swimming lessons," Deth said lightly.

"As many as you want. I'll turn you into the next John Naber." I doubt that he knew of Naber, the record holder in the 100 backstroke.

"Well," Deth said contemplatively.

He's considering my request. Wait for a moment. Don't sink the proverbial boat.

"It'll be a real once-in-a-lifetime experience," I posed, searching for any angle that might be persuasive.

"I can't believe I'm asking, but when are you going to try this?"

"Just over a couple of months. I want to time it for BC Day."

"I'll be frank; this conversation makes me wary. I think you'll fail."

"I know that's what you and some others will think, but even if we fail, we'll have captured the imagination of what's possible in the face of seemingly impossible odds. I can't help but think of the lives lost as this epidemic advances. We're at the beginning of what may prove to be catastrophic."

"I agree. The outlook is extremely grim," Deth stated confidently.

"Yes, but there's something hopeful in this swim. It's as though we're showing how we can overcome huge odds when people truly care about each other."

There was a prolonged pause on the phone. I waited for Deth to assimilate what must have sounded like some kind of Pollyanna hyperbole. It was the kind of stuff I despised, and yet I was spouting it ad nauseum.

"We have a saying: 'Hoe ouder, hoe zotter'. It roughly means, 'Wisdom doesn't always come with years'. What you're suggesting seems foolish at first, but it's deserving of further examination."

"So you'll con —"

"I'll consider it, yes. Give me a week to see if it's possible for me, all right?"

"I couldn't ask for more. Thanks, Dr. De —"

"I think it's really time you called me Serge, don't you?"

48

Meet the Crew

As the month of May wound down, classes finished for the year. It allowed me to hone my attention completely on swimming. With temperatures increasing both in and out of the water, I was able to stay submerged for up to 12 hours at a time. The monotony of the swim was also managed by mental gymnastics. My stroke and breathing were nearly automatic, so I worked out any problems in my head. I listened to my head's musical playlist, thought of food (a lot) and allowed my mind to wander sufficiently enough that I was cognitively engaged, but never so distracted that I ignored any possible peril. Still sticking reasonably close to shore, I was learning about twice-daily tides, the method by which they moved quickly along more shallow waters, how tides could become ripped and how to use them to facilitate speed. As well, I tried to nap every 4 or 5 hours I was in the water. Actually, it wasn't really a nap, per se, but rather a prolonged rest on my back for several minutes with closed eyes. I couldn't allow myself to fall asleep — that would be the end of me. With a few moments of stationary rest and a few swallows of my nutritional drink, I quickly grew cold and had to move my body to maintain my core temperature. Though I wasn't using any grease on my body yet, I was noticing that I had mostly adjusted to the cold waters — or as May was turning to June — the gratefully *cool* waters.

With the arrival of the Victoria Day long weekend on May 21st, beaches and outdoor pools had officially opened, and lifeguards were on patrol. I'd made a point of speaking with several of the beach lifeguards so that they understood what I was doing for many hours in English Bay. I was told not to venture past certain markers in the bay that were there for pleasure and other craft. Though the lifeguards expressed initial worry, they were satisfied that I was following the rules. I was glad the guards were on-duty — just in case. When I was feeling a little indulgent, I biked over to the heated Kits Pool and swam for 8 hours at a time, then during my break, I unpacked my satchel of food I'd brought for lunch: 2 loaves of bread, 500 grams of cheese and several Cadbury's milk chocolate bars, washed down with 2 litres of homogenized milk and a thermos of very strong black coffee. After 30 minutes, I went for a 3-hour swim at Kits Beach, which was conveniently adjacent to the massive 137-metre outdoor pool. Biking home, I'd fall asleep on the sofa within a few minutes. I had lost weight with the exertion of prolonged swims. It wasn't possible to compensate for the calories expended — I was using up to 8,000 calories in the water per day alone. Dropping down to 155 pounds, I had to be careful not to lose more of my fat stores, as those stores helped to not only keep me insulated, but body fat could be a source of valuable fuel.

The crew had been working constantly. Pete had established several important sponsors that were willing to donate some money and added a degree of prestige or perhaps legitimacy to the swim. He thought that it would be best if the announcement of the event was no more than 2 weeks before the attempt. Pete had prepared a press release that would detail our effort, and it would go to the papers at the precise time for maximum impact. Mrs. McBride had settled with Vaseline petroleum jelly for me to use in the swim, which was rather humorous, all things considered. Additionally, she had designed a special type of bathing cap that was triple-insulated. It covered my head much like water polo headgear, enveloping my ears, protecting the sides of my face and fastened securely under my chin. My swimsuit was also very different. On her Singer sewing machine, Mrs. McBride had created a suit that was more like shorts than my Speedo brief. In this way, it covered my groin and went half-way to my knee. The lycra fabric was quadrupled for extra warmth and though it was bulkier than my regular attire, she assured that it would work to keep me as warm as possible and prevent excessive heat loss from my mid-section. Lara's work on high-calorie and digestible foods were yielding positive results. She'd discovered that she could reduce blueberries by microwaving them to a thick, dense consistency, then add pureed tofu — high in both calories and nutrition. Peanut butter was another food that was whipped into drinks with other reduced foods; all easily tolerated during my practice swims. I couldn't risk having dangerous stomach cramps in the water, so foods had to be tried out in practice. We were extremely pleased that Dr. Deth — Serge — confirmed he would pilot the boat. When not working, he was pouring over all the oceanographic charts as he plotted out the complicated course for me in a way that would take advantage of the tidal currents. In spite of what he said, he was becoming a real mariner. Robby had decided that I would need some short practice swims with the boat and crew in daylight and at night. There would be an additional huge 25-30-hour dress rehearsal for swimming with the boat, managing any inclement weather conditions, practicing how food was given and most importantly to all of us, how to scuttle the swim and get me out of the water in an emergency. Robby was also managing all the disparate pieces; estimating the costs, arranging the Swim

Canada official who would ride onboard, working with Pete on funding matters, securing consents, waivers, and permissions with the help of my cousin, Ryan. I was grateful to have them busying themselves with planning the event as it enabled me to concentrate on the readying for the swim scheduled for July 30th. Until then, the crew agreed that it would be useful for us to meet every few Sunday nights at my apartment to do updates. The first one was on June 5th. I thought it would be gracious to make dinner for us and have a relaxing evening. The first to come over was not surprisingly Mrs. McBride. Her wide smile was most welcome as she stepped into my apartment. Her silver hair was piled into a French bun, which looked very chic. Her skin was rosy-pink, which nearly matched her blouse. Around her neck she wore a bright scarf of coral and blue. Hugging her trim figure, her wool pants were brown plaid. Mrs. McBride held a white swim cap in her wrinkled hands.

"Here, try this on," she urged.

"Now?" I took the cap from her we moved into the living room. On both sides it read, 'Swim for Life,' in large contrasting red print. "This is great, Mrs. McBride!" I exclaimed. "How'd you get this done?" I asked, simultaneously answering the intercom and pressing the enter buzzer for guests that had arrived downstairs.

"Dear, we Scots are very resourceful and penny-wise. Pete connected me to one of the nice young women at Speedo and after I told them what we're going to do, I sent my design along and they made us several caps for free. It looks very good; don't you think?"

"Yes, but I'm having difficulty getting it over my hair," I said, pushing clumps of hair under the latex.

"You'll need a severe cut, dear. To make it work properly. Wet hair will only make you colder."

Though I covered my hair with swim caps to keep my hair dry and my head warm, pulling off my cap after my swims revealed hair that was matted and moist from perspiration. Mrs. McBride was right. I needed to ensure that my hair was dry, and that meant I was due for a drastic hair-cut. I managed to get the cap on.

"My mother is always after me to get my hair chopped off, so I guess this is —" I was interrupted by Lara and Pete, who came through my open apartment door.

"Oh, something smells just scrumptious in here!" Lara commented. She then looked at me in my rather peculiar hat. "Fashion faux pas or au courant?" Lara asked archly.

"It's my swim cap that Mrs. McBride designed, and it's very au courant," I said as she hugged me, carefully avoiding dropping the wine bottle she'd brought.

"Well-done, Mrs. McBride," Lara praised my landlady. She laughed as I struggled to get the swim cap off. Pete gave me a hand with a painful tug to remove it (as well as a few strands of my hair). Lara deposited the wine on the counter and followed her nose to the oven. My cap might not have seemed stylish, but my best friend was. Lara wore an olive-green flight-suit with a wide brown belt and black boots. Her red hair shone and smelled of lemons. Beside her, Pete's incandescent smile beamed like a searchlight. As Lara investigated what was cooking in the oven, Pete gave me a long embrace. He looked slightly bleary-eyed, but that could have been due to taking his 'medication' an hour earlier. Pete had gained some weight, but remained pencil-thin. I noticed that though his hips no longer jutted into me when we hugged, he nonetheless was far from a normal weight. He wore a sharp navy suit with a bright white dress shirt, having come directly from work. His black shoes were polished to a mirrored finish. His glossy black hair had grown nearly to his shoulders, and he had kept his beard immaculately trimmed. Around his throat he wore pukka shells he'd purchased in Hawaii the previous winter. With all the considerable tribulations, Pete still cut a rakish figure. Viewing my well-dressed company, I thought about doing a quick change, but then Robby buzzed the apartment.

"Come on up, Robby," I said and pressed the button.

"Dear, you really should get that young man a key," Mrs. McBride said as she headed for the leather chair.

A few moments later, Robby arrived at the door, and I was surprised to see that he was joined by Dr. Deth, who shook my hand warmly, his eyes lingering on mine a few moments. If there was any tension on Robby's part, he didn't show it, though I'd never known my boyfriend to be jealous. Robby was dressed in jeans and a polo shirt and his companion wore shorts and a tee-shirt, so I didn't feel bad about being underdressed in my red fleece UBC shorts and lime-green cotton short-sleeve shirt.

"Come on in," I said, welcoming all the group members for the first time. "Serge, you haven't met Mrs. McBride. She's famous for swimming across —"

"Nonsense, dear. Oh, so nice to meet you. You're a cardiologist, aren't you?"

"Yes, that's right, Madam," he said, smiling warmly.

"Well, it will be very reassuring for the others to have you onboard."

"And you remember Lara?" I turned to see where she'd gone. Lara had finished closing the oven door, having inspected the sea-food lasagna that I'd made. She was making her way back into the living room where we'd begun to settle. She was chewing on some asparagus that she'd found on the counter.

"Of course, we spoke briefly at the meeting. You're the singer, aren't you? I'm Serge." He stepped towards her slowly. Lara appraised him quickly, noting the intonation in his speech.

"You speak French?" Lara managed to ask with a full mouth.

"I'm Belgian. I speak Brussels French and English."

"And Flemish, too?" Lara inquired coyly, extending her hand for a gentle shake.

He smiled warmly as he took her hand. "Yes, but not well. I'm surprised you could hear my accent. Most people in Vancouver can't figure out where I'm from."

"Well, Canadians *can* be Philistines when it comes to European culture," Lara said smugly. She managed to be flirtatious as she discretely picked at the asparagus stuck between her front teeth with her nimble songstress tongue.

After a few more hugs, I brought out a silver lacquered tray; on it were 2 large bottles of Pellegrino and some tall water glasses, filled with ice and slices of lime. I placed the tray on the glass coffee table. With everyone comfortably seated in the living room, Robby took out a pad of paper and a pen. "So, let's begin. We've just recently got a sponsorship with Speedo, a collaboration agreement with AIDS Vancouver, some dollars from Galloway's and a Swim Canada official. Uh … Lara's got a food plan, Mrs. McBride's created special swim-gear, we've got a pilot and doctor," he nodded with gratitude in Deth's direction. "I've got all the permissions from Fisheries and Oceans Canada, a permit for Ceperly in Stanley Park, signed releases … what else?" Robby thought aloud. "Right, Pete has all the press releases and media statements ready to go. That's about it …"

"Don't forget the swimmer," Lara stage-whispered at Robby.

"Yes, of course. Can the swimmer give us a progress report?" Robby asked.

"I'd be happy to," I said. "I'm spending about 12 hours in the water right now. I'm increasing the time by 2 to 3 hours per day, 6 days per week, depending on the conditions. That means that I'll approximate the distance in the next 6 weeks."

"You'll have just enough time to taper," Mrs. McBride stated. Tapering for swim events was something that she knew very well about.

"That's right. I've left 2 weeks to taper."

"Good," she said. "It's very important. That and being able to stay in the cold for longer periods of time."

"I'm getting comfortable with the cold water and soon I'll be using Vaseline to help me move up to 30 or 35 hours at a time."

"But you'll need to be in the water for much longer, won't you?" Deth inquired.

"I will, but if I can get to the 30-hour mark, that should be enough for me to complete the remainder of the swim. I won't necessarily need to swim the entire distance during practice in order to finish the crossing."

"So, if you manage to swim for 70 kilometres you'll be able to do the extra 10?" Lara asked.

"That's what all the distance swimmers say, and what the literature details," I answered. "It's like running, Lara. If you run for 5 K consistently, you can safely triple the distance."

"What's going to happen when you're swimming at night?" Pete wanted to know.

"Well," I started to respond, "I've done some swimming for a few hours before sunrise. It's probably more disorientating without a boat and lights to show me the way, so I don't think it'll be an issue for me — for us," I replied confidently.

"How are you going to manage with fatigue and staying awake when you need sleep?" Lara asked.

"You'll have to include caffeinated drinks to keep me from feeling sleepy," I said. "Like we talked about before, remember? Every hour should do it."

"Oh, yes, I've gotta figure that out." Lara looked a little stressed.

"Staying true to the course will be the concern we'll face onboard," Deth advised. "There's going to be some shifting and re-configuring along the way because of the tides and the ebb of the currents, not to mention the wash from other crafts, but we'll try not to add more distance than planned," he said with assuredness. I noticed that Lara was watching him carefully.

"And you'll be monitoring Sunshine?" Lara sharply asked.

"Monitoring the sunshine?" Deth looked confused with her question.

"No, I meant Shepard. You'll be checking on him medically during the swim?" Lara's tone was clearly one of worry.

"Well, not really. I'll be wrapped up in keeping us travelling in the right direction. You'll have to keep your eyes on him. With an endurance attempt like this the body *can* go into shock under certain conditions and start to shut down some internal organs."

Lara sighed deeply and reached for my hand. "Shut down? It's all very alarming, isn't it? We talk about the crossing here, but on the day ..." She squeezed my hand until it hurt.

"Lara, we've got lots of safety contingencies. The crew will be right there with him." Pete tried to reassure her that risks were mitigated by the practice swims.

"We won't really be with him. We'll be on a boat, Pete," Lara said curtly. "With no shower or toilets, correct, Serge?"

"We'll have a commode for you to —"

"A commode? No, I'm not peeing in a bucket. Christ, a full bladder, bouncing on top of the waves for 40 hours straight? Oh, God, I feel sick just thinking about it." Lara poured herself some water and took a draught. Once again she clasped my hand and looked at me. "When exactly is our dinner?"

"Peckish?" I asked, gently prying her hand from mine and moving to the kitchen to check on supper.

"I'm so hungry my stomach thinks my throat's been slashed," Lara exclaimed. With the exception of Robby, everyone in the room laughed at Lara's hyper-fast change from nausea to hunger; probably the only person in the world that remedied her upset stomach by eating.

A few minutes later, I placed a large, bubbling, golden, creamy lasagna on the table. It was filled with prawns, scallops, green onions, thyme, cream and Gruyere cheese. As it sat resplendent on a cast-iron trivet, Lara got to work and tossed a huge salad with arugula, red onions and roasted red peppers. Spring asparagus had been quickly sautéed and placed in a large blue bowl with wedges of lemon. A big loaf of crusty bread was sliced and put in a wicker basket. With the wine opened and the candles lit, the crew came to the table, pouring a glasses of cold Sauterne to accompany the meal.

"Bon appetite," Lara declared, quickly getting to work filling her plate.

"Iith gu leòir!" Mrs. McBride cried out, the small, soft-soft-spoken woman unexpectedly startling the group.

"Mrs. McBride?" Pete cocked his head in confusion."What did you say?"

"Eat plenty!" she explained. "It's a Gaelic saying, dear."

"Now, *those* are words to live by!" Lara said, hungrily diving into her lasagna.

49

Nothing Says Gay More Than Crème Brûlée

Nearly all of June was rainy, not atypical for Vancouver. The wet weather meant the bay wasn't as warm as it could be, but now that I had begun to acclimatize, the cool water wasn't adversely affecting my swims. I'd start my swim at 4 AM so that I'd be in the dark for 90 minutes. I was drinking Lara's concoctions which now included a heavy dose of caffeine. Rests were every hour for up to 5 minutes at a time, usually floating on my back. Frankly, it was good to look up, as so much of my time was spent peering into waters where I could only see my own hands and arms — in the daylight. Before dawn, swimming proved very challenging for me because I couldn't tell where I was going. Every 25 or 30 strokes, I checked back to the lit towers of the West End to ensure that I was on course. However, on the lee side of Stanley Park, there were no visible points of reference until sunrise, which made for a disconcerting swim. On occasion, I was frightened by a harbour seal and groups of waterfowl that didn't appreciate my presence in their territory. As before, I swam perpendicular to the shoreline for the most part, using tides and currents to help propel me. I found that my muscular legs were a boon for powering me when the tidal forces reversed and were not in my favour. My arms and shoulders were more developed than at any time in my swim career. Though I wasn't swimming the other 3 strokes, I had a sense that I was stronger and fitter than I'd ever been. My weight had alarmingly dropped to 150 pounds. That was 5 pounds less than my lean boyfriend. There was no insulation of fat, which was worrisome to me and to the crew. I tried to consume as many calories as possible, but gaining weight was proving impossible due to the calorie expenditure. There was simply no way for me to increase my weight when my body was now expending up to 12,000 calories per day on the longest swims. During my taper, I planned on regaining the lost weight, and most importantly, the lost fat stores.

On a few occasions, Mrs. McBride came down at sunrise to watch me swim. She wore a bright red sweater, which helped me to locate her on the seawall, depending on where I was during my practice. Several times she gave me valuable coaching on my arm position and freestyle stroke, which needed to be different in the rolling water as compared swimming in a pool where the water was flat. Corrections in my stroke might have seemed minor, however, over the course of so many kilometres, it could make a large differ-ence. I'd hoped that I might persuade Mrs. McBride to take a swim with me — now that the waters in English Bay were considerably warmed — to offer more "hands-on" coaching, but she graciously declined and instead called her out her strategies to me from the beach as I treaded the water during my break.

As before, my life was consumed with swimming. No longer doing endless laps in a pool, I was training for something more impressive than speed; endurance. More than any other time in my swimming career, I was focussed on the distances that I needed to cover 6 days per week. Failing to accomplish the distance in practice would mean that an attempt was impossible. Though I had adapted to the water, the sheer effort of the swims exhausted me. In fact, my life was only about 3 things — swimming, eating and sleeping. Robby accepted that sex was infrequent. Our evenings spent together found me passed out on the sofa long before the popcorn popped — not the best company — but Robby understood. I didn't go to the movies with Lara, nor did we run together. Our phone chats — once plentiful — were brief. Coffee dates and walks with Pete were put on hold. Almost everything that happened to me happened in the water, and as we eased into July, curious onlookers began noticing that I swam for hours in the bay. I'm sure that I must have appeared as an odd creature — submerged for a day in the ocean and when I staggered out, I shook with cold, my skin red as a pomegranate.

There had not been an announcement of my attempt. I had yet to tell my family that I'd been terminated from the team, nor had I told them of my bid to swim the strait. However, as the date approached, I knew that I owed them an explanation and I certainly didn't want them to find out from anyone else but me. On Sunday morning, I decided to tell my mother when I called her on the phone.

"Oh, that's terrible news!" she exclaimed. "What about all that lost income?"

"Mum, it's okay. They paid me out. I can coast for a few months until the fall."

"That's something, I suppose. You've been looking for work?"

"Well, Mum, I'm … uh … right now … for a while, actually, I've been training for an event. A swim event," I started explaining cautiously.

"But you're off the —"

"Yes, not for the national team, but a swim to raise funds for something going on here in Vancouver."

"For the AIDS?"

"Mum, not *the* AIDS, just AIDS. And yes, it's for AIDS Vancouver." She nonetheless surprised me with knowing more than I thought.

"Well, what kind of event?" she asked briskly.

"It's a distance swim."

"What … do you mean in a lake?"

"No, Mum. In the ocean."

"English Bay? With all those ships? No, that's too dangerous," she asserted.

"Actually, Mum," I took a quick breath. "I'm going to be attempting to swim from Ladysmith to Vancouver."

There was a prolonged silence on the telephone. I waited a few moments.

"Mum, you there?"

"You are not doing that."

"*Mum.* I've been training for a few months already. I've been swimming for a day at a time in the water. I've got a crew —"

"You haven't said a word about this. How could you? A crew? Who's —"

"It's Robby, Pete, Lara, Mrs. McBride and Dr. Deth — he has the boat."

"You've got to be kidding me," she said in horror. "That's no crew. Why on earth would Deth be doing this? Of all people, he'd know how stupid this is."

"Don't say it's stupid. I've been working harder on this than anything I've done in the pool. Deth thinks that it's possible that —"

"Your father's cardiologist is now giving swimming advice?" My mother's incredulity was palpable. "You know how ludicrous this sounds, don't you?"

"Yes, it's a bit hard to grasp, but Mum, I'm doing it, and with some luck, I'll land on the beach in Stanley Park for BC Day."

"I can't believe this hare-brained scheme."

"It's not hare-brained. We've thought everything out — the pilot boat, nutrition, safety measures." My defensiveness and irritation was fully in flight.

"Has Dr. Taylor checked you —"

"Of course, Mum."

"And he doesn't think you've lost your marbles?" Mum asked shrilly.

"No, Mum. He's been very supportive," I said firmly.

"Oh, is that right? Well, isn't that just lovely." My mother's sarcasm was unabashed. "I want you to speak with your father," she demanded.

"Why? I'm sure that he could care less about what I do in or out of the —"

"You know that's not true," she said unconvincingly. "Don't be so —"

"Mum, there's nothing else for me to say, so I better just say good —"

"Oh, so you're going to hang up? What an excellent way to end this conversation," she mocked, anger in her voice. "By breaking your mother's heart."

I could hear her start to sob.

Shit.

"Mum, why are you getting so angry? I'm not a child and I'm not doing this to spite you or break your heart, for gawd's sake."

I heard the click of disconnection. It appeared that my mother beat me to the punch and hung up on me for the very first time. I sighed heavily. Less than an hour later, my father — who was typically loathe to call me — phoned.

"Your mother's told me all about it."

Jezus…

"Uh, huh," I said flatly.

"What if the boat breaks down on the water in the middle of the night? Have you even thought about that? What then? And what does Deth know about engines?" he asked.

"Well, Dad, he repaired your heart. Can it be that different?" I posed. I hadn't thought about the boat breaking down. None of us had.

"Of course it can. Don't be a smartass," he said sternly.

"I'm not being —"

"You know, you've made your mother sick with worry. She's in the living room right now, crying into a glass of wine."

"Christ, Dad, it's 11 in the morning," I said. It was a little early for Chardonnay, even for my mother.

"She had to do something to calm her nerves. All right, I'll tell her that we've spoken and you've changed your mind."

"Dad, I'm not changing my mind. I'm going to do this. I've — we've — been working like crazy on this. It's all arranged."

"I'll ask you to do this, Number One," he started, then in typical fashion, paused for effect.

Kill me now. Hold me under the water until the bubbles stop.

"Yes, Dad," I said, impatient as usual.

"Think about our conversation and make the correct decision."

"Right, Dad. I promise to do that. Goodbye," I said and waited for his closing.

"Number One."

I hung up the phone, thought about screaming at the top of my lungs when the phone rang again. I took a breath.

"Now what?" I asked tersely.

"Sunshine? I've been trying to reach you."

"Lara? Oh, sorry. I was speaking to my parents. Argh."

"Shall I ask you how it went?"

"Please don't."

"Okay." Lara paused for a moment. "What do you think about Dr. Deth?"

"Huh? What do you mean?"

"Just tell me."

"Well, he did a great job on my father's surgery. He was very helpful with Pete, wasn't he?"

"Very."

"We're super-lucky to have him run the boat. He's obviously very bright. Um, he's nice-looking and has great hair. Why are you asking?" Judging how Lara had recently been flirting with Deth (I couldn't resist) at my apartment, I imagined that she wanted to know if he was interested in her. I didn't see that Deth gave Lara any indication of a sexual interest, which made sense — because he was gay as Nijinsky. I hadn't told her that Deth had asked me for coffee and had appeared at the pool a couple months ago and had touched my shoulders. I didn't want her ego to be bruised when she discovered that there couldn't possibly be a romantic interest.

"He asked me out," she said.

"Huh?"

"He wants to have dinner with me tonight. Isn't that odd?"

"Maybe it's a friendly gesture," I theorized. "I mean, we're all friendly now with the swim event."

"Maybe, but friendly's not the vibe I have."

Lara's "vibes" could be notoriously wrong.

"What did he say to you?"

"Well, he phoned me up, started talking about you and what a challenge the swim will be."

Of course. Deth was getting to me through Lara.

"Uh huh. And what else?"

"He thought it would be fun to grab something to eat."

"Okay. Everything sounds fine, doesn't it?"

"Do you think he likes me?"

"Lara, what are you in, Grade 8? Everybody that meets you likes you, so yes, of course."

"No, I meant do you think he likes me in *that* way?"

Lara's gaydar was as reliable as her cooking skills.

"Alright, Lara. I gotta tell you. I think Deth is gay."

"He is?"

"Isn't he?"

"Well," she sniffed, "he didn't ask you to dinner."

Not yet. He's too busy stalking me at the pool.

"Um, do *you* like him?"

"What's not to like? You're quite right. He's tall, thin and that head of curls alone is worth a few bad dates."

"It's true; he does have excellent hair." I recalled my first favourable reaction when I saw him at the hospital when my father fell ill.

"Yes, of course, Sunshine. And he's even French."

"He's Belgian."

"You're splitting hairs. He's French enough."

"Just think of your children," I added with a touch of drama.

"Stop being flip," she said with a serious tone. "Did he tell you he was gay?"

"Not in so many words. It's nothing he's said, but it's my sense."

"Maybe he wants me to be his soeurette?"

"Oh, Lara." I said, understanding her French reference. You'll have to tell him that you're *my* fag hag. There's only room for me, sweetie."

I could hear a small sigh on the receiver.

"I'll try to work that into the conversation — maybe over a crème brûlée. I'll see if he likes it. Nothing says gay more than crème brûlée."

I had to smile with that observation. "I dunno about that, Lara."

"You know, I'm beginning to think that I'm destined only to have gay men in my life," Lara said, resignation in her voice.

"Well, what's so bad about that?" I asked a bit too defensively.

"What if you only had straight men in your life?" she retorted.

"I see your point," I admitted. "I guess you haven't been doing much dating, have you?" I was thinking that if there was ever a time to be cautious, this was it. And, Lara's career had taken precedence over men for several years now.

"Sunshine, I was at the doctor for a check-up last week. He did an internal exam and announced I was dry as shoe leather," Lara said curtly. "*Shoe leather*. The nurse started to snicker. I was mortified. My doctor prescribed medication so that I 'wasn't like a sand dune up there'. I wanted to bolt from the examining room, but my feet were clamped in stirrups."

"So you'd agree you're going through a dry spell?" I asked, trying not to chortle at my best friend's misfortunate experience.

"Do you know what it's like to be told the Mojave Desert is in your vagina?"

"Well, not exactly. But it sounds as though you were hoping that Deth might end the drought?" *Might as well go with all the metaphors flying around.*

"I dunno. I thought that it might be possible that someone might want to date me at least a few more times before I'm dead."

"Lara, you're not even 30. I'd hardly say you were old." Lara was still 29 for 2 months. In my opinion, she had plenty of time to make some further dating errors.

"It's different for a woman, Sunshine."

"Listen, you sing like … like no one else, actually. You're becoming very successful. You're gorgeous, plus you've got a butt like Baryshnikov."

"He's got a huge ass. What are you telling me?"

"*Lara.*"

"Now you listen. According to my doctor, I have the reproductive organs of Mother Theresa." Lara blew out a large breath before continuing. "That's a horrible image, isn't it?" Lara sighed deeply.

"Well, it's not a good time for sex, anyhow. That's the biggest reason I went to the doctor; to talk. There's every reason to be cautious."

Lara was right. As the summer progressed, reports of AIDS consistently grew in Vancouver, with increasingly high rates of infection. The epidemic had taken hold in most countries around the globe affecting men and women.

"That's wise, Lara. At least for now. Speaking of 'wise', I told my parents about the swim. It didn't go well. My mother thinks I'm an idiot and questioned all of our intelligence, including Deth's."

"That's because she's afraid she's going to lose you."

"Huh?"

"It's a mother's prerogative to worry. Why wouldn't she? You're very important to your mother. It's natural that she's freaked out. I imagine all mothers would react the same way — excluding my mother from the equation."

"Of course. Sorry." Lara's mother had rejected her when she decided to be a singer rather than be a French teacher as was her family's wont. Her mother likened it to becoming a prostitute, which confounded me. Her mother refused to change her opinion, and it resulted in a cut-off relationship that hurt and angered her. The irony was that any mother would be proud to have Lara as their talented, caring and beautiful daughter. According to my studies of family systems theory, that could change. I hoped it would be sooner rather than later for Lara. She may have had conflict with her family, but there was no good reason for them to reject her for her own path. I didn't believe in destiny, as Lara knew, but if there was such a thing, she would have been fated to sing.

"My Mum doesn't have to worry."

"Right. This is the same woman who calls you several mornings a week to see if you're eating enough fibre?"

"Hmm. Perhaps I didn't do a good enough job to reassure her that all will go safely?" *No, of course I didn't. I was sullen and defensive instead.*

"Please. There's nothing safe or secure about this crossing. Your mother's got every reason to be concerned. It's dangerous and she's fearful."

"I tried to get her to understand all the precautions we're taking, but...."

"What did your father —"

"He said I was making my mother sick with worry."

"That's probably true. I'm anxious just thinking about me careening around in a boat for 2 days. Imagine how they feel when their son announces he's going to jump into the ocean in a skimpy Speedo and try to swim across 80 kilometres of open water? It's not a typical thing a child does during summer vacation. She's probably told herself that you won't be able to do it and that you'll risk your health trying."

My head flashed with the story that my mother used to read to me at bedtime: *The Little Engine That Could*, with the line, *"I think I can. I think I can."* That was one of my favourite stories, and a motto which I'd forgotten. I'll take my confidence from wherever I can, and I thought about how that simple tale could conjure up hope in unlikely situations.

"I think my parents will come around. They just need to get used to the idea."

"There's not much time for that."

Lara was correct. Time was closing in on all of us, with less than a month to go before we made the trek.

"Did you explain your practice sessions to get used to the cold, the special gear, the sponsors, your eating plan, how the boat will be near you, the lighting at night, Mrs. McBride's expertise? Did you?"

The pause provided the answer however Lara was patient for my response.

"Not really," I admitted. "I wanted them to be excited for us, not pan me as though I was a dope."

"You're not much of a therapist with your family, are you?"

"C'mon, you know with them I'm the Anti-Christ."

"Want some advice?"

"Gladly."

"Call them back, apologize for not speaking with them about this before and ask them for their understanding. And Sunshine," Lara added with the wisdom of her own personal experience, "just don't wait too long. Can you do that?"

"I think I can. I think I can."

50

Leap of Faith

During the first 2 weeks of July, the weather turned scorching hot, or for Vancouver that meant any temperatures above 25 degrees Celsius. After nearly 3 months of swimming outside for innumerable hours, I'd darkened to nut-brown — though mostly on the back of my body. The ocean had reached 19 degrees and in sheltered, shallow water, exceeded that number dramatically. As well, ocean currents from the southern Pacific region were drifting into the coastal waters and even at night the sea maintained a moderate temperature. On July 16th, I was set to do a 30-hour swim. It was meant to be my last long swim before beginning the taper in preparation of the crossing attempt. On Thursday night before the Friday swim, I was unable to sleep. I'd asked Robby if he minded that he stay at his place so that I could rest. But, it seemed that the worry of the next day's swim had me so tense that all I could do in bed was roll from side to side. When my alarm went off at 2:30 AM I was already awake. I must have slept at some point, but I truly couldn't recall when. I brushed my teeth, drank a half-gallon of orange juice, poached 4 large eggs, plopped them on toasted pumpernickel and ate a couple of bananas. After I collected my gear, I took the stairs to the lobby and nervously waited for Robby to arrive. Just after 3:30 AM, Robby appeared, bleary-eyed.

"Ready to go?" he asked quietly. Before I could answer, he said, "Deth should be getting everything together in the marina by now."

"Okay. And is Lara —"

"Let's hope she woke up. She's got all your food to stow onboard."

"Tell me about it. We can't go without her," I commented as we left my building and headed down to the beach.

"I'm sure that she made it to the marina." Deth moored his boat in False Creek, which was just past the Burrard Bridge. A few minutes later, we were at English Bay, the moonlight illuminating the high tide.

"This is usually the time that Lara's winding down after a show, not starting her day." I smiled at the thought. I would have loved to have seen Lara pulling herself together this early in the morning. I'm certain there would've been a plethora of expletives. My boy-friend and I stood at the edge of the water as the waves crested on the shoreline. We were alone on the white, deserted sandy beach. Before I was greased-up, he gave me a prolonged hug. I really didn't want to let go, but I removed my shoes and sweats, then placed them in my rucksack. My new swimsuit was put on before I left. It was white, so that I could be seen easily. I retrieved my earplugs, fitting them securely, then pulled my cap on effortlessly due to a new crew cut. The latex cap had been specially treated with a type of phosphorescent material that would glow for several hours. Next to put on were my swim goggles and finally Robby smeared my recently shaved-down body with petroleum jelly — a lot of it. I felt the heat of my body as the grease sealed the warmth in.

"Looks like you're ready to go." Robby stared at me. "You okay?"

"I'm a little nervous. When will you and Deth be in the bay?"

Robby looked at his watch. "Maybe half an hour or so. We'll find you." Robby's next step was to quickly get to the marina and depart for English Bay with Deth and Lara.

"Find me carefully, okay?" I laughed a little uncomfortably, not wanting to be run over by the pilot boat before I ever had the chance to attempt the 'Swim for Life'. *There's a bit of black humour.*

"We know where you'll be — just offshore Second Beach. Don't worry, Shep. We're gonna be right here, or out there," he pointed to the expanse of the ocean, black with only the moon providing a dim light scattered by the clouds. Robby gathered up my satchel and removed my car keys from the side pocket so that he could drive to the marina. I told him where my car could be found. He held my hand for a moment, then checked his watch. The crew was on a tight timeline. "I've gotta dash."

"Okay. Me, too" I said, relinquishing his hand, and smiling at my boyfriend as I began to walk into the ocean. I turned back and gave a thumbs-up gesture at Robby, adjusted my goggles, then edged my way into the dark sea, grimacing when the cool waters were about to come to my groin. Instead of inching my way, I leapt in, then pushed off with what felt was a turning tide and started a swim that would hopefully last for the next 30 hours.

The practice swim would prove more gruelling than I'd anticipated. After exactly 30 hours in the water, I crashed emotionally as well as physically and barely made it to shore. I was more exhausted than I ever recall being. I was woozy from riding up and down what had become heavy swells. Deth previously told me that swells could be flatter in the strait, but I had my doubts. Each hour, Lara blew a horn — a signal for my food intake, which was slightly annoying as I wasn't actually hungry. Eating or drinking each hour in the water was a challenging task. I was passed food from the boat on a long aluminum stick. It was hard to see when the ocean rose and fell. A plastic thermos with hot, sweetened coffee was thrown to me in on a rope that had a special loop holding the container. The coffee went a long way to warming my body temp, but what really helped was stroking the water. Lara and Robby kept eagle-eyes on me throughout, watching for any signs of fatigue — fatigue beyond what was anticipated as being normal for the swim. If I removed my goggles, I could see them onboard with Deth. Of course, Robby and Lara were the only ones able to take short 15-minute naps, but never at the same time. Deth had to stay alert the entire duration, though I can't imagine how he did it. Perhaps being a surgeon and working on-call made a difference, or maybe he'd drunk as much caffeine as me. That type of commitment was enormous, and I was very grateful. *Admit it, Deth's a really good guy even if you think he's a closet case and a stalker.*

I took several rest breaks on my back as I'd been practicing, but doing so made me more chilled. Having a boat near me was disconcerting as the shorter pilot-swimmer rehearsals. The lighting needed to be revised, as the glare made my head spin, though I was grateful for the direction it provided. I thought that being rather close to the shore created more waves and swells which were problematic, especially as I tired. As my biggest practice swim concluded, I ended where I started. The boat and I separated, with Deth returning with Robby and Lara to the marina. I barely managed to stand as I came ashore to a beach that was already getting crowded with sun-tanners. According to my Timex, it was just before 11 in the morning, July 17th. As I made my way up the beach, Mrs. McBride was jogging down to the water, greeting me excitedly, wearing her beacon-like red sweater. She carried a reflective silver heat-wrap given to us by Swim Canada. As I stumbled up from the beach, she immediately wiped the excess Vaseline from my body, first with a plastic scraper, then with a washcloth as I stood frozen. Then she wrapped the sheath around me, rubbing my chilled flesh. My body felt stiff. My skin was red as before, and was I having a hard time feeling my feet on the sand. This longest swim pushed me to my limits, but on the actual attempt, I had to be in the water another 10 hours or perhaps, with adverse conditions, even longer. Mrs. McBride brought me a thick towel emblazoned with the logo 'Swim for Life' (Pete's marketing genius) to dry myself off, as well as another set of sweats. She stowed my swim gear in a bag and helped me put on sandals, then assisted me to get dressed on the beach. People watched the queer goings-on with bemusement. I couldn't blame them; we were an odd couple.

"How did you do, dear?" Mrs. McBride finally asked.

"I got to 30," I said, my teeth chattering so forcefully I thought I'd break them.

"Let's move," she said, ushering me along quickly as we made our way to the Queen Charlotte. I was in a complete daze as we ambled up Denman Street. If Mrs. McBride hadn't been with me, I would have walked right out into traffic. Keeping the reflective blanket closely around me, we continued to the apartment and raised a few curious eyebrows in the process. We climbed the stairs to the 3rd floor. Mrs. McBride opened my door and gave me one further instruction.

"Get into a bath. Robby should be here directly, dear. Let me know if there's anything you need." Mrs. McBride had told me to get into a warm, but not hot, bath, slowly increasing the temperature. I did as directed. Shortly after the bath, the feeling had returned to my feet and hands. After drinking some warm water, I went to bed and pulled the comforter around me. I thought I could never get warm. My body felt like it was in shock. *Christ, I shouldn't be feeling like this.* I drifted off to a dreamless sleep almost immediately. When I woke, I was on my side. I looked at my watch and noted that 12 hours had passed. My other arm was numb, and I couldn't budge it. That's when I realized that Robby was lying beside me, his arms encircling my shoulders. He peered at me, his hazel eyes capturing my foggy ones. Before I could say a word, Robby grinned and whispered, "Well, that was one helluva dress rehearsal."

51

In The Boat Together

I t took me 2 full days to recover from my lengthy swim. We had gone to and from Bowen Island, though I wasn't really aware of the course. Two nights later, the crew gathered in my living room. Robby ordered a slew of Chinese food, and boxes of it were strewn over the dining table. As we finished eating, we worked through an agenda about the things that needed to improve for the crossing attempt. One was food.

"I thought my meal breaks each hour were more than I could manage. I think digesting the food made me a little groggy."

"No," Deth stated confidently. "I think you might have been taking in too much food." He addressed Lara. "Give him 25% less food, but keep it to each hour."

"All right," Lara agreed, making notes on her clipboard.

Deth stated to the group, "That should make a difference. He's losing up to a litre of perspiration per hour, so he's gotta take in warm, sweet and lightly salty fluids that help balance his electrolytes. Preferably with caffeine, as Lara's been doing." Deth ran his hand through his curly locks, casting his gaze on Lara for a moment, then on me as I explained how the onboard lights were disorienting. I got up and passed fortune cookies around, but only Lara took one.

"Robby, I understand lights need to see me, but does it have to blind me?" I sat back down beside him and waited for his response. Having a director as a boyfriend meant that he knew how to light me in a way that kept the spotlight from impairing my field of vision.

"We'll reduce the wattage and alter the direction of the light," Robby responded. "If the sea is calm, this is easy. If there's a swell, you'll have to manage with limited visibility. Next question?" Robby was all business.

"Okay, the boat seemed too close at times. I get panicky when it's too near. Can that be corrected?" I asked the crew.

Deth answered, "Well, we can pull back somewhat, but we have to adhere to the proximity rules."

"Don't forget," Mrs. McBride weighed in, "we'll have an official onboard who's going to dictate all regulations and ensure that we follow them to the letter."

"As well, we have to be close enough to use the pole for Lara to pass your food," Deth added. "I'm going to be very involved with the course, so you'll have to communicate with the crew if you're anxious about your position relative to the craft."

"Okay," I said, relieved that we were finding solutions.

"Can anyone repair a boat engine?" Lara asked abruptly. I was surprised, hearing her question after my father had raised the same query.

"I've never had a problem with the motor," Deth explained, shaking his head.

"That doesn't answer my question," she said firmly.

"No, I haven't a clue about outboard engines, other than knowing when to add fuel, of which we'll have to carry extra onboard."

"Do these things break down?" Pete asked naively.

"Everything breaks down," Lara said. "That's why I asked. We haven't talked about it before."

Mrs. McBride and Pete nodded and muttered that checking the motor and the propeller out was a good idea. Robby gave me one of his looks and blew out a large breath.

"Maybe I shouldn't have raised it," Lara expressed. "It could be bad luck." Lara put down a half-eaten fortune cookie, fingering the pink slip of paper it contained.

"No, we'll get it all checked out," Deth confirmed, smiling at Lara. "It's a good point. We need to think of every possible situation when we're out there."

Lara smiled warmly at the cardiologist, her brown eyes shimmering.

"Now, what's left to do?" Lara asked Robby.

"Well, we've gotta make all these adjustments we've talked about. We have a very strict sleep-wake schedule written out for you, the official and myself. Serge is the only one who'll be awake for the entire time. He's figured out a method of staying alert."

"Intravenous coffee and amphetamines," Deth joked.

"And Shep's gotta taper off and put on some weight," Robby poked me in the ribs. "All bone. He's never been lighter than me, and I don't like it one bit." He turned to speak with Pete. "What about the media stuff?"

"I'll make the announcement to the press on Friday. We've got a bunch of statements that are ready to go. Gloria Makarenko from the CBC is interested in 'Swim for Life', which is a huge advantage, especially considering the human against the sea angle. And, of course, this is doing what we had intended, drawing attention to AIDS."

"I won't have to talk to the press, will I?" I was tongue-tied when it came to the media, having been socially shy for most of my life.

"You might have to say a few words before the attempt," Pete guessed. "But I can coach you on what to say for maximum impact.

And, there's going to be coverage when you come into English Bay, for sure."

You mean, if I come into English Bay.

"Okay. I'll leave that to you. Thanks, Pete."

Deth said, "Robby and I will be going over the course-chart in the next couple of days to make any refinements. I think we can use a fresh tide to help us when we leave Ladysmith. The tides tend to run northeast, which will be a boon for the first 12 hours. They should run between 2 and 5 kilometres per hour, depending on where we are."

"So we all go to Ladysmith in your boat the day before?" Lara inquired.

Hearing her ask gave me new pangs of anxiety.

"Yes. We'll travel the route in reverse. Every bit of preparation will help."

"The course is confirmed with the swim official?" Mrs. McBride asked.

Robby and Deth looked at each other. Robby went to the map laid out on the coffee table and picked it up. "Yes," Robby said. "He'll begin the swim from Transfer Beach. We'll just be offshore, so he'll swim out to where we are. Fortunately, the water should be quite warm and it's fairly protected from winds. And here," Robby pointed out with his pen, "is Stuart Channel ... we'll head down the channel at slack tide and we'll double-back north and east in order to get past Thetis Island." Robby turned to Deth expectedly.

"This passage should be fairly calm to Thetis, but we'll have to watch the current through there, nonetheless," Deth added. "Things can change rapidly."

"Agreed, we have to have our wits about us." Robby said.

"Once we get through, we'll continue to head south past Reid Island. Porlier Pass is between Valdes and Galiano Islands, and it can run fast — very fast and treacherous — if the tide's not in our favour. We've completed all the calculations for the duration of the crossing, taking into account tides, currents," Deth explained. "Things we can't factor right now are the winds, but we've got an idea what the prevailing ones should be. I expect we'll have some surprises."

"Surprises?" Lara asked with arched brows. "I'd rather not be surprised out there."

"It's natural that there'll be things that we hadn't anticipated. We'll adapt where necessary."

"And if things really change, things that become dan —"

Robby interrupted Lara's concern. "If anything looks dangerous, Shep is pulled from the water, just like we talked about, Lara."

Lara nodded her head. "After he swims past those islands, then we're out —"

"In open sea." Deth finished her sentence. "From that point, there's nothing between us and Second Beach in Vancouver, except for 70 or so kilometres of water and few boats … a few massive boats," Deth stated seriously.

Robby folded the map into a square. "We've got it all figured out," Robby said proudly.

"What about the Swim Canada official?" Mrs. McBride asked.

"She'll meet us in Ladysmith, about an hour before we depart," Robby answered, putting his pen down on the table. "It's all come together, hasn't it?"

After sitting quietly and listening to the crew finalize the many details, I realized my part was relatively simple — swimming and eating was all I had to do. I looked around my living room. It was a curious sight. Young and old, frumpy and fashion-conscious, dubious and serious, worried and hopeful, apprehensive and excited.

"It's late," Robby declared. "I think our swimmer needs some shut-eye."

"I think we all do," Pete added. He looked extremely weary.

With that, the crew rose en masse and headed for the door. Lara came up to me, gave me a long hug and pecked me on the cheek.

"I'll call you tomorrow, Sunshine?"

"Deal," I said.

Dr. Deth moved towards Lara and me.

"It's dark. Let me walk you to your car," he offered kindly.

"Oh, I don't drive. Pete collected me, so I can get a ride to Kits with him," Lara responded. "But thanks, anyway."

"Pete," Deth called out, "I'll take Lara over the bridge, okay?" I caught Lara's eye. She appeared fine with Deth driving her home across the Burrard Street Bridge to Kitsilano.

"Sure. We're all in this boat together," Pete joked brightly as he cracked a smile, though fatigue was evident in his eyes. Perhaps Deth, noting his tiredness, was bent on doing Pete a favour. Robby was tired, too. Mrs. McBride was perhaps the one who was the most rested. The remainder of the crew had put in long hours for the practice swim. Now that we had problem-solved the logistics of the crossing, perhaps the most challenging parts were over?

After all the crew had left, I tided up the dishes. I looked for Lara's message in her fortune cookie and found it scrunched up in a tight ball and left on the side table. Picking it up, I unwrinkled the paper and I squinted to read it aloud in the dim light.

'If it seems that the fates are against you, they probably are.'

"Hah," I said, laughing to myself, balling up the prophesy and tossing the paper in the kitchen garbage. "Ridiculous. Don't you know I don't believe in fate?"

52

The Incident in The Water

The taper was a welcome reprieve. I still spent time in the ocean, but swim distances decreased till I got to 5 hours per day, which was still longer than most of my national team swim practices. I was pleased that I'd completely adjusted to the water temperature. By mid-mid-July in English Bay, the water was just below 20 degrees Celsius; further out in open water, a little cooler. For the night-time swim, I was prepared for a further drop in temperature. Certainly, it wasn't necessary to use grease during the taper phase because my time in the water was dramatically shorter. Some training days found me in the gym to maintain my strength, and other days I spent the entire day swimming at Kits, not paying attention to the laps, but focusing instead on the hours in the water. I was eating large amounts of food, but I wasn't able to gain an appreciable amount of weight. My physician estimated that I was at 9%, body fat; significantly less than the ideal 15-17%. Dr. Taylor and I were concerned about how the low-fat percentage would play out in the crossing. For that reason, I increased my calorie count in the remaining 2 weeks by eating limitless loaves of bread, plates of pasta, towers of pancakes, mountains of fruit, gallons of milk, buckets of ice cream and dozens of eggs. I was hopeful that I had sufficient time to add much-needed fat to provide both insulation and a fuel source for our fast-approaching watery adventure.

Pete had arranged a press conference as promised one week before our swim. We were meant to be at Second Beach at 3 PM to provide the press with the information related to the crossing. As per usual, I was looking forward to speaking to the press like bad cramps; the polar opposite of Lara's finesse with reporters. Pete, Lara and Robby would arrive at the beach by 2:30, and I was to come up to the press gathering from the bay, which Robby and Pete thought would make a dramatic entrance. I suggested that I remain in the water, as I was used to submerging myself far more than being visible. Pete insisted that I had my 'Swim for Life' gear on when I stepped out of the ocean and onto the beach for the reporters and cameras. Towels and tee-shirts with the same logo had been printed off and were going to be given out to the press and others that attended the conference. All of us were wearing the tee-shirts which, like my swim cap, were white with red print. Pledge donations and printed information about the swim attempt were also available. Pete expected that 80-100 people would show up at the beach for our announcement. AIDS Vancouver — as a co-sponsor — was going to be there, too, along with other sponsors such as Speedo. After Lara, Robby and I had a quick check-in at my apartment, (Pete had driven down with all the materials an hour earlier) we headed to Second Beach.

"Nervous?" Lara asked. She knew that I had performance anxiety whenever I had to speak in public. The three of us were walking from the Queen Charlotte. The day was unusually hot, which was great as far as I was concerned. The prolonged heat was beneficial for the swim the following Friday. I wiped sweat from my forehead.

"Yup, same old me. Like my stomach is in my throat. I'll feel calmer once I'm in the water." We continued to walk on a very busy Denman Street, quickly making our way to the seawall. I adjusted my rucksack, dodged a few pedestrians, then checked my Timex. I looked up at the flags in the small square at Morton Park. They were flapping heavily, though there didn't seem to be much of a breeze at street level.

"We've got plenty of time," Robby said comfortingly. It was his attempt to dampen my worry, though I thought he looked every bit as fretful as me. This was now more than a rehearsal. There were many things that had to go unerringly from this point onward.

"I want to make sure that I'm in the water at the right time." Pete told me that I was to appear from the sea at 3:10. "It's gotta be timed correctly," I added. We passed Denman and Davie and made our way to the crowded seawall.

"What a day!" Lara exclaimed, donning her sunglasses. "I can't imagine a better afternoon for a swim or to wag our tongues at the press," she said, walking with increasing energy and pace.

"I never get tired of this view," Robby commented. The deep-blue of English Bay opened before us as we moved onto the seawall. The skies were clear, though to the southwest there were a few dark clouds and a slightly rising breeze. Robby saw me looking over my shoulder. "We don't want any of those for next week."

"No. I'd prefer a fair-weather swim," I said. The sparse clouds and modest wind couldn't spoil a hot and sunny July day or a press confab.

We continued to walk for a short while. From the seawall, we could see the set-up at Second Beach. Dozens of people — presumably some of whom were the press — were milling around. "Okay. I guess I should change now." I unslung my rucksack. Lara and Robby accompanied me down to the sandy beach. Lara was right; the day was gorgeous, with the water gently lapping on the beach, making the wet sand sparkle in the powerful light. I removed my tee-shirt, shoes and shorts. Robby stashed them in my bag.

"I need my goggles."

"What about your cap?" Lara asked.

"Right, of course." I donned my red and white cap, then spat in my goggles, rubbed the saliva into the lens and put them on, adjusting them on my forehead. Again I glanced at my Timex. "I've got about 15 minutes." I stretched my arms over my head and then pulled each shoulder forward, up and back. "Pete said something about a signal, but I can't —"

"You should be able to see when Pete comes to the microphone. That'll be the time to make your way up, okay?" Robby briefly rubbed my shoulders and squeezed all the way down my arms.

"Yes. I remember." I bent down to stretch my calves, then twisted. I noticed a few beachgoers staring at us. We must have appeared freakish.

"Lara and I will head there now. By the time you swim out and over, we should be ready to go." Robby smiled at me warmly. "We better make tracks. See you in a bit, right?"

"Okay." I didn't hug them, but instead made my way to the water, feeling the fine, cool sand underfoot. I moved into the familiar waters, noting the warmth, swam out several hundred metres, began to make my way to the vantage point, then lifted my goggles so I could see the press gathering. Though I was some distance out, I determined there were at least 50 people in attendance. I treaded the water, casting a glance at my watch every few moments as I waited for my signal. It seemed to be taking longer than I thought. The dark clouds that had appeared previously were now threatening to obscure the sun. *Shit.* I felt an odd change in the air pressure. *What's the deal?* Suddenly the wind picked up force by ten-fold. *A squall?* Within moments, there was a gale that began to whip up the waters of English Bay. *Of course. Things can change in a heartbeat, remember?* I was shocked to find that the calm waters had rapidly changed. With each passing minute, there was not only a swell, but whitecaps that churned the waters into a frenzy faster than a swimmer could scream, "Mark Spitz". I started getting battered by the increasing energy of the waves. Over the chop, I could barely see the press on the beach. I could just make out Pete's image. He gave me the signal by moving to the microphone, but I had been pushed too far out — perhaps 75 metres and growing — by the waves. As I swam towards the beach, the fury of the squall resisted my forward motion completely, and I was pulled further into the bay. I couldn't see Pete or the people on the beach. The gale continued to blow southwest, or the opposite direction to where I wanted to go. *Okay, is this the part where I wake up?* The more I struggled against the opposing wind, the weaker I was getting. *Jezus, how could this happen?* Clearly, I was caught up in a rip. As the waves piled on the beach, it pushed the water back into the bay, and me with it. For several more minutes, the winds blew like a typhoon, and any attempts I made to come ashore were easily thwarted. In 6 or 7 minutes, I was at least 200 metres offshore when I heard someone calling out to me from a wooden rowboat. *This just gets better and better.* She struggled to come close to me as the oars dipped into the chop.

"Hey, come on, grab the line!" she hollered. It was the tall Amazon-like lifeguard from the Second Beach patrol, fighting against the wind and waves to get to me.

"No, I'm okay!" I shouted above the whitecaps. "I'm the swimmer that's due at that press thing!" I cried out, pointing to the now distant shore. The lifeguard couldn't hear what I was saying over the noise of the gale.

"Here!" she screamed above the noise of the wind and waves. "Take it!" The lifeguard tossed a buoy to me with a rope attached.

Resignedly, I took it and she pulled me to the boat. "Get in! Hurry!" she urged.

I held on to the leading edge of the wooden rowboat. With her considerable weight, she balanced on the opposite side and I pulled my tired body into the craft. "Thank you," I managed to say, thoroughly embarrassed. I took my goggles off and got in the centre of the violently moving boat.

"What the hell were you doing out there? You could have drowned!" The lifeguard had been put at risk for our press stunt and was furious at me.

"I'm sorry. I'll explain later, but can you please just get me to shore?" I pleaded, seawater sputtering from my mouth. "I've got a big entrance to make."

53

The Good Thing About Bad Press

"There's no such thing as bad press," Pete argued with Robby. They were talking in my dining room and referring to the article written in the sports section of the Vancouver Province newspaper the morning following the press conference. The story included an unflattering picture of me, staggering onto the shore of Second Beach with lopsided googles, looking utterly stupefied.

"Haven't you read this? It's like a disastrous theatre review." Robby pushed the Province at Pete. I sat in my leather chair and listened to Pete's narration.

Freak Storm Pushes Marathon Swimmer Out Into English Bay

If you happened to be looking out into the bay yesterday afternoon, you might have noticed a white and red buoy furiously bobbing in English Bay. In point of fact, it was a different type of 'buoy', namely Shep

Stamp, a 26-year-old distance swimmer and current Canadian record holder, who tried, but failed to swim a mere 100 metres to Vancouver's Second Beach for a press announcement. Stamp, whose last important win in the pool was years ago in Montreal, is attempting to be the first person to cross the Strait of Georgia from Ladysmith, on Vancouver Island, to the beaches of Stanley Park. It's laudable that Stamp's "Swim for Life" is aiming to draw attention and funds for AIDS Vancouver. However, if yesterday's disaster is any indication, it's hard to imagine how Stamp could swim across False Creek, let alone the strait. Caught up in a squall, he did make it to shore eventually, though 20 minutes late for his own press gab. Stamp never even got there on his own steam; rather the lifeguard that saved him from drowning rowed him ashore. Weather permitting, this scrawny swimmer and his non-professional motley-looking crew will try to swim a never-before-attempted distance starting this Friday, with the intent of completing the swim on BC Day.

"Well, it could have been a bit more positive. But he mentioned 'Swim for Life,' Pete said. "That's good." Pete dropped the paper back onto the dining table.

"Pete," Robby sighed tiredly. "He's saying that Shep's a gaunt has-been and we're a 'motley crew' destined for a fiasco. By the way, how did we become motley?"

"You don't care about your own theatre reviews, do you?"

"I try not to." Robby was usually proud of his work and was frequently indifferent to theatre notices.

"So, my advice is not to bother yourself with this trifle. The writer's a jerk. He didn't bother to inquire about the effort we've made coordinating Shep's swim, let alone acknowledge the dedication of his training for the past 3 months."

"The reporter was right about one thing, at least," I piped in. "It was a freak squall. But don't you think it's crazy that it happened when it did? What are the odds?" I pondered, recalling Lara's prediction for destiny and her fortune cookie message.

"C'mon. It was just an unfortunate and unexpected blast, nothing more." Pete shook his head. "It was probably a reaction from all this heat we've been getting."

"Yeah, but what if that happened when I was out in —"

Robby interrupted me with a snappy voice. "If you got caught up in something like that, you'd be on board in a flash — you know that. Exactly how many times do I have to tell you?" Robby's annoyance with my intermittent lack of self-confidence was showing.

"Until I'm reassured that I won't go for a voyage to the bottom of the sea," I said with as much snap as I could muster. I stood up and walked to the balcony and looked down at the street. I was breathing hard and felt my face burn. The room fell silent for several moments.

"I apologize. I guess I'm feeling the pressure of this, too." Robby spoke loud enough for me to hear. He stayed seated at the table fiddling with the newspaper.

"Who wouldn't?" Pete asked rhetorically, then called to me. "But the fact you were almost blown across the ocean might help generate more interest by showing how strenuous this challenge will be. I expect Monday the phone'll be ringing with questions and donations."

"You think?" I came back from the tiny balcony and gazed at Pete.

"It'll be a real summer event; a celebration. At the end of the swim, we'll have a party atmosphere. Lara and I've been planning it out. There'll be music, food, vendors, info booths and an area where we'll sell 'Swim for Life' goods. And of course people will be able to donate to the cause." Pete's excitement was a welcome and positive change.

"That's great, Pete," I said, still a bit hurt from my boyfriend's clipped tone.

"And, Shep, I do want to thank you —"

"No, it's not necess —"

"Quiet," he said. "I want to. This is a big deal. The *biggest* deal. It means so much to me." Pete rose from the table to give me a hug. As he embraced me, I smelled his expensive cinnamon soap. Even on a lazy, casual Saturday morning, Pete dressed in a faded denim shirt with pearl buttons, beige chinos and wore his trademark soft tan moccasins. He easily outclassed us all. "Personally, I have zero doubt that Aquaman can do this."

"We'll see." I looked over at Robby, who appeared sheepish. "Lately Aquaman is feeling a little wet behind the ears," I said wryly.

54

The Tanja

"It's really a nice-looking boat," I said, climbing into the cruiser moored at False Creek Marina. "It's really very … ah, sleek." I complimented Dr. Deth on his craft, which I knew nothing about. I had taken a jaunt to the marina for a closer look on Sunday afternoon. The vessel was a white and blue 26-foot cabin cruiser. On the starboard side, the 'Speedo' logo had been painted in large characters as per agreement. Though appearing small, the size of the craft was deceptive, as there were several compartments with plenty of storage and 2 sleeping compartments. The boat would need to hold a large amount of liquid and pureed foods which had been approved for the swim, plus would have to carry sufficient supplies and food for the crew. A light was now affixed near the bow of the boat, as was a swimming platform at the rear for access in and out of the water. Safety gear, ropes, and other items were kept in a crate, yet to be stowed. The seats were made of blue plastic, and there was room for 6 adults. The motor, much to my father's relief, had been tuned up and Deth reported that it "ran great". I was pleased and grateful that Pete had covered off all expenses regarding the crossing, including the tune-up, fuel costs, upgrades and new equipment. It was his gift to me for taking care of him during his illness. Deth's time had also been accounted for, though I didn't ask what the payout was. I had a chance to see the potty, which Lara would eventually *have* to use. The pilot would be further up front, and commanded an excellent view. "I couldn't really see your boat when I was swimming. Does it have a name?"

"Of course." Deth craned his body out of the boat and pointed to the hull. "There. Her name is 'Tanja', after my sister." Deth started cleaning the inside of the cabin with the contents of a spray bottle containing vinegar and water.

"Oh, that's a lovely name. Very European, like you," I said, smiling. "I bet Tanja didn't think she'd be guiding a swimmer the way across the strait, did she?" I fingered my Timex anxiously.

"Never in a million years," Deth said. "Nervous?"

"That's the question of the day. Yes, very. But I have a great crew, don't I? With good weather and some luck ..." I didn't finish my sentence. "Did you want some help with that? I'm good at wiping things down. My mother taught me. She's the Queen of Javex, you know. Never a bottle of bleach she didn't like."

Deth handed me the spray bottle and a roll of paper towels.

"Do *you* get afraid?" I asked, reeling off a few squares of towelling.

"What do you mean? Of the sea?"

"No, I meant doing those complex surgeries. It must be very stressful. You've literally got a life in your hands." I thought of my father's beating heart.

"Well, as hard as this is to believe, I've done so many heart surgeries, it almost gets to be ... well, not exactly routine, but familiar enough that it doesn't usually stress me."

"Really?" I asked. "I get stressed a lot, especially when I compete. I usually upchuck just before, not that you'd need to know.

I'm feeling it a bit now, just thinking of Friday." I scrubbed the top of the faux wood panelling.

"We *are* going over a day early. You might be able to relax more. I hear it's a very quaint town."

"Robby said that Ladysmith also has an incredible arts scene, but I'm pretty focused on the swim. I don't think I'd be settled enough to enjoy a play or be very good company."

"Lara is," Deth said calmly as he continued his task.

"Sorry?" I stopped cleaning.

"She's good company. We've been spending some time together."

"Have you? Lara never said." Hold on, *Lara's dating my stalker? The stalker you went to visit on a boat in False Creek? Reality check time.*

"She's very funny. I like that in a woman."

"You mean you like women?" My incredulity was showing.

"Of course. Why would you ask?" Deth seemed surprised.

"I thought that you might have been, ah, well, gay," I said cautiously.

"There's more to human sexuality than straight and gay, Shep. You should know that."

"Ah, so you mean that you're bisexual?"

"You said it a little while ago; I'm European. Some of us don't define ourselves in the same way as Canadians."

I was trying to figure out if Deth was inferring that I was a bourgeois oaf or not.

"I'm sorry. I sorta thought … at the hospital and when I saw you at the pool … I thought you might have been interested in, you know …"

"You?"

"Oh, no," I fibbed, instantly feeling my colour turn to scarlet.

"I didn't say I wasn't. Hand me the bottle," Deth said.

I may have been fluid in the water, but perhaps Deth was *as* fluid when it came to his sexuality. *So, Deth may or may not be interested in me. He might have been interested in Lara all along. Huh ... just when you think you've got it all figured out.*

I started to scour the seats with a brush in an effort to remove a stubborn stain.

"Uh, just wipe them down, please. You don't need to strip away the vinyl," Deth cautiously advised. "What does your father think of this swim, by the way?"

"Oh, well," I said, reducing the effort sizeably, "he thinks that by jumping into the ocean I'm murdering my mother. Though that thought's crossed my mind, I never thought of doing it by swimming."

Deth looked at me askance, perhaps missing my irreverence. "You close with her?"

"She annoys me at times," I started to answer his question.

"That's not what I asked you," Deth wrung his sponge dry into a blue pail. "Gay men often have close relations with their mothers. From my experience."

"Well, annoyance aside, I'd like to think that we have a very close relationship," I admitted. "You know, I have a distant father and a mother with an incredible sense of colour and design. Really, what chance did I have of being straight?" I joked. "I'm the complete stereotype."

Deth smiled at my assessment.

"Lots of straight men have distant fathers, you know. Your theory's a bit dated, if you ask me. Anyway, I just wondered what your mother thought about the attempt," he said as he continued to polish some of the metal fittings.

"To answer you, she's upset with me right now. It really pisses me off because I haven't done anything wrong. I'm just doing more or less what I've always done."

"Hmm. I'm no therapist, but I'd be frantic if my son told me he was going to jump into the sea for a couple of days."

"But you don't have a son," I commented.

"You don't know that, do you?"

"Well, I assumed."

"The thing about making assumptions is that they're very often incorrect. I *do* have a son. He's with his mother in Belgium."

"You mean —"

"I came to Vancouver to complete my fellowship several years ago. They remained there and after being in Canada for a few years, I didn't want to go back."

"Wow, I never knew."

"How could you? I keep some things private, including my son." Deth continued to polish the metal fittings near the front of his boat to a brilliant shine, stopping every so often to admire his work.

"How old is he?"

"Alex just turned eleven. Would you like to see his picture?" Without me responding, Deth put down his cleaning supplies and moved to the aft cabin where he brought out a small photograph album. Opening the binder, he scanned the pictures until he found several of his son. "Here he is." The boy was nice-looking with a thick head of curly hair, the colour light as wheat.

"He's a great-looking boy," I said, gazing at pictures of his son opening presents, camping, boating and playing soccer. "How often —"

"I bring him out a couple of times a year," Deth said pensively. "He loves to go out in the boat. Here's one of Alex and I going for a trip to Bowen. He loves it there." Deth smiled as he spoke of his son.

"And you're still married to his mother?" I asked, my surprise showing.

"Ah, another assumption. We weren't married. Karon wanted a child; I was happy to oblige. Truth is, I wanted to be a father, only if my role is mainly supportive. It works quite well this way. I have a place in his life that's very important to me."

"I see." I was constantly seeing there was more to a story and a person than what I thought. I finished cleaning the seats of the boat. "There. My mother would be proud," I said, looking at my completed job.

"Yes, I'm sure, but I've found it's best to do those things that make yourself proud." Deth's smile was wide.

"Ah, right, very sensible," I agreed.

For the next couple of hours, I helped Deth clean his treasured boat, stowing equipment, readying the life-jackets, sweeping the floor, sipping ginger ale and chatting with the Tanja's pilot as we prepared for the biggest swim of my life.

55

The Day Before

"The last time I was up before sunrise, I hadn't gone to bed yet," Lara complained as she and the crew hauled large plastic bins from a rented van en route to Deth's boat. One of the things that Lara carried was her battered guitar, perhaps for her to pass some time while on the way over and to sing during the crossing itself as she'd promised me. I carried the lightest articles, while Lara, Pete and Robby did the hefty lifting. They worked at stowing the heavily ice-packed bins in the holds. Lara had 6 crates of pureed food and litres of specialized caffeinated fluids that she'd packed into containers, all of which was to be carefully metered out each hour of the next day's swim. In addition to my liquid diet, Lara had added 4 loaves of bread and 1 kilo of peanut butter. If the waters were sufficiently flat, she was going to try to pass me bread and peanut butter on a kickboard to augment the pureed diet. For the crew, a caterer had created a variety of salads, grilled chicken, poached salmon, cheeses, pasta, fruit and several easy-to-eat desserts such as rice pudding and lemon bars. Like mine, the crew's food was packed with ice in large crates and stowed aboard. There were juices and milk as well as thermoses of tea and strong coffee to help everyone stay as alert as possible when on duty. As the sun began to rise, the boat was fully loaded with food and drink. Next to come were the personal items such as sleeping bags and toiletries — mainly toothpaste and washcloths — and extra warm clothing, just in case.

"Whew," Pete declared as he stood on the boat. "I'm exhausted."

Pete wasn't going to be on the boat, but would be waiting at the beach for when I hopefully came ashore. Of course, he had the reception party to organize and there were many things to finalize. Mrs. McBride, who had worked at creating warm swim gear, decided that the trek was too long for her, so she also was staying at home, promising to greet me on Second Beach with Pete. Deth had stayed the night on his boat, having completed a long shift at Royal Columbian Hospital. He'd ensured that the Tanja was fuelled up and ready to go. With all food and goods onboard, Pete said his goodbyes to the crew, tearing up in the process.

"I'll see you on August 1st," he said, then gave me a prolonged hug. "You'll never know," he whispered in my ear before taking his leave, with me wondering what the last part of his sentence might have been. We silently watched as Pete made his exit slowly, looking back once to give all of us a brilliant smile. Suddenly, my throat had a lump the size of the oranges Lara brought onboard. *This effort really started with Pete, didn't it?* I began to settle into my seat. Deth was at the controls at the front of the craft, drinking a large mug of black coffee. The rest of us were comfortable in the passenger section. It might have been a bit snug with crates jockeying for crew space, but we were happy and excited. Lara sat beside me, her elbow hooked in mine, with Robby on the other side, his hand gently gripping my own. *Perhaps they want to hold me down in case I make a run for it?* The sound of gulls screeching overhead in an azure sky interrupted my thoughts. They were quieted as Deth ignited the motor. Robby was asked to untie the tethered boat, and after doing so, jumped back in. Quickly seating himself, Robby placed his arm around my shoulders.

"We're off," Deth called out to the crew.

Yes. It's hard to for me to comprehend, but we're really on our way.

The water boiled at the back of the craft as Deth carefully reversed from the berth. A few minutes later, we were moving under the Burrard Bridge. The giant grey structure towered somewhat menacingly above us as we quietly sat in awe of the stylish Art Deco bridge. A short while later, we passed the Aquatic Centre, it's stark design contrasting the natural landscape. As the boat cruised into a calm English Bay, Deth powered-up the motor, and at 20 knots per hour, we started our 4-hour excursion to Ladysmith.

By the time that we got to our berth just before noon, Lara was seriously seasick. She meant to take a Dramamine, but in her excitement about sorting all the food items, had forgotten to take it.

"Land Ho!" Robby joked, as we put our feet on terra firma. Lara reeled down the gangplank with her overnight case, looking more than a little greenish.

The sailing had been relatively smooth, but in certain areas, the conditions changed — mostly increased swells — as we continued past the halfway point. That's when the motion-sickness affected Lara. To counteract the motion of the boat, Deth asked her to come to the controls and to look only at the horizon. It didn't work.

"Christ, I think I'm gonna jump into the water and swim to Ladysmith," she'd said, her queasiness giving way to irrationality, though understandable, given how she felt onboard. Deth directed her to lie flat on the prow of the cruiser, which she carefully did. That seemed to help, or at least it minimized the effect until we made port.

"Lara's gotta remember to dope herself up before we head out tomorrow. We're screwed if she's not able to crew the swim." Robby's concern was written on his beautiful face.

"She'll be okay," I said, believing that the medication would cure her sickness. *It must.*

Ladysmith was perched on a gentle hill and overlooked the sea. Founded in the late 1800's, it was a coal town with a good harbour. Rather sleepy, the town didn't grow as others in nearby cities like Nanaimo had. Perhaps for this reason, Ladysmith had retained its Victorian charm, complete with period buildings in the main part of town. Tourism and not coal, was one of the industries that kept the small town of 6,000 alive. Quaint and friendly would describe Ladysmith. I dislike small towns, though I found Ladysmith to be appealing. The hotel we stayed in was an old wooden home converted to rooms. It seemed pleasant enough, but I was so focused on my upcoming swim I wasn't paying much attention to anything else.

The hotel was very close to where I would start from — Transfer Beach. Shortly after getting some lunch, we all returned to the hotel to sleep for several hours. I was surprised at how fatigued I was, not having done anything of note for the entire day. The crew shared an early dinner. I wasn't hungry, but with Lara and Robby's encouragement, I ate a large, carbohydrate-laden meal of plain pasta with roasted vegetables and bread ... lots of bread. My loss of body fat had been a concern, though I had been able to regain 8 pounds, meaning that I did have some fat stores. At a lean 158, I retained muscle, but not much in the way of an insulating layer of fat, which was important for the swim. It would be critical that I was well-covered with Vaseline to compensate for the lack of body fat and to help protect against hypothermia.

After dinner, Lara, Robby, Deth and I strolled to the quiet beach. Like the rest of the crew, my eyes were on the weather. The forecast was for continued warm temperatures for at least 3 days and minor breezes across the strait; excellent news for us. As we walked, I noticed how the air was scented sweetly by the sea and the surrounding forests. The light lasted until just before 9 PM, and the sky at dusk was a blaze of purples and reds. Robby and I stopped strolling, sat on the crunchy dried-out grass and wordlessly looked out over the serene waters. Deth and Lara slipped away, strolling at the edge of the ocean.

"I wonder what's going on there?" Robby seemed curious at the sight of Lara and Deth chatting amiably as they walked slowly, pausing to take in the sky.

"Dunno, Robby." I shook my head. "I assumed Deth was gay; guess I was wrong." I thought about my early relationship with Lara. I was certainly confused about how I felt about her. Lara had the ability to make a gay man think differently about himself, but not through manipulation. Beauty of either sex can be a stimulating aphrodisiac, especially for those who are unsettled about their sexuality as I had been for many of my growing-up years.

"Well, he's just talking with Lara. It doesn't mean he's romantically interested in her, does it?"

"Oh, I think he is, Robby."

"That's great. Lara hasn't dated anyone for a while, right?"

"I think she has the same worries we all do. Dating today just seems so dangerous. I think she's been more focused on her career this year."

"You think Lara likes Deth?"

"She does. I mean, she told me that she liked him."

"You don't sound happy. What's wrong with her seeing him?"

"Well, nothing, but Lara's had problems with men. There's been quite an assortment over the years. Hairy beasts, married sailors, prison convicts, philanderers, oh, and that jester."

"What jester is that?" Robby's eyes were round with interest.

"A real jester. She dated a professional clown. Well, to be honest, she didn't know he was a clown at the time. I worry about her ability to make good choices about men." I pulled at the dry grass and chewed on a piece.

"Serge seems to be a good guy."

"I guess. No, you're right. He's a *very* good guy." I had to agree that Deth had been extremely helpful and supportive to not only our 'Swim for Life', but with both Pete and my father. I spat out some of the grass.

"Maybe this time?" Robby asked, a wide grin showing perfectly imperfect teeth.

"What, more Liza?" I asked pointedly.

"No," Robby laughed. "I just think it's time for Lara to go for someone, I dunno, more balanced. Not that a clown couldn't be balanced, no disrespect to him."

"Jester wasn't balanced, though he *could* balance on his head playing the wazoo while wearing a pumpkin costume on the pool deck."

My boyfriend's mouth dropped. "This is a real story, isn't it?" he deadpanned.

"Please, I can't make this stuff up."

I recounted the Halloween when Lara and I were swimming at the Aquatic Centre and she spied Jester — that's the name she gave him. Lara was stunned to see that the fellow she'd gone out with twice who told her he was "in banking", was wearing a pumpkin costume, which was understandable if he were at a Halloween party, but he wasn't. In a few moments, he put a wazoo in his mouth, then for reasons perhaps only a clown could know, stood on his head and began playing Dixie. This happened right on the pool deck and was one of the most bizarre things I'd ever seen. That was it. Lara broke up with him immediately. After I told Robby the story, his mouth was still agape.

"Wow. By comparison, Deth is kinda like the 'Oscar' of men, isn't he?"

"Well, if he's sexually fluid, he won't be any golden prize for Lara. She doesn't really —"

"Hey, look," Robby suddenly said. "Something's happening."

I watched Lara and Deth from our uphill vantage point. He took her hand as they turned into slow-moving black silhouettes against the tangerine late-summer sky.

"Huh," Robby uttered. Deth and Lara strolled further down the beach. "Watching them makes me think we stop talking and go back to our room," Robby suggested, with a quick wink of his hazel eye. He rose from the grass and grabbed my hand, pulling me up and giving me a quick kiss on the mouth. "Deal?"

"Deal," I agreed. We ran back to our hotel, giddy with laughter.

56

Lost in the Stars

*T*he waters were tranquil as I swam, stoking easily as the day turned slowly to night. The boat was close-by. I could smell the fuel fumes as it puttered effortlessly in the sea. My body felt cool, but not cold, as I continued on. Without warning, the water swelled, and I lost sight of the pilot boat. I swam up, then down the swollen sea. Suddenly, all around me was jet-black, with no pilot boat's light to guide me. I stopped swimming, treading water with difficulty, moving my goggles up to my forehead. The boat was nowhere to be found. I looked in all directions. Above me, the sky was inky, starless. I was alone in the blackness of the sea as it moved around me with increasing ferocity. A wave hit me hard and filled my mouth with brine. I gagged and coughed hard enough to vomit. The formerly cool water stung like ice. Water roared all around me, though there wasn't any wind. I panicked, looking in vain for the boat. As the ocean churned, I screamed for help, but in the desolation of the sea, my cries were unheard.

I woke, gasping. Robby was beside me, snoring lightly. My body was soaked with perspiration, and yet I was as cold as the water I dreamt I'd been swimming in. I pushed off the cover and swung my legs from bed quietly, not wanting to wake Robby. Padding to the washroom, I pulled down my boxers and sat down to pee. I was breathing hard; my heart raced. As I emptied my bladder, my Timex told me it was exactly 2 AM. I took a hand towel from the chrome bar and wiped the sweat from my chest and neck. Silently, I came back to the bedroom, slipped on a tee-shirt and sandals and left. A few moments later, I was outside under a sky filled with stars. It was staggeringly beautiful. Living in Vancouver, stars were often obscured by the city's lights and clouds. When I ran late at night on the seawall, stars were more visible on the darkest side of Stanley Park, west of the Lion's Gate Bridge, but that view paled in comparison to the starry spectacle I was observing. The boundless expanse of the stars and planets left me in awe. I lost myself in the stars. I stepped closer to the water's edge. The silence was broken as slight waves came ashore and I thought about what we were about to do, merely a few hours away.

Though I'd been far too stimulated to sleep, I nonetheless returned to my room after an hour under the starlight. I smiled when I heard Robby's snoring. Unlike me, my boyfriend's ability to sleep was extraordinary. Crawling into bed, I lay on my back, wide-awake. Staring at the ceiling wasn't nearly as interesting as looking at the stars. I waited to fall asleep, but at most, I dozed for a few minutes before getting up to brush my teeth. With the bathroom door closed, I used the toilet (for the last time in a while, most likely) and ran a very hot shower. I sat down in the tub and let the hot water from the shower penetrate my body. *I won't be warm again for a couple of days, so I might as well make this feeling last.* Towelling myself dry, I rubbed the steam off the mirror and gave my reflection a good, hard look. My skin was deeply tanned, except for the round circles where my goggles were worn, giving me a rather odd reverse-racoon appearance. My short hair didn't suit me the way it did Robby, but in a few months, it would grow back. I grabbed some loose skin beside my visible rib cage and gave it a jiggle. I looked deficient of fat, and once more I worried that it was probable that I'd run out of energy before I completed the attempt, though publicly I never admitted my biggest fear, not even to Lara.

"Can I come in?" Robby asked, gently knocking at the door.

I wrapped myself warmly with the towel and opened the door. "Morning." I smiled and kissed his mouth briefly.

"How'd you sleep?" Robby sat on the toilet to pee, just like me.

"Um, okay," I lied, wishing Robby believed I was well-rested.

"Lara and Serge are meeting us downstairs at 4 for coffee, so I'd better jump in the shower and get ready. We'll eat onboard the Tanja."

"And the Swim Canada official?"

"She'll be at the marina around 5:30 this morning." Robby finished tinkling, stood up and rinsed his hands. "By that time, you'll already be in the water just about 500 metres from us. We'll hook up with you as you start down Stuart Channel."

"Right," I said, suddenly feeling shaky.

"Okay, why don't you get your stuff together, and I'll be out in 10 minutes, okay?"

"Uh, huh," I said. I had a wave of nausea as big as any swell.

"Shep, are your nerves gettin' the best of you?"

"Yeah, I'm probably a little anxious to get going," I laughed uneasily. "Don't forget, you still have to grease me down, remember?"

"C'mon, how can I forget?" Robby's mouth turned into an evil grin. "It's what I've been living for."

"Long as you're happy," I said brightly, then left Robby to his tasks and started my own preparations, which were minor. After all, I merely had to pull on my suit, goggles, headgear and have my body greased with petroleum jelly. While Robby was taking a quick shower, I worked on composing myself mentally when the phone rang. This early in the morning, I thought it must have been my best friend.

"Lara?" I dabbed my chest with the towel as I held on to the telephone.

"My dear, it's me. I called to wish you the very best of luck!"

"Oh, Mrs. McBride. Thank you for calling, and at this early hour, too."

For a few minutes we spoke about the water temperature, correct arm position with the swells, and the impact of outgoing tides.

"Now," she said sternly, "remember to pace yourself, keep your mind occupied, sing songs in your head, or whole record albums, think of movies from beginning to end like we talked about — which one is it that you know by heart? *Casablanca*?"

"*The Wizard of Oz*," I answered. I'd probably seen it 50 times or more.

"Yes, of course. Well, while you're out there, you can also do some math calculations or whatever else it takes to keep your mind focused, dear."

"I remember, Mrs. McBride." *Math? Highly doubtful.*

"And we'll be there — Pete and I — to watch you swim the last bit. Oh, won't that be something to see! We'll be cheering you till our throats give out."

My own throat was feeling a familiar constriction.

"It means a lot to me, Mrs. McBride."

Robby appeared from his shower and walked into the room with brows raised in curiosity.

"Best of luck, dear. And we'll see you on BC Day."

"Hope so," I responded cautiously, worry in my voice.

"We all know you can accomplish this," she said with conviction. "And so do you. Goodbye."

The phone line went dead. I sat in the chair and exhaled deeply as I placed the phone in its cradle. "Mrs. McBride," I whispered to myself.

"Pep talk from your landlady?" Robby inquired. He was speedily dressing in dark-blue shorts and flinging on a 'Swim for Life' tee-shirt.

"Uh huh. I should probably call my folks, Robby."

"It's a little early, Shep." He looked at the digital clock. "They'll be following along when the swim starts."

"Huh? Whaddya mean?"

"We'll be sending updates to CKNW from the CB radio on the boat every few hours. Pete arranged a direct hook-up thing. Don't you recall that we talked about that?" Robby had indeed mentioned there would be radio coverage during the swim and then, with fingers crossed, TV reporting at the beach in Stanley Park.

"I'm sorry. I forgot all about it," I confessed.

Pay attention, for fuck's sake.

"Not a problem. We're on it." Robby tied his running shoes and flicked on the television, tuning in the Weather Channel. "You've had other stuff to think about, haven't you?" he asked rhetorically as he waited for the report. "Weather's looking good. Really good," he said, pleased at the forecast.

"Fantastic," I said, dropping my towel and after locating my special white swimsuit, tugging it on. "When I was outside a couple of hours ago, it was crystal-clear, and the stars were so incredibly —"

"You were outside?" Robby's voice was tinged with disappointment. "You should have been resting, Shep. You won't be sleeping for a long time now."

"I do *know* that, Robby," I said with more than a hint of irritation. "Sorry. I was having a hard time settling, that's all. I'm really very rested. Rested as I can be," I corrected myself. I hated to admit it, but he was right. I had only slept for about 6 hours; completely insufficient and not according to our plan. I put on a long black terrycloth robe, slipped into leather sandals and grabbed my swim bag. "Let's go."

The 4 of us crammed into a booth in the hotel's just-opened cafe. Lara and Deth certainly looked pleased to be with each other. I didn't want to ask about it. They had on their 'Swim for Life' tops, as did Robby, who, despite his shower, looked a little scruffy with a blonde beard. I looked queer; a black-robed monk wearing leather sandals.

"Dramamine?" I asked Lara.

"Check," she said immediately. "I've got enough for everyone to share," she said expansively.

I didn't imagine she'd want a repeat of yesterday. After a short briefing and a gallon of coffee, Lara gave me a long embrace, told me that she'd see me in a little while in the water, and we made our exit. Deth was hurrying to the marina with Lara to meet up with the swim official. I'd given Deth a urine sample with his physician's verification just before we had coffee. He was to provide it to the swim official who took it to the local lab in Ladysmith. Robby was going down to the beach with me to smear me to kingdom come with grease, which, in another situation, might have been rather enjoyable.

"You'll need gloves," I said, digging out a pair of surgical gloves that Deth picked up for us — well, stole, actually —- from the hospital. "This stuff won't come off easily."

We were standing on Transfer beach. The sun had not come up yet — not until 5:40 — though mauve light was filtering up from the horizon. There were no clouds in the skies. It was already 19 degrees and the water was dead calm. The odd person was out for a run or walk, and their curiosity was piqued at the sight of Robby rubbing a thick layer of petroleum jelly over my body from neck to toe.

"There," he said, admiring his handiwork. "You're done."

"Appreciated," I said. "Can you fetch my swim cap and goggles? Please don't get 'em covered in Vaseline or I won't be able to see," I said, standing as still as stone. I carefully eased my earplugs in as Robby handed me the cap, helping me to put it over my head. Robby fitted the cap completely over my ears and hooked it under my chin. I noticed my heart thudding in my chest. *Probably from all that coffee, right?* "Goggles now, please." Robby carefully put them over my cap and secured them to my forehead.

"I've never seen you look so slick," Robby joked.

After groaning at his observation, I said, "I've got enough oil on me to power Manhattan for the weekend."

Robby grinned. "I gotta run back to the boat," he said as he began collecting my gear and shoving my robe and other items in the bag. "You should easily be able to hear our signal."

"I can't even see the boat," I said.

"No, but you will in," Robby looked at his wristwatch, "about 10 minutes. When you hear the horn, jump the fuck in, okay?" Robby gave a hearty chortle. "I almost can't believe we're doing this."

"Hmm, I'm thinking the same thing." I shook my head, then gave my neck a massage, skin slippery with grease. *Gawd, I'm tight. Try to relax...*

Robby gestured at a black van with CBC emblazoned on the panel and two men with equipment were striding over to where we were.

"Okay, looks as though the media's here," he said.

Two men charged up to Robby and me with a video camera and microphone in tow.

"Hey, there. So, you're the guy that's doin' the swim to Vancouver?"

"I wanna know who we're talking to, gents," Robby inquired briskly.

"Oh, 'course. We're with the CBC in Victoria." He reached in and pulled out identification which meant nothing to me. Robby took a brief glance. The reporter was young, with a pushy demeanour.

His partner had a large, boxy television camera on his shoulder. The reporter pointed his finger at me, slicked with grease, wearing an odd swim cap and peculiar, bulky swim shorts and seemingly a bit queasy-looking.

"So, *he's* the swim-guy?" From his tone, I presumed he was surprised.

"That's right," Robby said. "He's Shepard Stamp."

"Guess we were expecting you to look a bit more, um, robust. Can we get some footage?" Without permission, the camera's red light turned on.

Robby looked at me and I nodded my head in the affirmative. After a short exchange, the reporter asked, "Will you do it? Do you really believe you can cross the strait? It's double the distance of any previous swim."

"The crew and I have trained very hard, so we believe that we're prepared for this attempt." I responded to the press exactly as Pete had instructed me to do. Pete said to respond like a politician, which meant, never give an absolute answer.

The reporter looked eager to get more from both Robby and me. Strikingly, he inquired, "And do you have AIDS? Is that why you're —"

"That's the type of rude question that doesn't deserve a response," Robby stated. "We're done." My boyfriend turned his back on the reporter and gave me a quick kiss which the CBC couldn't get on videotape. Ignoring the press, Robby said, "Listen carefully for the signal and we'll see you from the Tanja." With that, Robby dashed off towards the marina. The camera guy tried to get a couple more shots as I slowly made my way to the water's edge, waiting for the horn to blast.

57

The Crossing Attempt Begins

Just after 6 AM, I heard a horn that would shatter glass, or that's how it seemed to an agitated swimmer. I moved my goggles into place and slid into the tepid waters at slack tide. As soon as I started to swim, my considerable anxiety and nausea vanished. The Tanja was, as Robby promised, about 500 metres out. I caught up to the pilot boat easily, giving them a wave in the process. In the early morning sunlight, I could see the outline of Lara and Robby through slightly foggy goggles. As I looked up at the boat, they both gestured wildly at me from about 5 metres away, the maximum distance allowed. Deth was maintaining the gap expertly as he adjusted the power to the engines with the current. He matched my speed as we continued along the course. A couple of times, I caught a glimpse of the swim official, an older woman with a large helmet of brown hair. She was standing on the small deck wearing an orange life jacket. It was just a peek, but I could see her taking pictures, probably to authenticate the swim attempt.

The first few kilometres were swum southeast in Stuart Channel in waters that were thankfully flat and nearly warm. Swimming freestyle comfortably, my legs were flutter-kicking at a leisurely rate and I estimated my stroke count at the predicted 22 per 50 metres. Robby called out that I was swimming with the outgoing tide at over 3 kph, or faster than our goal of 2 kph. After I relaxed into the swim, I began to feel hungry after the first hour. At 7 AM, the boat sounded the horn, and I began to tread water. Quickly, Lara threw me a large thermos containing my meal. It was distinctly different not having to carry a belt with me to manage my food intake. The bottle was attached to a yellow nylon rope with a large metal clip. The swim official gave me a broad smile as she watched how I was given the food and appeared to note so on a clipboard. Lara's first meal for me was as planned: reduced blueberries, blenderized tofu, orange juice with salt. The meal had something different, though — an unfamiliar texture, though not unappetizing. "Hey, what's the grit?" I called out to my best friend.

"Toasted sourdough breadcrumbs from Paris Bakery," Lara hollered back. "I thought you'd enjoy some carbs!"

"You're doing great," Robby shouted down to me.

"Where we at?" I cried above the noise of the boat's engine and in-between gulps. Robby spoke with Deth briefly and then turned his head back to me.

"We're just about to change course soon — northeast to get 'round Thetis. Deth thinks were 11 K to Porlier Pass. Hopefully, we should be there at slack tide," he called out.

I did the math; it would be approximately 4-5 hours to arrive at the 650-metre passageway between Valdes and Galiano Islands. I did *not* want to be there unless the tide was slack or running with me. Otherwise, at 7 or 8 knots, the tidal current would make it impossible to swim through.

"Okay, that's better than expected," I yelled.

"Stop yapping and eat!" Lara cried out, hanging on to the chrome guard rails.

I did as directed and finished the food. I secured the clip to the bottle. As Lara pulled the bottle back, I gave her the thumbs-up sign, carefully adjusted my goggles back to the correct position without smearing them with Vaseline, and started off once more. Hour after hour, I felt comfortable, well-nourished, confident and secure in the light swell of Stuart Channel. With 5 meals in my gut, I was now past Reid Island and slowly approaching the pass. There was a change in the water. The tide that had been aiding in my swim speed was now beginning to ebb. The Tanja was now requiring more power to hold her position as I began to strain at my shoulders for the first time. There were a few small islands that I went by en route, and I began fantasizing about taking a breather on one of them — for about a day. Instead, I did what Mrs. McBride suggested; I played music in my head to pass time and to distract me from the fatigue that was gripping me in my arms and shoulders. My legs were counterbalancing my stroke and were fresh. My arms felt increasingly heavy. As if on cue, I heard the horn blast out 2 times — my rest break. I moved the goggles off my eyes and flipped onto my back. The sun was hot on my chest and stomach, and I was glad for the change in position. I managed to float on my back for 8 minutes. If I'd spent more time resting, my core body temp would have dropped, so I began again, swimming with the pilot boat in pursuit as we made the painfully slow approach to Porlier Pass. Close to 1 PM, pleasure craft were moving into the waterways of the channel. Even smaller boats tossed up significant wakes, and Deth tried his best to manoeuvre the Tanja in such a way those waves were minimized. *Waves aren't good for Lara, either. Hope she's been taking her Dramamine. I need her for a long time, yet.* The relative comfort of being in semi-protected waters was giving way to a fast tidal current coming from the pass. Something was wrong. In the centre of the pass, the water had churned into waves that towered above me and pushed me backwards. We were quickly getting caught up in the frenzied waters.

I stopped, pushed my goggles up and howled, "Hey, what's happening?"

Still about half a kilometre from the pass, the sea was whipping up considerable waves. At the top of each wave was a whitecap that slapped my exposed face — and hard.

"Shep, we've mistimed the tide a bit," Robby anxiously yelled. Lara bounded to the bridge to presumably talk to Deth. "Hang tight for a sec, till we figure out what to do," Robby turned to the swim official and held up his hand for a moment, then bolted to join Lara and Deth. I continued to tread water, maintaining my position in the water without being shoved back into Stuart Channel. I could hear the boat engine roar to hold its place in the water. Lara and Robby came back to the port side of the Tanja. "Okay, don't exert yourself —"

"Are you crazy?" I shouted. "I'm barely able to stay afloat!"

"We got to the pass too quickly," Robby yelled.

"What?" I cried back, spitting out a mouthful of saltwater.

"You swam too fast with the tide, and now we're here at the wrong time." Robby and Lara looked at each other, completely mystified. I thought I heard Deth yelling. Lara looked over at him. The official was watching everything with intense scrutiny. She had the ability to call off the attempt and have me hauled into the craft at her discretion.

"Say it again," Lara screeched to Deth. She turned back to me, "Okay, we're going to just wait this out for the next 10 or 15 minutes — that's what Serge says," Lara called out with the help of the electric megaphone that she brought along, not intending to hurt her voice.

"He'll adjust the boat to break you," Robby exclaimed.

"Jezus, Robby, I don't wanna be broken," I shouted.

"Shield you, I mean," he cried out above the noise.

"Better," I yelled. The roaring water was moving around me, and in different directions, as though I was a cork in a blender. It was impossible for the boat to shield me as the water was coming at me from many different angles. It seemed as though at any given moment I could be taken underwater, but that was mostly an emotional reaction. I knew I had the physical strength to ride it out. As I anxiously waited, I could see we weren't the only ones in trouble. There were a few sailboats languishing in the turmoil; one appeared to have a broken mast. Perhaps they, too, had a miscalculation with the tide. I continued to swim, but this time doing breaststroke to keep my head above the sea. The whirlpool of water swirled around me for a further 15 minutes, precisely as Deth had predicted, and I was left dizzy and disoriented. The sea began to flatten out. I moved my goggles back on and started for the pass, now only 200 metres away. I was deliriously pleased to be moving forward, albeit slowly. The beauty of the pass — with its towering, sandstone bluffs, emerald green cedars and arbutus trees with peeling bark — was lost on me as I fought to move through Porlier Pass. The remnants of the tidal current were bizarre and dangerous whirlpools that Deth wisely steered us away from.

"We're through the worst of it," Lara announced on her megaphone. The Tanja crew and I continued on, inching through Porlier Pass. I used my secret weapon — my kick — to help propel me along for the next few minutes. There was a change in vista as soon as we got past the head of Galiano Island. After nearly 20 kilometres, the expansive seas opened before us as we headed north and east into the Strait of Georgia.

58

The Big Struggle Starts

The strait was an enormous body of water for a swimmer used to doing distance swims in a 50-metre pool. At 14 hours in, with meal breaks, super-caffeinated beverages, rests floating on my back and with tired, aching shoulders, I continued to move along. The strait is a busy place. Many pleasure-craft, such as the Tanja, as well as sailboats traversed the waters, and especially during the long weekend. Several boats took notice of our efforts and screamed out their support from a distance. And though we were not close by to the BC Ferries, their wakes affected us even though they travelled routes several miles away. The swells created by ferries and other craft were daunting. Huge freighters plied the strait as well, and their massive size dominated the seascape even when we were a great distance from them.

The water was indeed cooler in the strait, and the small swells in Stuart Channel were nothing compared to the rolling seas that consistently rose up to 3 metres. One encouraging thing about the swells was that though I had to struggle a bit to swim up them, I found that I could surf down the swell, too. This meant that I used less energy and it increased my average speed. *Any small bit helps.* I closed my eyes as I swam, trying to imagine what it might be like after the sun set. With the sun slowing moving behind me, I swam for the next few hours with a developing fear of nightfall looming. We had practice-swum with Deth's boat at night, but this was a different story. By 9:30, the remaining shards of light barely illuminated the western sky as I moved northeast in an ominously darkening sea. As the night fell, there was a change in the water temperature that seemed immediate, though it was most likely my misperception. The horn sounded for my meal. I wasn't hungry; just tired. The horn sounded again and I stopped and treaded the dark-blue waters slowly. As the Tanja idled, Lara once more tossed me the bottled food with the expertise that had come from doing this many times since early in the morning.

"How ya doing?" Lara called to me after I chugged some of her pureed food.

"I'm okay," I said, mindful of the official observing my responses. "S'cuse me, but what's your name?" I called out to her. I thought it was about time I knew. The woman came closer to the port side and called to me.

"I'm Candice Kane," she answered loudly. "People call me Candy," the official said, and patiently waited for the penny to drop. I might have been in chilly saltwater for the past 15 hours, but even I found the humour in having Candy Kane as the onboard swim official. I smiled from earflap to earflap. "However, in my professional capacity, I prefer 'Mrs. Kane'."

Lara was beside her, secretly bulging her eyes and dropping her jaw in mock surprise. Mrs. Kane's name would be the type of irreverent thing that could set Lara into a fit of giggles. Needless to say, I had to be all business, and finished my meal, asked for a hot coffee to be thrown down and took a few minutes further rest by floating in the swelling waters on my sunburned back.

"Mrs. Kane, thanks for being the official on our excursion," I sang out.

"It's a pleasure, young man," she responded.

I nestled my goggles on in preparation of the continued swim.

"I'm going for a nap," Lara called out huskily.

"See you for dinner," I joked, then headed out once more.

The crew had entered the phase whereby regular rests would be taken. Deth had set up 2 small — and some would say claustrophobic — sleeping areas below deck that would be used for that purpose. Now that Lara had fed me, she would be the first to hopefully sleep for an hour. Robby would stay vigilant with Mrs. Kane, watching for signs of fatigue. Robby could rest when Lara was done, however, the official's rests were brief — only 15 minutes each 4 hours. Our pilot was the only one who was meant to stay awake for the duration. While Deth had pulled many hospital shifts where he was awake for up to 48 hours at a time, Robby had not. I hoped that with the frequent rests, Lara and Robby would be able to manage the pressure of the crossing.

As we moved northeast, any remaining fragments of light vanished. At 9:45 PM, Deth turned on the searchlight. It shone about 25 metres past the craft — more than enough light for me to see where I should be swimming. Not that I could see it, but I knew that Mrs. McBride's specially designed swim-cap would be glowing phosphorescently, and I would also be visible in the searchlight. My worries of swimming at night eased, and it was replaced by a wandering mind. I stroked the water monotonously and waited for Lara's exceptionally strong coffee to kick in. Even with the searchlight, I could no longer see my hand underwater as I pulled. From my 20 years of training, I knew that my stroke was correct by the streamlined position my body maintained. Any alteration of that — such as fishtailing — would be noticed by me and if not, Robby or Lara could provide feedback. Swimming is all about being efficient, by using a balance of muscular power and relaxation. Tension in the body causes resistance, and the less resistance I had in the water the quicker I was. The salty sea is denser than fresh water, so it made me more buoyant, and thus helped me to swim faster with the same force or energy expended. Though I'd been expecting the waters of the Strait of Georgia to be icy at night, I was pleased to find that there didn't appear to be a dramatic change. The hot temperatures had increased the heat of the ocean to nearly 19 degrees Celsius, even after nightfall. With my thick layer of Vaseline, I was able to maintain most of my body heat. When I stopped, I noticed how quickly I became chilled. With the sun down, it seemed that the swells had also decreased significantly. Other than seeing the rolling waters advancing towards me with the aid of the light, there was nothing much to look at. I was in visual connection with the boat. I could see it mostly with my peripheral vision; a steady, constant presence that went a long way to keeping me secure. Though my cap and earplugs muffled sound, I could hear the engine gurgling reassuringly as we plodded along. For the Tanja to travel with me at 2 kilometres per hour, the outboard motor was not expending a great deal of fuel. As per plan, I passed the time by playing and replaying 'Oz' in my mind, complete with soundtrack, Munchkins, Scarecrow, Lion, Tinman, Dorothy, flying monkeys, ruby red shoes, and of course, the horrible Wicked Witch. Replaying the film kept me entertained as the Tanja and I moved slowly through the night.

The sharp spot of light cut through the blackness and I played a mind-game; I tried to swim in front of where the light ended. I employed that game to urge me forward. Deth's charting of the crossing was taking us diagonally across the strait in a northeast manner. In the middle of the strait, the effects of the tides were lessened. Deth's calculations meant that the diurnal tides, which mostly ran northeast, would ultimately help push us into English Bay and to the landing point — eventually. In the meantime, I had to contend with stroking the water. Every couple of hours, my back would ache and so I would flip over and swim backstroke for several hundred metres. The first time I did it at night, I pushed my goggles off my sore eyes and saw a display of stars that were more dazzling than the previous evening. Being in the ink-black water under a chuppah of starlight astonished me. I stopped swimming so that I could take in the sight of the heavens. *Perhaps it's easy to understand why people would think of God when they looked at the night sky. I must truly be getting tired to think that way. Push on, McDuff.*

At 2 AM, both Lara and Robby had completed their rest breaks, then ate from the selection of food items onboard. No liquid diet for them, the holds were stocked with an array of delicious foods that were created by a caterer, including some luscious-looking desserts. Almost impossible to believe, Lara's large appetite was stunted by the motion of the craft, but she told me that she was taking her Dramamine. Robby refuelled the boat's engine. During my next meal, as I tread with an eggbeater kick in the sea, Lara informed me that Deth was going to take a rest.

"What? He can't. That's not what we agreed to."

"I know, but it's just a short break. He's exhausted, Sunshine. Robby'll take the course heading. He's showing him now," Lara said with confidence. "I think it involves a compass." Lara mugged at me.

"How long," I shouted to Lara, "will he rest for?" I was concerned. Deth was my lifeline, not funnily enough.

"Just a catnap; maybe 10 minutes, tops." Lara's voice was a little muffled due to my earplugs and thick swimcap, but I could hear easily enough in the eerily still ocean. "I've got a little treat for you," she said. For the first time since we started our trek, the water was dead calm. On a rope-attached kickboard, Lara was able to bend down and carefully pass me a piece of bread spread thickly with peanut butter, topped with slices of banana, and sealed in a waterproof bag. *My favourite treat.* She gently lowered it into the water and gave it a subtle push towards me. Picking the bag up, I removed the bread and peanut butter without getting the food soaked with saltwater. I shoved the board back towards her. The next part was trickier; not getting the bread wet as I continued the water polo eggbeater kick, which freed both hands. Stuffing it into my mouth, I was amazed how good it tasted. I washed it down with more of Lara's gruel, this time the mixture had less tofu and more fruit.

"Okay, don't forget to wake up Deth and for gawd's sake, tell Robby not to kill me," I said, only half-joking. I clipped the bottle to the nylon rope and pushed off.

The caffeine-laden drinks Lara passed me each hour were keeping me from falling asleep, but there was no amount of stimulant to help with the mental fatigue that washed over me like one of the previous swells. To combat this, I asked Lara to sing for me. She happily obliged, with some of my favourite songs that she'd performed over the past few years. Lara was a singer whose repertoire was boundless. She asked me what I wanted to hear, and during my short breaks, she hauled up her guitar from the hold and sang numbers she'd performed in clubs all over Canada and the states. A kind of quirky reversal, while I rested on my back gazing at the stars, my body bathed in the searchlight, my best friend performer — who was always powerfully lit onstage — was almost invisible to me, singing beautifully with only a soft guitar for accompaniment. She crooned, *'Summertime'* and ended on a high note that could surely have been heard in Vancouver, many kilometres away. Lara sang, *'Four Strong Winds'* or perhaps I should say she caressed the lyric. Rather than making me drowsy, her singing was something for me to look forward to; something for me to work for so that I could be rewarded by hearing her spectacular voice. Though I couldn't see them, surely Mrs. Kane, Robby and Deth must have enjoyed the live concert because at the conclusion of each song there was a hearty sound of applause. When Lara wasn't singing to me on my breaks, I put my own music on in my head. One of my favourite albums was, *'Judy Garland, Live at Carnegie Hall'*. I knew every orchestral note in that recording, having listened to it a thousand times. From the overture to Judy famously saying, "I'll sing 'em all, and we'll stay all night!", the 2-hour concert was burned into my consciousness. There were few vocalists that rivalled Garland — then or now. I put her historic album on my mind's turntable and told my brain to play each song; to hear every soaring number. It helped me to maintain my own rhythm as I swam, stroke after stroke. I probably knocked off at least 2 kilometres listening to *'Zing Went the Strings of My Heart'* in 4/4 time — a great time signature to swim to. Robby and Lara were onboard to support me, but Judy's incredible voice — booming, sweet, belting, soothing — was the one that helped me stay focused as I swam, especially as I moved through an arduous night.

"Shep … Shep!" Robby called out.

I heard his voice, but I was not quite connected to what he was bawling because I was listening to Judy sing, *'Puttin' on the Ritz'* — at least in my mind. The horn sounded, interrupting my musical interlude and I began to tread the water.

"We figure this is the last rest before sunup. Isn't that great?" Robby announced. Mrs. Kane was standing beside him, keeping watch on all proceedings.

"Good," I managed to say, avoiding the light that glared in my eyes. I massaged my suddenly cramping right foot. "Where are we?" I'd been swimming for 22 hours.

"Let me find out," he said, moving to the bridge to speak with the pilot.

"Tell me how you're feeling," Mrs. Kane shouted out.

"I'm good," I prevaricated. Actually, I was feeling tired and while not cold, various body parts were numb. The sunrise was less than an hour away, but for me, it couldn't come soon enough. Robby tumbled back to the starboard side of the boat.

"Deth says we're on course," Robby cheerfully called out.

"That tells me nothing," I complained. What I wanted to know was, how much longer.

"He figures we've got another 15 or 16 hours to go." Robby had read my mind. "By Deth's calculations, he says that you're swimming better than expected, or it might be that the tide is helping us move a bit faster than we calculated."

"Well, that's something," I responded weakly.

"You okay?"

"I'm okay. We will be able to see downtown soon?"

"No, we're a ways from that," my boyfriend conceded. "Not until we get past Point Grey."

When sailing on the ferries from Nanaimo, the towering skyline of the downtown core and my beloved West End could be seen once a vantage point had been reached. Because we were travelling from the southwest, that city perspective was cut off from sight presently. The view of the city was always such an impressive scene — day or night. *It'll be good to finally see that; to swim towards something visually is really going to help me. Sort of like Dorothy was finally able to see the city of Oz in the distance. Yeah, like that.*

"When will the sun —"

"I said, it's coming up in less than an hour."

In point of fact, because we were heading in a northeastern direction, I would be able to see the sun as it rose. I was looking forward to the warmth of the sun on my chilled body, though the cool water was helping to keep any muscle pain to a minimum. My shoulders, the ones that Dr. Deth was apparently so fond of, were now beyond pain, having pulled tens of thousands of times. The feeling had morphed into some other sensation which I couldn't really describe well — part pain, part frozen due to the water's coldness. My neck was also hurting from keeping it hyperextended during higher seas and for the sheer volume of times I'd turned it to breathe above the brine. Knowing that I was about two-thirds done was a relief as deep as the sea. I caught the hot drink that Robby threw me and drank it quickly. The heat of it was promptly felt down my chest to my stomach. I was in a losing battle with staying warm. I noticed that even when I wasn't on a rest break, I was chilled. Being cold at night was worrisome, with the risk of hypothermia perilously close. Because the large muscles in the gluteus and quadriceps can generate heat, I told Robby that I would try a few sprints to increase my core temperature. It would also help to move blood through my body.

"Careful," he advised me. "I'll tell Deth," he said, moving forward to the bridge, then called back out, "Just don't overextend your reach."

Robby gave me the go-ahead and I powered up my kick in a series of 4 sprints. Though it was fatiguing, the tradeoff was for greater body heat in all large muscle groups. *Better. A good trick for me to have when I need it.*

The crew found their own cadence onboard the Tanja. Deth was able to get several short, but helpful naps in as Robby kept the boat on the course he'd set. Lara's timely food delivery kept me fed and hydrated, with special warm drinks that proved useful in maintaining my level of alertness. Robby oversaw all the things in-between, and ensured that Mrs. Kane was satisfied with the required swimming regulations being met at sea.

I swam on, with the anticipation of the sunrise foremost in my mind. Seabirds know when the sun rises. With the sound of gulls screaming overhead — *maybe I look like a meal?* — the first strands of light were beginning to illuminate the eastern horizon. I took momentary glances, just to be certain that it was really happening. I was never more pleased to see the sunrise as I was that morning. The sky was an unforgettable violet and deepest blood-orange. As the minutes passed, the sea was reflecting the sunlight once again. I stopped for a few moments, as did the crew, to watch the stunning sunrise. The dazzling colours inspired me to push on, swimming for more than 24 hours in the strait.

59

Lara Takes a Dip

If I hadn't had been so tired, I would have been exhilarated to have gotten through the night swimming in the sea. But the truth was I had at least 6 or more hours to go. Just after 11 AM, the waters were rising with swells once more, as though with the sun would come a change in the waters. I'd been urinating on breaks, but noticed that I wasn't doing it as often. At this stage, I didn't want anyone to know about it, just in case it was a medical problem, such as the cold adversely affecting my kidneys. With the sun warming both me and the waters, I asserted that I could finish the crossing — at least to myself.

As the Tanja, her crew and I continued our watery trek, I felt something touch my hand. Peering through my misty goggles I could tell that I was in a mass of jellyfish. *Shit.* If I'd been stung, I hadn't felt it yet. I stopped immediately and pushed my goggles off my face and waved to Mrs. Kane, who was steadfast in observation.

"Trouble?" Mrs. Kane asked in a loud, forceful voice.

"I dunno," I cried out. "There's jellies all around me."

Robby stood from his seat immediately. Lara was on her sleep-break. "Have you been stung?" Robby's concern was evidenced by the look on his face.

"No, I don't think so, Robby, but these things are freaking me out. They're all around me." The jellyfish — Lion's Mane — were in a giant cluster of perhaps 10 metres or more across and at least 5 metres deep. Easily there were hundreds of them.

"Tell Serge to change course to get us —" Robby's bark to Mrs. Kane was interrupted by me.

"*Fuck!*" I cried. "I've been stung, right through the Vaseline."

"Where?" Mrs. Kane bellowed. She was probably thinking that I had to get hauled into the boat.

"On my hamstring," I said, grabbing my lower leg. "Oh, shit, feels like both sides, now." Deth was changing course slightly, and I breaststroked beside the boat.

"Get a credit card out, now," she yelled at Robby.

He did so, fishing out a card from his wallet. Mrs. Kane managed to clip it to the rope then tossed it to me. I grabbed the card and stuffed it under my swimsuit.

"Now, swim along and out of their way. Are you clear?"

"Yes, I think so," I answered, feeling panicked.

"All right. Go out a bit more," she advised.

I did as I was told, and swam out another 50 metres, perpendicular to the Tanja. With Robby darting looks between me and the official, I was certain I was away from the jellyfish.

"Take that card in hand — careful, don't let it slip away — and scrape where you've been stung. Don't be gentle, either."

I followed Mrs. Kane's instructions and was relieved when the sensation began to fade.

"Okay, I'm done," I said. Holding the card in my hand was a challenge due to my reduced hand dexterity.

"Good. Now stick that card back in your trunks."

"And now what?" I asked expectantly as I cautiously tucked the card away.

"Well, swim, of course," she said matter of factly. "That *is* why we're all out here, isn't it?" she said with a smile. "Keep that card safe and within easy reach. You could have a return visit from those pesky creatures." Satisfied that I was okay, she sat back down on her chair. Robby shook his head in disbelief and we proceeded on our slightly altered course.

"I'm gonna need more Vaseline. I've scraped a whole bunch off, and I don't wanna get colder."

Robby and Mrs. Kane sent an open jar of the stuff on a kickboard for me. I carefully smeared on what had been lost, doing my best to make sure that no grease got on my goggles. Satisfied, I started swimming. Mrs. Kane was correct. There were a few more stings that I had in the next several hours, but they were minor irritations. Robby kept watch to warn me of any, but in truth, only I could tell when I was in a mass of them by how my hand felt as I stroked the water.

As the sun continued to burn in the sky, my back was hurting from the direct exposure and I figured the Vaseline was magnifying the sun's power. My body was a study in contrasts. My back was searing hot, but my stomach was freezing. My head was warm from the swim cap, but my face felt as though it was encased in ice. My groin was not exactly toasty, but it was well insulated from the cold, however the front part of my quads were aching as though I had frost-bite. The biggest thing I experienced was fatigue. During a rest period, I nearly fell asleep not once, but several times. It was tempting to just let go and drift. If a large boat, freighter or ferry had come by, I fear it would have taken me out. The mental gymnastics it took for me to flip over to my stomach and swim was worthy of a Cirque du Soleil performance. After swimming for just over 36 hours, I was done. I stopped swimming and turned onto my back.

"What is it? It's not time for a break. Are you okay?" Robby asked. I think he could tell that my energy was zapped.

"Get me some caffeine," I pleaded. "I'm needing a pick-me-up. Some food, too."

Robby called for Lara to grab a drink and to throw me a banana to eat. She was clipping the bottle to the rope when she spied something.

"Sunshine, look!" Lara's voice rose with excitement. To the east, the tall bluffs of Point Grey were easily seen about 3 or 4 kilometres away. It was what the crew and I had been waiting to see. I grabbed the bottle and drank from it slowly. The bluffs seemed a little blurry to me. My fatigue was overwhelming. *4 hours or less. That's all. Like an extra-long swim practice. Hold on, and I'll be at the beach. Stay alert. Stay focused and keep pulling.*

"Hey," Deth called out. "We should be getting an incoming tide in about an hour. That's really going to help push us along. We might be ahead of schedule by an hour or more," he said with relief. Our course would find us going around the point and within the next hour and a half, entering English Bay. I readjusted my goggles for the last 6 or so kilometres. Mrs. Kane, seemingly reading my mind, feverishly cried, "Hang on, young man and keep swimming!"

An hour after we had rounded the bluffs of Point Grey, the towers of the downtown core came into view. The Sheraton Landmark was a tall and very welcome sight in the distance. There was building excitement on the Tanja. I was on my second to last break, guzzling Lara's potion, though I no longer had any hunger.

"There's a large crowd at Ceperly," Robby explained to a mostly non-verbal me.

Of course ... Pete. "The CBC's been covering the story."

"Covering it? How, from the beach at Ceperly?"

"No, even better," Lara shouted to me smugly. "Our own Dr. Deth has been giving out reports for the past 16 hours. He's been doing a play by play!"

"Great," I managed to weakly chirp.

"Isn't it?" Lara agreed enthusiastically.

Ironically, at the time that I should have been most energized, I feared I was succumbing to both heat and cold exposure. I'd completely stopped being able to urinate, and my head was reeling from the motion of the building swells. When we entered English Bay at 4 PM, the winds had increased and it was choppy, with visible whitecaps. *Of course, why would I have expected anything less?* We moved past Spanish Banks, then in another hour passed Kitsilano, though perhaps 4 or more kilometres above the beaches in the centre of the bay. A helicopter made several passes overhead, and its rotor blades made the ocean seethe dangerously. I was having lapses of alertness, and struggling to stay awake in the agitated waters. The wave action I'd been so worried about in the open water of the Strait of Georgia was ironically occurring in English Bay, with me finding it nearly impossible to swim up a cresting wall of water. My stomach started to churn as much as the sea. I didn't feel at all well. As we got deeper into the bay, I was aware that there was a flotilla of small boats that stretched out widely, like a long marked-out roadway that led to the beach in Stanley Park. I could now tell that we had made great headway as Robby picked up Lara's megaphone.

"Not even 2 kilometres to go, Shep," he announced as he worriedly watched me struggle with each stroke. My pace had slowed considerably. I was relying more on the action of the tidal current and waves to propel me forward than my own muscle power. Lara grabbed the megaphone and started shouting, "Stroke, stroke!" as though I was in a competition. It worked for a few minutes. The metric mile — 1500 metres — takes less than 20 minutes for me to swim in a pool. In the bay, it felt like each 50 metres was taking the same amount of time. I had no sense of whether I was moving forward with each stroke, though I was. When I looked up from the waters to where we were meant to come onshore at the beach, it seemed further away with every difficult stroke. *Was I making any headway in the swelling bay? It's like that Hitchcock trick that Robby told me about ... in Vertigo, right? Think, what was it called? Yes, the dolly zoom, where the camera zooms in for a close-up, but the dolly moves out. That's what this is like. I must be moving ahead, but why is it taking so long?* I tried to regain my focus, but concentration was elusive. I didn't have a death wish, but there was a part of me that was so exhausted that I wanted to drop deep into the sea. We were closing in the warmer waters of English Bay, which should have made it easier. It wasn't. I picked up my stroke, but with over 500 metres left before the beach, I was on the verge of collapse. I stopped and turned over on my back, which burned with pain. I didn't even have the energy to push my goggles off my face. I stared at the blazing sun. My eyes were watering inside my goggles. The salty tears stung where my face was blistered around the circumference of my swim goggles. My energy stores were completely depleted. Mrs. Kane noticed a broken swimmer barely staying afloat.

"I think he's about to go into distress!" I could hear her shout. "Okay, get ready, if there's no change, we're going to have to get him in this boat, pronto."

"Shep! *SHEPARD!*" Robby screamed at me. "Serge, I think we gotta stop, he's not looking good." He turned to me and bellowed, "I think we gotta get you out now!" He turned to Lara and roared, "Where the fuck is that rope?"

"It's there, Robby. No, there!" Lara pointed to somewhere that I couldn't see. When I caught her eye, through foggy lenses, I noticed she looked as helpless as me. I tried to clear my head, took a few deep breaths and called out to the crew.

"No, give me a moment to rest," I pleaded. "That's all I'm asking." I bargained that if I was unable to swim, I would permit them to bring me aboard without any struggle. Frankly, I had no struggle left. Robby had collected the rope, but I think he was reluctant to throw it to me. He knew that I was stubborn. Deth was at a dead stop, waiting for Robby and Lara's instructions. As for me, I floated in the waves a few minutes more, my body cold and unwilling to move. I felt such acute disappointment that I'd swum from Vancouver Island to English Bay, only to leave my journey unfinished. *What a disappointment I've become. Kicked off the national team and now failing at this crossing. Admit it, Thompson was right, I've become a hack. So close to completion and just don't have what it takes to close the deal. Great. And what about all the people, like Pete, that have to struggle to stay alive? This dip in the water is nothing in comparison, is it?* My head spun. The waves were unrelenting. *Because of the freighters?* I couldn't tell, but the waves were very large, and I was labouring. A large swell crested, lifting me up, then tossing me down hard. I came up, but feebly. Another one hit. I had no strength to come up from the couple of feet I'd gone under. For a brief moment, I thought about letting go and dropping deep into the ocean. Instead, I surfaced, sputtering seawater from my mouth. Because of the swelling waters and the large wave, I wasn't immediately visible to the crew, nor could I see them.

"I can't see him!" I heard Lara scream. "Jesus-fucking-Christ! He's gone under!"

I could see the blinding-white 'Swim for Life' tee-shirt flash in my field of vision as Lara leapt from the Tanja and dove into the sea. Her flip-flip-flops were also riding the waves near me — she hadn't taken them off before jumping in. Lara spotted me 7 or 8 metres away, afloat but dazed.

"For God's sake, Shepard, swim over to me now! Over to the platform. We gotta get you onboard!"

I heard Robby wail, "Lara, what the hell are you doing out there? Christ, we should have thrown him a line! Swim back to the boat! Serge, for fuck's sake, watch your position!" Oddly, I watched the scene from the water as Deth glanced furtively between Lara and me and grabbed the throttle controls of the boat, making sure the distance between the Tanja and us was both safe and regulatory.

"Get the life preserver and toss it out!" Mrs. Kane cried with urgency. In a second, I watched Robby throwing the life preserver into the water dangerously close to Lara.

"Are you trying to kill me?" Lara screamed at Robby. I saw and heard the mayhem onboard the Tanja, albeit stifled. Deth was now shouting at me, but I couldn't make out what he was saying. Or perhaps he was yelling at Lara? In the water with Lara, though flailing about, I suddenly realized how much I didn't want to get back into the boat. I wanted this as much as any win in the pool. Adrenaline surged, and it was exactly what I needed to reenergize myself.

"Mrs. Kane, please hold off!" I screamed as I continued to bob in the ocean. "Lara, stop! Don't come any closer!"

Lara ignored my pleas and started to swim the breaststroke towards me.

"I'm okay, please, stop!" I screamed. "Mrs. Kane, tell her!"

"Young lady, if you touch him, it's an immediate disqualification!" Mrs. Kane shouted.

"I don't care!" Lara swam towards me in the chop, but perhaps luckily for me, waves pushed her in the opposite direction.

"No, please, Lara! Help me finish this," I urged, treading water just sufficiently to keep myself from going under. "I can do this with your help," I begged.

The pair of us were metres apart, with Mrs. Kane eagle-eyeing each moment from the nearby Tanja. The swelling waters and severe chop made visibility problematic for her.

"What's going on?" Mrs. Kane shouted down to us from the Tanja.

"What does it look like? I'm in the goddamned bay trying to get him back in this fucking boat!" Lara shrieked. "Christ, look at me." Lara realized she had jumped into 250 feet of water in English Bay, surrounded by crashing whitecaps and numerous other hazards. "This is insane," she shouted. "Shep, come back with me," she pleaded, treading the water. She, too, was exhausted and impatient with my stubbornness.

"Lara, swim the rest with me. It's not far." I looked up at Mrs. Kane. "It's legal, right?" I called out to the swim official.

"As long as she —"

"Doesn't touch me," I finished Mrs. Kane's sentence and looked over at my best friend, who had no intention of going to the bottom of the sea with me. "Can you see the beach?"

"Yes, I see it." The crowds at Second Beach were now clearly visible, though the people were small as ants from our vantage point in the ocean.

"All right. You're gonna have to help me get there." I continued to tread water on extremely tired legs. We're gonna head straight for the beach. Deth won't be able to go much further." I called out to Robby, "Do we have a spare pair of —"

"Got 'em," Robby hollered, having quickly scoured my bag for an extra pair. Robby, whose swimming ability was rudimentary at best, pulled on his lifejacket just in case. There was no way that he was going to get into the drink willingly; it was far too dangerous for a swimmer with limited abilities. He threw the goggles to Lara, who nearly missed the catch.

"Tell me what I'm supposed to do," she said calmly as she fiddled with the swim goggles in her cold hands. It was hard to stay afloat in the waves and finagle the goggles. "And be quick, I'm already as cold as a nun's tits," she declared as she shivered in cool water wearing her tee-shirt and shorts — not an ideal swimsuit.

"Swim near me, that's all. I'm going to turn on the jets for one last burst," I said.

"Sunshine, I dunno if that's such a ..."

Looking at my best friend's brown eyes, I could sense that Lara had grave doubts about my strategy. The way I appeared, it was understandable.

"Trust me. It's the only way that we can finish this."

"Fire 'em up," Lara said as she pushed her goggles into place.

I looked at the Tanja, rocking up and down and side to side, where Mrs. Kane and Robby appeared worried. Deth was back at the controls, trying to keep the boat from colliding with us in the considerable chop.

This wasn't how our swim was to end.

I had hoped that this last part of the swim would have been a triumph, with me coming ashore strongly, victoriously. Instead, I was limping along with a mind that was in tatters, let alone my worn-out body.

"Okay, we're off." I gave Robby a final thumbs-up sign. He looked shaken at our turn of events. The boat began to slowly veer to the right. We were less than half a kilometre from the beach, but to me, seemed as far away as the stars I gazed at the previous night. I took one last look at my departing boyfriend and Mrs. Kane. The Tanja and crew had done their jobs beautifully, and now they made for the marina in False Creek. Robby was shouting what I presumed was encouragement to both Lara and me as the Tanja took off, though any words were unheard. For the last time, I realigned my goggles on my sun-blistered face. Lara and I shared a brief look before we swam, and then I started pulling my way for the final stretch with Lara 2 or 3 metres beside me. I believed that I still had reserves in my large legs, so with confidence that mostly came from the mountain of carbohydrates I'd been pushing down my throat, I began to kick. My arms were barely pulling against the water as I shifted all available power to my legs. Beside me, Lara swam strongly. It helped that I could see her when I took a breath. She was tired, too, but the two of us were steadily finding our way to Second Beach. With a heaviness that I'd never experienced, I swam — we swam — closer to the shore. The persistent bashing of waves and rolling swells made the last part of the swim perhaps the most difficult. My fatigue was showing up in every stroke; each movement of my body was laboured and effortful. I willed my legs to thrust as though I was a youngster swimming in Boulevard Lake under my mother's watchful eye. I pumped my quadricep muscles, used my large feet as flippers, plowed through the oppressive white-caps that relentlessly hit Lara and me in the face, especially when taking a breath. More so than any other time, my mind was shutting down. My ability to think was diminishing with each second. With Lara close by, I was just able to put one hand, then the other, in the water. There was no doubt that without Lara swimming beside me, I would've been unable to continue. With an agonizing pull that brought pain sharply to both of my shoulders and triceps, I willed my way to the end. Second Beach was 150, then 100, then a mere 25 metres away. The tide was gratefully in our favour, so Lara's speed increased and therefore so did mine, but not because I had strength. It was Lara's energy that pulled me along with her like a tractor beam from Star Trek. I hadn't any more jets to turn on. With less 35 seconds to realize our goal, I could hear the roar — not the sound of water this time — of people cheering us on to dry land. In another few seconds I took my last stroke of the water and my feet grazed the sandy bottom. We were now able to stand and walk to the shore. But, I was barely able to remain upright, so Lara grabbed me around the waist and kept me vertical for the next 5 metres until we reached the beach. On the shore, hundreds of people were there to welcome us. Dazed, I looked around. One of the first people to run up to Lara and me was Pete and the indomitable Mrs. McBride.

They and a few others whom I did not recognize formed a kind of greeting committee. A CBC video camera was being used to record our coming ashore. A microphone was shoved in my face.

"How you feeling?" the reporter asked.

"Glad that we made it," I gasped. Without being able to comment further, the reporter turned his eyes and the camera on Lara, who may have been weary, but looked fabulous, perhaps because she was in a wet tee-shirt. She was quickly pulled over by several other reporters. She *was* a name, after all. The press wanted to know how a Vancouver singer had crewed a successful swim crossing. In a few moments she appeared to be holding court. I continued to stand up with the help of Pete and Mrs. McBride who looked as surprised as me to have completed the swim.

"It's astounding, dear!" she cried, grabbing my frozen blue hands and rubbing them with hers. Mrs. McBride had a red terrycloth robe with 'Swim for Life' embellished on the back. She securely wrapped it around me, not caring about the remnants of the petroleum jelly, which seemed to have greatly diminished. She, like Pete, was wearing 'Swim for Life' tee-shirts. Pete embraced me so hard I almost couldn't breathe. I could barely stand, even with Pete's assistance, and he was aware of it. *He'd also had the same difficulty a few months back, hadn't he?*

"Aquaman is back, and better than ever," he said with affection, holding me carefully as he guided me to one of the beached logs I loved to sit on. Lara was caught up in a crush of people making inquiries about the crossing. I sat, unable to take off my swim cap, so Pete and Mrs. McBride removed it cautiously. My lips and face were blistered and swollen from the sun, the salt and the cold. My legs were red and covered in a plethora of sting marks from my unfortunate encounters with the jellyfish, though I was unable to feel pain. Paramedics soon made their way to where Pete, Mrs.

McBride and I were. In addition, there was a Swim Canada official who congratulated me and asked for a urine sample.

"I don't think I can give it," I swore. "I haven't been able to go for hours, but I'm going to hospital, so they can take one there, okay?"

"I'll see that they do," he said officiously, turning to speak to a paramedic.

The paramedics wrapped me in blankets and urged me to drink the warm, sweet tea they'd brought with them.

"Is Lara coming back?" I asked in a faint voice. I was fading quickly.

"Looks like she's chatting with that pretty Gloria Makarenko," Mrs. McBride answered. "I imagine that they'll be here in a few more minutes."

I hoped that I didn't have to speak further to the press. Besides my introversion, I didn't want to be asked the "difficult" questions. I don't think I had to worry. As Mrs. McBride pointed out, Lara was in the throng of reporters and appeared to be right in her element.

"Isn't that typical? I do all the work and she gets all the love," Pete commented.

"Tell me about it," I said, laughing, then coughing deeply from my chest.

Even though I was mostly out of it, I took a moment and looked around at Pete's incredible, big and colourful event. Red and white tents were set up for information, booths were occupied with staff from AIDS Vancouver so that donations could be made for each kilometre swum. Vendors were selling both food and goods, like our 'Swim for Life' shirts and towels. I'd had estimated that there were at least 150 people wearing our tee-shirts. Business seemed to be brisk, with hundreds if not a thousand people out on this spectacular and sunny BC Day. Upon closer inspection, I could tell that Pete had a red theme. In addition to the red and white 'Swim for Life' tee-shirts, there were fresh strawberries, apples, watermelon, cherries, rhubarb pie, red velvet cake, and raspberry smoothies. Of course, in the middle of this very red event, Pete was front and centre. Mrs. McBride continued clutching my hand and tearfully making saltwater stains on her wrinkled, weathered cheeks.

"We didn't know if you'd make it. There were reports that put it all in question, dear. Near the end. Your mother and father were worried to death," she added as she dabbed her eyes with tissues from her omnipresent purse.

"They've been following the swim?"

"Most certainly. The swim is big news; on the radio all day. Your family has been at the beach for hours. I must say, your sister's quite charming and very talkative."

"You've been speaking with my family?" I was gob-smacked.

"Well, of course. It must be frustrating for them, because they wanted to get past this crowd, but they're bound to be near —"

I interrupted my landlady because my family had successfully thrust by the masses and were coming towards us. "Hi!" I called weakly to them. I couldn't recall ever being so delighted to see my family. My mother seemed relieved to see me, attired smartly in a blue and white sundress and wearing fresh makeup. Dad appeared in a pair of outlandish blue flowered polyester golf pants and seemed a bit sullen. I guessed he might have been cranky at having to drive all the way into the city. My sister's face was a trifle pinched, but who wouldn't be short-tempered after spending the day with my parents? But, as annoying as they could be, I was certainly as maddening to them. I admit they surprised me by coming to see our swim conclude. My father *never* went to the beach for any reason unless it was part of a golf course, so I was duly impressed. My mother rushed over to me, her gait unsteady because of her high heels dipping unevenly in the sand.

"I think that was enough of a scare for a long, long time." My mother kissed me on my raw, blistered cheek as Pete and Mrs.

McBride curiously observed my family's many machinations. "You put us all through hell, you know. Worse than any teenager."

"I'm not grounded, am I?"

"Don't be clever with your mother," she said. "Are you all right? You look as though you had a struggle with a sea monster." My mother glanced at my injuries on my exposed legs, primarily from the nasty jellyfish but the subjection of the elements had left me looking as though I'd been towed underwater by one of the BC Ferries for a couple days.

"Well, it's true. I met a few monsters along the course," I said reflectively, thinking that mostly, those monsters were of my own making.

"It certainly looks that way," she said, appraising my damaged skin.

"I can't believe you did this," Lynda said as she gave me a warm hug. "It's simply incomprehensible, isn't it Dad?" Lynda looked at my father expectantly. I waited for my father's response. So far, he'd been a speechless witness to everything going on around him.

"It was a foregone conclusion," he said confidently. "I knew my Number One could do it." He cracked a slight smile, the corners of his mouth turned up a smidgen as he reached out and shook my hand.

"Thanks, Dad."

I almost didn't complete it, of course, but he didn't need to know that — not right now.

My legs began to cramp, and though I tried, I couldn't stand, so I collapsed on the log. The pushy reporter came back to me for some questions, but thankfully, the paramedics told me it was time to go, with no time for the reporter, which was a bonus.

"We've gotta date with the ambulance driver," Pete said to my family.

"Where are you going?" Lynda asked.

"He'll be taken to Emergency at St. Paul's, just as a precaution," one of the paramedics stated. "By the looks of him, he'll probably be there a couple days," the other medic offered his opinion. "Just to be on the safe side."

I stood up, more unsteady on my feet than my mother. "Thanks for coming down, it was a real surprise, a good one."

The two ambulance attendants hooked their elbows in mine and started slowly walking me to their vehicle. Media personnel were coming back to where my family was.

"We'll be along shortly," my mother called out. "These reporters want to have a word with us," she said. When I looked back she was adjusting her hair and putting on fresh lipstick for the interview. Pete walked with the attendants and me to the grass field where an ambulance was waiting to take me to St. Paul's Hospital. I squinted at the red and yellow lights flashing on the vehicle. It seemed fitting enough that I was going to where my father and Pete had started their story — in hospital, both sick and fearful that their futures had been taken away. But that story had been turned upside down. *Our story was about more than being sick. It was also about the ways that family and friends can band together to do the improbable.*

60

The Gathering

The paramedic was right. I was kept at St. Paul's for 4 days, having been diagnosed with hypothermia, dehydration and exposure. IV fluids were given with a dose of antihistamine for the jellyfish stings and bites to my (thankfully numb) feet by large salmon; that delicious fish was the speculation. If it was another type of fish that had been nipping my toes, I really didn't want to postulate what it might have been — I do have an active imagination. The IV kept dripping its medicines, slowly coursing through my veins as I lay in bed. Other than having very high electrolytes from swallowing most of the Strait of Georgia, I was doing better and recovering quickly. My mother, as promised, insisted that she come in and visit with me at the hospital for a couple of days. She brought enough chocolates to force-feed me until I felt ill, but the intent was good.

"Bend forward. I'll fluff your pillow," she instructed me.

"Mum, my pillow's fine," I said. Both my mother and sister seemed to have a pillow fluffing fetish.

"Just do as you're told and don't be stubborn. It's all in clumps and God knows if there's a nurse anywhere to help you."

I did as she directed, and she pounded the pastel green pillow before putting it at the small of my back. I propped myself up in the well-starched hospital sheets.

"I hope this bedding is clean," she sniffed, smoothing the linen.

"Mum, it's very clean. *It's a hospital.*"

Clearly preoccupied with something else, my mother stated, "Your father and I were worried sick."

"Mum, if you've told me once …"

"Clearly, it bears repeating. But your crew did well. For the AIDS, I mean."

"Mum, you don't need the *the* before the word. Just AIDS," I whispered.

"I see. Why didn't you tell me that before?"

She was dressed beautifully in a pink-blush crepe suit with gold-chain hardware on the sleeves. She moved to the bottom of the bed, picked up my chart and started to read it.

"What has Dr. Taylor said?"

"That I'll be fine. Gawd, put that chart back, Mum. What if one of the nurses sees you?"

"Hmmph, I'd love to see one of those nurses. What are they having down there, a coffee party?" She flipped over the page of the chart. There were several nurses at the end of the hallway chatting and laughing, which apparently was breaking my mother's care protocol — at least for her son. "So, what else did Bud say?" she inquired.

"Dr. Taylor says I'll be out in a day or so." My mother continued looking over the patient chart. "Mum, the chart?"

"Well, thank God for that. This time's been such a fret." After Nurse Mum's inspection, she placed the chart back, passed me a large red plastic container full of ice and filled it with apple juice from the bottle she'd brought, apparently mistrusting hospital beverages. "Here, drink. We've got to get some calories back in you."

My mother pushed the cup at me. "I don't need to get into a flap about you looking as thin as a stick, do I?"

"Mum, I'm not a stick. And, you didn't have to worry then or now. You never had to worry. The swim was all planned out, like I told you." I took the juice from her and swirled the ice cubes in the cup. I wasn't found of ice-cold drinks of late.

"No, it was a tragedy just waiting to happen," she scolded me. "Go on, drink," she beseeched.

I put the glass to my mouth and took a large swallow of apple juice. It was acidy, so sugar-sweet that it hurt my teeth. I was never fond of apple juice for that reason.

"Yeach," I said rubbing my tongue over my coated teeth.

"Stop complaining and keep drinking. Oh, by the way, you know your friend, that devilishly handsome Dr. Deth?"

"You mean the one I just spent 2 days with at sea? Of course, Mum."

"Well, it's official. I'm finally doing him," my mother announced triumphantly.

I inadvertently choked on my ice cubes and stared at her, unblinkingly.

"Mum, what did you say?" I coughed and put down my drink.

"I'm decorating his home. He's been asking for weeks. It's the least I could do for him. He's rather fond of green and red plaids, which won't work, of course. What was he thinking? Oh, *men*. Typical. He said it was a Belgium thing, or is it Belgian?"

"Uh," I started to answer.

"Doesn't matter. Regardless, I'll make his condo into something smashing. Anyway, I'll be in town for a couple weeks and hope it's okay if I stay with you when I'm doing the job."

"Of course, Mum, you're always welcome."

Just give me a day's notice so I can stash away my porn magazine collection.

"Thank you. I'm glad that you're in one piece, my son," she sighed. "It's been more than enough aggravation looking after your father." My mother bent down and put her arms around me for a long, tight hug. When she released me from her steely grip I felt a jolt of pain and heard a slight ripping sound.

"Mum, can you call the nurse?"

"Why, dear?"

"You just pulled out my IV with your gold chains."

I was set to be released on Thursday afternoon following the swim. I was seated by the bed in one of the most uncomfortable plastic chairs, anxiously waiting for my ride.

"Ready to go?" Pete entered the room with a smile.

"Am I."

I didn't have anything to collect, as Lara had brought me some clothing — my uniform of Levi's and a white tee-shirt — to go home in a couple of days earlier. I sat up slowly.

"Thanks for picking me up, Pete." I was happy that Pete was able to come as Robby was doing the preliminary design and casting at UBC on his new production.

"My pleasure." He placed his arm around my shoulder and carefully guided me down the halls of St. Paul's Hospital. It was my turn to be unsteady. As we moved down the long polished hallway of the old hospital, nurses took notice of the bearded, handsome and healthy-looking man in the blue seersucker suit that was walking me out. Now that he'd regained his vitality, Pete continued his tradition of turning heads. We headed for Pete's sexy black Porsche, and though the weather was hot and sunny, I couldn't help but think of the rainy afternoon I collected him from the hospital and began a series of events that changed all our lives.

"This reminds me of another time," I mentioned casually as Pete unlocked the car door for me and I got in. I unlocked his door and he slid onto his black leather seats.

"When you picked me up?" Pete asked. "It was pissing, wasn't it?"

"Uh huh. It seems long ago, but really..."

"I was never happier to be soaked by the rain." Pete smiled. He ignited the motor as I gazed at him affectionately. His glossy hair moved as he shook his head. I thought backwards in time. Much had happened over the past 6 months. Still, we were only at the beginning of a time where more devastating losses were yet to come. The fear that gripped the gay community was intensifying — all with good reason. None of us were out of danger — quite the opposite. We all were at risk to an epidemic that rivalled any plague.

I rested further at home as things fell into a predictable course once more. Robby had done a few interviews about the swim on the local news and there was some interest from stations in the states about what this swim had meant, given the pressing health crisis that was making American news headlines each day. I was proud that we brought attention to the issues facing gay and non-gay people alike. I was over the moon that through Pete's huge efforts, close to a half-million dollars in donations were secured to support clients at AIDS Vancouver. This was an incredible start for the needs that would rapidly explode a short while later. (Both Lara and I would eventually complete the volunteer training for AV. Though I'd not finished my internship, they were kind enough to allow me to do a counselling clinic with other practitioners. I was able to volunteer one day per week, and it soon became a busy and hectic day. I saw many people with AIDS, but also dealt with the "worried well", or those people, like me, who had every reason to be concerned. I also worked with family members, too. Unfortunately, I saw many clients whose families deserted them in their time of greatest need, and some who died alone because their families were ashamed of them. It horrified me that families could behave this way, but it was not uncommon in the earliest and even in the latter days of this disease. Lara opted to be a "Buddy" one day per week when in Vancouver, and made calls to men and women who were diagnosed and in hospital or living at home. Her advocacy for those affected grew, as did the increasing demands for care. Lara would sing in fundraisers more than a few times, drumming up dollars that directly supported AIDS Vancouver.)

Relaxing in my apartment, I was sipping on a hot tea when there was a knock at the door.

"Mrs. McBride, come in," I said warmly, ushering in my landlady.

"You do look much improved, dear." Mrs. McBride moved spritely into my living room and sat down.

"Thanks, Mrs. M. I feel well. Can I get you some tea?"

"No, I just wanted to remind you of the gathering for Tommy at 3 PM on Friday. I know you'd want to be there."

"Oh, yes, of course. I wrote it into my calendar," I replied. "Here?" I asked.

"Yes, he'd have wanted us to meet at the Queen Charlotte. We'll meet in my apartment," she said with a sorrowful lilt in her voice. "It's small. Just a few of us. His mother is also going to attend. She's been kind enough to wait for us to pull it together."

"I'll be there, Mrs. McBride. Can Robby and Lara —"

"Well, of course, dear. More than welcome; don't forget Pete. How's he doing, by the way? I haven't seen him in a couple of weeks."

"I know it's crazy, but the herbal treatment seems to be doing the trick," I said. It was true that Pete was much improved. At the St. Paul's LAV clinic, they said he was clearly out of danger and doing much better than had been expected. He believed that his cannabis was helping, and even if it were just a placebo effect, if believing made it better, then so what?

"I'm terribly glad. He's such a charming man. And, he's simply more good-looking each day." Mrs. McBride winked cunningly for effect. I liked that though she was older, the beauty of the male form was still something that she could appreciate. "Oh, we'll have some pinwheel sandwiches — salmon and cream cheese and some with watercress — at the gathering. And I baked a giant chocolate feathery-fudge cake with a chocolate buttercream that would make the Queen dance naked at Covent Garden. It's my mother's old recipe, though I've added a few of my own touches," she said pridefully, getting up with a wistful sigh, grabbing her lower back as she went to the door.

"Sounds delicious." I wondered if there were any secret, perhaps illegal ingredients, in her cake as I stood at the door with my landlady, friend and fellow distance swimmer.

"No disrespect, dear, but I believe you could use a piece of cake, couldn't you? Let's make sure that you have a very big slice." Mrs. McBride patted my concave stomach as she left for her apartment a few doors from mine.

I wasn't the only person that made the news rounds. There had been a certain panache with the swim crossing. For a brief time, it had captured the imagination of the city, much like Mrs. McBride's swim had in 1931. When Lara's work both on and off the boat (meaning in the drink with me at the end) became widely publicized, she was vaulted into the spotlight, albeit for a short time. She was touted as the singer that saved the day, or at the very least, saved the swim. What had Pete said? No such thing as bad press? For Lara, her time onboard the Tanja generated television interviews. How could she not mention her first album she was to record in Detroit for a winter release? With a few TV appearances, she was clearly more in demand for concert and club dates. Pete was happily lining up her calendar through to February of 1984. Lara was looking forward to getting back to work. As for her involvement with Deth, I hadn't had a chance to speak with her about what, if anything, was developing.

Perhaps the notoriety of being on the crew also helped Robby. Dr. Hockington wanted to capitalize on his exposure by giving him a play to direct at the Freddy Wood; Shakespeare's *The Merchant of Venice*. Robby was going to focus on the ardent — and in Robby's directorial hands — near-romantic friendship between Bassino and Antonio and give the audience a new way to think about the characters.

I was happy that for now, Robby's home was in Vancouver with me. We returned to a more contented way of life. Robby rewarded me for the swim crossing by taking me to see *The Right Stuff* before it closed. I enjoyed the movie even more the second time with him. When Alan Shepard, the first American in space, blasted off on a black and white Redstone rocket, I jabbed him in the ribcage and cried, "There, that's my namesake!"

My plan was to take the month off and then go back to school as I looked for work in the counselling field. I got back into the pool, though purely for fitness. The loss of being terminated from the national team was tough to reconcile. It hurt, and in my angrier moments, I fantasized about publicly outing Thompson as a duplicitous bastard, but instead I decided to do nothing. *Perhaps he's in his own kind of hell. Or maybe he's just in the park with Fleecy.*

On Friday, I stepped over to Mrs. McBride's lovely apartment for Tommy's gathering. She had been busy with more than baking a cake.

"Take a gander, dear."

She motioned me over to her dining table, where a large selection of photographs that his mother had provided. It seemed that Tommy had a life that I didn't know about. Mrs. McBride had arranged the pictures on a couple of storyboards. There were pictures of him as a young man playing the piano. Other snapshots found him with his mother and another man on vacation in Europe, including a shot of them at the Tower of London. Awards and certifications abounded for his creative work as a window dresser for The Hudson's Bay, Woodward's and Eaton's stores. Pictures of his Christmas displays were elaborate concoctions of a child's holiday fantasy come to life. I was amazed at the quality of his work spanning more than 15 years.

"I had no idea, Mrs. McBride. Did you?" I asked.

"No, dear. It took me quite by surprise." She looked with affection at the table.

There were a couple pictures of him with what appeared to be friends, but there didn't seem to be any romantic interests from what I could determine.

"Was there ever a boyfriend? Like the man from the picture in London?"

"Don't know," she answered plainly. "Oh, there's the door," she said, fixing the waistband of her black dress and moving towards the entranceway to greet her guests.

Pete and Lara arrived 20 minutes later, and Robby was going to come after he got back from the Freddy Wood and his meeting with Hockington. Pete was speaking with one of Tommy's work-mates and Lara came up to me as I fortuitously stood near the food.

"I never really got to tell you how sorry I was to hear about your friend." Lara had noticed the array of foods and the towering chocolate fudge cake on Mrs. McBride's beautiful antique sideboard. She picked up a small salmon sandwich and popped it in her mouth. "Oh, that's quite good," she cooed, then eyed the cream-cheese and watercress on crustless white bread.

"I'm sorry, too. Sorry that I didn't get to know Tommy better. In addition to being very talented, he was a very nice guy, but I think he liked being private."

"Private like you?" Lara scooped up several sandwiches and put them on a beautiful piece of china with a coral and white Greek key design.

"Oh, even more than me." I thought of how Mrs. McBride and I found him. It's hard to get that imagery from one's mind, as well as the fantastical apparitions — Tommy and a green bird — that appeared in my apartment.

"That's his mom?" Lara lowered her voice as she looked towards a small group gathered in an intimate-looking conversation.

"Yeah. Must be so rough on her. Mrs. McBride said he was the only child."

"She looks lovely," Lara commented. "But she's so very sad, isn't she? It's as though this gathering just stirs the loss again." Lara observed Tommy's mother, smiling wanly as people came up to her to offer their condolences. His mother was dressed in a dark-blue suit with a dove-grey blouse. Her face had the familiar look of pain — pain I'd seen on my father and Pete. As she stopped to look at all the pictures that Mrs. McBride had put together, she started to weep.

"Gawd. The poor woman," I said, thinking that I put my own mother through a hellish couple of days, but nothing could really compare to a life lost the way Tommy's had ended. Mrs. McBride went to comfort her, wrapping her arms around her sagging shoulders as she softly cried from a loss that was a few months prior, but to her was as fresh as today. *Lara was right. Pain doesn't just vanish, but it's with us all the time, just kept more hidden at times.*

"We did the right thing, didn't we?" Lara turned to me and put her plate down.

"Huh?" I was slightly taken aback by her question.

"I meant the swim. We had an obligation to make a statement, and we did." Lara's voice was defiant. "No mother should have to face this horror." Lara's eyes filled with tears as Tommy's mother was going round to all of the friends, expressing her thanks. "I'm not going to cry in front of his mother. I'm going to find our Pete," Lara said, grabbing several more sandwiches and moving to the other side of the room. Tommy's mother stepped closer to me, quickly wiping away a tear.

"You must be Shepard. I'm Beverly. Bev. Tommy's mother." She looked fatigued as though sleep was a commodity she hadn't had for some time.

"I'm so pleased to meet you, Bev."

"Hannah tells me you knew my son?"

"Oh, yes. I knew your Tommy for all the years that I've lived at the Queen Charlotte."

"Did you?" Bev smiled warmly as she listened.

"Absolutely. In fact, it was Tommy that helped me schlep a bunch of heavy stuff from the basement when I moved in. Right Mrs. McBride?"

My landlady stood comfortingly close to Bev.

"My word, yes. He was terribly strong." Mrs. McBride offered Bev a sandwich, which she declined. "Just like this young man," she smiled at me, "Tommy helped me with many things that needed doing."

"That sounds like my son," she said wistfully.

"Tommy was a great guy; I'm very sorry that he's gone." My words were insufficient to his mother. *What words could ever reconcile his death and her loss?*

"Thank you," Bev graciously replied. "Tommy was a special boy. I dearly loved him," she added. "Stubborn though he was. Very independent, too. Liked living on his own. I worried about him being by himself so much."

"I have the same type of mother," I said lightly.

"That's why I got him Floyd, or he liked calling him Floydie," she recalled.

"Floyd? I'm not sure I under —"

Mrs. McBride interrupted me. "Oh, hadn't you met Floydie?" she asked. "He was ever so chatty," she explained. "Couldn't shut him up!" she laughed.

"Yes, wasn't he lovely?" the mother agreed.

"I'm sorry, Floyd was who?" I asked.

"Why, the cutest, smartest little lovebird. Wasn't he, Bev?"

"Tommy adored him. Said he didn't need anyone as long as he had Floydie," she sighed. "He'd rush home from work, take him from his big cage and spend all his time with him. Floyd would kiss him, run down his shirt, snuggle under his chin or cuddle in his hand for hours at a time. Tommy preferred to be with Floydie more than anyone — even his mother." She smiled at her recollection. "When the little creature passed last year, he was heartbroken. Had cancer, you know. A shame; just 7 years old."

"Um … what colour was Floyd?" I asked innocently.

"Oh, he was such a beautiful shade of green, wasn't he, Hannah?"

"Just beautiful," my landlady agreed. "With peach on his head and breast."

"Sang out with a sweet chirp. Tommy could tell what each sound meant, though I never could. Perhaps you heard him in the hallway?" Bev inquired.

"Yes," I responded, absolutely astonished. "Now that I think of it, I think I must have."

"I'd like to think that my son and Floyd are somehow ... well, I know it sounds loopy, but ..." Bev hesitated, perhaps lest she be judged for her notion.

"I think you're right, Bev. I think that they found their way back together. I know it." My confidence in my statement took Mrs. McBride by surprise, but not Bev.

Tommy's mother looked at me with a wise and knowing smile. Her eyes were no longer tear-filled. Her mouth pursed to kiss each of my sun-burned cheeks.

"Thank you for being my son's friend." Bev bowed her head briefly and we watched as she slowly moved through the room.

"Well, that was ... something," Mrs. McBride stated.

"That was something else," I said shaking my head from side to side.

Robby came late to the gathering and found Pete in need of conversation. I grabbed Lara and we stole away to my apartment, but not before saying farewell to the grief-stricken mother. Lara and I entered my apartment. It was quiet and the light was beginning to fade. After pouring Lara a large glass of white wine, we had the "talk".

"Tell me," I started. "Have you slept with Deth?"

"You *do* know how that sounds, don't you?" Lara took a sip and smiled.

"Lara. C'mon, spill 'em." I was very eager to hear of any romantic news.

"Well, I don't want to ruin my reputation, but no, I haven't."
"Really?"

"You sound surprised." Lara's tone was dry as her wine.

"Stupefied," I said honestly. "But you're still interested in Deth, aren't you?" Robby and I both saw how she and he were "friendly" with each other at various times before our trek.

"I could be," Lara said, running her fingers along the edge of her goblet. "He's very nice."

"Yes, very nice, though I thought he was trying to pick me up. Just so you know."

"He told me." Lara looked at me directly. "Not every man that speaks to you is gay, you know," Lara admonished me. She had a long draught of her wine.

"Oh," I said sheepishly, "of course not." I rose to get the bottle and topped her glass before adding, "I was only thinking about you. I wouldn't want you to get hurt." I worried about Lara's choice-making on many occasions — everything from dating men on probation to sleeping with circus clowns.

"That's thoughtful of you. Look, I'm the first one to admit that I've screwed up many relationships. I figured I'd just wait this one out. See where it goes. I'm not interested in bedding down Deth, so to speak. At least not now." Lara twisted her long, shining red hair in her left hand.

"That really doesn't sound like you, Lara."

"What can I say, Sunshine? Ever since I sailed the seas, I've become a new woman. And isn't this just about the most worrisome time to be a single person with a high sex drive?"

"Oh, I agree. Terrifying. We just don't know what's ahead."

"Exactly. Really, I'm not in any rush. Career first," she asserted. "I have plans in the works and songs to sing."

"Hey, changing topics for a sec, I never asked you about something that I've been meaning to," I started.

"What's that?" Lara asked.

"Well, while you were on the boat, did you, um, ever wind up using   "

"I had to," she groaned, recalling her horror of using the onboard commode.

"I just went in the water … but eventually, I guess you had to —"

"Christ, Sunshine," Lara rolled her eyes. "I had to squat in a pail as though I was in Manila. And in front of Serge. Can you picture me, my shorts down, ass sticking up in the air, seasick, sitting on a plastic pail, rolling up and down in the waves, trying not to pee all over myself or vomit while holding on for dear life? It was not my finest performance." Lara's stern face seemed pained with the recollection.

"I'm sorry, Lara. Maybe not your finest performance, but it would have been an unforgettable one." I tried not to look too gleeful at the image of Lara's lost humility.

"There's absolutely nothing of me he hasn't seen. It's really quite traumatizing."

"Well, at least he's a doctor. It should make us all happy that you aren't dating that clown."

Lara laughed at the thought of Jester. "True enough."

"I don't know if I thanked you for jumping into the water. You saved the swim, Lara Jean." Lara's bold dive into the water plus her guidance at the most critical time were life-saving. "You must have been terrified," I added, admiring Lara's courage.

"No, it was pure impulse, Sunshine. We couldn't see you from the Tanja with all those weird waves. Like a toy boat in a sloshing bathtub; waves were coming from every direction. But if it wasn't me that jumped in, I suspect someone would have dived into the water and hauled your ass out."

"I figured that someone would have been Robby."

"Robby? Under pain of death. I think he was petrified of that water. The way it moved was like a vortex. He'd have shoved old Mrs. Candy Kane off the boat before he'd have taken the plunge."

"Robby's not the best swimmer, but still."

"Oh, it wasn't safe, Sunshine. It was you who swam, but for the rest of us it was agony to be vigilant when we were all so beat. Frankly, being exhausted felt dangerous; anything could happen to you." Lara's beautiful brown eyes looked reflective.

"I know it must have been unnerving. It was a lot to ask of you. I'm super grateful."

"The scary stuff will fade and then we'll think of it as an adventure. I'll never forget singing under a canopy of stars. It was extraordinary."

And neither will I. The shimmer of starlight and the soaring voice of my best friend, guiding me across black waters in the middle of the longest night of my life. I closed my eyes for a few moments, recollecting the thousands of stars that defied description.

"It was an amazing experience; right to the end. I didn't anticipate throwing myself off the boat and into English Bay, but that's why we have best friends."

As Lara finished her statement, the apartment door swung open. Pete and Robby had arrived, discussing *The Merchant of Venice* with great animation.

"Wine?" I asked Robby, who nodded vigorously. "I'll get Pete his special." I went to fetch an orange juice. In a few minutes, my friends and I were spread out over the velvet couch and heaped into chairs, talking about music, life, Shakespeare, sex, and above all else, friendship. As the light dimmed, I lit candles. Ever the observer, I noticed how my friends took on a softer appearance, subdued by the flickering candlelight. I was suddenly struck by the illusions that that life could bring. The wobbling light reminded me of the ghost I convinced myself I'd seen. But perhaps what I had seen wasn't a ghost, but an invention of my mind. Perhaps I had seen or heard Floyd and somehow forgotten. What we see, think and feel is just a piece of subjective reality, and not necessarily the absolute truth. Rather, it's merely the interpretation of our experience, fragments and memories that we cling to, holding onto them as true.

I peeled myself from the sofa to get some bottled water from the fridge. I liked hearing the sounds of my friends, chattering, laughing and whooping. As I went to collect the water, Pete was right behind me.

"Oh, hey, did you need —"

Pete put his large hand on my shoulder. "I need to give you something."

"Give me something?"

"Get your water and come back to the living room." Pete and I went back, though I sat in my brown leather armchair and he remained standing. The conversation level dropped in a few moments with others — including me — looking at Pete expectedly. Lara put her glass of wine down, Robby stopped telling his running story, and I wondered what Pete was up to. I didn't wait long; Pete took a large actor's breath, as though he was ready to perform a Shakespearean soliloquy.

"Two things. First, though we're missing a couple of people, I wanted to thank everyone for giving me my life back."

Pete's words hit hard. It was true that we nearly lost Pete, and was as true that the future remained uncertain. "And I don't mean just the physical care. Jesus, I never knew a man could be so grateful for his friends." Pete lit the dim room with his kilowatt charisma. "Being a part of the crew for the swim and putting on the event at the beach, well … I think it's helped me find my purpose again, and I'm not done yet," he laughed. "And the second thing …" Pete paused for effect. He moved to where he'd dropped his leather jacket and fingered the pocket without removing anything.

"What is it, Pete?" Lara's golden voice rose with curiosity.

"I've had some interesting talks with the lawyer for the swim. Actually, you recall that he's Shep's cousin."

"Right, second cousin, actually. Ryan. He's a terrifically bright guy," I added.

"Well, he wasn't just brilliant, he had the most beautiful blue eyes," Pete said dreamily. "I'm a sucker for blue eyes, as you know," Pete said to me.

"Or brown eyes, or green," Lara commented with a chuckle.

"Please don't tell me you made a pass at my cousin," I begged. "He's married with 3 children," I explained to the group.

"What do you take me for?" Pete tried his best 'scandalized' look, but we were all unconvinced. I've seen so-called straight men give Pete the 'look', so I was aware of his charming effect on women *and* men. "So, in addition to Ryan helping with the legalities of the swim, I took the liberty of discussing your termination from the swim team, and how it happened."

"Jezus, Pete, I assume Ryan now knows that I'm gay?"

"Gay as a Cary Grant and Randolph Scott sleepover. But don't worry, your cousin's suspected since you were 4 years old."

"Christ." I tossed my head back and sighed and Robby chuckled. He knew that people knew more than I ever told myself.

"All confidential, of course. Speaking to a lawyer is like seeing a priest, or you, I suspect. But I'm off on tangents. There's something that came into effect in 1982 called the Charter of Rights and Freedoms."

"It's the anti-discrimination bill," Robby stated, leaning forward in his seat.

"That's correct. It says that under the charter, no Canadian shall be discriminated against, including those who identify as gay or lesbian."

"Pete?" I looked at him with wide eyes, wondering what he had done.

"Ryan contacted Swim Canada regarding Shep's firing, and most specifically, the behaviour of Thompson towards him. The coach's language, his threats to contact parents, what he said about having a "faggot" in the showers. The things Shep told us about Thompson wound up being investigated. They spoke to several swimmers and they had similar stories to Shep's during the past few years. Isn't that amazing? Seems that you weren't the only one being targeted."

"And?" I asked nervously. "What did Swim Canada do?"

"Well, let's say that Swim Canada was rather apprehensive about having a human rights complaint lodged against them by a high-powered attorney before the Pan American Games. Really, it's not terribly good for their wholesome, sunshine and granola image."

"Okay, Pete, enough with the suspense, already," Lara said. "What's the result of talking with Swim Canada?"

"Ah, yes." Pete removed a letter from the pocket of his leather jacket. "Ryan received this via fax at lunchtime today. He sent it to my office right away. Would you like to recite it for us?" Pete passed the letter to Lara, who took it apprehensively. I felt my heart pound as she removed the letter from an envelope and began to read.

```
August 5, 1983
Dear Mr. Stamp,
After a careful investigation and review of
the circumstances of your contract, Swim Can-
ada is reversing the decision to terminate
you from the National Swim Team, and you are
reinstated forthwith. The funds to your pre-
vious payout may be kept. Mr. Thompson will
be on a leave of absence and his assistant
will be assuming coaching duties until fur-
ther notice. Please report to your team Monday
morning in preparation for the Pan American
Games in Caracas, Venezuela later this month,
which we have qualified you for, due to your
previous times in your stated events. Swim
Canada wishes you a successful competition.
Sincerely,
Jordon West
Cc Tom Thompson
```

"And that's why you never mess with fairies," Pete declared proudly.

The living room erupted into cheers and handshaking. The news took me by surprise. I didn't believe I would get a second chance, and had given up completely on the Pan Am Games. It hit me hard. I couldn't believe my friend had taken on Swim Canada.

"Sunshine! You're going to Caracas!" Lara cried out. She observed that I was looking odd. "Aren't you?"

The room hushed in anticipation of my response. I had only 2 weeks to prepare for an event that brought elite swimmers to an important competition. I had some doubts that I was ready. My body was depleted, and I had — for the first time — some shoulder pain when I swam. *But perhaps I could rally? I have a couple of weeks to get prepared. This is how I've wanted to end my career — going out in style at the Pan American Games, a once in a lifetime opportunity.*

"I guess I better bone up on my Spanish," I explained to my group of friends.

"That's the best news, ever," Robby commented proudly.

"Thanks, Pete. Is there nothing you can't do?" I shook my head in disbelief. He really was a gay superhero. Pete beamed. He always knew how to give the very best of gifts, and this was no exception. I don't think that anyone knew more about second chances than Pete. He also was mindful that at any time, our most precious gift could be taken away in a heartbeat, so opportunities missed could be opportunities forever lost.

"Well, we were just following the law," Pete said modestly.

There was a knock on my door. Robby opened it to Mrs. McBride, holding her massive chocolate feathery-fudge cake.

"I wondered where you'd gotten to, dear," she said to Lara and me as she carried the heavy, tall cake with inches of chocolate frosting. "Everyone has gone. No one really wanted dessert and I just couldn't be alone with this beast."

I suspected that Mrs. McBride didn't want to be by herself after a difficult gathering with Tommy's mother. I was delighted that she could be here to share the evening with us.

"It's absolutely colossal," Lara agreed. She looked hungrily at the impressive cake. There were a couple of slices missing and yet there was enough cake for a small army, or for Lara.

"I think we can help with that, Mrs. McBride," Lara said, relieving my landlady of the weighty dessert and carefully moving it to the kitchen counter. Lara pulled out a large knife, plates and forks. "I'll make you a nice cup of tea, if you'd like."

"Oh, dear, I'd much rather have some of that lovely wine, if you don't mind. It's been a rather difficult afternoon."

"Coming right up," Lara responded, pouring my landlady a glass of white wine in my best crystal goblet. Clockwork Carrie slumped comfortably on the velvet sofa as we waited for Lara to slice the cake. I told Mrs. McBride about my reinstatement. She was nearly as excited as me.

"That's news I've longed to hear. All the way in Caracas? We'll be watching on the telly, won't we?" Mrs. McBride asked the group, who nodded and voiced their agreement. After a few minutes, Robby, Pete, Mrs. McBride and I moved to the table as Lara cut generous pieces of the sumptuous, dense cake and placed them on glass plates from France — my favourites. Lara was the first to take a forkful of the rich, decadent cake to her mouth. "Oooh, I think I'm in love, Mrs. M." Lara's eyes rolled backwards in what looked like ecstasy to me.

"I think she's found the substitute for sex," I whispered to Robby, who was also enjoying a large piece of moist chocolate cake himself.

"This is just mind-blowing, Mrs. McBride. What makes this so delicious?" Lara asked between bites. Pete caught Mrs. McBride's eye and gave her his best wink.

"Oh, just reams of chocolate and a few touches of Scottish love, dear."

After we stuffed ourselves with cake, my company left, including Robby, who had an early call at the Freddy Wood Theatre Saturday morning. At 10 PM, I dropped my Levi's and went to bed, then stared at the ceiling. I stayed in bed for an hour, turning from one side to the other. It was hot in the apartment. Frustrated, I got up, found a pair of athletic shorts, a clean tee-shirt and put them on. I slipped on a pair of running shoes and headed out the door. I noticed the night air was humid as I walked down to the beach. Of course, Denman Street was still busy, with people having a drink or carousing. I jogged to the seawall, where many people were walking, some were in the water, taking an evening dip to cool off. I slowed to a walk and continued along the seawall towards Second Beach, where the lights diminished. As I passed the beach, it grew progressively darker. I pondered all the things that had happened. From the winter, when my father had nearly died, to Pete, who had become a benchmark for our mobilization to draw the community-at-large's attention to AIDS, a great deal of turmoil had occurred. I was witness to the tragic loss of Tommy's life and the dramatic resurgence of life in my father and Pete. I'd been removed from a swim team in a shameful manner only to be fully reinstated after a collective triumph with my friends in a 2-day, unforgettable adventure. I'd understood the repercussions of living without friends due to my own fears. And I understood the crucial role that friends played in order to accomplish things that were considered, at best, improbable. I stepped faster, then moved once more to a light jog. As I ran, I took notice of the ocean moving close to the sandy shores of Third Beach, where a giant wave had swamped me during a violent winter storm. *That huge ice-cold wave was the beginning of something, wasn't it? But I don't believe in fate; I gotta keep reminding myself of that.* The salty air served as a reminder of our watery expedition. I always felt contemplative when I looked out over the sea in day or at night. But now that I had run for 15 minutes or so and was a distance from the West End, darkness shrouded me. Siwash Rock was in sight, standing as a weathered and silent, soaring sentinel to the coming and going of the tides. Instead of staring out at the bay as I usually did, I cast my eyes to the heavens. Though much dimmer as compared to when we were out in the waters at night, I could nevertheless see the stars and galaxies hundreds and millions of light years away. In the warm night air, I stopped running on the seawall to reflect on my place in the world. Looking at the flickering starlight, I thought how our existence on earth is merely a flash in comparison to the immensity of time. Though we are small, our lives are not insignificant, but as important as any of the stars that continued to dazzle me, glittering across the infinity of space.

61

Epilogue

In April of 1984, and only 8 months after the gathering for Tommy, the mysterious killer that was in our midst had been confirmed as a retrovirus with origins dating to the 1920s. A test to screen for the virus was developed with the declaration that a cure could be found in 2 years. In the meantime, precautionary measures were recommended for all people, regardless of gender or orientation. After 1980, AIDS began an outrageous killing spree that would result in an astounding 35 million global deaths. As Robby had predicted, the community would be challenged like never before. Ordinary people became heroes as they cared for those who others may have wanted to forget. The struggles we faced in the water paled in comparison to the battle that many faced and many more lost.

Just 11 years after the swim crossing, there was an estimated 23 million people infected with the virus responsible for AIDS. At the time of this writing, more than half the population who were HIV positive were receiving HART treatments, or over 19 million people around the globe.

There is recent evidence that cannabis use may halt the HIV infection from transforming into AIDS, so Pete's life may have been unwittingly saved by Mrs. McBride's home-grown herbs. While the daily pharmacological treatment for HIV renders the virus unable to be transmitted and saves lives, there remains no cure.

Made in the USA
San Bernardino, CA
23 August 2019